THE MOSCOW
CONNECTION

THE MOSCOW CONNECTION

A Novel by
ROBIN MOORE

Affiliated Writers of America/Publishers
Encampment, Wyoming

Published by

Affiliated Writers of America, Inc.
P.O. Box 343
Encampment, Wyoming 82325

ISBN: 1-879915-11-1
Library of Congress Catalog Card Number: 94-78955

Manufactured in the United States of America

This is a work of faction—fiction based on fact. The historical events chronicled herein may be hard to believe—believe them, they happened, though in most cases were successfully expunged from official records.

Mother Russia's fatal flaw is her refusal to recognize the fatal flaws of her corrupt progeny.

Three couriers were arrested in Frankfurt on August 10, 1994, deplaning a Lufthansa flight from Moscow. They were escorting more than a pound of plutonium worth a quarter of a million dollars to outlaw terror states seeking to acquire nuclear capability. Was it a coincidence that Viktor Sidorenko, Russian Deputy Minister of Atomic Energy, was aboard the same flight?

DEDICATION

This book is dedicated to my beautiful and loving wife,
Mary Olga, who stood by me during the
three years this work was in progress and twice read
and helped revise the manuscript.

ACKNOWLEDGEMENTS

During the three years it took to write *The Moscow Connection*, the extensive travel and research was made possible and pleasant by John and Gloria Strong.

Important technical assistance was rendered by Alexander N. Rossolimo, president of International Strategy Associates, Newton, Massachusetts.

At Petrovka 38, Militsia Headquarters in Moscow, I was greatly aided by many good and knowledgeable Militsia friends. And, of course to Valerie, sturdy boxer who whipped all his American police opponents and gave me his red Communist Party card when he quit. The Moscow Crime Writers Association also gave me considerable assistance.

Peter Grinenko, a special investigator at the Kings County District Attorney's Office specializing in Russian affairs, provided much insight into Russian criminal activity in America.

My lovely Moscow interpreter, Nina Martinova, was most helpful in the field research that went into the book.

The Harvard University Russian Research Center provided continuing orientation as this work unfolded and the author owes thanks to its associate director, Dr. Marshall I. Goldman, as well as to Marvin Kalb who first made me realize Russian ICBMs could be bought for a price after the failed coup, and to Janet Vaillant who introduced me to the Center and provided translations of Russian documents.

There were many other advisers, guides and editorial assistants over the years this book was in the works. I particularly acknowledge my final editor, Jay Fraser, who brought this novel to its present state in ten days which we hope will shake the world, or at least the reading public. In the earlier days of writing this book, Anthony Schneider worked closely with me as editor, reducing 800 odd pages to manageable proportions. Marie Reid proofed the manuscript at a critical juncture. And of course there was The Duke of Hoboken, Joe Koehler, whose encouragement never flagged. To everyone involved, I express my heartiest thanks.

GLOSSARY OF TERMS

ANASHA	Refined hemp, widespread jail and camp drug like hashish or marijuana.
AT-LARGE	Outside prison, free, or escaped.
EZPREDEL	Literally, 'on the edge.' The state of 'everything goes' in crime and business. Virtual anarchy.
BITCH	A hardcore criminal who defected to the prison camp administration and used to beat up and rape other prisoners into subservience.
CIS	Commonwealth of Independent States, formerly the Soviet Union.
COCKEREL	Or goat. A prisoner turned forceably into a passive homosexual.
CROSS	A camp or jail infirmary.
COBRA	A woman adept at performing fellatio.
DELO	Big deal
DGIGIT	Literally means a 'knight' in Georgian language. Used as a slightly mocking term for a typical Georgian, black stubble, swarthy, hard-eyed.
FRAYER	Second in power, the underboss of a thief-in-the-law.
FOOL	A prisoner with a privileged easy job; laundryman, librarian, tool keeper, etc.
KOBEL	The 'male' role in a lesbian relationship.
KODLA	A thief's gang.
KENT	A common prisoner.
MENT	Short for "Militsiaman," corresponds to American "cop."
OBSHAK	A thief's money bank.
PCHAK	A long, thin, curved fighting knife.
SCREW	The female role in a lesbian relationship.
SHMON	A search of prisoners.
SIX	Leader of criminal footsoldiers.
SKCHOD	An authoritative thief meeting.
THIEF-IN-THE-LAW	A hard core authoritative criminal, not necessarily a thief, recognized as a leader by other gangsters.
TRUMP SIX	Advanced six, checked for loyalty to thieves.
ZIRHICK	A prison guard.
ZONA	A territory of the prison camp.

PROLOGUE

The thief-in-the-law who would be known and feared as Yaponchik, the Jap, was twelve years old when he killed his first man.

It happened in Samarkand, in the middle of Soviet Central Asia, in 1948. He was called Slava, diminutive of Vyacheslav. His father Kyrill Yakovlev, ethnically Kazakh and thus of descernable oriental caste, came to Uzbekistan with his wife and son to find work. In the Republic's famous city, Samarkand, he toiled in a factory where the Kazakh workers were well aware they were employed to process great quantities of drugs from the poppy plant and hemp which grew plentifully in the area. The head of the plant was a rich Uzbek communist named Mamatadgi, one of the bosses of a powerful drug family. Uzbeks hired Kazakhs because they could pay them less and control them. The Kazakh community in Samarkand was small and uninfluential.

In the city there were good gymnasiums where coaches taught the youths boxing, wrestling, and gymnastics. Slava was a bright student at the Russian school but his real love was training with the school's boxing coach, a big German with a broken nose and solid as a rock. The coach liked the stubborn, thin Kazakh boy, who would never turn his face away even under a shower of blows from a stronger enemy.

"You have fighting spirit, boy," the old German used to say.

"That's what counts, muscle will follow. Always know exactly what you are going to do and strike without a second thought. Remember, your enemy is afraid of you too, no matter how small you are."

One terrible night had irreparably changed Slava Yakovlev's life—for the better, he recognized in retrospect; otherwise he might never have broadened his horizons beyond Samarkand. He and his mother had worried all evening when his father didn't come home. Finally the front door of their adobe house swung open. His father staggered inside and fell to the floor. His face was a bloody mess, one eye invisible under a large gory tumor, teeth missing; he could only let out a wheezing groan—his ribs were broken in several places.

Slava and his mother wept looking at him and managed to put him on his bed and ease off his dirty shirt. After he found a partially comfortable position on the bed and took several sips of cold water, Kyrill Yakovlev told them what had happened.

The Uzbek, Mamatadgi, refused to pay the Kazakhs their monthly wage. Only Kyrill had protested. At a sign from Mamatadgi, his muscleman started beating him with an iron rod. None of the workers protested—none came to his aid. Finally, after an hour of punishment he managed to crawl home.

In the morning his father stopped groaning and Slava found him dead. That day the boy stole into the home of a neighbourhood Militsiaman on duty. From a bureau drawer he took the pistol he had often watched the policeman clean.

At seven that evening dusk was a bright and violet color as it could only be in Samarkand. Mamatadgi was alone in his plant checking the account books and counting the money that had just come in from the traders in Namangan Valley. They were a day late with the payment for several hundred pounds of opium and a ton of refined hemp or *anasha* so he had delayed paying the wages to his Kazakh workers. That was fine; they would get their money tomorrow or even better a few days later so they couldn't identify the Uzbeks from Namangan with the salary delay.

Mamatadgi was round shouldered, with a big Iranian nose, black slanted eyes on a wide swarthy face. A gold tooth sparkled in the left upper corner of his mouth when he smiled or smoked a cigarette. His lower lip was fleshy and hung forward, giving his face a contemptuous look. Friends and enemies alike called him Old Jackal Mamatadgi.

The boy did not knock. He pushed open the door to the counting house with his foot and then stood on the threshold, hands behind his back, the twilight sky silhouetting his dark figure.

Behind his back Slava clasped the big pistol with both hands.

Jackal Mamatadgi looked up from his desk. The gold tooth flashed as he spoke.

"Hey, Sonny, what do you want?"

"I'm Slava Yakovlev. My father, Kyrill, worked for you."

"So do a lot of people, boy. Now what do you want?"

"He does not work for you anymore. My father died this morning."

"Poor child," Mamatadgi grumbled. "I'm sorry."

Slava's grip on the pistol behind his back tightened as he saw that Mamatadgi sensed danger.

"But what did he die from?"

"You ordered him killed because he wanted the money he earned."

"No, no! You are wrong, by Allah!" Mamatadgi started rising to his feet.

"Sit where you are!" Slava ordered, drawing his hands from behind his back. Mamatadgi faced the barrel of a silver pistol, the gun looked huge in the boy's small hands. The steel of the barrel was worn with dark pitted cavities, obviously from frequent use.

"Hey, boy! Do not joke. It can fire! You're a bad boy! Allah will punish you and your family! What's more..."

Suddenly Mamatadgi was upright behind the table. "Here, I'll give you some money."

Mamatadgi opened the strong box beside him. Heaps of rubles and other currency lay inside. Under them was the weapon, an Uzbek curved *pchak,* a blade of stainless steel. He put his hand inside the strong box as if reaching for money and drew the *pchak* out of its leather scabbard.

Slava was on the verge of fainting. His mouth was dry and hot, his eyes blurring. The pistol was as heavy as a lead ball. Suddenly the old bandit, deadly *pchak* in his right hand, lunged at him. Slava jumped back as the arc of the knife just missed his right arm. Terror crept into his pounding heart as Mamatadgi poised for another stab at him. Instinctively he squeezed the trigger. The huge pistol blew a lightning bolt of fire and a cloud of smoke.

"Bastard!" Mamatadgi yelled, again swinging the *pchak* at the boy. But the bullet had broken his spine and he only managed to fall on the table, stabbing the *pchak* into its wooden surface.

Suddenly the gun felt as light as air. Mamatadgi's face was close to Slava's, on the table, his wide open black eyes filled with hatred.

The second bullet went through the lower part of the brow. The back of Mamatadgi's head flew off and in a split second the bloody mess plastered itself over the wall behind the desk and safe. The body collapsed backwards, books and accounts tumbling after it, the table remaining clean, only the *pchak* sticking out of it.

At that moment Slava began to become The Jap. He walked around the table, stepped over the body and calmly took all the bills from the safe and stuffed them in both his pockets. He didn't know what was in the leather sacks but took them anyway, only later to discover they were filled with gold dust. Then he put the gun in the strong box, now empty of value, and closed the metal lid. The Militsia, when the police were finally summoned, would start looking for a common robber in town and perhaps interview the Old Jackal's many enemies and the drug dealers with whom he traded.

Meanwhile Slava and his mother, with the power of the money he had taken from Mamatadgi's strong box, would be long absent from Samarkand.

BOOK
ONE

❧ ❧

THE UNDERGROUND KING

CHAPTER ONE

⋘ ⋙

The snowdrifts surrounding Tulun labor camp were deep enough for a man to sink into over his head. Fir trees around the prison had been cut down to create a half-mile-wide clear firing zone, beyond which the dense Siberian forest loomed in the distance. Every day fresh fallen snow was shoveled beyond the outer white mounds by a gang of shivering inmates. Great heaps of it reached up to the guard towers where sentinels with machine guns stood shivering and watching the desolate prison yards and bleak landscape through icy binoculars.

These troopers were guarding ten long barracks where many of Russia's incarcerated criminals were lying on bare wooden berths wrapped in all the clothing they possessed. They huddled together in an attempt to save precious warmth, bringing their knees closer to their chins and trying to sleep.

A two-story brick and cement structure was the camp's internal jail, located in the center of the perimeter, where the officers on duty also slept after watching TV and downing their half-bottle ration of second grade vodka.

Tulun camp near Irkutsk, one of the largest cities in Siberia, was currently home to 500 prisoners including five thiefs-in-the-law or criminal bosses, each with his own gang of about 30 musclemen led by an underboss or frayer. "The easiest thing to do in the USSR is to go to jail," the proverb went. And when a prisoner was asked what he did to get sentenced to fifteen years and answered "nothing" the rejoinder was, "Impossible, they only give you ten years for doing nothing."

In the biggest, deepest underground coldcell of the camp's internal jail the most important individual in Tulun, the master criminal known as The Jap, was wide awake, drinking cognac and gazing pensively into a crackling fire.

The Jap had been placed in this coldcell, especially prepared for him at great expense borne by his generous bribes, upon his arrival at the camp. He had never been obliged to visit the working zona where common criminals shared wood and concrete unheated barracks twelve months a year, out of which winter comprised eight months. The average temperature was rather stable—that is twenty-five degrees below zero Celsius.

Subdued lights and the fire gave the cell a cozy atmosphere. Two comfortable chairs faced the fire. Fur rugs had been thrown on the hardwood floor and hung against brick and mortar walls. In an adjoining cell a sauna bath had been created and a third cell served as Jap's wardrobe and storage area. A color television and VCR stood on a table against the wall.

A bottle of cognac shone dimly against the flames in the fireplace. Beside it sat a long plate with slices of fresh smoked rabbit meat, salmon and Armenian basturma. A deep wooden bowl was filled with cucumber and tomato salad in olive oil.

He was dressed in a white shirt and simple black jeans, and wore a thief's trademark gold Rolex watch on his left wrist. His feet were bare—he liked to feel polished wood and furry skin while walking.

The Jap was just over fifty but looked at least five years

younger, a characteristic of men his age belonging even in part to the Mongoloid race. Though not tall he was stoutly built, slightly bow-legged with broad shoulders, a short neck and long, powerful arms. His face was broad with slanted-eyes above a smashed boxer's nose. His mouth was thin and cruel, his hair still naturally black and thick.

The jail commandant, Major Karamushev, did his best to make the Jap's incarceration comfortable—and was thus assured a comfortable future for himself and his family as a result of his notorious prisoner's gratitude and largesse. The adjoining cold-cell was connected to the Jap's quarters by a thick oak door and the sauna was fashioned inside. A gigantic iron cauldron was found after a widespread search of the villages within a hundred miles of the camp and placed next to the sauna to serve as a pool. The Jap enjoyed sweating profusely on wooden planks for an hour or two and then plunging into the ice cold water which filled the cauldron.

The guards seldom entered his cell for fear of staining the carpets. Even the commandant always took off his boots when, as happened so often, he visited Jap in his underground apartment to enjoy cognac and lavish snacks of food and watch a videofilm or have a twist with girls brought from the nearby women's camp. They also talked business. And there were many facets of the Jap's affairs that needed to be handled on the outside which added to Major Karamushev's coffers.

The Jap was known as "The Underground King" to the common prisoners who slept in the crowded barracks above. They endured interminable freezing winters and savage beatings administered by overzealous guards and sadistic criminals ceded the authority to punish any infraction of the rules laid down by the inmate bosses. These were slaves condemned to hard labor until in most cases they perished long before their sentences had been served.

But the Jap was not just a bandit, not merely a savage killer whose very name terrorized his targets of extortion. He was of the highest rank in the criminal world, an authoritative thief-in-the-law whose foraging minions, even with their boss in prison, were feared throughout the Soviet Union and Eastern Europe.

At the top of the criminal pyramid stood the "thief," a distinction which could be granted only by the meeting of authoritative "thieves" who would create a certificate, a diploma of sorts equivalent to a Doctor of Jurisprudence or a Ph.D. in the academic world. This charter was signed in the nicknames, which were inseparable from their "thief" titles, by the gathering of "thieves" who recognized a new member of their order.

The thief, according to the "law" could not work—that was below "thief" dignity—he could not profit other than by criminal business, could not serve in the army, could not marry or if he did his wife must be subservient and invisible, he would always oppose authorities and jail administration, organize his own gang inside camp and rule common prisoners charged with minor crimes. His sacred weapon was his knife, the *pchak*.

The Jap refilled his glass and sipped slowly, savoring every drop, his nostrils flaring as the warmth of the liquor filled his gut.

Grimly he mulled over the declining state of his business affairs. A strenuous effort by his outside organization to obtain an early release for him had resulted in the Moscow Chief of Police and Jap's enemies in the PolitBureau cutting off his communication privileges. No longer could he rule his enterprises by decrees passed on through frequent couriers. The door to the sauna room in the neighboring refurbished cell opened and a half-naked woman stepped out and walked proudly into the Jap's living room cell. Her big belly was almost hanging over the rim of the wide guard's belt which held up the leather bath breeches above leather slippers. Her over generous breasts were nevertheless firm. Her shrewd slavic face featured a small upturned nose, slightly slanted brown eyes and a wide mouth with full lips. An air of self-confidence attested to a hard life accepted with forebearance. She proudly displayed the numerous tattoos covering her skin telling stories from her lurid biography.

Jap loved to hear Maria tell the stories behind each of her skin adornments as he sat near his fireplace with his legs stretched to the heat. The oldest tattoos, which she unabashedly revealed, were acquired when at about fourteen the gang of Moscow hoodlums who ruled her area would undress her in some back alley or hallway and violate her in turns; they laughingly inscribed tattoos on her large bare buttocks and other parts of her body by means of a rusty nail. These early decorations had faded with age as later on in the camps her flesh was introduced to more sophisticated examples of tattoo art.

The designs covered her back, shoulders, buttocks, thighs and breasts. On her back was depicted several church steeples representing each of her sentences. A wicked dagger on her left shoulder was reminiscent of when she had stabbed an abusive boyfriend, almost to death. The bright, eight-pointed star on her right shoulder, Jap recalled, was the sign of her high rank among female prisoners and of active lesbianism. She also sported numerous men's names in handsome script along arms and shanks—these were the names of her many criminal lovers. Now she had risen to the top of Tulun's social order.

Maria walked to the crackling fireplace and put her back to the heat. Jap gestured at the second glass of cognac on the low table eagerly anticipating what was to come. She took a few steps and picked up the glass, returning to the heat and sipping the drink.

Jap smiled at Maria standing bare breasted between him and the fireplace. He pictured in his thoughts the two butterflies on her thighs representing two escape attempts while a red and blue rose on the inside of her left thigh simply stated she was a good lay.

Maria and Jap held their glasses up and drank and then they both looked down at the smooth, polished, pinewood floor covered with the skins of bears and lynxes—denizens of the local forests. They grinned knowingly at each other. He did not require much furniture apart from the three low tables: one for the TV and videotape recorder, another for the stereo system, and the dining table. Jap grew up in Central Asia and did not favor European-style furnishings. Blankets and pillows lay in a neat roll in the corner—Jap favored sleeping on the floor.

"Do you want to hear my news from Moscow first?" she asked with a saucy look on her face.

"Is there anything I can do about it tonight?" Jap asked. Resignation to his circumstances and anticipation of what was about to come lowered his tone.

With an impish grin Maria shook her head, swallowed her drink and kicked off her slippers. She walked across the fur rugs to the Jap who put his drink down as she started to take off his crisp clean shirt. His wardrobe was in a third cell, also connected to his living area. The laundry was taken by the guards to the women's camp five miles away. The Jap liked well-ironed, light-colored shirts, fresh ones everyday.

Soon she had stripped him naked and he lay on his stomach facing the fire feeling the fur of the bear rug against his loins as she slid out of her leather skirt. Nude, she positioned herself above him, one knee between his thighs the other outside as she began to knead his rippling back. He sighed deeply and gave himself up to her ministrations as strong fingers sought out the tight knots that had formed in his muscles.

The first time she was brought to his cell from the neighboring women's camp by Major Karamushev, along with several other girls, Maria had proved to be a sexual impresario. She soon became keeper of Jap's quarters and he became intimate with her life in the women's camp. He quickly learned it was shockingly different from the men's facility.

Her revelations always excited him in a strange and erotic way - particularly the tale behind the tattoo displayed on Maria's left buttock: a female hand holding a severed penis, blood dripping from its base. She had proved herself once in a most violent gesture, not to be forgotten by guards throughout the prison who were prone to frequently rape and force submission on female inmates. And now, as Maria's sensuous massage commenced, she reached between his thighs, fingers slyly twitching in his groin eliciting a pleasurable moan from him. She knew how to draw out the erotic manipulations and finally when he could wait no longer her expert motions brought him to a groaning climax.

His sexual tension relieved by Maria, Jap pulled on his pants and shirt. She fastened her leather skirt around her waist and filled his glass again as he stared contemplatively into the fireplace. "You know me too well, Maria," he said softly and then suddenly his tone changed. "Now, what have you heard?"

"A girl was recently sent here from Moscow. She found out that I was, well, close to you, and began boasting about Tofik's gang, saying that soon he will take over all your business."

"What?" Jap asked incredulously.

"She told me that her former lover, a Georgian, one of Tofik's *sixes*, left her to go to New York just before she was arrested as an accomplice to extortion. According to him Tofik's gang is stealing your business in America."

Jap's lips compressed into a thin line, the black pupils of his eyes glittering. "I suspected that one of the other thiefs was trying to move in on my American contacts but this is the first I have heard confirming my suspicions. What else did she say?"

"Well, she just boasts. She said her boyfriend and one other man are meeting in New York to take over some kind of a printing business."

"Printing!" Jap jumped on the word. "Did she mention anyone by name?"

"I don't think so. She said they have already killed one of your men last month in New York."

"Ask her if she heard the name Zekki Dekka." Jap stared angrily at the fire and then continued. "Tofik is here, in Tulun. We are supposed to be working together. This isn't the first time I have had reason to believe he is trying to steal my business on the outside."

"What is this printing?"

Jap was silent for some moments. Finally he began to talk as though trying to explain something to himself. "An American came to me through trusted channels. It was eleven years ago, in November 1979, the very day our astronauts came home after 139 days in space. The American wanted the thiefs-in-the-law to help drown the communists in a tidal wave of billions of counterfeit rubles which they would provide. Our economy, a self-perpetuating joke anyway, would be ruined. It was the American's idea, and he was right, that we, the thiefs-in-the-law, would take over authority in a financially ruined Russia and split the empire into warring factions."

Seldom had Maria seen Jap so concerned. She wanted to allay his fears, but there was nothing she could say or do but let him talk. "Three times we were ready to receive the flood of rubles and launch the operation, and three times the Americans changed their minds. I realized this was a plan coming from the highest level of the United States government. While I still had regular outside contact, I heard the American, I never knew his name, is still using Zekki as his contact with our *organizatsiya*." Jap rose suddenly and refilled Maria's glass.

"Two men you say?"

Maria nodded.

"Probably already in America by now. So it seems we have two problems." Then he turned to Maria. "Such loyalty must be rewarded. I will get you out of here, Maria. I promise."

She smiled up at him mistily.

"But now we must get word to Pavel. I doubt very much that he knows what you have just told me, and, if it is true, we must act fast."

"Jap, there is a girl who received a good conduct citation from the guard captain and will be going home soon. I can give her a message to take to Pavel."

"When does she go home?"

"In a few days. The captain got her pregnant and she goes back to Moscow in time for an abortion."

"She must find Pavel at Peking Restaurant and tell him we have a problem in New York. Tofik's men are trying to move in on our business with the Americans. Pavel must warn Zekki Dekka and our people in New York. They must eliminate the problem. Tell her to remind Pavel that Tofik always sends two men. He must dispose of both problems."

Maria nodded. "Two men," she repeated.

Jap strode across the room to a metal box. Taking out a gold coin he handed it to Maria. "Give this to your friend. It will buy her an airline ticket to Moscow. I want Pavel to have my instructions immediately. Afterwards, he and I can discuss strategy."

"They will permit you to see him?"

"This is a most intricate matter. Karamushev tells me that the First Secretary of this Irkutsk region, Nickolai Martinov, has the power to ease the restrictions on me and help me get out of here. He also tells me that Martinov has a daughter, Oksana, in Moscow who is studying at the Maurice Thorez Language Institute. Tell your friend that Pavel must find Oksana Martinova and find a way to put her to use for us."

"You think he can do that?" Maria asked in disbelief.

"Pavel is the most resourceful underboss in my entire *organizatsiya*. He will know how to do this."

"Jap," a worried look came over Maria's face, "you know I hear many things. What is happening on the outside that makes resentment of you spread throughout Tulun?"

Jap shrugged. "What do you hear?"

"Some thieves-at-large send word to their people here in Tulun that important PolitBureau members are working to free you."

Jap smiled slyly. "We must get First Secretary Martinov on my case."

"Some business people outside are afraid you will take over when you are at-large again. They want you to be killed here."

"You heard that? From whom?"

"Not directly from the girl of any thief here. It's just a feeling I get from the rumors."

He shook his head in self-reproval. "I should have listened to business the moment Karamushev brought you to me today instead of . . ." he shrugged and smiled at her fondly. "I have been here too long. Outside matters become secondary to immediate gratification."

Jap paused as though considering his own words and then sighed. "Have Karamushev bring you back tomorrow, after you have passed my orders to your friend. We will take a sauna together and maybe play chess. The important thing is that your girl passes on my orders. And tell her Pavel will arrange and pay for the abortion. He will also make sure she is well cared for afterwards."

"That will make her very happy, Jap."

Together they walked to the cell door.

Jap shook the heavy slab on its hinges. "Maria, this thing we are working on in America, it is something big and nobody is going to get in my way, not Tofik, not anybody. This girl must get to Pavel immediately. She must tell him we have two problems which may jeopardize our American operation and which we must dispose of."

The bolt clanked as it drew back and the crunching sound of the heavy door swinging open echoed inside the cell.

"I will make her understand, Jap," Maria called back as she followed the guard out of Jap's abode.

CHAPTER TWO

⋖⋗ ⋖⋗

S pecial Investigator Peter Nikhilov dashed out of the nearly
deserted Brooklyn District Attorney's office, jumped into his
car parked in its privileged spot on the street directly in front
of the Municipal Building, and sped south through the midwinter
night on Ocean Parkway. Wipers at full speed cleared the windshield of the slush splashed on it by the tires of the cars Peter shot
past. He glanced at the dashboard clock. Another ten minutes and
he would be at Brighton Beach.

It had been a year since the last time Hugh McDonald had
called him. Now, out of nowhere, the former CIA operative, his
ally in a Soviet investigation for which Peter had been borrowed
from the New York Police Department, had rung his office. Peter
was just about to go home for the night when Hugh's urgent voice
crackled, "Meet me at the Kiev Restaurant, Brighton Beach as
quick as you can. I badly need your help."

Out of habit Peter turned to the police frequency on his radio
and as he was approaching the point where Ocean Parkway termi-
nated at the Atlantic Ocean he heard the matter-of-fact dispatcher

announce a double shooting at the Kiev Restaurant on Surf Avenue, Brighton Beach.

Peter reached Ocean Parkway's junction with Surf Avenue and found himself looking at the Atlantic surf spewing white foam out of the night as it pounded the sand. He spun a turn left and drove east, paralleling the boardwalk, which was nearly deserted in the chill winds which whipped up and down the ocean.

There was nothing unusual about murders in Brighton Beach, also known as Little Odessa by the Sea, named after the Russian crime capital on the Black Sea. But what was the over-age intelligence operative doing in the middle of a killing? Two murders according to the police frequency.

Peter parked as close as he could get to the Kiev Restaurant on brightly illuminated Surf Avenue opposite the boardwalk. He placed the police department plate under the windshield, and stepped out of his car, locking it electronically behind him. A crowd of curiosity seekers milled outside the entrance to the restaurant controlled by several policemen. As he looked around, a middle-aged man with thinning white hair and a ruddy face appeared in front of him.

"Hugh!" Peter greeted his erstwhile partner. "It's been a long time."

"Good to see you, too," Hugh responded as they shook hands.

Breathlessly the older man wasted no time. "This has turned into a helluva situation. We've had our eyes on these two Russians," he gestured at the Kiev Restaurant, "for several days. They contacted a member of the Iraqi United Nations mission we had under surveillance. Now they're dead."

"I know. I just heard about it over the radio as I was driving here. So who are you working for now?" Peter asked.

"NEST. Nuclear Emergency Search Team. Our duty is to prevent a nuclear emergency from occurring. Our fellows keep a close watch on the terror state missions to the United Nations as possible sources of nuclear terrorism. My particular target is a fellow called Azziz in the Iraqi mission."

Hugh and Peter were both watching the entrance to the Kiev Restaurant on well-lit Surf Avenue behind the boardwalk as they talked. Unlike most of the bars and restaurants that lurk along the side streets, the Kiev faces the Atlantic Ocean, resting among the art deco apartment buildings in which affluent Russian emigres reside. The crowd milled around the closed doors hoping for a view of the corpses being carried out. "So why did you call me?" Peter asked.

"I needed someone who could speak Russian—fast. Earlier this evening I observed these two Russians enter the Iraqi mission with Azziz and when they left without him an hour later, I followed them out here to Brighton Beach in the subway. Naturally, I thought of you and called when they went into the Kiev Restaurant."

"You were lucky; I was in my office late."

"I would have gotten you on your beeper and you would have come to me."

"Yeah, I suppose I would."

"When I called I wanted you to help me find out who these guys are. I had just hung up the phone from calling you when I heard a lot of screaming and shouting. By the time I got out of the phone booth and back into the restaurant these two were dead. God damn it, if I'd just waited a little longer to call you I'd have witnessed the murder."

"And maybe been blown away yourself. In Little Odessa they don't care who they kill."

"I need to find out who these guys were."

"Well, let's see what we can find out."

"Thanks. They would never have let me in," Hugh lamented. "And proper channels would waste precious time. By the way, Peter, don't mention to anyone that I followed these two out here from the Iraqi mission to the UN. That surveillance is top secret."

"The time may come when I'll have to say something. But we'll deal with that later." Peter Nikhilov pushed his way through the crowd, and flashing his Brooklyn DA card he walked past the two policemen guarding the door. Hugh followed him closely.

Inside, they walked across the gaudy imitation of "Peking," an elaborate Moscow restaurant. The Kiev seemed cavernous, deserted as it was except for a knot of police officers and homicide detectives. Big plain clothes detective Lieutenant Tom Egan looked up from the staring eyes of two corpses. "Jesus Christ, Nickeloff," he mispronounced the name. "How the hell did you get here so fast? I didn't call the DA."

"Hello Tom. Meet Hugh McDonald. An old friend from a special assignment with the Agency."

"Pleased to meet you, Hugh." Then back to Peter, "No shit, Nickeloff, how did you get the word?" He looked at Hugh suspiciously.

"Instinct, Tom. A cop's instinct."

"Right," Tom said unconvincingly, still eying Hugh while Peter Nikhilov gazed at the two corpses under the overturned table. He was a lean, sandy-haired man who appeared to be in his early forties. His tweed sport jacket, black knit tie, button down slate blue shirt tucked into gray worsted slacks, and polished brown loafers gave him more the appearance of an eastern university-trained prosecutor than a former detective now attached to the Brooklyn District Attorney's office as an investigator.

Police photographers were taking pictures, moving cautiously around the pools of blood surrounding the victims' upper bodies like ill-shaped, crimson halos.

"The work of a typical Chechen assassin," Peter said, still studying the bodies. "Use at least three times as much gun as you need to do the job, or a hand grenade. Any ID?"

"Only this." Egan gestured to a uniformed officer standing beside the corpses. His gloved hand clutched a sheaf of crisp hundred dollar bills. "With this kind of paper you don't need ID."

"No witnesses I suppose?"

"There must have been fifty to a hundred people in here when it happened. But," Egan shrugged hopelessly, "*Ya nechevo ne znayu*—nobody knows nothing. Nobody even admitted to hearing the shots."

"The shooter may have used a silencer." Peter knelt beside the upturned table and examined the bodies. "They haven't been in this country long enough to buy American suits and shoes. Look at them. Probably Georgians from the Caucasus. Any weapon yet?"

"We're checking the trash cans nearby," Egan said.

Peter studied the bodies a few moments longer and then stood up. "By now the perpetrator is already at JFK waiting to get on a plane to somewhere in Europe, probably Frankfurt, from where there are two flights a day for Moscow."

"Exactly what I was thinking," Tom agreed.

"This hit was ordered from Russia," Peter declared. "I'm sure of it. The black hand from Moscow reaches right into Brighton Beach. It's a matter of style. We'll never find the killer unless an informant comes forth, which is extremely unlikely."

"Just as I was hoping we were going to have a quiet new year," Egan bemoaned.

"Think you'll be able to identify them?" Hugh gestured at the bodies.

"Sure, eventually," Egan replied. "They're transients. It may take awhile before someone starts looking for them."

Peter looked at the bank notes in the sergeant's gloved hand. "I wonder if it's fake," he said, taking a closer look at the sheaf of bills clasped in the sergeant's fingers without touching them. "Tom, check those bills out."

At that moment a swarthy, heavy-set man with greasy black hair and a few days' worth of black stubble on his cheeks and chin came out of the kitchen door, exploding in Russian. Peter answered him in equally rapid gibberish and after some moments patted the man on the back, calming him down.

Peter turned to his two companions. "Niko, the manager here, is understandably upset. This is the second massacre, as he calls it, that has occurred in his restaurant this winter."

"Did he see who did it?" Hugh asked.

Peter laughed aloud. "Of course not. To see is to die." He jabbered in comforting tones to the restaurateur whose business was ruined for the evening. Then he said to Hugh, "Let's take a ride over to the airport and give the place a toss. We just might see someone who sticks out." It was a perfect way to get Hugh out of there before anyone could start asking questions.

CHAPTER THREE

⟪⟫ ⟪⟫

A s Peter Nikhilov drove quickly north on Ocean Parkway out of Brighton Beach, Hugh admired the quietly luxurious blue gray leather interior of the detective's automobile. "Does the Brooklyn DA give you a Lincoln Town Car to cruise around in?" he asked.

"No. This is mine," Peter replied.

"Not bad. Even at the Agency we couldn't drive a new Lincoln or Cadillac."

"I give the DA two days a week working Russian cases. The rest of my time is my own. Gorbachev's Perestroika is good for business if you speak Russian and know how the people operate."

"What kind of business do you do with the Soviets?"

"Middleman."

"For instance?"

Peter shrugged. "Here's one venture. Aluminum is currently selling for $1300 a ton in the West. The controlled Russian price of aluminum is 1300 rubles a ton. Right now we can buy rubles from," he paused discreetly, "certain Soviet institutions for 30 to the dollar." Peter grinned broadly. "So if we can pay $400 a ton for aluminum in Russia and sell it a couple of hundred miles away in Finland for $1300 we make a nice profit."

"Then why isn't everybody doing it?" Hugh asked.

"Because we thought of it, and because the Ministry of Metals can only sell to state-approved Soviet enterprises for internal use."

"So how do you fit in?"

"I convinced the Ministry of Health that the international AIDS epidemic was spreading fast to Russia and that the company I represent was prepared to manufacture and distribute condoms cheaper than any company in the world. Each condom would come individually packaged in aluminum foil."

A wide grin came over Hugh's face. "I begin to see the light."

"All communist bureaucrats are corrupt," Peter went on. "The higher up they are, the more successfully corrupt. The Minister of Health and the Minister of Metals quickly convinced the PolitBureau of the great service the condom company will do the people of the Soviet Union. My condom company now purchases unlimited aluminum in Russia, sells it next door in Finland for a profit of about $1000 a ton, imports aluminum foil from the Dutch and latex condoms from Taiwan, puts the package together in Moscow and sells at a slight loss per condom but enormous profit on the sale of thousands of tons of aluminum."

"Don't the authorities catch on?" Hugh asked.

"The ministers allow it, for good reasons of course, and they are, after all, preventing an AIDS epidemic in Russia."

Hugh just shook his head, and Peter was silent for several minutes, staring out the windshield which was constantly cleared of the splattering late winter slush by high speed wipers. Then Peter asked, "You must know other people making money off of this."

"Yes I do. What businesses do ex-cops, and," he paused and gave Peter a significant look, "ex-Green Berets almost always go into?" He paused and grinned. "I'll answer my own question.

They go into security and arms dealing. We have files on every arms deal made in the world, who is buying what, for how much, and from whom."

"Interesting," Peter allowed. "Who's the boss of NEST?"

"There's no one boss like the Director of Central Intelligence or FBI Director. It's run by the Federal Energy Department out of Las Vegas in conjunction with the nuclear weapons testing program. We're coordinated by the FBI but many of the operatives are ex-agency guys like me. Energy department scientists make up the emergency search teams. The nuclear terrorist possibility is a growing global threat. It probably will get completely out of hand in just a few more years." He paused again giving Peter a speculative glance. "I think about you once in a while. Special Forces people are valuable, especially rare ones who speak Russian like a Russian born into it. And demolition experts with Soviet nuke installation experience in East Germany."

Peter nodded. "There was nothing in the record that indicated I ever did such a thing, was there?"

Hugh smiled enigmatically. "No. A few things get left out of Special Forces service records. But there are still those of us who know."

The lights of JFK International Airport glowed ahead of them on the Van Wyck Expressway. Peter was obliged to slow down in the traffic. "Are you on a recruiting mission?"

"Not yet. Just thinking."

For ten minutes Peter drove through the boulevards leading to the various terminals. Finally pulling up directly in front of the Lufthansa boarding area Peter slapped his police plate under the windshield as he slid out of his car. Hugh stepped onto the sidewalk and they walked inside. A cursory glance at the ticket counters indicated that most of the passengers were already ticketed. They started up the steps to the waiting lounge on the second floor.

Peter, followed by Hugh, strode toward the boarding area and stopped at the security gate. From his pocket he took out what appeared to be an oversized pocket watch, bigger and thicker than the old-fashioned rail conductor's timepiece, and placed it on the tray beside the electronic frame as he walked through. Peter retrieved it after being cleared, and slipped it back into his pocket.

"So you managed to appropriate a sneaky Pete chronolog shaped charge," Hugh remarked.

"Tells the time everywhere in the world at a glance."

"Airport security would have heartburn if they knew."

"It's become a sort of security blanket." He winked. "Nothing like knowing the time in Moscow and Tokyo."

Peter's head turned as he watched the passengers about to board the eleven PM flight. "Of course there are other flights the killer could be trying to board," Peter said. "But the Moscow Mafia like Lufthansa because they have Stoli vodka—lots of it—in first class. And once they board a foreign airline they're out of America."

"Really. I didn't know. I go on when I want. And arrest if I want. Nobody's ever tried to stop me."

"Well, take an area and look around. Just don't tangle with a suspect."

Peter watched the boarding gate which was about to open, and Hugh wandered nonchalantly throughout the waiting area. He looked into two bars but saw nothing of interest. Finally, as it was close to boarding time, he walked to the elevator which had a small plaque above the call button indicating the First Class Club.

Hugh was soon inside the subdued interior of the preferred waiting section and almost instantly froze. There, in the dimly lit far corner of the room, two men caught his attention. A dapper man with a waxed mustache, hair parted in the middle, and wearing striped pants and black coat with grey cord piping brought back vivid memories of former operations. With the boulevardier type was a swarthy, bushy-haired individual with the cruel look of the Soviet Caucasus natives, the real assassins of the Russian underworld, imprinted on his face and posture.

Hoping he hadn't been noticed Hugh turned, strolled from the club, and once in the boarding section on the lower floor he made for the Lufthansa gate. Peter was standing, watching the crowd about to board, when Hugh came up to him and mentioned his find. Peter nodded and the two of them proceeded back to the VIP club.

Inside, Peter glanced into the corner briefly. "That's Zekki Dekka. As usual, he looks like he's going to a diplomatic convention. I never saw the character with him before but he looks like a Chechen. They've got to be the ones. Let me handle this alone, okay?"

"I'll keep out of your way, Peter," Hugh promised.

With a smile on his face Peter walked across the rapidly emptying club to the surprised pair. Standing over the two he began to address them in Russian. Zekki and his companion looked up at the detective in surprise.

After some rapid fire conversation Zekki Dekka suddenly recognized Hugh McDonald standing aside. Without any salutation and as though seeing the ex-CIA man was an everyday occurrence the obviously aggrieved Zekki blurted to Hugh in English, "Hey, Hugh! Tell this detective he's way out of line." He gestured at the dark-skinned man next to him. "I can vouch for this man's whereabouts all this day."

"You've been in here all evening?" Peter snapped.

Zekki threw a hesitant glance at the blonde older woman attendant at the desk. "No, we just came in a few minutes ago."

"I'd like to take your friend over to Brighton Beach, the Kiev Restaurant."

Zekki glanced at his watch and feigned innocence at the sudden mention of the place. "Impossible. He's got to be on board his plane to Frankfurt in five minutes."

"Frankfurt will still be there tomorrow," Peter replied. "I also want him for questioning at the Brooklyn DA's office."

"On what grounds?" Zekki asked.

"Two Soviets I believe to be from Georgia were murdered, almost certainly by another Soviet citizen. I have been hearing about a man nicknamed Chechen prowling around Little Odessa —looking for someone. I think your friend here is the man we're looking for."

The subject of this conversation looked back and forth between Peter and Zekki as they talked. Suddenly the suspect stood to his feet, a burly man of over six feet, and scowled at Peter. A torrent of harsh Russian words came from his mouth.

"Zekki," Peter said in a warning tone, "tell your gorilla I can now arrest him for disorderly behavior. I want to see his papers. Now!"

Zekki quickly muffled the man, who pulled out a packet of papers and tickets from his inner pocket and handed them over.

"This passport looks forged." Peter shook his head. Russian passports indicate ethnic origin. "This man is no more a Russian Jewish emigré named Josef Zilinski than I am."

"He's under the protection of the New York Agency for New Americans," Zekki replied. "You know what they can do to any cop accused of anti-Semitic actions."

"What are you doing masquerading this Chechen as a Jewish emigré?" Hugh demanded.

"He has full accreditation with NYANA and his travel documents are all in order," Zekki insisted. "Detective Nikhilov interferes with Mr. Zilinski at his own political risk."

A club attendant walked over to them. "The flight to Frankfurt is boarding now," she said urgently.

Peter knew he had to let it go. Damn, he thought. "OK. I expect I do not have probable cause to detain him. But you, Zekki, I want you at the Kings County District Attorney's office tomorrow morning at eleven A.M. Sharp!"

"I'll be there, Peter Nikhilov," he gave the name its proper Russian pronunciation, 'Nik HI lov' and grinned knowingly. "I assure you."

As the emigré stood up Peter added a few words in Russian. The only word Hugh caught was Yaponchik. A look of surprise and even fear came over the suspect's hard features. Then he and Zekki, followed by Peter and Hugh, left the VIP lounge. Peter walked with them all the way to the gate and watched as the suspect handed his ticket to the gate attendant. Once his feet were inside the boarding ramp the swarthy one turned and showed his teeth in a huge grimace at Peter before turning and scuttling down the ramp to the interior of the airliner.

The dapper Zekki Dekka waved. "Until tomorrow then." He turned and strolled away.

Peter looked after him shaking his head. "I'm going home and send a fax to the guys at Petrovka 38 about this scene. Come with me for a drink and then I'll drive you into the city."

Peter lived in a neat house in Forest Hills convenient to the airports and his office via the Brooklyn Queens Expressway. He pulled into his driveway and led the way to his back door which he unlocked.

"You're all alone here?" Hugh asked as they entered the kitchen.

"Depends," Peter replied enigmatically. He switched on the lights. "Go ahead." He gestured toward the well-lighted stairs to the basement. Some basement, Hugh thought as he took the last steps into the brightly lighted comfortable office and sitting room.

"This is the command center," he said proudly. Along the wall to Hugh's left as he stood at the bottom of the steps was a display of photographs, paintings, framed letters, and a green feltboard to which were pinned a myriad of small colorful commemorative pins and medals. The wall was as Russian as St. Basil's. In fact there was a picture of Peter and some friends standing in Red Square, the colorful onion-shaped domes looming behind them.

Peter pointed to some of the pictures. "That's my great-grandfather." Hugh nodded at the picture of the stern-looking uniformed old man. "He was a general in the Czar's army, one of the first to be executed by the Bolsheviks."

He pointed to the photograph of a bosomy, lace shawled, grande dame. "That was my grandmother. She took my mother and aunt to the family home in Kiev. They grew up in the Ukraine and then between Stalin's forced famine and the constant hunting down of suspected Czarists—" he stopped himself short. "In any case to make a long and bitter story short, the women in my family found their way to America."

"Was your father American?" Hugh asked.

Peter shook his head. "I was born in Germany. Dad was captured by the Germans during the war, so were a lot of Russians and Ukrainians, men and women. Since my parents were not Jewish they were allowed to work and they met in Germany where I was born close to the end of the war. They swore never to go back to Russia while Stalin was dictator."

A bitter look pinched Peter's face. "Roosevelt made a deal with Stalin at Yalta to send all Soviet citizens back whether they wished to return or not. Dad hid out with us in Germany for a couple of years after the war." There was a pause and Peter went on hollowly. "But the Americans found him and turned him over to the Russians. We never heard from him again."

"Yalta," Hugh spewed the word in disgust. "Roosevelt was a sick old man."

Peter shrugged. "I was lucky. My mother and grandmother and aunt were able to immigrate to New York. I grew up in Brooklyn."

Peter opened a door to a back room and switched on the lights revealing a well-stocked bar. "Help yourself while I get a fax out to Moscow Militsia headquarters. They need to know who's on his way." Peter sighed, thinking of his decision not to detain the Chechen. "The hassle the DA's office would have to go through if I had arrested and held him isn't worth it."

"So you are still an active detective?" Hugh asked.

Peter sat down behind his computer. "Being helpful to the Moscow cops is good for my business between Moscow and New York."

"Can I make you a drink?" Hugh asked.

"Sure, a gin and tonic?"

"In the winter?"

"That's my drink."

Peter wrote and sent the fax message to Moscow and then took the drink Hugh made him.

"Is your mother still with you?" Hugh asked.

"I bought this house for her after my aunt and grandmother died, but she's in a nursing home now. She and my wife never got along anyway but no sooner did mother go away than my Irish Catholic wife, who wanted this place to herself and finally got it, decided it was really me she couldn't stand and she took off."

"And you are alone here?"

"In the day this office is a busy place."

"Maybe I could shed some light on the Zekki Dekka situation."

Peter shot a surprised look at him. "We know he is a master forger."

"And counterfeiter," Hugh added. "The Agency got him out of prison to work for us."

"Why the hell did you do that?" Peter snapped.

"The Agency had a plan to destabilize the Soviet ruble," Hugh went on.

He took another long swallow of the drink he had made. "Anyway, we were going to counterfeit huge amounts of rubles."

"And you never followed through?" Peter asked.

"We almost did. It was during the darkest days of what President Reagan called the 'evil empire.' Remember when they shot down Korean Flight 007 in 1983? There were several very high up U.S. government agents aboard. Among the two hundred and sixty nine people killed was Congressman Larry MacDonald who was a special friend of the President's and member of the House Foreign Affairs Committee."

"So the CIA boss, Bill Casey, put the operation back on the front burner again," Peter concluded.

Hugh nodded. "Red Rolf and I even went so far as to spring Zekki Dekka so he could help us etch the high denomination ruble plates. He is considered the most skilled forger and counterfeiter in the business by the experts."

"And then, once again, you were ordered to scrub the mission," Peter filled in, "leaving Zekki on the outside for me to contend with. Thanks a lot." There was a mock bitter tone in his voice.

"What if the CIA plan was actually carried out many years later, say right now?" Hugh posited. "By some of the guys who originated it. On their own."

"Then Zekki Dekka would be the main man to watch."

"That's what I think, too," Hugh said.

"Well, let's keep in touch."

"Will you work with us, Peter?" Hugh asked.

"I'll help by keeping a close watch on Zekki. Beyond that we'd have to talk."

"There are a lot of experienced old duffers like me who need guys like you. If you'll watch Zekki and follow the murder investigation, I'll be very grateful."

"You got a deal, Hugh. I'll run you back to New York and then I'm going to stop in at the Russian Samovar and see what new lovely talent has come over from Russia. Russian women understand cynical bastards like me. And vice versa. I may be a part-time cop but one of these days I plan to start another family."

He pulled out his ponderous pocket watch. "Almost midnight in Manhattan." He held it tightly a moment. "I have a hunch I'll be putting this little gem to the use for which it was created."

CHAPTER FOUR

⋖⃛⋗ ⋖⃛⋗

It was at the end of her first year at the Maurice Thorez Language Institute in 1988 that Oksana Martinova and her closest friend, Tanya, had just successfully passed another set of tests in German and English and received their students' maintenance fees. They enjoyed sharing their secrets and found pleasure in reading English books together. Now, with the term exams behind them on this beautiful fall day, they decided to buy a bottle of light wine, a pack of cigarettes, perhaps some chocolates, and go to Oksana's apartment that her father kept to provide comfort on his trips to Moscow for PolitBureau and Party meetings.

They walked through the streets of Moscow. Sunshine broke the pink autumn haze into opaque mild light creating a mood of lightness and relaxation. At the corner of Arbat Street they came upon the flea market and waited patiently in line on the sidewalk to enter the small liquor shop.

Everything imaginable was for sale at the tables set up on the wide sidewalks and although champagne bottles were displayed in profusion, Tanya insisted they wait in line. There was no telling what you might find in the street bottles, she warned, and pointed out to an inexperienced Oksana the furtive swarthy men lurking at side-street corners. Each sidewalk merchant had his own racketeer who took a percentage of the day's sales in return for 'protection' from other menacing racketeers.

Finally it was their turn to step inside and examine the bottles of wine and vodka standing on well-stocked shelves. The old, bewhiskered, tired-looking storekeeper recognized Tanya and when she voluntarily overpaid for two bottles of Soviet champagne he did not ask for her weekly ration stamp.

Not far away from the shopping center was Oksana's apartment located in a block of five-story houses.

By eleven o'clock that night one bottle of champagne was empty, the other quickly going the same way, the cigarette supply exhausted. Oksana's loneliness in Moscow was only gradually receding. She still missed her home on Lake Baikal and her family apartment in Irkutsk. She was a Siberian girl at heart and the overpowering massiveness of Moscow depressed her. For her father's sake she studied hard at the language institute in which she had been enrolled shortly after her mother's death during the worst winter at home she could remember. She was desolate at the school and completely dissatisfied with the callow young men she met. They pawed her awkwardly and made her feel as though she were some kind of an object to satisfy their physical desires.

Her unhappiness deteriorated to despair at the turn her life was taking. But above all else she had to please her father after the loss of her mother. She was making every effort at her command to become an outstanding English and German interpreter.

Tanya helped her adjustment to Moscow life. Now, as they sipped their wine, the girls' talk shifted to aphrodisiacs and drugs in general. "Know what?" Tanya said suggestively, "I've heard that if you add a little Demerol to wine it produces some wild fantasies, you see all kinds of exciting visions."

"Like what?" Oksana asked.

"Guys give it to girls at parties to arouse them, make them sexy."

"Do the guys get aroused?" Oksana asked.

"They are always horny without any Demerol," Tanya laughed.

"You know this guy, Igor, in the German group?" Oksana asked. "When he is talking to me his gaze is never above the level of my breasts."

"Yeah," Tanya chuckled. "I doubt our guys will ever recognize us by face portraits."

They laughed happily. It was so nice to sit opposite laughing, small lovely Tanya in the kitchen, stretching out long slim legs in black nylon stockings. Then, impulsively, Tanya stood up and went to her floppy black pocket book. "Let's see if Demerol in wine really does do something for a girl," she laughed. "I have a box here." She shook several tablets into her hand and returned to the table refilling their glasses with the last of the sparkling wine.

She dropped the pills into the two glasses and stirred them with a spoon. As they sipped the wine they kept on chatting, but soon began to feel sleepy, laughing easily and losing track of the conversation.

"Time to go to bed," Oksana finally said, "or we won't get up tomorrow for class."

They both went into the bedroom, Oksana feeling dazed and uninhibited. She managed to pull her blouse and brassiere over her head and drop them on the floor. Then she stripped her skirt, stockings, and thin white underpants off her body in one smooth motion and flopped onto the bed wriggling under the blanket.

Tanya undressed in much the same way and slipped in with her. Tanya was shorter than Oksana, blonde, with a diminutive, well-proportioned body. The blankets felt cold and alien, producing shivers. They embraced each other without any further thought. In half an hour they felt warm and cozy, but there was more. The sensuousness of their two young smooth bodies against each other was bewildering to Oksana, something unexpected.

Waves of tenderness and heat passed between them. Their minds were floating and light as air, their thoughts going in languid low circles, like yellow merry autumn leaves flying from a tree in the garden mist.

Oksana's eyes drifted to Tanya and she made not the slightest move as her friend put her warm moist mouth on her right breast, full lips closing over the nipple. Tanya's tongue depressed the nipple back deep into the breast flesh, moving over it in circular movements. Oksana gasped in surprise; she couldn't believe what Tanya was actually doing with her—she had never imagined that such intimacy between her and another girl could ever occur in her life. Nevertheless, her breasts grew firm, and her nipples became erect as hot waves rippled along her spine and melted in her pelvis, somewhere in the cloying depth between her hips.

Tanya was already embracing her, their legs locked together in reflexive, sliding, sinuous movements. Tanya took Oksana's left breast into her mouth, slipping her hand all the way down her tender stomach letting her fingers caress soft curly hair and into the moist hot opening. The two girls felt and saw nothing any more but the hot curves of breasts, thighs and buttocks. Their mouths met in a kiss, tongues flicking wildly against each other.

Tanya's mouth was going down the length of Oksana's body. "No, do not do that, no . . . please."

Then, "Yes, please go down right there, oh, what are you doing?" Oksana heard herself moaning to her more experienced girlfriend. She pressed Tanya's head tighter with her palms, squeezing her with her thighs. Oksana's breasts swelled, caught tightly between her own arms, the exquisite waves of heat choking her as her spasm-stricken throat emitted wild, guttural, greedy, triumphant, long outcries followed by ferocious rocking of the body.

Later Oksana, following Tanya's softly murmured instructions and encouragements, bestowed the same ultimate pleasure on her first lover as she had just been given, thrilled at eliciting Tanya's climactic cries of exquisite sensation.

Finally, as the first white light of dawn shone through the window, the two girls fell into a sleep of deep exhaustion.

Waking now in the morning they both felt an enormous surge of joy and satisfaction; laughing and embracing each other they exchanged congratulations being now true lesbians. In the shower together, under the pinpoint needles of hot water, caressing soaped bodies, they again found themselves aroused and spent several hours in the bath and emerged exhausted once again, almost numb from such overexposure to sexual excitement. Class studies were therefore happily missed that day.

The affair continued unabated for a year. They met at least twice a week at Oksana's apartment or at Tanya's, to study their lessons and practice speaking English and German together. Sometimes during the lessons they would feel building desire, making each girl mad with need; they would go to the bedroom and almost tear away each other's clothes—bras and other garments flying all over the room.

Reading many books in English where lesbian activities were described, they improved the technique of their lovemaking, trying all possible ways of excitement—even the puncture of nipples and clitoris with tender needle pricks.

They discovered that the lesbian community in the Institute of Foreign Languages was really vast, comprising at least a hundred girls. But most preferred to remain true to just one lover.

Boys in the Institute were really curious about Oksana, trying to guess whom she was dating, but in vain. Girls were devilishly smart covering up their homosexuality, but the traces of their lovemaking were hard to conceal—time and again they would appear in the classes with livid spots on their necks, especially Oksana from Tanya's voracious mouth. But the origins of these bruises remained obscure to the boys.

After a year the situation with Oksana's personal affairs began to change. Tanya started dating a boy who was a jealous type and demanded as much time as possible with Tanya, which limited her meetings with Oksana.

So Oksana succumbed to the pleas of Igor, a fellow student who constantly followed her and appeared at her side. Finally Oksana agreed to go out with him one evening. But after several dates with Igor she dropped it. Igor was no better than the other urgent males she invited up to her apartment after going out. His hands and fingers lacked the elastic tender electricity which she had come to crave. He would climax too soon and had not the least experience in bestowing the vast pleasure of erotic kisses so expertly developed by generations of lesbians.

Oksana and Tanya, as their relationship waned with Tanya's discovery of males who knew how to use their manhood to best and fullest advantage, decided to go out for a final dinner together.

It was seven o'clock of an early spring evening in 1991, during their third year at the institute. The "Peking" restaurant was filling with customers. Clouds of smoke from hundreds of cigarettes, some the smooth American Marlboros, others the harsh native hemp, wafted among the intricate Chinese columns. A blaze of Chinese colored bas reliefs combined with traditional Buddhist designs, complicated nets of flowers, dragons, lions, and horrible masks of pagan Mongolian gods to decorate the walls and ceiling. The restaurant was equipped to entertain and feed about a thousand guests at one time and did capacity business every night.

The visitors included numerous guests from the "Peking" hotel above the restaurant, foreigners of all stripe from Vietnamese, Koreans, Japanese and Uzbeks to Europeans and the growing number of Americans filtering into the Soviet capital looking for business opportunities in the wake of Gorbachev's proclaimed "Perestroika" and "Glasnost."

KGB and Militsia officials mingled with Mafia and Communist Party bosses and their underlings along with Moscow students, prostitutes, and all manner of con men.

Oksana and Tanya occupied a small table in the far corner near a small fountain in a wall basin. The hall was already full of customers, numerous groups giving parties, ordering supper, talking business over a bottle of green chartreuse liquor and coffee, prostitutes hunting for clients, and visitors tasting exquisite cuisine.

The buzzing hum of voices filled the air with the clanking of dishes, glasses and forks; the luminescence of cigarette smog surrounding the chandeliers increased in density as the evening went on.

Oksana and Tanya spent about an hour sipping coffee and gossiping about the students and instructors at the Institute and then they caught sight of a woman sitting down at the neighboring table. Both girls stared unabashedly at the unusually tall and lean woman's well-proportioned figure, with her handsome face artfully made up. A wave of dark hair cascaded over her delicate shoulders. She wore a white blouse which contrasted with her dark eyes and hair and was tucked tightly into a golden silk miniskirt, slit to reveal upper thighs of long slim legs in black stockings. She was accompanied by three not quite sober men. Oksana was annoyed to see one of the men with the palm of his hand on the lady's thigh under the table trying to move it further up. The expression on the black-haired slim woman was one of absolute indifference as she argued with another companion. Occasionally, as though brushing off a fly, she pushed away the guy's hand poised to disappear under the skirt, and threw out a sharp word or two at him. The other two men laughed.

With a sympathetic glance Oksana's eyes met the woman's dark-eyed gaze as she seemed to study the two so-innocent appearing young girls at the next table. A knowing smile passed between them and Oksana felt an immediate attraction to the older woman. She was intriguing and charming. Oksana couldn't help trying to imagine what she might be doing out with these three unseemly men, but Tanya wanted to go, probably because she had spent most of her rubles, so she and Oksana laid out the money for the check and a tip and stood up to leave.

Oksana and the woman were giving each other farewell glances as Tanya said, "I will stop by the toilet," and walked down the aisle between the rows of tables toward the entrance. Oksana shrugged, turned and followed her to the toilet. The place seemed empty and Oksana waited while Tanya finished in a stall. Moments later they started to leave but it was not going to be as easy getting out as it was entering the toilet. The exit was barred by the most strange creature, a dwarfish, incredibly dirty, old man clutching a wooden crutch with his left hand. His clothes were ill fitting and badly stained. He wore a dirty gray cap on his head. The expression in his small, red tinted, squinting eyes was both moronic and vicious. A dirty bristle covered the lower part of his face.

Tanya and Oksana stared at the apparition in horror. No normal imagination could project the existence of this nasty goblin in the center of Moscow, in an expensive restaurant. Yet here he was, his right arm hidden in the sleeve of his jacket. But as the two girls stared, appalled, the little monster shoved his fist through the sleeve. A long, thin glistening blade emerged. The girls froze.

"Now girlies," the bizarre creature croaked, "let us not be in a hurry. We have time to play."

The blood drained from Oksana's face and glancing sidewise she saw that Tanya was paler than the toilet wall. The evil-looking gnome advanced toward them, mouth aquiver, red eyes glaring. He looked to be wondering which girl he would molest first as Oksana and Tanya backed into the wash basins and could retreat no further.

"What the hell is going on?" A woman's sharp tone cracked out.

The two girls and their antagonist turned toward the door of the toilet. The lean, dark-haired woman was standing in the entrance way in a seductive, self-assured pose, one arm on her hip, the other holding a long brown cigarette. Her high heels gave her figure an even taller look.

"Get away slut. We donna wantya here," the gnarled one snapped, his knife blade still pointed at Tanya and Oksana.

"Ah ha!" she exclaimed as though it were all clear to her including how she would handle this weird situation. She placed the cigarette between her lips, inhaled deeply and blew out a cloud of smoke. Then, with an outstretched hand, she languidly shook the ashes from her cigarette, took a casual strolling long step toward the pig-eyed gnome, and delivered a sudden, shocking, powerful right-leg kick at the breast level. The old man was much shorter and her high heel caught him at the base of the throat.

His knife flew to one side, his crutch to the other. The goblin went over backward losing his balance, one leg shooting out from under him and straight up in the air. He collapsed backward into a stall where he lay motionless.

"Let's get the hell out of here," their rescuer said. "Come on, we'll catch a cab."

Once in the cab heading away from Peking restaurant the girls learned their savior's name was Nadia. In the next few minutes the girls discovered that they owed their gratitude to a professional prostitute.

"I entertain men for 500 rubles a session," Nadia stated nonchalantly. "And you girls?"

"We're students," Oksana answered.

"Where did you learn to kick so beautifully?" Tanya asked.

"My husband used to beat me when he got drunk, but I was never shy. I learned how to strike back."

Oksana invited Nadia to come up to her apartment to talk further but had to apologize for not having anything to drink. Nadia laughed, gave the cab driver an address, and soon she stepped out of the cab and returned with a bottle of cognac. The three girls went up to Oksana's apartment, Nadia smiling wanly as she went along with her newly found friends.

CHAPTER FIVE

Yaponchik, the Jap, had risen to his thief-in-the-law power after fate intervened in his life taking the form of Galina, Party Chairman Leonid Brezhnev's daughter. Galina's first husband was a bear trainer, whom she had met at the circus. He was a burly, kind man; Galina was a renowned slut. After a number of long-suffering years the circus performer went to his father-in-law and said he had no guts to beat his wife. Therefore he wanted a divorce. During their years of married life Galina had taken numerous low-class lovers and frequently did not come home for several days at a time.

Brezhnev sighed, gave his consent, and to reward the young man for putting up with Galina during their marriage he appointed him a director of the New Moscow Circus.

Yuri Churbanov was a common investigator in the Special Crimes Unit of the Militsia at Petrovka 38. He was twenty-eight years old and as handsome as Apollo. The moment Galina met him at a Militsia reception she was consumed with an insatiable lust for Yuri. Churbanov succumbed to his own lust for power and married the forty-year-old fat, ugly, moustached daughter of the Communist Party General Secretary.

Brezhnev, at heart a generous and mild person, lavished gifts, ranks, and prestige upon the new family martyr, husband to his daughter. Thus, in a short period an ordinary policeman became a General and an associate of the Minister of Home Affairs, General Shelokov, the most corrupt figure in Brezhnev's inner circle.

Yuri cultivated the rising figures in Moscow's criminal elite and soon learned that a recently made "thief-in-the-law" known as Yaponchik, The Jap, was one of the most reliable assassins in the Moscow Mafia and a personal henchman to the Mongol. There was never any thought on the part of the Militsia of arresting these high level criminals. All of them, and the Mongol in particular, were protected by powerful members of the PolitBureau and deputies of the Communist Party who profited handsomely from these connections.

Late one fall night in 1974 the Jap was entertaining a beautiful, very young blonde girl who had just arrived in Moscow from Minsk, the capital of Belorussia. He loved blondes and wanted to be the first to take this one. He was therefore seriously annoyed when there was a sharp knock on the door to the apartment he thought was a secret location. Angrily, his *pchak* in hand, he went to the door and shouted through it for whoever was there to go instantly or die.

"Militsia!" came the answering shout. "Vyacheslav Kyrillovitch Yakovlev, open up!"

The Jap was shocked to hear his real name. Very few people in Moscow knew him as anything but Yaponchik, the Jap. He cracked the door and to his amazement when the Jap looked around his door he saw General Churbanov standing outside in civilian clothes. He had seen the son-in-law of Brezhnev twice before since Jap's mentor, the Mongol, conducted direct affairs with Minister Shelokov himself. Without hesitation the

Jap returned the knife to its sheath concealed under the top of his pants and followed Churbanov out to the street and into a gleaming black sedan, driven by a uniformed Militsiaman.

"It has been reported to me that you are a serious man. This is a serious matter. So you behave accordingly."

The Jap nodded silently, still impressed that Churbanov knew his real name, and made an obedient face. He knew how to seem loyal and friendly.

The car stopped near a high building on Kotelnik embankment, not far from Taganka. It was half past twelve at night. The monstrous gothic structure of a cathedral-like building of at least twenty stories towered in front of them, its peak concealed by the night fog. Together they mounted the wide marble steps to the massive sets of wooden doors through which they strode and the Jap found himself in the lobby of a hotel, which occupied the central part of this Soviet skyscraper.

The elevator took them to the fifteenth floor. Very few people indeed knew that this hotel, luxury apartment and office building in the center of Moscow concealed the most exclusive brothel in the capital at its upper stories. The amenity was reserved for party leaders. Mafia bosses of the highest level were not strangers here either.

At the entrance to the apartments which made up the brothel, they were met by two impeccably dressed and groomed men—the place was under the meticulous supervision of the KGB.

Routinely checking Yuri's credentials the sentinels virtually jumped away from him realizing who he was, and Yuri led Jap inside. The evening was in full swing. The long hall of the apartment was filled with a dense cloud of cigarette smoke and exuded the unmistakable smell of *anasha*, a virulent cannabis grown in Central Asia.

Half-naked young girls in teasing underwear were everywhere, sitting in men's laps, cigarettes and drinks in their hands, or wandering around the place entertaining a horde of guests. Companies of middle-aged men with reddened happy faces, wearing informal suits, their neckties and shirt collars loosened, passed among the lively girls sitting with their legs as high as possible revealing the pleasures they had to offer. The spacious accommodations echoed with women's laughter, inebriated male cries of excitement, and the blare of Western jazz music.

Yuri was met by a short fat man in a blue shirt, obviously a gypsy—black haired, gold chain around his short, hairy neck. "In here," the gypsy breathed. "Do not make any noise."

The three of them entered a darkened empty room with heavy red curtains at the far end concealing yet another chamber. The gypsy approached the curtains cautiously and parted them enough to make a very narrow opening. He gestured for Yuri and Jap to come closer. At first the Jap could observe nothing, partly because it was dark behind the curtains, partly because Yuri was peering between the draperies, his tall, broad back obstructing the slit into the next room. Suddenly Yuri spun around. Even in the dim light the Jap could see his handsome face contorted in rage, his eyes cold and cruel slits.

Jap moved up to the curtains and peered inside. At first he could distinguish nothing specific in the darkness and then he made out a number of moving, naked bodies, several girls were performing fellatio, two girls lay on the floor with their clients on top pounding into them vigorously in time to their stentorian breathing.

All of a sudden his attention was riveted on three people in the far corner. A woman in her mid-forties, fat and somewhat hairy with a big belly, was bent over forward supported by her hands and feet on the floor, her huge, shapeless breasts heaving to the rhythmical movement of an even more hairy and fat man behind her while simultaneously she was devouring the organ of another man lying under her head, his legs apart, as he snorted and tried to heave himself into yet another rhythm.

Something seemed familiar to the Jap about that female figure as she abruptly rolled on her back, spreading her legs widely, her ponderous gut moving upwards as her huge flabby breasts fell apart. For a moment Jap saw the wide, fleshy almost-moustached face of the woman before the swarthy man who had been lying on his back below her straddled her head. The second hirsute player in the sordid drama climbed on top of her and continued his activities in the more conventional position. Now once more her face could not be seen behind the bare heaving buttocks . . . but for Jap he had seen enough. He suddenly felt cold sweat on his forehead and up and down his spine. It was no joke, no mere perverted performance for special guests allowed to look behind the curtains. The woman was none other than Galina Brezhneva, Yuri's wife, daughter of everyone knows who. . . . Shit! She had gone too far. He turned to Yuri.

The gypsy was frantically trying to explain. "I could not help it! She would not listen to me, you know when she is drunk. . . . Well, I called you right away. Besides. . . . Besides," he licked his lips, "they paid her . . ."

"What!?" Yuri almost shrieked, "what did you say?" He seized the gypsy by the collar of his shirt, tearing at it in utter fury.

The gypsy bent his face closer to Yuri and whispered hurriedly and fervently. "They paid her! In diamonds! She would sell us all to the enemy, together with Papa himself, for a handful of those bloody stones!"

Slowly Yuri became rational, his face composing itself. He shoved back his hair with the palm of his hand. Jap was frightened, but his face remained emotionless. Yuri stuck his finger into the Jap's breast.

"You saw it all, heard it all." Anger and disgust still distorted his tone of voice. "I want the asses of those two bastards, no matter what, I want their fucking asses! You will learn their background, where they come from and then they must never be found. But before they die . . ."

"I understand," Jap said. "I am serious, I understand. They won't ever be found—and they will suffer, I can promise you that. No one will know anything. You can be sure."

Yuri nodded, his breathing slowing. He took the glass from the gypsy's trembling hand and threw down several greedy swallows of vodka. Then to Jap, "If you need anything techni-cal—weapons, anything—just call me." He handed the Jap a white card with only a number on it. "Just add one to each number and you'll reach me."

"I will need an asphalt roll," the Jap said.

"What?" Yuri and the gypsy asked almost as one.

"An asphalt roll," the Jap repeated. "There are many roads in Russia that need paving," he added, a wise look on his face. "And one other thing, if you like. One of your police surveil-lance cameras."

The scene that took place a few days later was preserved for the edification of Yuri Churbanov. At a remote construction site in a half-built house, the two Georgians were hanging with their hands tied up to an iron pole that ran across the ceiling. After their seizure by Jap's men as they left the Georgian restaurant Iveria, forty kilometers from Moscow, unaware they had eaten the last meal of their lives, they were brought to the prepared place. First they were beaten to a pulp; then Jap's meanest Chechens, the most vicious ethnic group in Russia, raped them in turns, then made them perform oral acts on each other under the pistol barrels. After that they were hung by the hands, several dozen cigarette butts were put out against their bare buttocks, and finally their genitals were mutilated. During the torture sessions Jap studied their identification documents minutely. Both of them were KGB officers from Georgia, a colonel and a major, people of Eduard Shevardnadze. The diamonds they gave Galina had come to them as bribes.

Jap had learned much from his gangsters operating in the south about Shevardnadze, head of the KGB in Georgia. He had accumulated tremendous power. He was taking bribes from all the mafia bosses whose criminal activities took place within his sphere of authority. He also had another even more insidious and profitable operation working for him.

KGB had full data on criminal activities of high-ranking Communist Party officials. According to a secret regulation issued by Krushchev after Stalin's death and the collapse of Secret Police Chief Beria, KGB was ordered to wipe out all records of malfeasance on the part of Communist Party officials. This applied all the way down to the lowest rung of the Communist hierarchy, city district chairman. Thus party leaders were free of any legal control in the state and had almost unlimited power to operate as they pleased. All traces of their crimes which might come to the public eye or the attention of the police were exterminated immediately as were any further reports on party officials the Militsia might gather during the course of an investigation.

But Shevardnadze restricted his officers from destroying the incriminating material and encouraged them to collect extensive reports on illegal activities on these party apparatchiks who thought themselves immune from the law.

He systematically blackmailed Georgian Communist Party leaders, corrupt beyond imagination, and thus obtained considerable wealth, hiding it in Swiss banks and into legal enterprises run by the Italian and Sicilian Mafia in southern Europe. His closest associate was the First Secretary of Stavropol Regional Communist Party Committee, a simple-looking peasant guy with a strawberry in the bald spot above his right forehead named Mikhail Gorbachev. But Gorbachev was not that simple. His lust for bribes earned him the nick-name "Purse" in Stavropol.

The Jap learned more from the documents he found on the two KGB agents, information which assisted him in interrogating them, making them think he would spare their lives if they told him everything. He quickly realized that Shevardnadze was a highly dangerous person which was all the more reason why these KGB men must disappear without a trace, or his own life would be at grave risk.

The two Georgian KGB agents kept talking between fainting spells from losing blood. They offered Jap enormous ransom in money and jewels for their lives but he was not impressed. Both of these KGB men, who had made the mistake of earning Yuri Churbanov's undying enmity when they romped in the whorehouse with his wife, were rolled in a tarpaulin and dragged from the unfinished house to the dirt road in front of it where a roller and a heap of hot asphalt were waiting.

The victims were thrown into a pit in the road and the Jap's musclemen started to shovel hot asphalt upon them. When the two were completely covered and the paving material was piled high above them the roller drove over it. But the smooth black surface creased and rippled suddenly, something was moving ferociously down there. The Jap's guys added several more shovels full of asphalt and the roller made a few more passes and finally everything was still. More pavement had been added to Russia's roads.

The Jap did not appear in any of the photographs since he took them all. He destroyed the negatives and presented the pictures to Yuri Churbanov. In his magnificent office at Petrovka 38, Militsia headquarters, Yuri studied the photos, an expression of deep satisfaction on his face. He listened attentively as the Jap, sitting opposite him in a deep leather chair, poured out the information he had gleaned about Shevardnadze.

"This is interesting," he enthused. "This is hell of a fuck interesting. Papa will love hearing about this."

At the time Jap could not even imagine that he had granted Shevardnadze an invaluable service instead of bringing down his career.

By his blackmailing activities as KGB General-Lieutenant in charge of Georgia, he not only gained enormous profits but also amassed a whole army of bitter enemies. Georgia Communist Party officials decided to rid the republic of the head of the KGB. A Communist Party Congress in Tbilisi, capital of Georgia, was scheduled and every member of the Congress had secretly agreed to vote for his immediate discharge. Later, when he was out of office, Shevardnadze would be made to pay for humiliating the deputies and, with coercion by mafia hoodlums, he would be pursuaded to make up their financial losses.

Brezhnev himself was informed by the head of the Georgian Communist Party that Shevardnadze was unacceptable to the members and that he was not the right person for the office he had despoiled and used for personal gain.

Late at night on the eve of the Georgia Congress, the "not right person" was put on a plane by Churbanov's men and brought to Moscow. Shevardnadze was rich and practical but not a greedy man. He arrived in Moscow with two briefcases full of diamonds and within the hour had presented one to Shelokov, Minister of Internal Affairs, the other to Brezhnev, head of the Communist Party of the USSR. The same evening, as the leader of the Soviet Union ran the diamonds through his fingers, he made a telephone call to Tbilisi and issued his orders to the key members of the Georgia Communist Party.

Shevardnadze returned to Georgia in the morning. The Congress of the Communist Party was underway when he arrived. At this remarkable assembly, once more the unshakable unity of the Communist Party and common working people was evident. The Party confirmed its intention to follow the course of the great Lenin to further victories and labor achievements in the name of prosperity for the Soviet people and world peace.

The worthy son of Socialist Georgia, the true Lenin-type communist, Eduard Ambrosy Shevardnadze was elected the First Secretary of the Communist Party of Georgia; his predecessor resigned due to serious health problems.

CHAPTER SIX

By the close of classes in early June, she received an appointment as an interpreter for the Hotel Russia in the center of Moscow—for summer practicing of language capabilities. At last she was beginning to interpret for foreigners, and it was then that she started to realize what the institute was all about.

Maurice Thorez Institute of Foreign Languages, named after its founder, the head of the French Communist Party, was fundamentally another department of the KGB masked by the cover of an education establishment. By the time students had graduated they became arms of KGB one way or another; about one fourth would become KGB officers. The career of the interpreter was impossible without KGB protection. In return numerous translators and interpreters rendered to KGB all kinds of minor services—information about foreign guests for whom they were interpreting, searching through their luggage in hotel suites when the guests were absent, planting packages of drugs into foreigners' suitcases when KGB wanted to provoke a scandal, and many other services.

Oksana confronted this situation the very first day of her new assignment. Her group, consisting of five students, three girls and two male youths, was called into a room at the institute to face a young man with an expressionless face wearing a neat formal gray suit. Oksana noticed his gaze focusing on her legs encased in new flesh colored silk stockings.

"So Comrades," the KGB man began, "tomorrow begins your first day of work and we, 'soldiers of the invisible frontier,'" the phrase rolled proudly from his tongue, "will assist you and teach you not to make mistakes."

A lecture on ideology culminated in the observation, "Westerners can be very amiable and friendly, but you should remember, that under masks of friendliness hide potential enemies."

The young zealot went on for two hours warning against dissidents, traitors and CIA mercenaries. The students were instructed to report on every move and word of the guests and to look for drugs, pornography materials (especially *Playboy* magazine) and bugging devices.

Finally, they were given the numbers of the suites in the hotel used by KGB officers in their surveillance work. When the group was dismissed the officer motioned Oksana to stay behind. In his eyes Oksana read abject physical desire and fury that it could not be fulfilled on the spot. Tenseness at being in a situation she could not control gripped her.

The KGB officer seemed as ill at ease as she was. "Comrade Martinova, we count on you . . ." he stopped abruptly, swallowing saliva forming in his throat.

"Sorry . . . In what respect?"

"Well . . . you are an attractive young woman. Some foreign men will invite you to their suites . . ."

"So what?" she replied taking charge of the conversation. "Are you jealous?"

"You must refuse those proposals," he said sternly.

"Do I look like a whore or something?" she cried belligerently.

"No! I didn't mean it that way."

"Well, if you don't mind, I must go."

The officer sprang to his feet and demonstrating surprising agility reached the door ahead of her. "By the way, my name is Marat . . ."

"Nice to meet you," Oksana replied curtly and walked from the room feeling his wicked stare between her shoulder blades.

In the days that followed Oksana was amazed at the scale of surveillance KGB maintained at the Hotel Russia. The vast cement cavern at the base of the hotel building was occupied by a technically highly developed electronic surveillance center. Two thousand girls, graduates of KGB schools, took turns sitting there twenty-four hours a day with earphones on their heads, each girl listening for twelve hours to the specific suite to which she was connected. When something interesting was occurring, she would switch on the tape to record all kinds of audible information—beginning with conversation and ending with the gasps and heavy breathing of the inevitable sexual episodes. Many of the tapes, because of the men involved, were highly sensitive on a diplomatic and intelligence level.

These operators arrived at work through an underground passage from KGB premises across Red Square and would leave the same way. Neither hotel personnel nor guests ever saw these operators of the "invisible frontier." Oksana learned about this core of silent female monitors from a lesbian friend among the operators. Later on Oksana realized that all the other Moscow hotels where foreigners stay were equipped with such bugging centers in the underground rooms. Furthermore, the majority of high level hotel personnel were either KGB or Militsia people. Even prostitutes in the halls and in the hotel bars and restaurants were KGB informers—otherwise the doormen would not let them in the building to carry on business.

Oksana found interpreting highly interesting. The foreigners would reach the hotel mainly at night when the planes from western cities arrived at Sheremetievo Airport. It was pleasant dealing with the amiable and friendly visitors. Foreigners were free and easy, well-dressed and had money. The last thing they were thinking of was spying. They came attracted by Perestroika propaganda to do business, and make contacts and friends.

Little did the foreigners realize that from their first steps into Moscow, KGB surrounded them, impersonating doormen, interpreters, waiters, parlor maids, barmen—it was an ubiquitous presence, unseen, silent, polite, but attentive, cunning and recording the least trifles, and of course understanding! It was not, however, the kind of understanding the foreigners had been looking for. One thousand years of oppressive Russian culture capped by seventy years of atheism had bred an inborn mistrust and suspicion of foreigners, and even their own people, in the Muscovite psyche.

Marat was devious with his five students. One of the men, Paul, was already a KGB junior lieutenant. He was Marat's inside spy watching for any sign of party disloyalty on the part of members of his group.

Oksana was happy in her job; she enjoyed conversing with foreigners. Her usual working hours were at night, by day she slept in her apartment—occasionally succumbing to the advances of a lesbian friend, although this was something she sought to outgrow. Her life was on a straight course, she reported to her father, who occasionally came to Moscow for Polit-Bureau meetings. But as it usually happens, the tempest that was to enter her life came swiftly and unexpectedly.

It was well past midnight when Oksana met Anders Prahl. She was sitting at the interpreter desk not far from the doors to the north ground floor of the hotel; there were four entrances although this was the main reception area. Suddenly she caught sight of something most unusual.

Two men passed through the rotating glass doors. One was a porter carrying no luggage which was unusual. But the second man was a weird one. He seemed to be seven feet tall, a giant; his shoulders were twice as broad as those of an average big man. Well-muscled, hairy, obviously unusually powerful arms hung from his shoulders, his legs as thick as columns and also heavily muscled. His thick white hair spread out, untamed by comb or brush above strong chiseled features in his wrinkled manly face. A great beak of a nose and small eyes almost squeezed out of sight by heavy brows and high cheeks, gave him a hawk-like appearance.

The complexion of his face and body was dark tan which could only be the result of many years' exposure to severe wind and sun. He had no belly at all and walked with a youthful light stride. All these details were easily visible because the man was almost devoid of clothes, wearing just blue silk trunks and a sleeveless T-shirt. He stopped in the middle of the reception hall and cast a piercing stare at his surroundings. The hall was almost empty.

In half an hour the entire interpreter group was sitting in chairs surrounding the strange patron, who was soon wrapped in a blanket and smoking. His mountainous figure towered over the students, the self-made cigarette between his wide, thin lips emitting strange odorous smoke. The golden cigarette case with cigarette paper and powder tobacco were his only luggage.

He introduced himself and explained his plight in English. He was on his way for a vacation in Athens. It was a warm early September night when the airliner made a stop at Moscow's Sheremetievo Airport and he decided to debark. While exploring, looking for a bar, the plane took off without him.

Oksana stared at this huge, vital, and confused man. *I've never met such a man before, this Anders Prahl is a real Viking!* she said to herself. For a moment she wondered what might be the size of the Viking's . . . and then cut her thought of it off, blushing and feeling strange heat deep inside.

Meanwhile Prahl talked on to the translators, other girls and boys on the summer assignment from the Institute joining them. He described his perilous job on the North Sea working the offshore oil rigs, and told of his years of strenuous labor which, the young people decided, accounted for his formidable physique.

After several minutes of talk Prahl made his way to the bar draped in his blanket and bought a large bottle of vodka for the last of the dollars in the pocket of his trunks.

"What are you doing?" Oksana scolded as she followed him to the bar, unable to leave him, as if tied to the Viking by an invisible cord. "You won't have money left to pay for the room."

"To hell with room," Anders boomed. "Warm chair, cigarettes and good drink are all I need; at sea for many months you learn quickly the value of simple things—warm fireplace, hot bath, an omelet . . . perhaps an understanding woman."

He smiled at Oksana and took the bottle from the bar. What struck Oksana most forcefully was that the Viking was the first man she had met who looked at her without any sign of wanting to slip his hand into her panties. She had seen that greedy, speculative look in stupid eyes so many times and for so long that the absence of this element in Viking's gaze surprised her, and attracted her even more.

Again they were sitting in the hall, Viking drinking vodka right from the bottle as if seltzer water, without snacking despite the sandwiches that had been brought to him.

"Russians are good fellows," the Viking waxed garrulous. "I've never been in Russia before but I've met Russians many times at sea. And at sea if you meet a man you know him in five minutes. Scum you see at once. I saw no scum among true Russian seamen." He paused, thinking over what he had said. "Well" he amended, "I saw several times really bad guys on Russian ships, not like other sailors; my Russian friends later told me that they were KGB bastards. They are giving the sailors hard times."

"What ship was that, do you remember?" asked Paul, one of the students.

"Drop it, pal. I am a simple man, just an old Scandinavian seagoing fireman." He took another long pull from the bottle. "But I've seen enough to know at one glance which one of you five is on the invisible leash. The only thing I tell you—in real bad situation among real tough guys you go down the drain fast. Think it over."

An uneasy silence fell over the group; the Viking had revealed the junior lieutenant so openly that everyone was frightened. Formally it was their task to persuade foreigners that secret police had nothing to do with interpreters—democracy everywhere, long live Gorbachev! But the truth was so obvious, the wisdom and might of the man so unshakable, that no one uttered a single word.

Two girls soon left under some pretext in order not to get into trouble, then another one walked out of the hall with a second boy saying their working time was over.

The junior lieutenant, Paul, went directly to the KGB suite on the second floor to report the Norwegian's unseemly behavior and blatant disrespect for the secret police and open anti-communist propaganda. Secretly he was furious that the Viking had spotted him that easily in front of the other students.

Oksana and Anders Prahl talked for another two days. She brought food from home so that the Viking was not hungry as he lived in the hall. The hotel would not give a penniless client accommodations but let him sleep and wash up in an empty room. His documents and a suitcase and money were returned from Athens and Viking called his wife to transfer money to the post office in the Russia Hotel. Now he was a valued guest, paying in hard currency.

Oksana would not follow him to his room, knowing about the KGB bugs so he spent most of his time sitting in the hall, talking with her about his rugged life at sea. She was entranced with the Viking and his visit was extended until he could get an exit visa from Moscow.

When Nadia stopped at Oksana's apartment as she did unexpectedly so often, Oksana told her all about him.

"Maybe you should bring me to him," Nadia suggested. "Old men really like me and you say he has hard money."

Oksana felt a strange surge of jealousy and resentment which told her that she was feeling more than friendship for Anders. "He isn't an old man, he is more vital than any of the boys I've ever met. He's a real man!" Nadia caught the look on her friend's face and laughed merrily.

"Well, I hope you get a taste of his manhood before he goes. It's what you need to get straightened out, you know."

On Anders Prahl's last night in Moscow he and Oksana occupied a table for two in a special booth with red leather walls, having the best supper the Viking could order. He was in a dark-blue formal suit with a snow-white shirt, wearing diamond cuff links and a gold pin in his black necktie. His torso towered above the table, the waiter on his feet eye to eye with his customer.

Oksana wore her one evening dress which displayed bare shoulders to which her long black tresses fell. Her halter top revealed a hint of the cleavage between her full breasts. Anders was going to leave by early morning plane for Athens and she wanted him to remember her. Both were feeling awkward and not very talkative, regretful at parting forever.

"I'll leave you my address," Anders said. "Though I do not

know, I'm at sea eight months a year and, to speak frankly, my wife won't be happy to hear a young girl calling me."

Then he shrugged and smiled warmly. "But hell knows, maybe life will take a twist, you will need me, someone in Northern Europe, and I'll do my best to be there for you. The word of an old sea dog, you can rely upon such a one."

Spontaneously Oksana reached a beautifully turned arm across the table, taking his hand in hers. "I know I can, Anders. You are the most . . . most real man of all those I have ever known. Most guys, of all ages, think only of themselves, they do not even know how to please a woman, no manhood . . ."

"You have a boyfriend?"

"Well, I had several, but—that was no good, so . . . see?" she hesitated, then gave him a look begging for understanding—"I like lesbians more; and I do not know—" she blurted, "maybe this is wicked?"

Anders stared off to the side of the table, underlip caught in his teeth for a moment. Then, "No—no I do not think it is; after all you must follow what you feel at the moment, but give the future a chance to shape the course of your life."

He leaned earnestly across the table holding her soulful brown eyes in his snapping Nordic blues. "But you must remember, Oksana, that you should be on the alert always— even in a quiet sea there sometimes out of nowhere comes a giant killer wave." He paused and nodded. "Never forget that he is lucky who has his belt always leashed to the railing . . . Thus you can count only on your own self. No one will tie this leash for you."

A self-depreciating grin came over his face. "Enough morals for this evening. Have some liquor. It is good, especially with chocolates."

"What about you?"

"I'll order hot vodka with sugar and pepper—true sea style."

They left the restaurant after midnight, not observing Marat and Paul seated behind a far corner table watching them. The killer wave was already rising on the horizon, invisible but ready to inundate many in its wake before crashing down and dispersing itself.

Oksana and Anders were standing outside the restaurant in the hall of the second floor. It was dimly lit. No one was around. Common sense told them it was reasonable to part here, but both of them wanted to prolong this moment a bit longer.

"We can go to my room for a last drink," Anders said shyly.

"No," replied Oksana, "I've told you the rooms are bugged. Besides, we had many drinks today, you'll miss your plane again."

He shrugged, put both hands on her shoulder and kissed her gently. "*Do svidaniya*. That's one Russian word I wish I was not saying. Goodbye," He smiled sadly.

Oksana took a deep breath, her heart pounding. "No, do not leave like this. I want you to make love to me before we part."

Somberly Anders consulted the floor, biting his lips. "See, Oksana . . . I really am old, you could be my daughter. I do not want to offend you in any way, you made my unexpected stay in Moscow beautiful. But . . . no way can I do this." He turned to walk away but she seized his arm.

"Wait . . . Do not refuse a young, fervent girl! You are not a Viking then! Why are you like that?"

Anders turned, bewildered by her outburst. "How did you call me? A Viking?"

"You are."

A moment passed in silence. "Forgive me, Oksana," he said at last. "I made a mistake. I myself forgot the real course of life. You are justified, you are right, I should have asked, begged you. It's just I am so much older."

"I only want an older man. I will look for a man as old as my father when I am ready to marry."

"Okay . . . so you say the room is bugged?"

She nodded, then replied. "There is a tourist bus outside the hotel; it is open and empty. It will be at least another two hours before the passengers will come . . . no one will guess." Her voice was adamant and hard, as if she was planning a bank robbery. The old giant, powerful man though he was, felt suddenly weak before the passion emanating from this beautiful tender young woman, so frank, open, honest about her desires.

"Wait then. I'll get my things in the room, you get into the bus first so that we won't be seen together, I come in a few minutes." He shook his head, his voice taking on a tone of wonder. "By Odin, in a bus, who would think . . ."

It happened on the back seat of the Moscow Tour Bus in the middle of a fine late summer night. At first Anders and Oksana smoked small portions of hashish, filling the salon of the bus with a musky sweet odor; their heads became dizzy, an air of unreality pervading the scene.

Oksana remembered only his powerful torso, great rock hard muscles of chest and shoulders, but smooth as marble, warm and ecstatically sensuous. She could not recall the moment she let her evening gown slip away from her body, feeling soft and hot in his giant palms. Strangely they were not coarse as they caressed, running all over her back, buttocks and through the valley between her breasts; she felt the powerful sweet strokes inside her moist thighs and spread her legs seizing him in between them, locking her ankles at his back. His arms went on moving caressing her entire body, pressing and generating live electricity.

Oksana cried out softly, catching his shoulder muscle with her teeth. His palms locked on her hips directing her pelvis to the powerful manhood she so craved. She bit him deeper, thrusting herself against the huge hard penetrating organ reaching to unbelievable depth inside her and then withdrawing for another, smooth, indescribably delicious thrust. Her round

59

sweat-glistening hips urgently met his in a rocking, mind-dazing rhythm and for the first time she understood what it meant to achieve orgasm at the exact moment her man was filling her with his essence. She had read about it in English books but now, gloriously, she knew the experience to the fullest.

For an hour they lay there in the back of the bus totally exhausted, their clothes a heap on the floor, the Viking's enormous yet trim figure hardly finding space enough on the cushions of the back seat, Oksana nearby, on the floor, slim wet shining legs outstretched. She knew unbelievable relief and a lightness of soul and fitness of body as if song birds piped their melodies inside every cell of her physical being. He was a special man, and his inner warmth radiated a special kind of feeling within her.

Early in the morning, their rumpled clothing pulled back on, Anders and Oksana stood near the bus. A group of sleepy tourists were lazily boarding the bus which would deliver them to Sheremetievo Airport.

His luggage already on the bus, the Viking was still trying to say *"do svidaniya"* to Oksana. But neither of them could manage the words of parting. Only when the bus was on the verge of leaving, the driver impatiently looking out the door at him, Anders reached into his pocket and pulled out his silver cigarette lighter. He took her hand in his, pushed the lighter into her palm closing her fingers around it. "Think of us when you light a cigarette. I do not say good-bye. We will be together again."

"Please, Anders, yes," she begged.

A serious look came over his face. "Oksana, beware of the killer wave. Keep the belt leashed to the rail."

And then he was gone, and Oksana watched the bus roll down the slope to the highway along the Moscow River embankment and dissolve into the stream of morning traffic.

CHAPTER SEVEN

⟨⟩ ⟨⟩

The phone was ringing as Oksana entered her apartment. "This is Marat speaking." The KGB officer's voice had a stern ring to it. "Comrade Martinova, we must meet to discuss some business. I will be waiting for you in our suite at Hotel Russia on the second floor at three this afternoon. Please do not be late."

By the time she was admitted to the hotel lobby by a KGB man posing as doorman she had composed herself. After all she had done nothing. Her short affair with Anders could hardly be a pretext for big trouble, she thought. But she was mistaken.

Marat was waiting alone for her sitting behind the table, relaxing in an arm chair. He greeted Oksana pleasantly, as an old friend, and motioned her to sit down in the straight backed wooden chair opposite him. His eyes greedily devoured her full figure and classically beautiful face. Uncomfortably sensing this stripping gaze, hating his false friendliness, Oksana felt sick.

"So, Comrade Martinova," he began, lighting a cigarette, "or maybe just Oka for short, you do not mind, do you? I am not much older than you."

"No, I do not mind." She shook her head, mouth dry as dust.

"Fine. We are off to a good start." He leaned forward, tapping his cigarette above a porcelain hotel ashtray. "So, Oka, how are you today?"

"I suppose . . . I suppose you want to talk business." Oksana tried to conceal the nervousness she felt wondering how much Marat knew about last night with her Viking.

"Yes. Let us talk business." He fixed her with a long, hard stare. "So . . . we would like to know everything you learned from Anders Prahl."

"What is there to know? He answered all your questions in the airport the night he missed his plane . . ."

"See, Oksana, we are interested in what you can tell us about him. You are a Soviet woman, no? You want to help us?"

"Yes."

"So?"

"Well . . . He spoke mainly about his work, things that happened to him at sea."

"Yeah, we have all this stuff already. Halls are bugged too, you know. We even have your conversation in the restaurant— where you made a surprising confession. You do not like men. Maybe you are a lesbian. We know what you talked about near the door to his room before leaving for this cozy bus." Marat gave her a hard look. "Would you be so kind to relate your conversation there?"

Oksana felt her face burning but she replied evenly, "There is nothing to relate. I simply do not remember, that is all."

"Yeah, but of course, you were so busy fucking your brains out there was no time to talk at all."

Oksana sprang to her feet, shaking. "This is none of your

business, none of your damn business! What do you want from me?"

"Truth, nothing but the truth. Calm down please. Let me remind you, first, that in this country everything is our business. Second," he threw a hard look at her, "our criminal code has an article against prostitution."

"What?"

"Yes, of course; would not you agree that you screwed the old man for his money? Leave all this crap about love aside. By the way how did he pay you?"

"Bullshit!" she dredged up the term. "You must prove that."

"Oh, there will be no deficit of proof," he answered smoothly. "We have tapes of all your talks, we have videotape—very interesting by the way—of what you have done to the guy inside a bus. We can also search your apartment, and you can be sure we'll find what we want."

Oksana felt she was close to fainting. She knew KGB methods. In the search they would plant a pack of dollars or crones or marks and later claim they found it. No one would believe her. A prostitute? She had been stupid to act so openly.

"What do you really want from me?" she asked.

"I've told you. This guy pretended to be a fool missing his plane. What was he up to?"

"You are trying to say he was a spy?"

Exasperation tinged his tone. "Do not play tricks with us! You know everything about him. Why did he give you his address?"

Oksana could hardly believe what she was hearing. "You are building a spy plot on empty speculation. Anders Prahl is no spy. You are just trying to make yourself important. Do you think I'm stupid? You have no proof. I see no point in this talk anymore."

"I see . . ." He frowned and appeared to be reflecting on matters. Then, "Well Comrade Martinova, I must tell you, we were mistaken in your true face. Looks like you are not a friend of ours. That is a pity. The investigation will proceed. We will question you again and I hope you will be more cooperative."

The young KGB officer, trying to act like a seasoned interrogator stood up from behind the table. "You are free to go but do not leave the city. If you change your mind, recollect something and decide to cooperate—you have my phone number."

"I doubt that." Her voice was cold. "Goodbye."

"You will regret this lack of cooperation," she heard him say as she left the suite, feeling weak and sweating. All she wanted was to get back to her apartment.

Two days later Oksana was sitting in the presence of the Dean of the Institute of Foreign Languages. A short, bald, fat-bellied man of about sixty, he paced back and forth having just informed Oksana she would be expelled from the institute for reasons of state interests. The following week she could come to pick up her documents.

"Your behavior, student Martinova, is most shameful. You have betrayed the high privilege of being a Soviet interpreter. As the dean of the language institute I cannot permit you to affect our students, your colleagues, in this wicked way. Do you have anything to say in your defense?"

Oksana desperately wanted a cigarette but such was forbidden in a meeting of such gravity in the dean's office. She was wondering what other measures KGB was preparing. Take away her apartment? They were capable of that although, of course, it was in the name of her father, a member of the Council of Deputies. She shuddered at the thought of his being drawn into this situation.

"Student Martinova, do you hear my question?" he fussed.

"You have no right to expel me. I have done nothing—"

"Most regrettable that you do not repent," he interrupted her.

"I am not obliged to give you reports on my personal life."

"Disgusting!" he pronounced. "And you come from such a loyal Soviet family."

"Do not touch my family." Her voice rose in pitch. "I have done nothing against Soviet law or the rules of this institute. Why do you believe any filth they say about your students?"

"They?" he shrieked. "What do you mean, they?!"

"KGB."

A spasm of fear passed across his face. "Comrade Martinova, we have nothing else to talk about. Leave the premises immediately."

Oksana called Marat the next morning. His voice was formal.

"What are you going to tell me?" he asked coolly.

"Well, you said if I recollect something . . ."

"Ah ha, so you did. Excellent. We'll meet tomorrow evening."

"In the hotel?"

"No. I'll give you the address. The matter is too confidential. Your Norwegian seaman turned out to be not that simple."

Oksana wrote down the address. It was near Arbat Street, in the labyrinth of side streets of the ancient Moscow area.

"Make sure no one knows where you are going," he cautioned. "And do not be late."

It was early evening as Oksana walked through the Arbat and made her way between the stalls lining the main street of this perpetual flea market, the hawkers promoting their wares in a vain effort to sell her something. Turning off Arbat she trudged up the hill to an old five-story gray wooden house and in the vestibule she looked at the mail boxes and bell buttons. She checked the number Marat had given her and pressed the button to ring the bell on the fifth floor. It appeared the other apartments in the building were empty. All the buildings around were abandoned and marked for reconstruction.

Marat, wearing the three-piece gray suit that was the civilian KGB uniform, met her at the door. His face was gloomy and serious. The apartment consisted of one long, dark hall with three doorways, two of them locked, the middle one open to a sparsely furnished, narrow room. The window at the end of the room overlooked the wall of the opposite house whose proximity shut out most of the fading summer light. There was a carpet on the floor, a huge oak table in the middle of the room and several armchairs facing the table as though in preparation for a conference. In one of the chairs Oksana saw Paul, sitting with crossed legs, smoking and staring at her.

Oksana turned from Paul to Marat. "What did you call him for?" she asked sharply.

"He is, or was, your group officer." He gestured toward the empty chair facing the table. "Sit over there."

When they were all seated Marat asked, "So . . . what are you going to tell us?"

"I . . . I am ready to help you. I'll do what you ask of me, but you will have to let me stay in college."

"We have nothing to do with the institute. It was their decision. We merely reported your little scene with a potential foreign spy in the bus. What else have you to say?"

Oksana was speechless for a moment. Liars! They ordered the dean to expel her for no reason at all. From what she had heard the dean say she realized the old fool was just following orders.

"You bastard!" she yelled. "What do you mean you have nothing to do with it!?" Oksana leapt to her feet. Marat slapped her hard on the face first with his palm and then with the back of his hand. Blood ran from her nostrils. She fell back in the armchair, covered her face with her hands and wept bitterly.

Then she gasped through the sobs, "You animal! You have no right to hit me—"

"Shut up, slut! You listen to what we say! Read this, and sign it!"

Marat pushed a sheet of paper and a pen across the surface of the table. Her fingers trembling, she took the paper and in the dim light read it. It was a contract between an applicant of female gender and KGB of the USSR, which stated that an applicant agreed to attend a secret KGB women's school for six months. She swore on pain of prison camp never to reveal any information regarding her training.

At the end of the course she would be granted special assignments as a female KGB operative. A dotted line for her signature followed.

Horrified, she remembered Nadia telling her about giving special instruction to KGB girls in the art of fellatio, making real little cobras out of them, as Nadia put it. The girls were all beautiful and under the age of twenty-six. These girls practiced Nadia's teachings on specially privileged KGB officers, who also taught them all the techniques of sexual intercourse.

So this was it, she thought hopelessly. They wanted to turn her into a state-employed whore. Between sobs she asked, "What does this mean, special assignments beyond the country border?"

"Sounds attractive, eh?" Marat chuckled. "Well, it means if you pass the courses you can even find yourself in the harem of some Saudi Arabian prince. We have a very limited number of good agents there."

Oksana was silent for some moments, dabbing at her bleeding nose with her handkerchief. Marat and Paul eyed her silently.

"If it sounds attractive to you, sign it yourself." Her eyes blazed. "Some Arabian prince will be happy to bugger a good white agent like you!"

Both men caught their breath in shock and surprise. Then

Marat leapt to his feet and rushed at her from behind the table yelling, "You, dirty whore, I'll teach you obedience!"

Oksana jumped from the arm chair, overturning and pulling it between them as she tried to escape through the door. Paul joined Marat and they both seized her. Marat tore off her dress in a single violent tug. Then as she struggled and kicked fiercely they toppled her down on the floor, handcuffing her wrists around a leg of the heavy table. Her screams brought no response from within or without the building.

Paul forced her legs apart. Her struggles only excited them more. Oksana felt pain pierce her. After each of them climaxed they turned her on her stomach, twisting her hands around the table leg, and continued their assault from the rear. Oksana lost all sense of time as the pain swept through her just before she lost consciousness.

When she came to she was lying on her own bed, obviously they had taken her home to her apartment. Her dress was torn and the dirty rag that was left of her panties had been stuffed in her mouth. With her dry, numb tongue she pushed it out and her eyes moved around the room, stopping in horror at the sight of Marat standing beside her bed, smoking. Seeing her awake he started speaking.

"Listen, girl, these are no jokes," he began menacingly. "You are in a man's game. We want you to work for us. Think it over. If you fight us anymore," he paused giving her a hard stare, "we turn you over to a gang of rovers somewhere in the country. They will fuck you far harsher, make tattoos on your boobs and buttocks with nails. Do not leave the apartment until we are back. One wrong move—and you will not want to go on living."

Traumatized, she turned away from his filthy mouthing. Then he left and she heard the door slam after him. She tried to rise but her bruised eyes caught sight of herself in the mirror at the foot of her bed. She gazed at the strange creature with the red and blue alien face, lower lip hanging, her blouse torn to the waist, blue spots on her breasts where fingers had grabbed, her skirt ripped and dirty, stockings hanging in shreds. She felt pain in her pelvis and genitals and its sharp surge reminded her of what they had done to her. She fainted again.

When she awakened she could not remember what time or date it was. No thoughts passed through her mind now. She crawled on all fours into the bathroom, turned on the tap and watched hot water fill the bathtub. Pulling herself into the hot water, still in her torn and dirty clothes, she lay there motionless for several hours. Gradually she returned to reality but her mind refused to go back over the preceding events as she removed her clothes, now rags, and washed herself. Finally she climbed out of the tub, wrapped herself into a blanket and collapsed onto her bed, still refusing to remember anything, sinking into the comforting dark abyss of sleep.

Oksana woke up in a few hours, her head aching. She went to the kitchen and found a half-full bottle of vodka in her refrigerator. She drank it all, as a drunkard might go after a badly needed drink. In a few moments she felt warm and more at ease. She lit a cigarette, still wrapped in her blanket and sat smoking, trying to think things over but her mind still rejected reality.

She had lost track of time when the sudden ring of the doorbell jerked her back to the present. She sat still, staring out through the small foyer and the front door beyond. The bell rang a second time but still she sat silently. Who the hell is that? Maybe Tanya? No, Tanya was cross with her and afraid. Maybe Nadia. She knows about such men, Oksana thought hopefully. She would know how to deal with these KGB beasts.

The bell rang a third time and then, to her horror, she heard something that sounded like a key being inserted into the door lock and realized that she hadn't fastened the chain. She could only huddle under her blanket and stare out toward the door. She heard the door lock give way and the squeak of the hinges as it was swung open. Eyes wide with fright, she saw a shadow cast by the hall light outside through her open door and onto the floor of the foyer.

She was shocked and terrified to see Marat and Paul and some other, older-looking man, maybe in his middle forties, wearing a black coat, push their way into her apartment. Paul and Marat each carried a thick bag. The horror was back.

"Hey, hostess, here are guests!" Marat said merrily as if they were all good friends. "You must know that no door lock can resist the 'invisible frontier.'"

She heard her own trembling voice hoarsely cry, "What do you want?" She knew she must try to keep the note of fear from her voice which almost failed at the sight of the invaders.

"Have a good drink, make good talk; by the way this blanket around you is really great." He turned to the older man. "Didn't I tell you, Colonel, the chick is cute?"

"Please leave me alone," Oksana begged. "Haven't you done enough to me already?"

"Now that is a hard attitude for a pretty girl like you to take," the one addressed as "colonel" said. He stared at her and at a gesture Marat stripped the blanket from her, leaving her nude before the three invaders.

"Please, go away," she cried. "This is against the law. KGB or not, there is the law." But in this older man's small, colorless, gleaming eyes she could see what her fate was to be. Paul and Marat threw her onto the floor and the older man with deliberate motions reached into his bag and took out a full syringe, squirted a few drops out of the needle and suddenly plunged it into a vein inside her elbow. She screamed until Marat held a hand over her mouth. She tried to bite his fingers. He laughed as he dug his thumb and fingers into her cheeks holding her head inert. He didn't have to hold her very long. Suddenly a feeling of euphoria came over her as she felt first weak, then mellow, then bemused.

Paul helped her to her feet and led her naked around the room for all three to see. She wasn't really conscious of the actual words which expressed what the colonel, who would be given the honor to go first, was going to do. She heard herself laughing at the suggestions as the older man opened his pants completely exposing his hardness to her and asking her to be his little girl and sit on his lap. She allowed him to reach out for her, pull her down on his lap, and slip inside of her. She offered no resistance feeling somewhat in a dream state as he bucked up and down, putting his drink down and pulling her to him with both hands. She was aware of Marat and Paul verbally encouraging the colonel and in only moments she felt him climax.

Marat wasted no time pulling her into the bedroom and pushing her back onto her bed, standing over her and clutching her buttocks in both hands thrusting himself into her. She noted with a derisive laugh, which infuriated him for a moment, that he took even less time than the colonel to reach his release and then Paul, the junior member of the trio, had his turn.

Afterwards, walking naked around the apartment she followed their instructions, mechanically fixing the food they had brought, pouring cognac and giving them plates as they slipped their hands into her crotch, fingered her nipples and the colonel, still smoking a cigarette, once again drew her down on his lap, surprising her at the vigor with which he entered her a second time. They all tried to pour cognac down her throat as they repeatedly violated her and finally between the liquor, the continuous feral sexual activity, and the aftermath of the drug injection, she slipped into a state of total unconsciousness.

CHAPTER EIGHT

<figure>⤜⧫ ⧫⤛</figure>

W hen Oksana opened her eyes the next morning the sun was shining brightly through the window of her bedroom, the curtains drawn far apart. She was lying naked on the floor, her legs spread. Her thighs were wet and sticky and she ached inside as she sat up slowly trying to recollect what had happened the night before. Slowly the memories came to her.

What appalled her the most was to recall that she had willingly succumbed to their abusive behavior. Shamefully she remembered the effect of the drug they had injected into her.

Oksana gazed absently out the window at the sun. She put on her shirt but didn't have the strength or dexterity to button it and sat for several hours, smoking and dropping the ashes on the floor all around where she was sitting. Her apartment was a disgusting mess, empty bottles everywhere and something like dried sperm on the carpet and her thighs, legs and bosom. She remembered their vile juices burning her throat and larynx.

She had always thought that after one climax a guy was finished. How little she knew.

So she was finished. She had made a grave mistake. She should have called her father right away, several days ago when she was unjustly expelled from the Institute. Indeed, she had actually initiated a telephone call to Irkutsk in the far reaches of Siberia.

It was an interminable process. Long before the call to her father could be put through, as she contemplated how best to confess the Viking affair and certain other intimate details of her life, she cancelled the call.

She was also afraid to ensnare Nickolai Martinov in a fight with the KGB which, she imagined, could even involve the PolitBureau. She began to realize for the first time that the Soviet Union was more apt to crush the life out of its citizens than to help them fight State-induced injustice. Meanwhile, she had been determined to get out of this mess on her own.

And look what had happened. She had in two days become a disgusting, lascivious creature, a monstrous whore—even to look in a mirror was torture. Self loathing was the hardest cross to bear and she wished the drug they had injected into her had made her forget everything that happened as well.

Oksana tried to rise to her feet, clutching onto the handle of a bureau drawer above her, but the drawer collapsed to the floor, its contents spilling out around her. She started to look through the objects. One of them was her dad's straight razor with a keenly sharp blade.

She stared at it for some moments. Waves of guilt and despair coursed through her consciousness as the desperate idea formed in her head. There would be no questions to Nickolai from KGB. It will be best for her father this way.

Oksana put the blade to her left wrist but couldn't bring herself to slice the vein. Then she placed the blade flat to her skin, savoring its cold, metallic touch. She held it thus until the blade turned warm to her skin temperature and she no longer felt it. Then with a sudden, resolute move she turned the blade perpendicular to her wrist and slashed it deep into her flesh, a dark hot stream of blood gushed from the slit, staining the left arm and flowing to the floor in heavy drops.

Vaguely Oksana was aware that her front door was effortlessly swinging open and her last conscious impression was seeing Nadia appear in the room. Nadia had always reacted quickly and now she assessed the scene confronting her in a split second kicking the blade out from between Oksana's fingers.

Nadia fell upon her, clutching Oksana's bloody wrist to staunch the flow of blood. Oksana was too weak and feeble to resist as Nadia hauled her to the kitchen, seized a dish towel and fashioned a tourniquet on Oksana's wrist above the sliced vein. Nadia pulled open every drawer in the kitchen and found some first aid supplies, applying what bandages and medication she could find to the wound. Oksana sank to the floor again, like a rag doll, staring in a daze at her cut wrist.

Then Nadia phoned a friend at the hospital where she worked part time, and told her to bring sedative, antihistamine drugs, and antibiotics with syringes and solutions to the address she gave. Nadia's mate was stunned, but Nadia accepted no arguments and in an hour the medical supplies were delivered. Nadia did not let her bewildered friend in, but gratefully accepted the package of medical supplies and immediately gave the shocked girl an injection of antibiotics and wound a proper tourniquet with sterilized gauze on the wound. Then she put Oksana in a hot bath, washing her thoroughly with soap and disinfectant.

At the end of the bathing she held Oksana's mouth open and poured half a cup of cognac down her throat. She wrapped her in several blankets, as if the young woman were a baby, and put her to bed. The effect of sedatives combined with alcohol caused Oksana to sink into the oblivion of relaxing slumber.

As a finishing touch, Nadia painted the bruises on her friend's face with iodine solution to make them disappear sooner.

Now Nadia had time to examine the apartment. From her own strife-filled and adventurous life Nadia possessed the experience of a retired police officer. It was clear to her that Oksana had been drugged and raped by several men. The bruises around the syringe mark suggested the rapists knew little about injection technique and therefore were not drug addicts, but people who used drugs on others. They would have been Militsiamen or worse, KGB. Three glasses with remnants of cognac told her that three men had violated the young girl. A bottle of cognac, almost untouched but uncorked, indicated the perpetrators would be back.

Nadia had yet to meet the first KGB man—and she had slept with many—who would forget an unfinished bottle. Proverbially it was said that a real KGB officer works with his liver rather than his head. This was to be expected; the founder of the secret police, Felix Dzerzshinsky, was a heavy drug addict himself, as well as being a drunkard and molester of young girls.

Thus, Nadia now realized, staying in Oksana's apartment was dangerous for both of them. Nadia did not risk booking a taxi by phone—dealing with KGB you always had to be conscious of electronic surveillance.

She left the apartment, caught a cab in the street and, giving the driver a large tip, she asked him to wait for a while. Back in Oksana's apartment she packed some of the girl's clothes and toiletries so that the rapists would think Oksana had left on her own. She ran down to the cab and dropped them inside then went back and half-carried, half-led the barefoot groggy girl wrapped in her blankets down the stairs of her building and out into the cab.

Nadia explained to the bewildered driver that she was a

physician and taking her alcohol-poisoned patient to the hospital.

At the hospital Nadia took Oksana up to the ward tended by her friend, the nurse who had delivered the medical supplies to the apartment. For several hours they worked on her, rebandaging the razor cut on her wrist and covering her bruises and welts with medications.

Their final ministrations included a thorough douching and a dose of the so-called "morning after" pills which Nadia herself used frequently. Then they gave her an injection that brought her back to her senses and Nadia assisted her from the hospital by a seldom-used back entrance to the railroad station and three hours later they arrived at the *dacha* of one of Nadia's closest female friends. The surprised woman looked at the dazed girl with Nadia, asked no questions, and together they put her to bed on the living room couch.

In the safety of her country place they tried to decide what to do next.

"The most rotten things, my girl," Nadia was saying, "are not behind you, but ahead. These three bastards committed a terrible crime against you and they will never forget you. I do not know what to propose. I always tried to stay away from KGB. I had trouble enough with the Militsia."

"What will they do next?" Oksana asked fearfully.

"They will look for you—secretly. But they won't find you here."

"You're sure?"

"Nothing is one hundred percent. But they are just a bunch of arrogant drunkards with too much power. I took you away just in time."

"How did you get in?"

"These guys left your door open for when they will come back. I just pushed it to get in. Quite a sight I found."

"They will know someone helped me."

"It will take time for them to put things together. They will be acting on their own, without help of KGB machine. Officially they have nothing against you. On the contrary, they are afraid their bosses will learn about their crime. I have fucked a lot of KGB and I can tell you the main thing they are afraid of is open public information."

"Maybe I should try to go home to my dad. I was afraid to but he will know what to do. He is a high-ranking party official."

"Who is your dad?"

"He is First Secretary of Regional Committee . . . People's Deputy."

"Region of what?"

"Irkutsk."

Abruptly Nadia reacted. "Of all Irkutsk Region? I think I do know the guy who can help us."

"How?"

"See, it is best your dad will not learn what happened to you until everything is taken care of."

"Who is this guy you think can defend us against KGB?"

"Not all KGB, remember. Just three sperm-blinded jerks who use their official standing. The older one, you say, they called him colonel?"

"Yes."

"Hmm. Bad, but we'll handle it. You will stay here while I go to Moscow tomorrow. Your new friend, Sofia, will watch out for you. We'll take these bastards down. I won't let them make a whore out of you, it is enough I am a whore."

The Baikal Restaurant, one flight of stairs above the big Moscow shopping mall in the popular Arbat market area, was a favorite eating place for celebrities and the city's criminal society alike. Tourists were always lined up to get in and stare at the famous patrons. Three nights after her rescue, at seven in the evening, Oksana was sitting inconspicuously with Nadia at a far corner table in the restaurant. Nadia ordered champagne and a big chocolate: this was her favorite snack. She dropped a piece of chocolate in the wine and watched it float from the bottom to the surface, surrounded by golden bubbles. They lingered some time before Nadia, looking up, said, "Ah, here he comes."

Oksana followed her glance and saw the man approaching them making his way through narrow passages among the tables. It seemed he was no stranger here; many people at the tables turned their heads and greeted him. The man was rather tall and well-built, with wide shoulders and a big head. His face was wide, with a thin, straight nose. Small gray eyes were half covered by lids, giving him a sleepy expression. His hair was light-colored and severely combed back from his forehead, his face was clean-shaven and he wore an expensive custom tailored suit. When he reached the table, Oksana sensed the subtle odor of expensive eau-de-cologne. Big white teeth shone in a moderate smile. This was Pavel.

"Hi, girls," he said in a pleasant, low voice. "What's up?"

"Hi, Pavel." Nadia lit a cigarette. "It is nice you do not forget old women."

"You would be hard for anyone to forget. You're a sun ray on a cold day," he said, sitting down with them. Oksana looked curiously at Pavel but said nothing.

The waiter was already at their table. Pavel ordered himself a carafe of cognac and sturgeon with salad. Orders at the restaurant usually took an hour or more to reach the customer due to its great popularity, but Pavel's order appeared at once.

The girls refused dinner, but Pavel ordered coffee and dessert for them. He ate slowly, with impeccable manners, wide white napkin tucked behind his collar.

"So, you are Oksana," he said after a short silence.

"I am." She took a cigarette from Nadia.

Pavel looked deeply into her face, observing the traces of bruises under the cover of cosmetics. He nodded.

"You can call me Pavel." He poured himself cognac, tasted it, took a long swallow and placed the glass beside him as he went on eating.

"I was shocked by what Nadia told me." He shook his head as if in disbelief and chewed up another bite of the sturgeon fillet. "I am not a man without capabilities, but I want to hear all the details from you . . ." He held up a restraining hand as she started to protest. "I understand, this is hard. But I must know everything if we are to settle this matter."

"How shall I begin?" Oksana asked.

"There will be no talk here. We finish supper, chat a little, but real talk will be in another place."

Pavel smiled pleasantly, turning to Nadia and tapping her tenderly on the knee.

"Sounds reasonable," Nadia agreed. "Where shall we go?"

"I'll show you." Pavel was merry, accepting greetings from men who came up to the table. It seemed to Oksana that if permitted, the guys would kiss his hand—so much admiration tinged with fear shone from their eyes. At last Pavel stood up. It was already ten o'clock. He left a hundred rubles banknote as a tip, though the check was half that. "My car will be at the opposite side of the street near the theater in an hour from now," he said briefly. "Have a good time, order yourself some champagne. Do not be late." And he walked away from the table.

One hour later Nadia and Oksana stepped into a black Volga sedan, Nadia sitting up front beside Pavel behind the wheel, Oksana in the back seat. There was little conversation as they drove up Gorky Street heading away from the city center. Soon they were on the highway connecting Leningrad with Moscow. Oksana couldn't help noticing the car following them. Pavel chuckled. "In my business it is always prudent to have friends close by."

Within an hour Moscow was left behind and the car was speeding among endless fields and forests passing through the small town of Klin to the north of Moscow. The highway was empty except for the car trailing them. By the end of the second hour they were nearing the banks of the Volga River. In this upper flow, close to its source, the Volga was magnificent. It was a mile wide, with swampy banks covered by the dense, low forest. The highway bridge across the Volga was two kilometers long and of solid construction. To the west loomed the railway bridge of the Moscow-Leningrad Railway which ran parallel to the highway.

Crossing the bridge the road ran for a mile between lines of century-old poplars. Here Pavel slowed down and stopped the car at the curb. At Pavel's direction Oksana stepped out of the car, wrapping herself in her black cloak. Already, though only September, it was getting cold. She followed Pavel and Nadia into the pine forest on this bank of the Volga and looked out at the islands covered by thick bushes and trees which seemed, in the moonlight, to be floating over the river.

Several big country mansions could be seen on the opposite side of the road.

"Whose houses are these?" Nadia asked.

Pavel pointed at the most magnificent one. "This one belongs to the director of Moscow regional vegetable storage base, Givi Gigauri."

"No kidding!" Nadia exclaimed. "I know that fat guy."

"He is in Byturka Prison right now—under investigation."

"He'll break through, he's shrewd," Nadia said confidently.

Pavel led Oksana and Nadia to a spot where they were out of the wind and could see the waters of the Volga reflecting the moonlight in a silver, shimmering ribbon.

"So," Pavel said, "Oksana, I would like to hear the whole

story all over again, from you. Do not omit the slightest detail, do not be in a hurry. We have plenty of time. No one will bother us." He nodded toward the escort car from which three glowing cigarettes shone through the windows.

Little by little, pausing sometimes, Oksana told her story, including the details of her lesbian affair with Tanya. She stood with her back to her two companions and spoke into the darkness of the night, into the eddies of the wind, into the majestic flow of the great river. Pavel listened attentively, smoking, sometimes asking abrupt questions, but not interrupting the girl.

When Oksana finished at last, a silence fell over the trio for a moment. Pavel took out another cigar and lit it thoughtfully.

Nadia lit a cigarette for herself. "Quite a tale. No?"

"Yeah," Pavel nodded. "Yeah. Well, we have to live with it. Life is life. Now Oksana, as far as I understand, your aim is not only getting out of the mess, but revenge, too?"

"Precisely." Oksana's voice was cold, sharp.

Pavel liked her reaction. "So let us be clear with each other. I am . . . say a business man. In Soviet mentality an outlaw, mafia boss, okay. Now, girl, if you are with me against them—I guess we shall win. But you will never be on your own again. We will be connected by a common affair forever, till death do us part as they say in the ceremony." He puffed on his cigar contemplatively.

"I do not mean you will actually participate in my business, but you will be one of us—and when the moment comes I will ask you to help me. I will ask nothing from you that you will be incapable of performing, but it may happen that helping me you will have to put your life at stake . . . think it over."

Oksana answered at once. "I understand." She paused and lit a cigarette with the big silver lighter, staring at it a moment. "The wave has come. Time to leash the waist to the railing."

"Sorry?" Pavel look puzzled.

"You can rely on me," Oksana replied. "I will never forget your help."

Pleased with her answer, Pavel nodded. "Nadia, dear, open the glove compartment. There is a flask of cognac there, bring it to me." Nadia found it and brought it to Pavel.

"Thanks," he said and sipped from the flask then offering it to Oksana. She took a sip too. The bargain was sealed.

"I can make them disappear without a trace, chop them into slices and roast them on a fire, bring you their heads, pricks in their mouths. You just say."

Oksana was silent for a moment. Then, "Just—no traces."

Pavel nodded. "And you can also render me a great service."

"What do you want?"

"The KGB scum will be destroyed and you will be readmitted to the institute. Then you will introduce me to your dad."

"You want my father to be corrupted?"

"Are you so naive to think that a Communist reaching such standing is not already corrupt? Your father will simply help me in a certain matter in return for what I am doing now."

"So you will have to tell him all this filth," she stated bleakly.

Pavel smiled in understanding. "We shall omit details about Viking, this is your personal affair. But we will tell him about your trouble and that you are not guilty of anything. Your dad will understand there was no legal way of solving your problem."

Pavel sipped from the silver flask and handed it to Oksana who followed his example. "You can probably cause these guys to lose rank because of scandal but then the whole KGB will be against you. They can prove any lie they make up is the truth. They will prove you were a prostitute from early girlhood; that it was you who raped these three innocent KGB true family men and tender fathers."

Pavel paused and gave her a speculative stare. "Though of course if you are afraid, or . . ."

"Cut it out," Oksana snapped. "It is a settled matter. Dad will help you, I promise."

Pavel nodded and took another long drink from his flask. They talked for another hour discussing details in the dark night, the dense forest, and the bend in the great river surrounding them. The ends of their cigarettes glowed brightly in the wind.

CHAPTER NINE

⊰≫ ≪⊱

Calling Marat at the KGB office suite in the Hotel Russia was an emotionally draining prospect but Oksana realized that Pavel's plan was dependent upon the success of her ruse. Nadia stood beside her at the telephone in her apartment encouraging her.

"Hi, man," Oksana crooned. "How are you doing?" She put all her feminine wiles into that first question, trying to sound sleepy, cozy, relaxed—a young sexy slut, just out of a warm bath, her blanket wrapped around her. Oksana could picture Marat's lascivious smile and imagine his mind working, expecting to be praised by his superiors for recruiting a new female agent. She smiled wryly, standing there, phone in hand, covered with her severe black cloak in the middle of the shambles he had made of her apartment, her face pale and swollen. She loved taunting the man who would die for violating her.

"Good to hear you," he replied. "How is it going?"

"A little rough, not what I expected."

"But you liked it?" There was a note of disbelief in his voice.

She forced a chuckle. "Did you? What was that shot you gave me?"

"It got you high. It's better the second time." There was still a hint of suspicion. "How about the papers you were to sign?"

"That's why I called. I want this settled."

"You really want to work for us as an agent?" There was open disbelief in his tone.

"If I can make it through this far, I can do anything. I'd like to hear more of what's expected of me."

"We were pretty tough on you. I'm sorry."

"You showed me what you can do. I suppose it was some kind of a test," she replied.

"Being an agent is tough work sometimes." Now he was sounding like Marat the zealot again. "But you can be a true heroine of our country," he went on enthusiastically.

"It sounds exciting."

"The colonel liked you."

"Oh, he did?"

"Yeah, he said you could be one of his best agents." He paused. "Are you all right? Please don't be mad. We can do great things."

"It was pretty abusive, you know. I've never done anything like that before. You could have been more gentle. I mean three guys and all that . . ." She let her voice trail off.

"I guess we all got sort of carried away. Some women, you understand, like it that way. Really. But when you become one of us we'll make it up to you. You will be a valuable and respected agent. One of us," he finished proudly.

"What do I do next?" She injected the right amount of faint-ness in her voice, realizing how weak she still was.

Eagerly now he took the bait. "Why don't the three of us get together again and talk more about it, Oksana."

She allowed a dubious tone to creep into her voice. "We just talk this time?"

"Of course, Oksana. Comrade Martinova. This will be a serious business meeting. I promise."

"When?" she asked.

"How about later today?"

"I am resting."

"When do you want to meet with us?" Marat's open anticipation brought a sardonic grin to Oksana's lips.

"Please let me rest another day or two."

"Okay . . . you will be at home?"

"We will not meet here again," she snapped, letting her true emotions out.

"I understand. I'll give you a call. Behave yourself."

She restrained her rage at the supercilious admonition. "I'll be here. Give me a few days."

But Marat couldn't wait. He called Oksana early the next afternoon. The three of them would be waiting for her in the Arbat apartment at eight o'clock that evening.

It was half past seven when the white Zhiguli sedan stopped in an Arbat side street. Pavel was sitting in the front seat. The matter was too serious to be assigned to anyone else. The driver looked to his boss beside him for instructions. Misha, the gunman, sat beside Oksana in back, his long black coat covering his clothing. He appeared to be in his late thirties, with jet-black hair, a gaunt man with a deeply lined face, chin and cheeks black with stubble, eyes in a perpetual squint as though burned that way from long over-exposure to the sun.

Pavel turned in his seat to Oksana. "Sit in this car quietly and under no circumstances leave it without either Misha or myself. The address is correct?"

"Yes, I will never forget it, you may be sure."

Pavel was sure. His men had checked it out in the early morning, right after they had returned from the banks of the Volga. Oksana knew nothing about it nor was she aware that the three blocks around the apartment had been alive with Pavel's men since six o'clock, marksmen posted on the roofs covering the KGB hideaway with long range rifles. By seven it was reported to Pavel that the three individuals in whom he was interested had arrived, acting as if on a holiday.

Pavel opened the front door of the car and stepped out going around to the trunk and opening it. He took out a big, black foot locker and with Misha carried it into the front door of the semi-abandoned house.

Quietly they ascended to the fifth floor and Misha placed the box in the hall outside the door to the KGB apartment. He was wearing a black cloak that reached down to his heels concealing the field Kalishnikov machine gun he was carrying under it.

Pavel approached the door of the apartment, checked the number, took out a small metal rod with a hook on the end and inserted it into the keyhole. It clicked and the lock silently opened. "Ah Switzerland!" Pavel sighed. "What technical devices they make. By the way," he asked in a whisper, "Misha, have you been to Switzerland?"

"No. Only to Afghanistan."

"Yeah, it is a difference . . . Never mind, be a good boy and I'll see you have a nice shopping trip to Switzerland."

Marat, Paul and the colonel were sitting in the armchairs around the solid oak table. On it stood bottles of vodka and cognac, platters of snacks and cigarette packs. The men appeared relaxed, smoking and in good moods after drinking several glasses of cognac as they waited for their dark-haired passionate beauty.

A rustling sound came from outside. "That must be Oksana," Marat exclaimed, excited as he jumped to his feet.

The curtains hanging at the door parted. The three pairs of eyes burning with lust in anticipation of Oksana's arrival suddenly widened in shock as a hand gripping a 9mm Luger Parabellum automatic pistol protruded into the room; its barrel was capped with a silencer. Marat froze.

"Hail to fervent hearts and clean hands, as Papa Felix used to say," Pavel announced with the KGB obligatory reference to Felix Dzerszhinsky. He entered the room, Misha after him. "How are you doing, comrades?"

Paul and the colonel sprang to their feet beside Marat. Misha made a menacing gesture with the barrel of a Kalishnikov automatic rifle, poking its barrel into their faces.

"What do you want?" the colonel asked hoarsely.

"Be seated, please," Pavel continued in a calm tone of voice. Then, mock-depreciatingly, "I am, after all, neither a general secretary nor a KGB chief. No need standing in my presence. What we need is to talk."

"Who are you? What do you want? I am a KGB colonel. I can have your bloody asses. Lower your weapons, immediately!" the colonel blustered.

Pavel chuckled, extending the Luger further in front of him. "It seems, Colonel, you do not grasp the situation."

"What the hell do you mean?"

"Just what I say. Now, let's not waste time. I am a business man and an affair of profit brought me here. I will make it clear, only do not shout any more or you'll attract the attention of my marksmen on the roof opposite this window and they will let daylight into you before you make another fart. And that would be a pity because we must come to an arrangement—and we will. I never met people with whom I could not agree, that's because of my mild character." He smiled grimly.

"Bastard," muttered the colonel, although in a low tone. "How dare you oppose KGB. We'll make mincemeat out of you! What criminal gang do you belong to?"

"Well, Colonel, I won't beat about the bush. Several days ago you and these two fuckers raped a girl, inflicting upon her severe emotional and physical damage. That was a mistake, a deadly one, and it will cost you."

The faces of the three men went ashen; Paul and Marat started trembling.

The colonel sank into his chair, suddenly totally sober. "What are you?" he asked. "Her relatives?"

"Yes, in a way. We are all children of one and the same family, if you get it, and won't permit even God Himself to maim our people."

"We . . . we can make a deal," the colonel pleaded in a subdued voice.

"Yeah, sure, that is what I started to say when you interrupted me by your shouting."

"What do you want us to do?" the colonel asked, all too clearly understanding his position at last.

"Now we are hearing reasonable talk." Pavel nodded to Misha. "You see how hard-core commies suddenly become easy to bargain with when you stick the muzzle of a gun in their faces?"

Once again addressing the colonel, Pavel continued. "We do not want much. First, the file on Oksana Martinova this lousy prick to the right of you has created. Second, the tape of the bus scene. Third, just one phone call."

His lips trembling, Marat mumbled, "The file is not here."

"Yeah? Shall I look for it?"

Marat, who had collapsed into a chair, sprang to his feet and rushed to the table, opened the drawer and took out a neat file folder. Briskly he handed it to Pavel. Misha kept hard eyes and muzzle of his machine gun on the KGB men.

There was not much material inside. A photo of Oksana with a tall, rugged white-haired man, institute testimony, several notes made by Marat and transcripts of recordings of conversations constituted the file.

"Where is the tape itself?" Pavel asked.

"It is not here. It is at the surveillance center."

"How about the videotape?"

"There was none . . . "

"Are you sure?" Pavel stuck the barrel of the luger under Marat's chin. "Think twice before answering a second time."

"There was no tape," Marat shrieked. "It was a joke, just a joke. How could you make such a tape at night, you need a special camera, we had none. I'm just a lieutenant."

Pavel nodded. "Aha. Just as I thought. Okay."

Misha had been staring at the colonel for some moments with burning eyes. "Look at this respected KGB officer—a rapist of young girls."

"Scum," the colonel pronounced glaring back at Misha. "Total Caucasus scum . . . "

Misha took a sudden step toward the colonel and swung the machine-gun barrel into his face. The sickening crunch of broken bone matter totally unnerved Marat and Paul, who cried out in horror as the colonel fell backward over the armchair to the floor with a crash, his face broken and bleeding.

Pavel was shocked. "Mikhail, are you mad? Calm down. We have business to handle."

The colonel reached up to the armchair and painfully pulled himself off the floor. His voice burbled through the blood streaming from his nose and mouth. "I do not know what this madman is talking about," he cried.

Suddenly Paul fell on his hands and knees, slithered across the floor to Pavel and screamed out, trying to embrace his knees. "He is lying. He gave Oksana the shot. He raped her. I did not. Do not kill me. I'll do anything, anything. I did not rape Oksana! I swear! It was his idea," he pointed at Marat, "when he saw her with the Norwegian . . . "

"Shit! He is lying!" Marat shrieked, close to fainting.

Pavel kicked Paul away from him. "Misha, keep your barrel on these two." Then to Marat, "And you, fighter of the 'invisible frontier,' stop yelling, I am not deaf. If we listen to you, no one raped her. Now, you, call the dean of the institute."

"The dean? What for?" Marat asked. "He must be at home."

"You tell him KGB made a terrible mistake. Student Martinova is a true, devoted KGB agent and that if he expels her he will lose his job."

Pavel placed a cellular radio telephone on the table in front of Marat. "We will not bother your internal surveillance center with this call," he said. Marat hastily found the phone number in his address book and in a few minutes was talking to the dean, stammering and trembling. He went on for some minutes extolling Oksana's virtues and her value to KGB ending with, "Give my best wishes to your wife and tell her I am sorry to bother you at home. Have a good night."

"This is it," Marat said. "We did all you asked for, what else do you want?"

"Nothing," Pavel replied taking back the radio telephone.

Marat started to cry and beg for his life. Pavel stared at him pitilessly. "Did you show that young woman any mercy?" Pavel asked. "No," he answered his own question quietly. "You terrorized her, you gang-raped her. And you planned to do it to her again tonight. Now, I will give you an idea of what it is like to be raped."

Marat saw Pavel point the silenced pistol at his groin and screamed, throwing himself to the floor but not before Pavel fired his shot. Shrieking in agony, clutching the wound, Marat lay on the floor, blood forming a trickle under him on the floor. Pavel turned to Paul who was wailing, crying, and calling out for his mother.

"She cannot help now," Pavel said evenly. "You will never rape again." Paul grabbed for his groin as though that would stop the bullet that smashed through his hands and plowed into his genitals. Screaming, he fell helpless beside the twitching bawling Marat.

The colonel sank to all fours and crawled to Pavel and Misha. "Don't. Please don't. I was forced . . . "

"Misha, the choice is yours." Pavel let out a mirthless chuckle. "My personal preference would be to let him die the way he deserves, contemplating his sins by fire."

"Yes, you are right, as always, Pavel. We'll do it your way."

Misha suddenly turned on the babbling colonel. With finesse he flicked the selector switch on the weapon to single shot and fired two well placed rounds to the crotch. The KGB colonel collapsed head first beside the two screeching young men.

"Now," said Pavel. "Bring in the trunk. Quick! Before someone hears the laughter of these jackals."

They opened the trunk and poured one can of gasoline all over the room, then put another two in the middle of the KGB apartment. Pavel also shook a box of ferrous oxide mixture with aluminum powder over the twitching moaning bodies. Under the fire's heat a moulding aluminum-ferrous mass would form, it cuts through layers of tank armour and would make the bodies unrecognizable even to the point of melting the bullets inside, obliterating all traces of evidence.

They quickly left the apartment and once out on the street a confederate in a car at the other end of the block made a sign to the gunman on top of a house nearby who in turn waved to the marksman. A phosphorus incendiary bullet was shot into a dark window.

The hot wave of a thunderous explosion shook the building, and a crimson oven of fire raged through the fifth floor of the decrepit gray apartment house. Loud echoes sounded all over Arbat. Pigeons streaked skyward in packs.

In the car Pavel handed the file to Oksana. "There you are. Nothing serious in it, but I advise you to burn it at home and flush the ashes down the toilet. There was no video tape, just as I thought."

"Thank you, Pavel. I will always be grateful to you. How did it go?"

"I won't tell you a thing so that if you are ever questioned you will not fall into a trap. I can only say that you will not suffer anymore. They died like dogs, on their knees, begging for mercy."

A fire engine raced past them, siren screaming, heading to Arbat where the column of thick oily smoke was rising into the evening sky.

"How can I repay you for what you have done for me?"

"You know what I want, that is all; if I need something else from you it has been paid for. You belong to our family now."

"What family?" Oksana asked.

Pavel laughed. "You'll see. We will take a trip to Irkutsk together sometime soon and visit your father. We will help you and you will help us. You will personally visit our leader who is temporarily residing near Irkutsk. He will like you."

"Who is he, Pavel?"

"You will know soon enough." Another fire truck screamed by them. Pavel looked over his shoulder as it hurtled toward the smoke rising from the middle of the city. "Yes, Oksana Martinova, we are bonded by fire and death."

Oksana shivered and Pavel took her hand gently. "You have nothing to fear from us. But I am interested to know, what do you think of this system we live under? The Communist Party, KGB, PolitBureau? I know, your father is a party boss. And because of you he will help us. Are you really Comrade Martinova, ready to carry on the next generation of Lenin's ideals?"

Almost violently she shook her head.

"Well, you and I think much alike, Oksana. And we are going to make certain that your English studies continue either at the institute or privately."

The car stopped not far from the American Embassy, on the Garden Ring. "Out you go, girl," Pavel said to Oksana. "Go home by Metro; do not forget to burn the file immediately. I trust you, it was not easy to get it, so do not let me down."

"I won't."

"I know. You are a grown up woman now and you have seen how things happen. I will give you a call when the time is ripe. Start preparing your father for our visit. *Do Svidaniya.*"

The car took off. Oksana walked along the sidewalk in the stream of the nighttime Moscow crowd, holding to her a simple blue cardboard file with white tapes.

CHAPTER TEN

⟨⟫⟩ ⟨⟫⟩

The Russian emigré tourists around Peter Nikhilov industriously snapped pictures of the Statue of Liberty under the watchful eye of a New York Agency for New Americans official. They had been herded to the Battery at the lower end of Manhattan to make an obligatory pilgrimage to the symbol of the freedom they had achieved by getting out of their former mother country. Peter was gratified that he had resisted the temptation to skip this Saturday morning outing after the long night with his friends from the Moscow Militsia who were in New York for the first boxing matches scheduled between the Moscow and New York police departments. As luck would have it he spotted Zekki Dekka with an obviously Caucasus-bred hoodlum, swarthy, with blue-stubbled cheeks and jaw.

Peter pointed his specially instrumented camera at the Statue of Liberty across the harbor. Unlike all the emigré amateur photographers with their cameras trained in the same direction, the image he was seeing on his viewfinder was of a scene located at a ninety degree angle to the camera's normal line of sight. He adjusted the

trick lens bringing into sharp focus a picture of Zekki and his bur-
ley companion in the ill-fitting suit that Zekki must have just purchased for him from a Brighton Beach second-hand clothing store.
He snapped the picture of the two of them and then turned the
zoom to rest on a perfect head shot of the man posing as an emigré, but almost certainly an assassin brought over to do a certain
job for Zekki. He took three shots and noticed through his viewfinder that Zekki had spotted him.

Letting the camera fall on its strap to his side Peter ambled
toward Zekki as the NYANA representative scribbled his initials
on the fake emigré's forged papers indicating that the subject had
indeed viewed the shrine to freedom.

"Good morning, Zekki," Peter greeted the forger. "Lady Liberty
is indeed inspiring."

"Ah, Mr. Nikhilov, and I see you are busy looking for trouble in
the oppressed Russian Jewish community."

"And I see you've brought over another Caucasus import."

"He is certified by NYANA."

"Your documents must be really a work of art to make anyone
believe this is a Jewish emigré." He laughed. "How much did you
contribute to NYANA to certify this *dgigit*?"

The blue-jawed goon looked up at the one word he could
understand. In Russian Peter addressed him. "Do not let your
sponsor here talk you into anything illegal, like murdering someone, because I will personally see to it you never get out of our
prisons."

"Intimidating a poor, friendless Jewish immigrant!" Zekki cried
as his companion stared open mouthed, startled by the display of
street Russian by the American.

Zekki made as if to summon the NYANA representative. "Go
on," Peter taunted. "Call Mr. Epstein over and tell him the Brooklyn DA's office is harassing one of the downtrodden killers
NYANA is certifying as a recently freed *refusnik*."

"Some day you will go too far, Nikhilov."

"And you already have, Zekki." The Caucasus goon gave Peter a menacing look and took a step toward him. Peter grinned. "Go ahead, Zekki. As the man said, 'make my day.'" Then in Russian, "You will be watched closely, *Dgigit*."

Zekki hastily restrained any impulse on the part of this product of the Caucasus to revert to type. A sudden series of beeps emitted from the area of Peter's belt. He strode away from Zekki and, recognizing Hugh McDonald's phone number displayed on the beeper, he strode to the nearest pay station and put through the call to Hugh.

"Something important came up," Hugh said breathlessly. "I took a picture yesterday which I want you to check."

"Meet me in the lobby of the Beverly Hotel on Lex and 50th Street in two hours," Peter snapped.

The Beverly Hotel attracted Russian officials and that was where the Moscow Militsia Boxing Team was ensconced during the New York stay of its four city tour. Hugh McDonald was waiting in the lobby. Peter took a seat on the sofa next to him. "What's up, Hugh?" he asked.

"We've been keeping a close watch on the North Korean mission to the United Nations. Twice we've seen a distinguished-looking Russian, I've learned how to spot Russians," he added parenthetically, "go in and out. The second time, yesterday, I got a telephoto shot of him. The FBI agents at Foreign Mission Control couldn't identify him. They said he was definitely not an accredited diplomat at any mission. I thought you might help me ID the guy."

"If I can't, the guys upstairs getting ready for the fights tonight may be able to help."

Peter studied the picture Hugh handed him and shook his head. "Let's go up to General Major Bodaev. Maybe he can help us."

Minutes later Peter greeted the general in his suite and, wasting no time, showed him Hugh's picture. Bodaev let out a surprised grunt. "He's here in New York now?"

"That's right." Peter shook a mock admonishing finger at the Militsia general. "He's twice visited the North Korean mission. I thought you people were no longer messing with the North Koreans."

"My Government is not," Bodaev replied. "This is one of the top members of a powerful Georgian criminal syndicate. He is also a minor member of the Chamber of Deputies which makes him immune from arrest. We would love to build a case and put him away. He is college educated and well connected. The leader of his *organizatsiya* is known as Tofik, whom we put in the labor camps for ten years, but his gang has only gained in power." He tapped the picture. "This is Edward Gardenadze. I wonder what he's doing in New York."

"Yes, and at the North Korean mission," Hugh said, after Peter had translated the general's words.

"Let's see if I can supply a tie-in," Peter said. He handed over the picture he had just taken on the Battery with his trick camera.

"I don't know him. Looks like a product of the Caucasus. I'll have the others take a look." He picked up the phone and in moments the senior members of the Militsia boxing team were assembled. As Bodaev handed the pictures around, Peter introduced Boris Burenchuk, a slender neatly dressed man in his mid-thirties, to Hugh. Boris, recently promoted to major, was the Militsia's public affairs officer as well as a detective, Peter explained. Boris immediately recognized the politician criminal. So did the tall coach of the boxing team, Major Yuri Navakoff. But nobody could identify the Russian hoodlum with Zekki until Captain Valerie Kutuzov came into the room.

"Valerie is our star boxer," Bodaev said proudly. "No American is going to beat him." He handed Peter's picture to the young Militsia officer, who stared at it and nodded.

"Yes, I've seen him twice in lineups of murder suspects. He is a Georgian who joined the Moscow gang of Victor Kalina."

"Kalina!" Bodaev exclaimed. "That's the bastard son of Yakovlev or Yaponchik as they call him."

"Yes. I have heard of the Jap," Peter replied. "What do you figure his son's goon is doing here with Zekki Dekka?"

"We have files on him," Valerie said.

"How about if I fax this picture to the Sly Fox in Moscow?" Peter suggested.

"Good idea," Bodaev agreed. "What time is it at home?"

Peter pulled out his chronolog. "Eight o'clock tonight."

"Impossible to get Vladimir Ivanovitch before tomorrow then."

Hugh McDonald was unable to understand what was going on and Peter explained. "They all know your man but mine seems to be somewhat of an enigma. Colonel Vladimir Ivanovitch Nechiaev is the Chief of Detectives at Petrovka 38, Militsia headquarters. They call him Sly Fox. I'll fax my picture to him and we'll see what comes back."

"What do they say about this politico-crook visiting the North Korean mission to the UN?"

"Just that it is nothing official."

"At NEST anyone going into a terror state mission is suspicious," Hugh replied.

"Do you know where this Gardenadze is staying?" Peter asked.

"One of the men followed him after I took the picture but lost him in the sprawl of Brighton Beach."

"Are you interested in going to the fights tonight?" Peter asked. "I've got a bunch of extra tickets and five or six of New York's cutest Russian girls to bring along as a cheering section."

"No thanks," Hugh declined. "Now that I have the ID I needed, the next step is to find out more about this Edward Gardenadze. Could you ask your friends in Moscow to send us a dossier on him? We know that North Korea is trying to build nuclear weapons. Maybe he's some kind of a link to unofficial dealing in plutonium."

"I'll do my best for you, as always."

Peter sat a few rows above ringside at the Long Island Coliseum surrounded by the pretty Russian girls he had recruited to cheer for their countrymen in their bouts with the New York Police Department boxers.

Captain Valerie Kutuzov beat a furious tattoo of left jabs and right cross punches on his adversary.

"Va—LAY—ri!" the girls shrilly repeated, cheering him on.

The bell signifying the end of the third and last round saved the American fighter from further punishment. As Valerie returned to his corner he flashed a smile and waved at his cheering section. Excited screams greeted the gesture. Major Yuri Navakoff, the Russian coach, threw a towel over Valerie's shoulders. The referee walked across the ring and held Valerie's arm high, signifying his victory. Applause and cries of joy broke out. Valerie's defeated opponent walked across the ring to the Russian corner and the two boxers shook gloves. The Russians had won four out of five bouts and now they were ready to enjoy the party afterwards at a nearby restaurant taken over by the New York Police hosting the event.

Peter was proud of his efforts on behalf of the Militsiamen. There were enough Russian girls to please all of them and when the New Yorkers mixed with the Russians Peter was the official interpreter.

Just before midnight the New York Police Commissioner appeared. He congratulated General Bodaev on the Russians' victory and then strode over to Peter Nikhilov, who had just invited one of the Russian girls to come to his home for a nightcap after the party."We have a major problem, Nikhilov." The commissioner's face was grim. "Maybe you can help. I have been trying to reach you. You're not wearing your beeper."

"I thought I had the night off. What's the problem Commissioner?"

"There's been a homicide that may have severe political repercussions. A Russian politician, visiting this country unofficially, was murdered a couple of hours ago. We haven't notified the Russian Consulate yet. I thought you could do the honors."

Peter smacked his forehead with the palm of his hand. "Oh Jesus, I should have figured it out sooner. Same pattern."

"What are you saying?" the commissioner asked.

"Was the name of the victim by any chance Edward Gardenadze?"

"How did you know?"

"And it's too late to get to the airport."

"What's that got to do with it?"

"Another killer blows this country. We've got to talk to General Bodaev."

"I'll have to apologize for being unable to protect his member of their congress or whatever they call it in Moscow."

"In this case Bodaev will be delighted. But there is something most serious going on."

"Can you explain?"

"Later." He turned to his Russian date telling her he would have to work tonight but would make up for it. Bodaev was hard put to express any regrets about the murder when he was told of it by the commissioner and the two of them discussed the procedure to follow, with Peter interpreting. It was a great relief to the commissioner that nobody of importance in Russia would be distressed other than the Georgian criminal *organizatsiya* for which Gardenadze was obviously on a mission.

Peter took the opportunity to urge the commissioner to send him to Moscow during the summer to organize a chain of communication and cooperation between the New York and Moscow police. Bodaev enthusiastically seconded the request and the commissioner, now that an expected diplomatic and political problem had been lifted from his shoulders, agreed to use all the influence at his command to finalize such an effort. The party continued but Peter left with the commissioner to explain the full significance of the murder as he saw it.

On Sunday morning Peter and Hugh discussed the murder at length. Twice, unofficial Russians had visited terror state missions to the UN. Twice these same Russians had turned up dead. Both times Zekki Dekka had in his charge a typical Caucasus assassin. What was the Moscow connection here?

CHAPTER ELEVEN

The chilling revelation that there really is a Moscow Mafia was the final lesson in Oksana Martinova's education as an English interpreter. She sat gazing out the window of the Moscow-Irkutsk passenger train at the the great snow-covered plains which seemed to be floating backwards, dissolving into the bright mountainside behind them. Lofty Siberian pine and fir trees towered above the barriers protecting the tracks from snow drifts.

The train was gaining speed after losing several hours in a heavy snowfall and was due to arrive almost on time at Irkutsk Railway Station. Up front over a hundred passengers were packed into each car. The inevitable fight between two drunken soldiers returning from military service had accounted for the destruction of one toilet and yet another smashed window through which icy streams of air chilled the cars. But where Oksana sat, in the first-class carriages at the rear of the train, the cars were clean and luxurious, with comfortable couchette compartments for two, filled, for the most part, with local government officials.

She wore a loose fitting black blouse tucked into black slacks. Her long legs, slim beneath the traveling pants, were thrust into ankle-length fur-lined boots.

Smoking a thin, brown cigarette she gazed out the window. It was a terrible bother to have to travel by train for four days when the flight took only one, but storms had grounded all air traffic in the region and it was imperative that she reach her destination as soon as possible.

Four years ago when her mother died during a particularly harsh Siberian winter, her father, First Secretary of the huge Irkutsk region of Siberia, had arranged for her to leave Irkutsk and go to Moscow where she was admitted to study English at the Maurice Thoriz Institute of Foreign Languages. She was young and naive, the lovely daughter of a powerful party leader, all things bright and beautiful, adventures of youth awaiting, with a promising career ahead.

Now she was returning to visit her father on behalf of a notorious Soviet criminal, Vyacheslav Yakovlev, known as Yaponchik, the Jap. She could hardly believe the things that had happened to her these past six months culminating in this visit home with Pavel, Yakovlev's chief associate, who sat in the compartment directly behind her. Pavel was a courtly companion at meals. Perhaps in his mid-forties, she thought, he was quite handsome and his attire was impeccable, Western in style. He combed his sandy-colored hair straight back, and with his sharp features and blue eyes he certainly didn't look like a gangster.

Oksana looked up, sensing someone staring at her through the open door of her compartment. It was a young man who had tried to strike up an acquaintance with her since the train left Moscow several days before. She had conversed in a non-committal manner with him in the corridor but refused an invitation to join him for a glass of cognac in his compartment. Misha, Pavel's stony-faced bodyguard, black cloak hanging to his heels, appeared beside the young man, nudging him away.

Even as Oksana was contemplating the events in her young life which had precipitated the long train trip to Siberia, Vyacheslav Yakovlev was eagerly awaiting news of the efforts to secure his release from the prison system. The size of his mighty *obshak* made it possible for him to buy relatively luxurious surroundings at the labor camp but his power was withering away after nine years of his fifteen-year sentence.

As the train sped towards its destination at Irkutsk the sharp silhouettes of labor camp turrets appeared in the distance. Pavel, Misha, and Oksana went together to the dining compartment for breakfast. Pavel chuckled at the moonfaced, well-fed waiters, mentioning that to get such a job one needed the influence of the KGB or Mafia. Waiters gained profits by selling their food supplies to the hungry population at the stations along the way where the train stopped. In Siberia these kitchen employee entrepreneurs acquired valuable skins of marten, sable or mink in exchange for lumps of meat. The people of these remote areas did not see meat or eggs for months, eating little besides frost-bitten potatoes and turnips.

While they were having breakfast, the train stopped at a small station and a few old women stepped up onto the dining car, bargaining with the waiters. With the stops no more than five minutes in length they had to act fast and be shrewd enough not to be defrauded by the train's kitchen personnel. As the train started to shudder into motion they all jumped from the carriage. One shaggy *babushka* waited too long and was afraid to jump from the moving train, still clutching a large bloodsoaked parcel of pork. As the train gained momentum the voices of her companions fell behind. The next stop was a hundred miles down the tracks, it would take her a day or two to get home and the meat would be spoiled without refrigeration.

The old woman's hysterical wails echoed through the dining car as she ran back and forth in the narrow passage between the tables, tears running down her wrinkled cheeks. The waiters laughed and shouted at her to jump.

Oksana dropped her napkin in disgust, told Pavel she would be in her compartment, stood up, and started after the crone. The anguished cries ceased as Oksana forced several hundred-ruble bank notes into her clenched fingers.

"Here, Babushka, do not be upset," Oksana said in comforting tones. "You'll get home. This will do it."

The bewildered woman counted the money with wet fingers as with her arms she pressed the pork to her breast. She had never seen, much less held in her hands, such a sum of money and was so astonished she even forgot to thank her lovely young benefactor.

Later in her compartment Pavel sat down beside Oksana and once again went over what she must tell Jap. He was meticulous in all business matters.

"First, the assignment in New York was carried out successfully. Second you will give him all the details of the arrangements for his release. You will also tell him that Zekki Dekka in New York has the plan ready to go forward, and then he will give you information for me."

"I know," Oksana said. "You've gone over it already."

"Yes. Sorry. I just like to be certain. Even you may not be able to see him again after this."

It was almost noon when the train pulled up at Irkutsk Station. Although the sun was shining brightly, the platform was still covered by wet melting snow that had fallen the night before. The dilapidated old brick and cement building of the city's railway station towered in front of them; it was built more than a century before and looked like a cathedral.

Not many people were on the platform. Oksana stared around, drawing her cloak against her shoulders. Pavel's eyes darted about the station until he saw a short square figure approaching them in brisk strides.

Oksana ran to the man, splashing through puddles of melted snow. The next moment she was hugging him and he lifted her feet off the ground in a joyous embrace.

Arms still around each other, Oksana and her father approached her travelling companions. Pavel was at least a head taller than Martinov but the two men looked strikingly similar except for height and age. Misha was silent, his thick black cloak fastened up to the throat.

"Daddy," Oksana said. "This is my close and trusted friend, Pavel."

Martinov stretched out his rough wide paw of a hand.

"A pleasure to meet you. Call me Nickolai."

"Your daughter has been telling me some very complimentary things about you. I am her true friend, though not the closest one, actually."

"Aha." Martinov turned to Oksana. "He speaks well, my dear." He looked at Misha. "And who is this *dgigit*?" he asked, recognizing him as a Georgian.

Misha did not utter a word, watching the secretary attentively.

"This is my secretary," Pavel replied without blinking an eye. "He has the most precise handwriting."

"Really?" Martinov asked with a coarse chuckle, recognizing a gunman when he saw one.

"Yes. Writes with both hands most expertly."

"And from any position?"

"Certainly."

"I see. And who exactly are you?"

"I am a businessman as Oksana has no doubt explained to you."

"Yes," Nickolai acknowledged. "Well, I of course am a politician only involved in State business."

"I understand. I have come to discuss some matters of interest to both of us, if you do not mind."

Nickolai turned to a group of his men standing under the roof of the station. He pointed at the luggage coming off the train which Misha was now approaching and they walked over to help him.

Soldiers and smiling, newly-released prisoners from the surrounding labor camps were waiting in lines at the small windows of the booking office. In front of the station was a pickup truck, two jeeps, and a new American Cadillac. From the extensive research Pavel had done on Nickolai Martinov, he knew the Cadillac was virtually a tank. It had been reinforced with armor at the machine plant in Toliatti on the Volga. Martinov pulled open the door for Oksana and gestured Pavel and Misha inside as he sat in the rear seat beside Oksana. Misha took a middle jump seat and Pavel sat in front with Nickolai's old retainer whose name Pavel already knew was Tuva.

"Where are we going?" Oksana asked.

"Out to the country estate. I ordered your things to be put in the second floor room you always loved."

It took almost an hour for the convoy to reach the outskirts of Irkutsk, a large city founded in the second half of the sixteenth century by Russian Cossacks. The area was enormously rich in fish, wild poultry, and fur-bearing animals. It was also the site of a productive gold mine. Under the Tsars the city had bustled with numerous Russian, Chinese and English trading houses, restaurants and shops. In those days Irkutsk residents would become indignant if less than fifteen kinds of fish were not on display in the market stalls. Now, communist austerity had killed all that, the big paper plants poisoning many of the fish in the region's rivers. The city became grim, empty and hungry. Its chief distinction was as capital of the labor camp region where thousands of Soviet citizens were enslaved and worked to death in the forbidding climate.

Three hours after leaving the railroad station they arrived at the gates of Martinov's estate on Lake Baikal. The driver pressed the remote control button on the dashboard and the gates slid smoothly apart, automatically closing behind the vehicles.

Pavel followed his host and Oksana through the front door into a magnificent reception room. Chandeliers of crystal and bronze were hanging from the fifteen-foot-high ceiling. The shining parquet of the floor was carpeted by several white skins of polar bears. Gold-framed landscapes and portraits hung on the walls along with lavishly decorated Mongolian and Chinese swords, shields, and helmets. Redwood heavy antique furniture stood in the corners of the room. Two wide staircases met in the middle of the second floor. No Western hotel palace could have been more lavish.

Martinov chuckled as Pavel's head turned, taking in the opulence. "Yes, my friends, I like beautiful things."

As Oksana mounted the thickly carpeted staircase, Pavel and Misha followed their host across the reception room, through another set of double doors and into a courtyard. They walked along a path among great cedars until, coming around a bend in the forest, they saw a large barn-like structure surrounded by a sturdy ten-foot-high iron picket fence.

"Now there's a nice spot, quiet and no fuss," Martinov said. "Easy place to work. No one ever bothers me when I am in my office. You will soon see why."

As they approached the building it appeared to be a long wooden stable. Martinov's driver, who had preceded them, slid the bolt of the double doors aside and pushed them open.

111

Inside there was an iron grill, to their right and halfway down the barn a wooden wall from floor to ceiling. A strange animal smell came from behind the grill. Martinov walked over to what seemed to be one side of a cage and taking an iron pike that was leaning against the grill, he rapped with it on the metal mesh. Instantly a roar came from inside the cage and a great striped beast slunk into the light.

"Do you like cats?" Martinov chuckled. "That is a Siberian tiger, makes the kind you find in India look like runts of the litter."

Pavel and Misha stared dumbfounded at the animal, which let out another mighty roar so powerful they could feel the vibration of the blast.

"I lost three men capturing this cat," Martinov continued. "Well, let's go into the office. I can assure you we will not be disturbed and perhaps we can get started on our business."

He led the way to a door in the wall which divided the barn and on the other side was a single room the length, breadth, and height of half the barn with a glass wall at the end overlooking a grassy field and the trees along the bank of the lake. Animal skins covered the hardwood floor and shelves of books and trophies lined the other three walls. In the middle of the office was a huge wooden desk looking out over the view.

"Shall we have a drink? Vodka or cognac? I think cognac actually." Martinov turned to the Mongolian at the door. "Tuva, we'll all have cognac, and then be sure that we are not disturbed."

After they had finished their first glass of cognac and Martinov poured a second, the First Secretary gestured out the window. The Siberian tiger was prowling about, looking in at them. "Now, let us discuss the matters that caused you to bring my daughter all this way to see her old father again. I'm sure it wasn't because you have always wanted to visit our Sacred Sea," he nodded toward the bank of Lake Baikal.

"Oksana felt that you might be disposed to return a great service Misha and I were able to do, saving her career, reputation, and her virtues."

Martinov darted a steely glance at Pavel. "What do you know about her virtues?"

"When she was, um . . . compromised, I helped her to preserve them."

"What happened to Oksana?"

"She was in trouble with KGB."

"My Oksana? Why didn't she call me?"

"Why don't you ask her? She was in a bind with some rather vulgar operatives. Scum. We got her out of it." Pavel let Martinov assimilate the information for a few moments, then added, "I'm sure you are well aware why I'm here."

Martinov settled himself behind his desk, the bottle of cognac in front of him, and began the discussion. "I have talked to the chief at Tulun Camp and made inquiries about Yakovlev, the Jap, as he is known."

Pavel lounged in a leather armchair beside the desk. Misha sat attentively in the straight chair on the other side of the desk, casting uneasy glances every so often at the tiger slinking back and forth on the other side of the glass wall.

Pavel played his first card. "You and Jap have something in common, you know."

"We do?" Martinov sounded surprised.

"Yes. You both rose to power through the good will of Comrade Brezhnev."

"Jap knew him?"

"Certainly. You know the story. General Churbanov of the Militsia, the Secretary General's son-in-law, and Yakovlev were close associates."

"I think I did hear that," Martinov allowed. "Of course out here, five time zones away, we know little of what goes on in

Moscow." He poured the three glasses full of cognac again and they all drank to Jap.

"Now," Martinov continued, "Churbanov is behind bars and you are asking me to use such influence as I have to seek early release for Jap. Do you understand the political risk I take as an advocate for this thief-in-the-law?"

"You have done it before," Pavel countered. "Several times, I'm told, you have been contacted by a chief of camp on behalf of a prisoner who paid everyone well and secured his release. The camps are a big source of revenue for you, unlimited free labor, and once in a while someone like Jap comes along and you make a real killing."

"Unfortunately his case is the most difficult," Martinov said. "He has enemies as well as friends in high places."

Martinov recited the many difficulties inherent in securing Jap's release. Pavel listened and then said wearily, "I am prepared to offer one hundred thousand rubles."

Martinov cried out as though stuck with a knife. "Do you take me for a beggar, risk all that I have for that?"

"How much do you want then?"

"One lemon."

Pavel laughed. "One million? Why not make it two?"

Martinov smiled condescendingly. "That would be nice, but one will be enough . . . to start."

"Two hundred thousand," Pavel offered.

After much debate a price of five hundred thousand was agreed upon. Martinov poured three more glasses of cognac and sighed. "And do not worry. Your Jap will stay in Tulun in the best shape possible until we can get him released."

Pavel nodded in satisfaction and reaching into his pocket he pulled out a small leather pouch and started to turn it upside down in front of the First Secretary, then paused. "Remember when you did something like this for Brezhnev?"

The surprised look quickly disappeared from Martinov's

face as a sparkling six- to eight-carat square-cut yellow diamond fell on the desk in front of him.

"To seal our bargain," Pavel said.

Martinov stared at it for some moments. He licked his lips, downed his glass of cognac and seized the stone. "Where did you get such a beauty?" he gasped. "This didn't come from any Russian deposit."

"Very rare," Pavel agreed laughing, handing his host the pouch. "It came from right men in right places. And so it goes around."

Martinov caressed the stone a moment, dropped it back into the small leather bag and turned toward the door. "Tuva!" he shouted. "Get the cat in for his supper. We're going to the sauna."

With the tiger back in his cage Martinov led Pavel from his office along the bank of the Baikal to the sauna house. Misha refused the steam treatment, and the two of them sobered up, sweating in the steam and bathing in the natural mineral pool on which the sauna house had been built.

That night the parlor was filled with servants and Martinov's highest placed retainers and fellow party bosses with their wives. The men were wearing black formal suits and the women their most lavish dresses. The table, with its white table cloth, silver candlesticks and gold service utensils, was set as for a king, and indeed Nickolai Martinov was the king of his Siberian region of Irkutsk approximately the size of France.

He was seated in his chair at the head of the table, Pavel and Misha at his right side as the honored guests.

Oksana made her entrance, walking slowly down the formal staircase dressed in a white silk blouse and a tight knee-length black skirt; her hair was gathered in a bun at the back of her head. She was escorted by two men in evening wear to the seat at her father's left, directly opposite Pavel.

"This is a smart young man," Nickolai said as he chewed on his favorite smoked bear meat nodding at Pavel.

Two cooks brought in a narrow silver dish six feet long containing a great sturgeon recently caught in Lake Baikal and immediately refrigerated for the arrival of Oksana.

It was baked in the oven, stuffed with mushrooms, vegetables and whole chicken; the pool of sturgeon oil around the fish was deep yellow and warm, leaves of fennel and parsley floating on it. The guests cheered the arrival of the prize fish and the corks of champagne bottles began popping.

Oksana gave Pavel a questioning glance. He smiled and nodded. As the wine was poured Pavel raised his glass. "Your father is a most reasonable man. Here's to a profitable relationship for all of us!"

CHAPTER TWELVE

❧ ❧

Oksana barely managed to suppress the trembling of her hands as the stark brick and concrete walls of Tulun's internal jail came into sight behind the barbed wire and gun turrets. Misha, sitting in the front seat beside Martinov's driver, turned around to give her what he thought was a reassuring smile. Actually, his stubble-covered face was incapable of more than a distorted grin. He gestured to the brick structure just inside the gate to the right. "All these camps are the same. That's the crematorium."

Oksana shuddered, staring at the pall of gray smoke hanging over the single stack.

The gate swung open and Major Karamushev met the car inside the compound. Misha jumped out and opened the back door for Oksana. She stepped out, looking about her uneasily.

"It is a rare pleasure to have the daughter of the First Secretary of the region visit us, Comrade Martinova." The jail chief eyed a suede bag which dangled from Oksana's right arm. "Slava Yakovlev is eagerly awaiting your visit."

Karamushev bowed and escorted her from the warm interior of her automobile past machine-gun carrying guards through iron double doors into the administrative section of the concrete and stone building.

Descending a flight of stone steps she walked briskly after the officer, holding her head high as he opened the final hinged iron slab of a door. Suddenly she found herself in the unexpected opulence of a pleasant chamber reminiscent of her father's den with animal skins hanging on the walls and thick fur carpeting on a smooth wooden plank floor. A crackling fire gave a cheerful glow to the surroundings and on a long, low table rested cognac and wine bottles, crystal glasses and plates of sandwiches. The place didn't seem like a prison cell at all but rather the den of a comfortable *dacha.*

Beside the burning fire at the back of the room stood an elegant, slightly oriental-looking man. He held a glass of cognac in his hand, and as she stepped into the warm chamber a polite smile lit up what would otherwise have been an inscrutable countenance. He wore a freshly pressed blue shirt and black jeans. His feet were thrust into fur slippers.

He put down the glass and walked towards her, taking her fur coat and hanging it on a brass hook beside the door.

"So you are Oksana," Jap said warmly. "How beautiful you are and how I have looked forward to this visit."

"Comrade Yakovlev," she held out her hand. "I bring you good wishes from your friends and my father, Nickolai Martinov."

Jap took her hand and bent his head, kissing it gently. "Please call me Slava," he said with a chuckle. "I am not a communist, never was, and this comrade business is about to disappear anyway."

"All right, Slava."

"Would you like a drink after your long drive? I'm sure our

friend," he smiled and gestured toward the jail chief, "will join us."

Karamushev accepted the drink as Oksana shook out her long raven tresses, a gesture which drew rapt attention from both Jap and the jail chief. As she pulled off her boots the full extent of her perfect, youthful figure was evident, bosom enticingly swelling the bodice of her black dress. Her trim skirt falling just to her knees outlined her thighs above sheer silk stockings which sheathed long, excitingly turned legs. Both men sharply caught their breath.

Oksana smiled at Karamushev and reaching into her bag took out a square blue velvet box, and handed it to him. "My father asked me to give this to you."

The major snapped it open and his eyes feasted on two sparkling blue-white, pear-shaped diamonds. With a gasp he said, "They are beautiful, my dear. I shall treasure them and always be mindful of your father's esteem."

To Jap, Oksana said for Karamushev's benefit, "Your wife Olga sends her love and wishes for your early release." Part of the jail chief's excuse for permitting this visit was that Oksana was a family friend unconnected with Jap's business. Turning to Karamushev she said, "In my car is a hamper of food and some special wine. Can you arrange to have it delivered here?"

"I will see to it this minute." Clutching the velvet box in his right hand Karamushev walked out through the metal door in the cell leaving Jap and Oksana alone.

"That was very generous of your father to send such a gift to the jail chief," Jap said.

"Pavel provided the diamonds."

Wistfully Jap said, "I wish it could be arranged for my loyal frayer, Pavel, to come here and see me. There is much happening outside that only he knows about."

"Even my father cannot bend rules so your associates can visit. If he makes too much effort, your release could be in jeopardy." She smiled. "So I, a young woman and friend of your wife, to whom I have never been introduced incidentally, am allowed. My father himself could not come."

"Of course not," Jap replied. "He must be politically watchful. Besides, it is a delight to have so lovely a visitor."

"Pavel gave me many things to tell you," she said when the door was closed. "He wanted no writing, so I memorized everything."

Then, businesslike, as Jap poured her a glass of wine she said, "Pavel is in Irkutsk. He says you are losing power within the *organizatsyia* in New York and here."

Jap nodded somberly and she continued. "He and my father have met every day for over a week. The phone lines and fax machine between here and Moscow are very busy with messages that concern you. And now, even as we are together, they are arranging for payments to friends in the Council of Deputies and the prosecutor's office. Before this spring is over they think it likely you will be back in Moscow."

"Tell Pavel no matter how much it costs, I must be out soon."

"He says he is working as fast as he can. There is also the problem that in Moscow the People's Deputy from Samarkand is trying to have you transferred to a camp in Uzbekistan."

"That must not happen," Jap said flatly. "Tell him I am working from within to keep a transfer from being approved."

"Most important," Oksana went on, "he said to tell you the New York assignment was complete, but there are others from the Georgian crew in New York trying to cut into your business with the Americans. He asks if he should have your men there complete more assignments."

"These Georgians belong to a thief-in-the-law here in Tulun. I have warned Tofik not to let his men touch my businesses on the outside. Tell Pavel to do whatever is necessary. We may

have trouble with Tofik's frayer in Moscow, Givi, but hopefully not. I am not looking for a war with him."

"I will tell him, Slava."

"Any more about my release?" Jap asked eagerly.

"My father telephoned and talked to People's Deputy General
Director of the Institute of Eye Surgery, Svyatoslav Federov."

Jap nodded approvingly. "He is the richest and most highly
respected physician in Russia."

"Yes, and renowned for his international practice. He wrote
a personal plea to President Boris Yeltsin for your pardon."

Oksana leaned closer to him. "My father wrote his friend,
the Chairman of the Commission on Human Rights of the
Supreme Council of the USSR, and personally talked to the
Minister of Internal Affairs on your behalf."

"You are magnificent, Oksana." Jap reached for her hand
and held it in both of his.

"When I am back in Moscow I will continue to remind these
people," Oksana continued.

"And when a beautiful and brilliant woman like you deliv-
ers the message, that makes it one hundred times stronger."

Oksana's eyes sparkled at the compliment, delivered in this
underground prison cell which was nevertheless pleasant
enough.

"Pavel wanted you to know that through his sources, the
Assistant Chairman of the Supreme Court of the Russian Federation, A. Merkushev, has committed himself to help you. It is
Merkushev who must present the petition for mercy and
clemency on your behalf to the court."

"You certainly have been reaching the highest seats of par-
doning power in the country."

"Yes, and Pavel suggested that I personally go to see an old
friend of yours, People's Deputy of the USSR, and such a
famous singer and actor, Josef David Kobzon. I will be thrilled
to meet him."

121

"And I am sure he will be thrilled to meet you." Jap's eyes twinkled. "I know Josef well. He loves nothing in the world as much as beautiful women."

"Pavel said that when he finishes paying for everything you'll need to be printing your own money and fortunately Zekki Dekka is ready in New York to put the printing operation together."

Jap leaned forward intently, taking her hand in both of his. "Zekki Dekka must immediately make arrangements for shipping the presses and material to Moscow. As soon as I am out, we must start our operation. I see communism turning to anarchy before the end of the year and we must be ready to move."

Jap breathed heavily at the import of the message he was sending. "Be certain that Pavel understands the importance of keeping our future trading partners, in particular North Korea and Iraq, in line. And we must continue to eliminate all competition. Soon after I am at large I will go to America," he asserted.

"Perhaps you will need an interpreter you can trust in America," Oksana suggested.

She was thrilled to hear Slava reply, "Yes, I'm sure I will. I am too old to learn English. You make your father get me out of the Soviet prison system and I promise that you will go to America. That's settled. Now, enough of business. I want to hear a little about you. What do you do with your life?" Oksana described her life as an interpreter at the Russia Hotel and under Jap's questioning revealed how she and Nadia had met and become friends.

At that point Major Karamushev returned with the hamper of food and wine. Although Jap was absorbed in her story he was too polite not to offer some food and a drink to the jail chief who cheerfully accepted. Their conversation drifted to inconsequential subjects such as her long train trip to Irkutsk.

On his second drink Karamushev, unable to take his eyes off

Oksana, once again made reference to the interference he was experiencing from Moscow in regard to prisoner Yakovlev.

"Resist it, Chief," Jap boomed heartily. "Soon enough you will be retired and leading a rich man's life."

"I would retire now, but then what would happen to you?" He gave Jap a humorous questioning look. "I do hope you will find a way to get released soon so we can both get out of this devil's playground." Then, taking a final shot of cognac, Karamushev left them alone together.

"Now, go on with your story," Jap said eagerly. "I could hardly wait for that old rascal, always looking for another excuse to extract payment, to leave so you could get back to this interesting tale."

As Jap listened intently, Oksana glossed over her brief sexual episode with the Norwegian and dwelled on the mental and physical abuse inflicted on her by the three KGB officers.

The Jap was angered by the revelation and savored the account of their deaths which Pavel had reluctantly described to her so she could pass it on to Jap. "It won't be long before all these State-licensed rapists, torturers, and murderers pay dearly for their excesses."

Oksana put out of her mind some of the deeds she had heard attributed to the Jap.

Silently they sampled the delicacies Oksana brought with her, sipping the fine wine from Nickolai's cellar. Then Jap looked at her quizzically. "Tell me, doesn't it seem strange that you, with an elite education and background, are part of an organization considered illegal by the State?"

Oksana sipped her wine thoughtfully a moment and put the glass down. "I will never forget what was done to me by, as you put it, State-licensed rapists. There was no place I could turn to seek relief from further abuse. It was as though the State considered me at fault. Then, at some point after the Arbat fire, I experienced what you might call an epiphany."

Jap nodded in understanding. "One thing I do a great deal of here is reading. I want to hear about your epiphany."

"It came down to what was good and what was evil. In my life I couldn't believe that the Communist State I had been brought up to respect would not only condone what was done to me by a colonel and two young KGB officers, but seek to punish me by expelling me from the institute."

She shook her head as though in disbelief. "I tried to kill myself and it was Nadia, the prostitute, and your associate Pavel, who saved me from a system which almost destroyed the naive young girl I once was. I do not regret the bargain I made with Pavel."

"You did the right thing. Those three would have ruined your life. As Dostoevsky wrote, 'He once did me a grave injustice and has never forgiven me since.' They would never have forgotten what they did to you as guilt and fear fermented in their heads until they killed you."

Jap waited patiently for her to go on, encouraging her with his total attention. She took another sip of wine, discovering a reassuring quality about her unlikely companion despite his savage reputation, and found herself enjoying conversing with him.

"I am coming to realize that good and evil are not so clear," Oksana mused. "Most people rely on religion to make that distinction, but formal religion was denied me although mother tried to give me some feeling for God and Jesus even as my father, a devout communist and atheist, was ordering churches destroyed. You can only judge good and bad by what happens to you personally."

"You are right, Oksana," Jap agreed. "Morality, like everything else, is subjective."

He took a deep breath and again reached for Oksana's hand, which he held in both of his as he looked into her soulful brown eyes. "This epiphany of yours makes me trust you totally, Oksana." Jap let go of Oksana's hand and stood up, walking around his cell, pouring himself a glass of cognac and filling Oksana's wine glass.

"You have seen at first hand, Oksana, that the Communist Party in Russia is dying, it just won't lie down yet."

Oksana nodded. It was only on this visit home that she realized her own father owed his influence, wealth, the comfortable apartment in Moscow, to unbridled corruption.

"The party is rotted through and through," Jap continued. "One kick, one political or military upheaval, and overnight the entire structure will collapse." The intensity in his slightly slanted black eyes as his words came forth conveyed his belief in the prediction. "I must be on the outside before that happens so I can take advantage of the turmoil."

Jap paced back and forth across his cell and finished off the cognac in his glass. "I am at a tremendous disadvantage not being able to communicate. At least I am glad to know Chechen was successful in New York, and by now I'm sure Tofik knows too."

"Anything else?"

"Pavel thinks that some of Tofik's Georgians from Givi's crew are still trying to go ahead with the operation in Moscow. Do you want Chechen to do anything more?"

"Do nothing, nothing at all," Jap was suddenly agitated. "Pavel must make Chechen behave in Moscow. We do not want war." Jap was silent a few moments and a slow smile spread across his face. "Tell Pavel to try and plant a man in Givi's organization, Misha would be the best, he's a Georgian like them. And tell Pavel that Victor must try to gain at least a temporary peace with Givi."

Oksana's natural curiosity had been aroused. "Who is Victor? A businessman like you?"

"Victor Kalina is my son by a woman I did not marry." He smiled sadly at Oksana. "He is trying to be a businessman but he is young and makes mistakes. The Militsia caught him in the middle of a drug deal and he was lucky to get only three years, thanks to the help of my political contacts."

"So he went back into business when he got out?" Oksana asked.

Jap sighed and nodded. "It is fortunate I will be out soon because Victor has tried to directly compete with Givi and Tofik and my son isn't ready for that."

"You are really very proud of him," Oksana observed. "Have you seen him since coming here?"

"He was allowed to visit me in Tulun twice before General Yuri Churbanov, Brezhnev's son-in-law, was jailed himself," Jap replied evasively.

For another hour they talked and then Major Karamushev came to escort Oksana back to her car and driver. "I am sorry we cannot make this a longer visit, perhaps overnight." Oksana ignored his confidential grin. "But as I said, questions about my friend Vyacheslav Yakovlev keep coming from Moscow."

"We are trying to take care of these things, Major Karamushev," Oksana said. "My father asks if there is anything we can do for you?"

"Tell him that when I see trouble coming I will let him know promptly," the commandant replied.

She turned to Jap. "*Do svidaniya,* Slava. May our next meeting be in Moscow."

Jap walked with her to the iron door. He held the back of her hand to his lips. Impulsively she kissed him on the cheek. "I'll tell Olga you send your love." Then she briskly followed Major Karamushev into the outside hallway.

Jap listened until her high-heeled boots clicking on the concrete floor beyond his cell could no longer be heard. He returned to his inner lair, poured some cognac, and his thoughts turned to Olga.

They had met quite by chance back in 1978, almost four

years before he had been condemned to the camps. He had always resolved to obey the thief's law against marriage—until an hour after he met her. She had been, was still, a good and loyal wife to him. Fortunately she had always enjoyed her own busy life in the company of the upper levels of Moscow business and social circles. His generous gifts of money, and muscle when needed, had greatly contributed to Olga Yakovleva's prestige and the deference she commanded among her associates.

Josef Kobzon was responsible for their meeting. The renowned singer had sounded his usual arrogant self when he called Jap on the phone. He treated the thiefs, including Jap, with such impudence that one might think all these gangsters were indebted to him instead of the other way around. They had intimidated theater owners and movie producers into making a star out of Josef David Kobzon.

"We'll meet at Cinema House in half an hour," Kobzon announced.

Cinema House was situated in the side street not far from the Belorussian railway station, close to Gorky Street, in the center of Moscow. It was a big, square, three-story building with a sub-street-level restaurant, several intimate bars and an exhibition hall.

Jap met Kobzon in the restaurant at a small table in the corner. They discussed their illicit matter quickly, Jap promised to carry out his share of the bargain, and Kobzon left. He was the most in-demand performer at concerts and government affairs of that day. Jap stayed for a while to finish his drink. Then he stepped into the hall and was about to enter the cinema where the latest Fellini movie was being shown when he saw Olga. She was standing in the corridor, dimly lit by red lamps, repairing her hairdo in front of the mirror.

Jap was captivated by her gracious figure, short blonde hair and handsome, lean face with grey eyes and thin, yet promising lips. She wore a tailored brown chamois suit; the skirt was tight, falling above her knees, grey stockings and high heels making her figure even more shapely and long. She sensed his glance and turned her head. Jap was looking at her with an unwavering stare. In her face he saw irritation and arrogance.

She abruptly turned away and went downstairs.

Jap thought a few moments and then followed her; his brain was burning with desire and he felt his heart pounding loudly. Downstairs he found walls decorated with plates of grey marble, the lights were dimmed by brown shades. He saw another bar and several closets in which guests could hang coats. The bar, lit by a green light, was empty, not even a barman attended it. His eyes fell on the door to the restroom.

Jap felt himself on the brink, reminiscent of the incident so very many years ago when he was pointing the pistol at the old Uzbek bandit. He had guts enough then to pull the trigger. What was wrong with him now? With that he pushed open the door of the ladies' restroom and strode in. The lady was standing in front of the great wall-mirror, near the sink. Seeing Jap's reflection before her she did not blink an eye.

Jap's face was serious, even solemn. He approached her from behind slowly, without any hasty movements. She turned and faced him, her slim buttocks resting against the sink. For a moment their eyes met. Then Jap lowered his glance. Her long slender legs in grey silk stockings were firmly planted against the tile floor. Jap put his hand under the hem of her skirt and slid it up the silk and elastic inside surface of her thighs. She pushed his hand away with a strong slim hand and slapped him so hard across the face he nearly fell backwards.

She remained standing in front of him, not uttering a word and eyeing him quietly, her face expressionless. The next moment he slapped her back; a streak of blood ran out of her nostril. She gasped, but did not utter a sound and closed her eyes. Jap gently thrust his hand between her thighs again, rumpling her skirt and pushing it upwards. She seized his shoulders with her long meticulously manicured fingers, his palm already reaching into her silk panties. Unbelievably, she lowered her hands and unbuckled his belt and opened his trousers. There was no possibility of either denying the other now as she moved just enough to allow the entrance he sought.

In half an hour they were sitting together in the bar, wet, slightly embarrassed, but unrepentant, comfortably disheveled in their appearance.

"What is your name?" she asked taking out a cigarette.

He clicked his lighter and lit it.

"Ja . . . " he began. "Er . . . Slava," he uttered.

"I'm Olga," she said.

One week later, forsaking the *thief's* law, Vyacheslav and Olga were married. She was seven years younger than Jap and as different from him as could be. She was a head taller, slender to the point of being almost skinny. She always kept her blonde hair cropped short.

Olga was an associate director of the Hotel Russia and therefore a well-off woman with wide ranging connections. She knew full well who Jap was and what kind of "business" he was operating. She had married him anyway.

Jap lifted his glass. "To Olga," he said aloud forcing his thoughts from the unattainable Oksana as he drank the cognac.

CHAPTER THIRTEEN

❧ ❧

Boris Burenchuk, promoted to the rank of major in the Special Crimes Unit before the boxing tour of America, had been assigned his own office upon the team's return to Petrovka 38. It overlooked the inside courtyard of Militsia Headquarters at Petrovka 38, an uneven asphalt surface broken by the twisting roots of huge linden trees. Several Militsia drivers stood by their cars, their red-banded visor caps pushed back on their heads, bunches of keys hanging by chains from their belts beside the brown leather pistol holsters. It was turning cold in Moscow this late October day and most of the Militsia men were wearing their overcoats.

Boris had been waiting all afternoon for the call summoning him to the office of Colonel Vladimir Nechiaev, chief of detectives of the Criminal Brigade. His door was half-open and the hum of voices drifted from the narrow, brightly lit corridor. The Special Crimes investigators passed to and fro, from one office to another, cigarette smoke lingering after them.

Unlike many of the other officers who wore their ties loosely in

131

open collars, Boris's brown tie was knotted neatly. The gray blazer draped over the back of his chair instead of worn on his back was his only concession to the office's musty atmosphere. The empty holster for the Makarov handgun hung under his left armpit. The weapon was locked inside his safe.

On the desk in front of him, surrounded by the mounds of paper, stood his typewriter with a sheet of closely typed lines hanging out of the roller. This was the last page of his assessment of the triple murder of KGB agents. The Special Crimes Unit had been in uneasy cooperation with KGB trying to solve the crime. "The Arbat Massacre," as the press referred to the case had broken at summer's end and now, almost two months later, the case was virtually "null and void" in Petrovka 38 terminology.

Trying to prove himself worthy of his recent promotion, Boris had catalogued all the facts of the case. Some unknown perpetrators had killed and incinerated three KGB officers, a colonel and two lieutenants at their own premises, a secret operative apartment in Arbat, in the very center of Moscow.

He had studied every detail and witness report. Dozens of people had heard the blast, but nobody had reported any suspicious or unusual circumstances. The Militsia's usual informants expressed only surprise and perplexity. Criminals were businessmen. What was the purpose of challenging KGB so bluntly?

In accordance with KGB protocol, the agency had waited over two weeks after the blast before reporting to the police that three of its operatives were unaccounted for. It was another two weeks before dental records of the missing KGB agents were turned over to the Militsia and compared with the teeth, even more fire resistant than metal, which were carefully preserved at the crime scene. Finally positive identifications were reached. The forensic pathologist's report also noted blackened shards of bottles and glasses suggesting a drinking session, not uncommon with KGB. Colonel Nechiaev had ordered his men to probe deeper into the backgrounds of the victims, but KGB supplied sparse data, refusing to allow Boris and the other Militsia investigators access to any tapes that might have been recorded from the scene of the crime before fire destroyed the bugs.

Meanwhile the city prosecutor kept up steady demands for results in the investigation which further exacerbated KGB-Militsia relations.

Boris Burenchuk, self-effacing and diplomatic, was Ukrainian, a graduate of Kiev University, and thus entered the Moscow Militsia with a negative image. As a "Uke" he had always extended himself to be courteous and accommodating. Working in public affairs, he accumulated a record of positive media coverage for the police.

On a hunch, General Alexi Bodaev, chief of the Criminal Brigade, promoted Burenchuk to major, and assigned him to take over the case.

It was six o'clock in the evening when the call came through. Boris strode down the long hallway of the third floor of Petrovka 38 and walked into the relatively spacious office of Colonel Nechiaev. He was excited at the prospect of Sly Fox, as the colonel was known to police and criminals alike, officially turning over all aspects of the Arbat case to him.

Waiting in Nechiaev's office was the tall, lean Major Yuri Navakoff wearing his trademark stone-washed denim suit decorated with the American flag he had been given at the boxing matches above the left breast pocket. He specialized in street crime as a plainclothes officer. Nicknamed Americanski, he looked like "Dirty Harry." Yuri carried a big gun. Nechiaev poured vodka generously into the glasses in front of each officer at the table.

"Well, men," he held up his glass, "may the moment be cursed when," his tone took on an acid tinge, "these warriors of the 'invisible frontier' put their bloody finger into our investigation."

Everybody threw back their glasses except Boris who sipped his politely. By now his comrades in the Militsia regarded his reluctance to drink with forbearance. He was, after all, a Uke and thus an inscrutable type.

Nechiaev poured each of his men another glass of vodka. "On my part I must tell you that I have a distinct impression that this freakish homicide was motivated by unique circumstances. If Jap, Yakovlev, was not in Tulun I would have had him here for heavy interrogation. This killing has the trademark of a Jap hit."

"Could he have had visitors and given them instructions?" Boris asked.

"He is not allowed to communicate with old friends. I gather his wife, or a friend of hers, was allowed in to see him last week but that was long after the Arbat killing."

Nechiaev was silent then added, "Let's hope he serves out his full sentence, another five years." Nechiaev turned to Boris. "Major Burenchuk, I leave the disposition of this grotesque affair to you with one last bit of advice. This is no ordinary murder. No one, not even a madman, lashes out at KGB like this unless they have good reason and a lot of power."

Boris nodded. "Yes."

"I tell you," Nechiaev mused, "this Arbat atrocity is only the outer doll of a criminal nest. I know KGB will be a hindrance in this investigation, but you break through that outer shell and you will find something very interesting. And possibly very important."

"I am doing comprehensive background checks on the victims," Boris said. "I will start by questioning once more the students of Paul Varankov's group at the language school and report to you in two or three days at most."

"And one more thing." Nechiaev studied his empty vodka glass. "I don't think it is connected to the Arbat case so I didn't mention it before but it might well be one more doll in the nest. Our colleague Peter Nikhilov told us when we left New York that the homicide of Deputy Gardenadze was closely connected to the murders of two Georgians who were shot in Brighton Beach two months earlier. In both cases the suspected killers, Chechens, were seen by Peter with the same man, one Zekki Dekka, who Peter believes has ties to our dear Yaponchik. If you have reason to arrest a Chechen try to find out if he knows anything about what's been going on in New York recently."

Nechiaev upturned his empty glass with a wry smile, set it down and filled it along with those of the other detectives. "Things have a way of being connected. The New York murders could be the beginning of a war in our streets."

The following day Boris Burenchuk summoned the eight language students from the dead KGB officer's group to meet with him separately in one of the least intimidating interrogation rooms at Petrovka 38.

None of the students reported anything strange on the eve of Paul's disappearance. Two of the boys reported that he seemed happy when last seen that evening.

"Happy about what?" Boris asked. The students shrugged. "Late summer, pretty girls," they replied. "The institute is known for cute girls."

Throughout the interviews Boris sensed a hesitancy to talk about a certain aspect of Paul's background. Then when he made it known that the Militsia was well aware that Paul was a KGB lieutenant they nodded. None of the students wanted to volunteer any information about KGB.

The last witness, Oksana Martinova, interested Boris particularly. She was dressed with sophistication, her black cashmere sweater revealing a full figure. He couldn't help but notice that Oksana was a very attractive woman. He was struck by an indefinable sense of pain that he detected in her deep brown eyes.

Oksana waited to be invited to sit which she did in an unconsciously provocative manner, nonchalantly pushing the chair back from the table between them. He glanced over at one long nylon-encased leg crossed over the other then looked away. There was a self-possessed, almost a haughty demeanor in the way she carried herself.

"May I smoke?" she asked.

Boris nodded and she took a pack of cigarettes and a large silver lighter out of her pocketbook, offering him one which he declined. The lighter, when snapped into flame, was a virtual blow torch. It must belong to a man, he thought, probably one who spends much time outdoors. Boris affected a tired and inattentive attitude. He was imitating Nechiaev's manner which was so effective in bringing inadvertent admissions from witnesses.

Oksana's testimony was shorter than that of the others, her answers brisk and precise.

"So . . . You did not know him well you say?"

"That's right."

"But you two have been studying together for several years. How come you did not become friends?"

"Being in the same study group does not necessarily mean friends, let alone something else."

"Did you know he was a KGB lieutenant?"

"No, I didn't have the slightest idea," she replied. Boris noted that she was the only one in the group who denied knowing this aspect of Paul's status.

"Did anything special strike you when you heard of his death?"

Oksana shook her head.

"No strange details came to mind?"

"None." Her voice was firm.

"He was killed together with his superior, Lieutenant Marat Ogurtzov. Did you know the man?"

"Yes, he was KGB instructor in the Institute. He used to tell us a lot of nonsense about foreigners and teach us how to steal and spy."

"You did not like him?"

"Show me the one who did. He was a disgusting creature."

"He had enemies?"

"Probably. Everyone tried either to help KGB or stay away from them as far as possible."

"Which did you prefer?"

"Distance. I always had conflicts with Lt. Marat Ogurtzov because of that."

"Such as?"

"He would approach me and ask me to look through the suitcase of a foreigner when he was out of his hotel room."

"And what was your response?"

"I told him he was the secret agent. He could do it himself. My job is interpreting not searching luggage."

Boris laughed. He started to like the girl. There was solid firmness in her makeup, very rare among so many young women.

"I guess that would not make him happy?"

"Of course not. He even complained to the dean of the institute that the Marxist upbringing of students was not supervised closely enough. The dean gave me, in particular, a hard time."

"Oh, yeah. KGB is like that." Boris was on the verge of telling her what problems KGB creates in Militsia but restrained himself. This girl had a way of making a man want to open up to her, he thought. "Did you see Paul and Marat together often?" he pulled himself back on track.

"Several times."

"Anything unusual on the eve of their death?"

"I had that day off," she replied.

"Okay. Did you ever see any one of them with this man?" Boris passed a photograph over the table to Oksana. She stared at the picture without expression, a trail of smoke rising from the cigarette between her fingers. The colonel appeared impeccably uniformed and groomed, a slightly reckless look in his eyes and chiseled features. This image contrasted sharply with the real man she had encountered—puffy face red from drinking, strangely colorless eyes, sticky greedy hands that pawed her naked, drugged body as he raped her. She handed the photo back to Boris.

"No, I've never seen them together. Who is that by the way?" Her voice wavered slightly, Boris noticed. Although she claimed not to recognize Nazarov in the photograph it seemed to him that she knew him.

"That was Colonel Nazarov, the third victim." He breathed deeply and pushed his chair back. "Okay, that's it for today."

Boris rose to his feet dumping the contents of the ashtray in front of her into the wastebasket. Then he took his jacket from the back of his chair and slipped first one then the other arm into the sleeves.

Casually, appealing for her consideration as though personally deeply puzzled and curious, he asked, "Comrade Martinova, tell me unofficially, how does it happen? A man lives, studies, has mates and girlfriends, works in KGB or something, and then one lovely late summer evening, for some unknown reason, he is murdered. And no one, not friends, colleagues, nor relatives can shed the first ray of light on this tragedy?"

Oksana shrugged indifferently. "Ask KGB, he was their protegé. They must know a lot more than they pretend."

"Why are you sure KGB has reasons to cover the truth?"

"I am not sure of anything, anything at all," she replied. Then, "May I go?"

"Certainly. It was nice meeting you. Have a good evening."

Oksana arose and walked briskly out of the interrogation room. Boris stood in the doorway watching her go. He noticed the admiring stares of the officers she passed. As she walked out through the gray door at the end of the smoky corridor, he was convinced she knew considerably more than she had revealed.

CHAPTER FOURTEEN

❦ ❦

I t was customary during *skchods*, meetings between thiefs-in-the-law, that all present be naked to the waist so that no one could conceal a weapon or wear a bullet-proof vest. So, when Maria emerged from the sauna in Jap's cell shortly before the night's meeting was to begin, she wore only her usual leather split skirt gathered at the waist by a wide belt. Inside the sauna, the four other Tulun organized crime bosses—Maxim, Tofik, Potma and Josik—sat sweating heavily. As soon as they had relaxed and plunged into a cold bath, the meeting would begin in earnest.

Jap sat in front of the fire, calmly eyeing the sauna door.

"They say they will be ready in half an hour," Maria said wiping the sweat from her large breasts and underarms with a towel.

"They take their time," Jap commented.

Tonight's *skchod* had not been Jap's idea, but with rumors circulating around Tulun that his power outside was being eroded by rival gangs, he felt it imperative to confront the lead-

139

ers of those gangs, several of whom were in Tulun with him. According to the prison's unspoken thief-in-the-law protocol, when the meeting was called, Jap would ask Tulun internal jail commandant, Major Karamushev, if he and his friends could enjoy a sauna together after a long day of work. Jap's was the most luxurious underground cell in the compound, and the only one with a sauna. Karamushev gave his consent, as he always did, and after the common prisoners had returned to their dark, cold barracks for the night, armed guards escorted each of the four thieves to Jap's underground cell.

The sauna door opened and four shirtless men entered the cell, their tattoos and scars, denoting criminal authority, clearly visible on their glistening torsos. The Jap received them and they all embraced each other with warm greetings. Maria prepared four carpets for the visiting thiefs to sit on and brought another two bottles of cognac and four wine glasses to the table on which was an appetizing display of salt fish, slices of fresh smoked rabbit meat, and even black and orange caviar. Jap occupied his place with his back to the wall behind the table.

Tofik, the Georgian sat beside Jap, his skin adornments discernible through the dark hair that covered his chest and back. His largest tattoo, made when he was a young man, depicted an eagle with wings spread across an outline of the Russian boundaries signifying that he was a bandit who traveled all over the country in the name of crime. Beside him sat Potma, a lean but powerful thief with a crimson dagger tattooed across his clavicle piercing his neck, the handle on one side, the blade protruding from the other side of his neck which threatened vengeance to the unfaithful girlfriend. On the other side of the table was seated Josik, head of the St. Petersburg Jewish crime gang. Next to him sat Maxim, the eldest of the five, an old thief from Odessa whose entire body was covered with a web of intricate tattoos.

They drank a toast to bring the meeting to order and then

Tofik, a former professional wrestler with ape-like arms and a mountainous belly, spoke.

"We must pick the chairman. I think this time it will be Maxim. He is the oldest among us."

At all previous meetings the Jap was chairman. Picking the chairman was the regular procedure—as if at a Communist Party Assembly. That was thiefs' democracy. Jap let this surprise go by unnoticed and reacted immediately. "I agree, Maxim is a reasonable person."

Jap noticed the face of Potma, a powerfully built Belorussian, change for a fraction of a second. So! They thought they would startle him by this proposal, make him show disapproval. More than ever Jap realized how really bad the situation was. Something serious must have happened in Moscow since Oksana's visit. He thought fast. Who had closest ties to Moscow now that he was being denied access to outside information?

Maxim operated in the south on the Black Sea. The burly Potma was from Minsk with Polish connections. Josik was a Leningrad Jew, a city rat, thin, gaunt, who had fallen behind the bars by some mistake—he was running a huge business in Leningrad, controlling the artworks and icon trade with Northern Europe and Finland. Such people usually do not go behind the bars—they are invincible as are almost all millionaires in the Soviet system. Josik was very young by thief's standards— only twenty-eight. Jap alone knew that Josik had bought his thief title for the price of $50,000 U.S. hard currency at an authoritative meeting which issued him the signed certificate.

Tofik was the only one connected to Moscow. All Georgians were in awe of this city, it attracted them as honey does bees. Tofik did business with drug dealers and pimps but he had powerful connections with the trading mafia. They dealt in foreign currency and Tofik knew about the counterfeiting operations an American had been negotiating with Jap.

Maxim was elected chairman and Jap soon realized the others did not have serious business to discuss. Nevertheless, Jap took the opportunity to stress what he deemed important. "We must work together, not fight each other over business questions," he went on earnestly. "America! That is where the strength and vitality to feed our system will come from."

Jap's first choice was for a peaceful alliance with the other thiefs. "Working closely together our future profits are unlimited."

"Sounds nice," Tofik replied. "Our crews will be one big syndicate, ruled by a council of associate members and supervised by a chairman."

When Potma, in a bitingly sarcastic tone, said, "I guess Jap, that this chairman will be none other than you?" Jap read which way their brains were working.

"If that is your will," Jap replied meekly but in fact seeming to tug at the bait.

"Yeah, the way you run things here!" Potma exclaimed.

"What do you mean?" Jap shot back. He noticed Maxim had bitten his lip at Potma's unreasoned outburst. According to the "law," Maxim, as chairman, should restrain Potma, a younger thief.

But Potma was allowed to go on with his harangue. "I mean . . . I mean who do you think you are? Some kind of fucking king or something?"

Jap gave Potma a cold-eyed stare which should have warned him to back off. "It is my hope that when the five of us are at large again we will form a council of leaders to settle our disputes."

"And you will be the chief, the chairman of the council, I suppose," Potma sneered. "With your underground kingdom you consider yourself better than the rest of us." He gestured around the luxurious coldcell.

"I consider I am a thief who doesn't need to listen to this

shit from a slime like you." Jap's tone was low, even, and menacing. "Now would you kindly shut up and stop yelling or you'll bring in the guards."

Potma sprang to his feet and stood in the middle of the cell. "Here!" He pointed his finger at the spot in front of him. "Stand here. I will talk to you."

Jap pushed over the table in front of him. Wine glasses and bottles crashed to the floor. He stepped over the shards and faced Potma. It was a thief's axiom that fist fights are for fools. The thief's weapon was a knife, but they had no knives there. Potma was taller and more broad-shouldered, with a powerful muscular neck and a big round melon of a head. The Jap was shorter but stouter, his fists as big as beer mugs. An uneasy moment passed.

Then Maxim rose to his feet and stood between them. "Break," he ordered. "As chairman I order you to break. This is no place and no right time for a fight."

Jap stared at Maxim with glowering eyes. Bastard, he thought. You planned it all. Your phony peace mission destroys my authority. Tomorrow it will be all over camp that some lousy petty thief abused the Jap and got away with it. Then the legend of the defeated Jap will spread out from Tulun Camp to every thief-in-the-law and their crews in the Republics, Europe and even America.

There was no turning back now. If the Underground King let Potma get away with insulting him, it would undermine his authority forever.

Jap looked from one to the other of the four bare-chested men. The speculative glint shone from their eyes, mouths compressed, stubble beards working with twitching muscles in their cheeks and the corners of their lips. They all saw themselves as supplanting him as top authoritative thief here at Tulun and later in Moscow, Odessa, Kiev, Minsk, and Tbilsi when they were at large. Jap would have preferred some sort of negotiations but he recognized that diplomacy would only degrade him now.

"All right," Jap said to Maxim, his tone conciliatory. "I think I let him drink too much cognac. He's not used to such quality drink." Jap sensed Potma's temper rising as he faced him with a depreciating smile on his face. "You are a lucky guy, Potma, because I have an easy heart. Apologize now, admit you were wrong and we shall return to our affairs." He took a step back from the seething thief.

"Why should I?" Potma addressed Maxim as if the Jap were not there. "I am not afraid of him. Why should I apologize?"

While they were arguing Jap pushed his hair from his forehead with his left palm; but it was a maneuver. He pressed his wrist against his forehead and the bracelet of his gold watch unfastened, the watch went loose. When he lowered his arm the watch fell to the floor, the heavy gold smashed on the floor and the crystal popped off. "Fuck!" Jap exclaimed. "My watch."

He bent down to pick it up. But it was not the watch he was after. Beside the overturned table lay a broken wine glass. In a lightning move Jap seized the jagged weapon, jumped at Potma who was arguing heatedly with Maxim and before the thief could defend himself, Jap drove his razor sharp crystal instrument with both hands into the pit above Potma's left clavicle. The weapon made a wet sucking sound as it was drawn from flesh and sinew. Potma's screams filled the cell as Jap threw the improvised weapon behind him, pushing his victim in the breast at the same time.

Potma staggered back against the door and then dipped forward, rage burning from his eyes, his right hand clutching at the base of his neck on the left side; suddenly his right hand slipped away and the wound opened like a purse. A thick red fountain spurted from the deep gash, the power of the geyser of blood was so great that it dashed against the low ceiling and with almost equal force ricocheted back into the room in a shower of big dark red drops. Everything and everybody was immediately speckled with hundreds of red spots, the column of red squirting upwards as if there was a pump inside Potma's body. It spattered the lamp bulb and the illumination in the room turned crimson as if in a night bar. Red streams ran down the walls, across the screen of the TV set, and stained the naked torsos of the four other men.

Potma collapsed face forward. His body jerked twice and then he lay still. The fountain subsided but blood still ran from the body covering the floor and soaking the carpets. For another moment there was shocked, awed silence. Jap was the first one to start wiping his face, smearing blood with his hand. Suddenly Maxim came to life and seized Jap by the throat.

"You fucking bastard!" he screamed. "What have you done? What hell of a fuck do you think you have done? The chief will have our asses for that!"

Contemptuously the Jap pushed him away, his face obscenely composed considering the grisly scene he had single handedly created. "Potma defied every thief's law we swear to obey. I could not allow him to live after the disrespect he showed me. You are all aware of that." He fixed the chairman with a knowing stare. "Is there some reason you did not control him?"

Maxim silently studied the crimson puddles on the floor at his feet. Josik stood at the side of the cell, shaking all over as if in a fever, moaning incomprehensibly, his eyes fixed on the Jap who stared back at him pitilessly.

Only Tofik remained taciturn. Wiping his blood-spattered face indifferently and looking at the floor, as though speaking to himself he said, "I always knew Jap was a man, a real thief, not like all that scum."

Then Tofik lifted his head. "Hey, you two, Maxim, Josik, shut up and sit down." He turned. "Jap, you hear me, Jap? Pour us some more cognac . . . shit, there is blood even in my

145

glass . . . It is dry in my throat, give a good drink to Josik or he'll stain his pants and the cell with a substance somewhat different from blood . . . Maxim! Old fool, be seated. I tell you; what hell of a fuck chairman are you? Hey, Jap. Call your tattooed slut from sauna, *khe-khe* . . . We need some cleaning here . . . "

Maria entered the room and her jaw fell gaping. She couldn't hold back the shriek of surprise and horror. "Holy Virgin—Oh hell, oh fucking hell. What shall we do now?!"

"Bring us another bottle," Jap said reflectively. "We have things to discuss . . . "

CHAPTER FIFTEEN

⊰⊱ ⊰⊱

The next morning the four surviving thiefs-in-the-law were summoned to Major Karamushev's office. While Karamushev was lower in rank than the chief of the camp, the chief did not want to be responsible for crimes, especially murders, committed in his prisons, so jurisdiction was given to his second-in-command. The commandant was also a convenient scapegoat if anything dire were to happen.

Major Karamushev's office was small and neat. On the wide, oak desk his pens, papers, and a glass inkwell were precisely arranged.

A portrait of Felix Dzerzshinsky, founder of Chekka, the Secret Police, hung on the wall behind him and bright yellow chrysanthemums in flower pots sat on the sill beneath the room's only window, adding some cheer to the barred, frost-covered glass.

The four thiefs-in-the-law who sat before Karamushev had already submitted written testimonials of the previous evening's events and had been questioned individually by his staff. Now they were to answer questions from the commandant directly, and he would decide whether or not to continue the investigation. Karamushev leaned back in his chair. A lean, sharp-featured man in his early sixties, his blue watery eyes and thin covering of gray hair made him look like a content grandfather. Only the commandant's black uniform, military belt, and leather holster with its standard issue Makarov pistol belied the benign, happy impression he gave. He thumbed through the testimonials and then studied the emotionless faces of their authors. All four of them read as if they had been written by the same man. According to the reports, the five thieves had met to take a sauna bath in the internal jail. While they were talking and relaxing, Potma had excused himself and committed suicide by cutting his neck with a piece of broken glass. It had all happened quickly, the reports agreed, and by the time the men came out of the sauna to investigate the noise they'd heard, Potma was dead. They had called the guards immediately and assisted the jail administration in all possible ways.

"Well guys," Karamushev said at last, "I guess you understand that the four of you—or should I say five of you—have made me look like an ass to the authorities. What do we do now?"

"We're helluva fuck sorry," Tofik offered. "But such an accident, such a tragedy . . . we can scarcely believe ourselves."

"Well, I don't believe it," the major retorted. "The guards claim they heard nothing before they were called by Jap, ah, I mean prisoner Yakovlev."

"We would never mean any harm, Commandant," Maxim said soothingly. "We loved Alexi like a brother. That was a tragic suicide . . . "

"I know, I know," Karamushev cut in impatiently. "You all love each other. Though sometimes one of the lovers gets killed at the meeting of love. That's what I could never understand about your 'thief's law.'"

"If you did, Commandant, you'd be one of us."

The commandant glowered at Maxim. "You had better stop that crap with me. I want no trouble within Tulun's regime of confinement; I give you no trouble in your business. Remember, I'm an old worn-out fart. I want to reach my discharge without problems. This is the last time I am talking to you in this manner. Next time the one who remains alive will talk to me hanging from the ceiling handcuffed to a rail by his wrists. And he can be sure he won't get away with a lousy suicide tale. Do I make myself clear?"

"Beautiful," Tofik chuckled.

Karamushev pressed the button on his desk to summon the guards. "Now go out and be good boys and behave yourselves."

Later that day Karamushev visited Jap's apartment. All traces of blood had been obliterated. Even the carpets had been changed. Jap nodded silently and, motioning him to sit down, he poured a glass of cognac for the jail chief. After drinking it the commandant leaned toward Jap.

"Now Listen, Jap," he said in confidential tones, "something is brewing here."

Jap sipped his drink. Impatiently Karamushev continued. "So you don't want to tell me? Fine. But I expect you to warn me if there is going to be trouble."

"I don't know yet, but you are right. I will not be your guest forever, you must realize. What is happening here, in your camp today is preparation for tomorrow when we all will be at-large again. And it may be that the elimination of this thief-in-the-law," he thumbed his chest, "is the objective of the others in Tulun Camp."

"When will you know what is really happening, may I inquire?" Karamushev clearly showed the concern he felt for his own future.

"Don't worry. When I know you will know."

"I'll be waiting to hear."

"Tell the guard outside to follow my instructions tonight," Jap said as the commandant stood up to leave.

Karamushev nodded and left the cell.

It was almost dawn when Jap left his quarters. The guard brought him to the cell where Josik was sleeping.

Jap tapped Josik on the shoulder. Josik sat up promptly although it took a few seconds before he was fully awake. When he saw the Jap standing close to his bed his eyes widened and he started to tremble.

"What do you want, Jap?"

"Do not be afraid, man," Jap said soothingly. "No harm meant. We just need to talk."

"About what?"

"I want to know, why was that *skchod* called?"

"I don't know." Josik shrugged. "Regular procedure. Time was ripe."

"Ignorance," Jap said wearily. "You know what Lao-tze used to say?"

"Who?"

"Lao-tze, the Chinese philosopher. He said that ignorance is the worst of crimes. You say you don't know. But I am not so ignorant and I want to tell you a story I do know. Two years ago, in Moscow, in Peking Hotel there was an authorized thief meeting. Rolik Kabadgan, the Armenian, was the chairman. Among other things they granted a thief title to a very young man who has never been to jail, never killed an enemy, never was truly tested by severe law of the thiefs. But this young guy had 50,000 American dollars, hard currency, which was divided up at the meeting and they said okay, and gave him the certificate with their signatures. But that was the business of their consciences, after all they did not obligate themselves to do business with him."

In the dim light cast by the single lightbulb hanging in the hall, Josik could see the Jap's eyes glinting dangerously, and he shuddered as the Underground King went on.

"Do you know, Josik, what happens to such fake, cheating thiefs in jails and camps when the brotherhood learns about it? They are crucified on a wall and stabbed to death in the gut."

"You won't . . . " Josik pleaded.

"No, I won't. But let me tell you what another philosopher, Gratian Baltazar, said. 'Truth belongs to few and must be kept in the temple of silence.'"

"Yeah, yeah, that was a wise man. What do you want?"

"Oh Josik, what do I want? I know the truth about you, but I will keep it in the temple of silence if you will be on my side. So what about this meeting?"

Josik did not hesitate. "That was Maxim's idea. Potma and Tofik supported him."

Jap was astonished. He never suspected that Maxim, the wise old veteran, was after him too. Obviously he was mistaken. This was bad. He was losing his grip on the jail and on his people outside.

"Why Maxim?" he asked hollowly.

"Maxim got word from his guys in the government that you will be transferred to a camp in Central Asia. The Uzbeks there have something against you."

An image of Mamatadgi, the back of the Uzbek bandit's head plastered on the wall behind him, and young Slava cleaning out the strong box flitted across Jap's mind. The families there carried grudges for many generations. Uzbeks are the main drug dealers and would reward the man who killed Yakovlev, the Jap.

"Maxim decided you are a dead man anyway so he calculated that if he kills you himself he would inherit your authority in jail and on the outside and strengthen his connections on the drug market. But Maxim wanted to do it by Potma's hands.

Potma himself is just a fool—was a fool. And Tofik . . . Tofik wants his Georgians to take over your crew's counterfeiting operations in New York and Moscow."

"How did he know so much?" Jap repeated wonderingly.

Josik took several deep breaths and looked up at the Jap, as if for approbation. "Tofik is most dangerous to you."

Jap nodded and quietly exalted in the knowledge that Tofik's men in New York had been killed.

Even more dangerous than Tofik inside the camp was the lack of intelligence he received from his outside crime family as opposed to the apparently reliable sources of information commanded by Tofik. The frustrations of not being able to run his operations personally were building up enormous pressure within his mind and psyche.

Jap had been out of circulation too long. Now he knew what he had to do. He must provoke something serious in Tulun, a strike, an uprising, anything to prevent his transfer to Central Asia. The Jap leaned close, his face inches from Josik's terrified eyes. "Now, Josik, here is what you will do. One of the people in your gang must insult one of the guys in the barracks in such a way that a member of Maxim's gang, or Tofik's, will be killed or maimed. Understand?"

"Fuck it, Jap, that will . . . you know what will follow?"

"No other way, Josik. Either we survive or . . . remember, if they kill me you will be next. You are too weak, besides, they may learn what I know—you are not a real thief-in-the-law and I am not the only one who knows. Everything will be okay if you just do what I say."

Josik, eyes popping, nodded his head in vigorous agreement. "Okay, Jap. I'll do what you say."

"We have very little time left. We must work together." He raised a finger cautioningly. "Temple of silence."

With that Jap left as abruptly as he had appeared.

CHAPTER SIXTEEN

It was an easy drive on a springtime Sunday afternoon from New York's Upper East Side apartment house where the beautiful blonde Russian defector Lena lived, across Manhattan and through the Lincoln Tunnel to the port city of Hoboken, New Jersey. Health Club Mills, a large clothing warehouse, was ten blocks west of the river. As Peter Nikhilov parked on the street near the building he noticed a huge sea-land container backed up against the loading dock at the side of the warehouse. "Looks like a lot of clothing is on its way to Moscow," Peter commented in Russian to Lena, who sat beside him.

The girl gratefully snuggled close to him and replied in her native language, "Not until I get what I want."

Hugh McDonald was waiting at the emporium's entrance and led them inside. Ruddy faced, with rimless glasses, Hugh wore a gray suit and blue on blue tie and shirt that gave him an anonymous appearance.

"A lot of Russians are here," Hugh said as they entered the

warehouse. "Today's a special sale for Soviet diplomats and offi- cial employees. They're stocking up for their annual visits home."

Peter gave Lena a pat on the shoulder. "It's all yours, darling. Take back to the apartment everything you can carry."

"Ooooh," she squealed in delight. "I love you." And with that Lena scuttled into the frey of bargain hunting Russians tearing through the sumptuous stocks of clothing.

Hugh looked after her, smiling broadly. "She's quite a morsel. How did she get here from Russia?"

Peter chuckled. "The way many of them do. Some older-type American on business met her in Moscow, fell for her, arranged for her visa, bought her tickets, and set her up here in an apart- ment. It didn't take long for her to find more interesting employ- ment. And now—she's a New Yorker."

Peter watched her holding an angora sweater against her bosom and smiled fondly. "All these Russian girls take care of each other, find high profile jobs like checking coats at the Russian restau- rants until something better comes along, pick up rich boyfriends, and help one another with immigration problems. Almost all of them are only one step ahead of the Immigration Service, which opens the poor girls up to various types of abuse and blackmail. I help them as best I can."

"No wonder you're not married," Hugh joked.

"Actually I may surprise myself one day. They're great women. Anyway, I brought Lena along for a cover."

Standing in front of bales of T-shirts, sweat suits, and sweaters, out of hearing in the burgeoning throng and excited cries of Russ- ian bargain hunters Peter said, "Okay, Hugh, this should be safe enough for you. What the hell is up?"

"We've been keeping a close watch on old Zekki which isn't easy since he has no fixed address or telephone we can tap. He's kept five of us busy tailing him."

"And what are you finding?"

"Well, he's big in the delegates' lounge at the United Nations.

He seems to know the rich Muslim delegates and twice we've seen him with a North Korean observer. That ties in with the murder of Gardenadze after he left the North Korean mission. Those who try to compete with Zekki die. Zekki is cultivating outlaw states who are trying to acquire a nuclear capability."

Peter shrugged and looked around the emporium. "What has NEST got to do with this place?"

"We followed Zekki here last week. He stayed quite a while, talking to Joe Koehler, the guy who owns this place. It turns out the Duke of Hoboken, as everyone calls Joe, ships out one container a week packed with about fifty thousand dollars worth of merchandise. The buyers pay Joe in advance right here and sell the stuff in Moscow and St. Petersburg for five to ten times more than they paid for it."

"So what? That's what Perestroika and Glasnost are all about. I've got some Russian associates who'd love this. So how does Zekki fit in?"

"I don't know, yet. But what we do know is that a plate to print the face side of hundred dollar bills was lost by or stolen from the Printing and Engraving Division of the Treasury Department. We also know that two of the people Red Rolf and I implanted in the money printing section some years ago have not been seen for over a month. That may be somehow connected to Zekki."

"I thought it was rubles you were going to counterfeit."

"Red came up with the ingenious idea that if we could catch the Russians red-handed passing multimillions in counterfeit U.S. hundred dollar bills through European banks we could ruin their precious hard currency exchange."

"And that plan got approved as an operation?" Peter asked incredulously.

"No. We just set it up in case it were. But, obviously, it is now out of control. An authentic plate is missing."

Hugh was interrupted by shrill cries of delight as several Russian women pressed suede suits to their chests chattering about how they had always wanted suede suits and for only fifty dollars!

"Go on with your theory about Zekki, then," Peter said when the ladies had quieted down.

"I'll make it short. Zekki is not in the clothing business yet the Duke told me, once we got acquainted, that Zekki was interested in purchasing an entire container of merchandise and shipping it to Russia."

Peter nodded thoughtfully. "That is indeed out of character. What he wants must be the container, not the clothes."

"That's got to be it. Smuggling. And Red Rolf has quit the Agency. So it could be that Red Rolf and Zekki Dekka are planning to activate the operation for their own benefit. Zekki would be the ideal man to supply the obverse side of the hundred dollar bill."

"They would need well-connected Russians to make it work," Peter said.

"And heavy printing equipment to run the intaglio process," Hugh added. "A container could carry a lot of equipment with clothing packed around it."

"Why don't we go have a word with the Duke," Peter suggested.

They walked over to the cash register where Hugh introduced Peter to the proprietor of Health Club Mills, a jolly individual in his early fifties, revelling in the success of his business.

"Looks like you're selling the place out, Duke. What's with the container backed up to your loading dock?" Hugh asked.

"The container ships out for Helsinki tomorrow with everything I don't sell today. I've got ten new factory buyouts coming in tomorrow afternoon. We move it fast."

"What happens after Finland?" Peter asked.

"When the container reaches port, a truck from Huolintakesus— Hey," the Duke cracked, "you know how many loads it took before I could say the name of the Helsinki transportation company?"

"So what happens?" Peter pursued.

"The truck picks up the container and hauls it to St. Petersburg in six hours or if it goes all the way to Moscow that's twenty-four hours."

"And the buyers are on hand to unload and distribute it?"

"They sell the garments as fast as I can get them there."

"What about customs?"

Joe laughed. "That's their responsibility. I hear the customs men and their families are the best dressed people in Russia."

Peter turned to Hugh and both nodded just as the loud hissing of air brakes and a squawking honk sounded from outside the front door. "That will be another bus from the White House," the Duke grinned.

"From where?" Hugh's tone registered surprise.

Peter laughed. "That's what the Russians call the big white apartment building they own in Riverdale where so many of them live."

"Yeah, they chartered a couple of buses to bring them down here." Joe turned to one of his assistants. "Hey Tom, keep the beer flowing."

"So, Duke," Peter moved closer to the proprietor of the clothing warehouse and went on in confidential tones, "I do a lot of business in the Soviet Union. Can I buy a container load from you, say, in the next month, for my Moscow outlets?"

"That's what I'm in business for. Come by anytime and we'll plan a load. I guarantee you the lowest prices anywhere."

He waved at the babbling crowd of excited Russians, men and women of all ages, pouring through the front door, pummeling the merchandise and drawing draughts of beer for themselves. "I can only sell in quantity to people who will take the merchandise out of America. I buy the goods for fifty percent less than any other outlet as long as the merchandise leaves this country."

"Would it be okay if I put a little machinery I need to get to Moscow in the container with the clothing?" Peter asked.

Joe Koehler gave Peter a long, questioning look, picking up

Peter's meaning in a New York second. Joe did not answer. Lena came up to the checkout counter, a suede suit laid across two arms full of clothing. Peter turned away from the Duke toward her, and in Russian he said, "Lena, meet the Duke of Hoboken, Joe Koehler." Then to Joe, "I told her I'd buy her everything she could carry out of here."

"Beautiful girls these Russians," Joe remarked. "Total it up, Tom," he said to his assistant.

Then he turned to Peter. "Come by tomorrow, or whenever you like and we'll discuss that shipment. And to answer your question, if you buy the clothes, it's your container. So I guess you can put whatever you want in as long as you take fifty thousand dollars' worth of my merchandise. I sell you the merchandise and assist you in finding a container and a price for shipment to Russia. I deliver my merchandise FOB Hoboken Ramp. It's an inland bill of lading out of here. It's your responsibility, or the shipping company, or whoever, to complete the international bill of lading and the customs declaration of contents for shipment on to Russia." With that he turned to a Russian couple and helped them sort out their purchases.

"What do you think of my theory?" Hugh asked as they made way for others at the checkout desk. Lena stayed and sorted out her purchases, and Peter and Hugh strolled off to find a place to talk.

"Zekki couldn't find a better way of bringing presses, ink, chemicals and paper into Russia to print counterfeit money," Peter said. "But there's got to be one hell of a powerful protective organization on hand there. There are a few honest cops in the Militsia but they don't have any customs authority. Zekki sending printing equipment and paper and ink out of New York is not a U.S. customs violation. It is a Russian customs violation to bring it in. That type of equipment and supplies are Russian contraband but there is really nothing we can do at the New York end to stop this."

"Like I said, we had it set up once. So Red Rolf and Zekki may have already established their Moscow connection, maybe even with Jap himself, or at least his gang." Hugh gave Peter a long speculative look. "What do you know about the Jap? I heard you say something to Chechen at the airport about Yaponchik."

"My informants tell me he's getting out of prison soon."

"Just think of the diamonds, platinum, priceless icons, to say nothing of strategic metals they could buy for counterfeit and sell in the West for legitimate letters of credit and real money."

Peter shook his head scornfully. "They could print it there but spending it is when they'd get caught. If they're smart they'll go for one big deal. What single buy for fifteen or twenty million in counterfeit money can be resold overnight for real currency?"

"A nuclear weapons deal."

"Right. Now, those Russians who were murdered in Brighton Beach and Gardenadze too must tie in somehow. They were all dealing with outlaw states."

"Remember, one of the men who got shot had hundred dollar bills."

"Fake, as I suspected. And bad fakes, laser copied."

"Right. And Zekki seems to be developing nuclear customers. Will you help us?"

Peter nodded slowly. "I already am. I'll get my Moscow operation in gear over the summer. Maybe I'll even start with a container load from the Duke. I'll need access to all your files on this subject."

"You'll get everything you want from us, I promise."

"I also want access to your files on weapons sales worldwide."

"Why weapons sales? Ah, don't tell me."

"You don't expect me to work for nothing, do you?"

"No. Of course not. Anything else?"

"Yes. I'll need to work out a Moscow assignment with the Brooklyn DA. The NYPD Commish is with me."

"We'll help there, too, if you need it. Everything you need."

Peter then found Lena, and taking one of her clothing bags over his arm, led her through the throngs toward the exit, saying good-bye to Joe and paying him on the way out. "We'll be in touch," Peter said. Already there was a line up of squirming Russian women trying to get into the two small toilets. Others made for the empty lot outside, squatting behind the huge sea-land container. The men were relieving themselves of the free beer they had consumed on the street outside the warehouse emporium to the consternation of the police officer assigned to keeping a boistrous crowd in order this bright early spring Sunday.

CHAPTER SEVENTEEN

C hechen was happy to be back in Moscow. The American detective at the New York airport had shaken him and for a few minutes he had been sure he would be arrested and tried for murder in America. All the way to Frankfurt he had sipped vodka and looked forward to smoking *anasha* again. He had never been able to adjust to New York although he learned enough English to get by and do his job. He hated dressing in American clothes to avoid standing out in a crowd. He especially didn't like the soap and showers that kept him from smelling like a Chechen. He believed in the tradition of his ancient Mongol raider ancestors that bathing washed away luck. Not that he had minded the mission. Yaponchik always paid Zekki Dekka well, and Chechen in turn made a tidy profit from his American forays.

So it was good to be living in the Chechen Brigade section of Moscow again. The money from the New York job would keep his family back home eating well for several years.

His only real problem at the moment was that he had run out of refined North Caucasus hemp and for the moment was out of cash.

However, he knew where to go to get money. He walked at a brisk pace along Vernadsky Prospekt, hands in his pockets, gazing straight forward, shoulders rigid. He was wearing a thick lambskin coat, the short white fur of the wide collar emphasizing his dark face covered with several days of black stubble. The black fur hat sat deeply on his head, covering his ears and forehead. Chechen had just emerged from the "University" metro station and was now striding purposefully along the prospekt. The bright state of his inner world, anticipating heavy hemp smoking soon to come, was belied by his mean looks. Passersby jumped out of this Chechen's way.

He was now just a few minutes' walk from the building in which his fellow member of Pavel's crew, Misha, lived. It was a huge fifteen-floor structure near Vernadsky Prospekt belonging to Moscow State University inhabited by students and tutors. Misha occupied a room on the 10th floor, paying tribute to the supervisor of the building in hemp and money. For Misha it was a good cover. Who would think of looking for a notorious gunman among the students of a prestigious educational institution?

Inside the building Chechen made his way through the crowd of students to the elevator and pushed his way into the car. It took him almost ten minutes to go up ten floors as people were entering and leaving the car at every floor, sometimes holding the door open for a friend to dash down the hall and jump in. The throng was made up of girls and young men of all imaginable skin colors and dress. The building was a big swinging place, the center of a flourishing black market. On the tenth floor he knocked on the wood panel door to Misha's room.

"Come in. It's open," he heard Misha shout.

Chechen pushed the door open and walked in. The room was brightly lit by a single bulb screwed into a ceiling plug. It was small with a window overlooking the city, tattered paper hanging from the wall. Misha was sitting on a wide mattress which covered a considerable portion of the floor. Two teenage girls were sitting facing him on a blanket. They were heavily made up with cosmetics, wearing short skirts and black stockings. One girl was stripped to the waist and the sight of her pear-shaped standing breasts caused a throb in Chechen's groin. He figured she was a student as there was a notepad and textbook beside her. Several bottles of beer stood on the floor nearby. The three were playing Rishkit, a Russian card game similar to strip-poker. Misha was winning.

Seeing Chechen, Misha sprang to his feet and strode over to his caller. He was wearing a clean white shirt, under which a striped military T-shirt was visible.

"What's up, Arsen?" he asked, addressing Chechen by a common Caucasus name.

"I see you are having some fun." He cleared his throat. "I need some cash. You remember?"

"Sure. How much was that? I was drunk when I took it from you."

"Two lumps. You have it?"

Misha stood up and went to his coat hanging on the wall, produced a bunch of crumpled bank notes and handed them over to him. Chechen counted them and looked up questioningly.

"Listen, Arsen. I can give you the rest in American bucks if you do not mind."

"Hell no. How much?"

"I got a hundred dollar bill. You'll be a big man at the hard currency shops. You are lucky today."

"Okay. I'll take it."

Misha reached into his pants pocket and produced a crumpled-bank note and Chechen took it. Almost instantly alarm bells went off in his head. He had spent enough time in America to get used to U.S. currency and this banknote was wrong, no good. He felt it with his fingers. The paper, though crumpled, felt too smooth and slick. He held it up to the light and examined it. The image was okay, in fact perfect. But this was no bank note from the U.S. mint.

He grabbed the notebook beside the topless girl, turned to a clean page and rubbed the bank note fiercely against the paper. He had learned a few tricks in America, not the least of them to spot counterfeit high denomination bills. Not a trace of a smudge of green rubbed off on the clean white paper.

"What's wrong?" Misha asked watching Chechen's actions suspiciously.

"Laser printed," Chechen cried. "A Jewish trick, Zekki warned me." He dropped the banknote and yelled, "you tried to cheat me! Where did you get it, son of a bitch?"

"Take that back, and be quick." Misha's voice was husky with anger at the insult.

"I'll fuck your mommy for pulling such tricks!" Chechen reached for the gun in his inside breast pocket but Misha punched him in the jaw with a quick right-hand blow before he could raise the weapon. Chechen lost his balance and fell backwards over the girls, beer, cards and heaps of clothing. The girls crawled off to the corner of the room screaming. With a swift movement Misha darted a hand to the shelf and grabbed a vicious looking stilleto. Chechen was kneeling, trying to get to his feet when Misha sprang at him and stabbed the blade into his buttock. No matter how much hemp he had smoked that afternoon before running out, Chechen felt a sharp pain surge through him. Awkwardly he jumped to his feet but collapsed back against a shelf and fell again. The girls fled the room still half-naked.

Chechen rose to his feet, his gun extended in front of him. He felt sticky warm liquid running down the back of his right leg and a searing pain in the buttock. But what he saw numbed his senses. Misha was standing back against the window, bloody knife clenched in his left hand while in the right hand he held a faceted ball of grey steel, the size of a large orange. Misha's fingers were pressing the spring lever to the iron stem sticking out from the top of the ball.

Chechen's eyes dropped to the floor at Misha's feet and he saw, glistening in the mess of blankets, cards, and bottles, the small bright steel ring that kept the grenade on safety when inserted in the stem. The field grenade in Misha's fist was activated and he had only to let his fingers go to blow half the floor away.

"Drop the gun, Muslim shit!" Misha said. Staring at the grenade Chechen dropped the gun and it fell with a muffled thud onto the blanket. "Hey Mikhail. What are you trying to do?" he asked. "It ain't bloody jokes," Chechen went on. "Okay, I apologize, I was wrong, brother, if you want to hear me admit it."

"All right." Misha sounded appeased. "And do not ever say that again. I'm a Caucasian as you are and you better not insult me and make me mad."

"Now put the ring back in the grenade," Chechen said urgently.

"I can't," Misha answered abashed. "Once you pull the ring it can't be put back on safety."

Chechen's face turned ashen. "How long will you be able to hold it?"

"Don't know, the lever is pretty strong. An hour at best."

A cold sweat broke out on Chechen's forehead. "I'll help you get dressed. We'll go someplace and drop it. Just don't make any sudden movements. Hell knows what it will blow up."

"In Afghanistan one orange like this would tear a truck into pieces. Give me my coat."

It took a few minutes to get Misha dressed. Finally he dug his right hand deep into his coat pocket.

"How does it feel?"

"Fingers getting numb. Let's hurry."

But they got stuck in the elevator for another fifteen minutes. At every step Chechen's heart sank, sweat soaking his spine. Misha's gaze was absent and tense. When they finally reached the ground floor he was sweating too.

At the guard's post they were agonizingly detained again. A noisy group of students entered the building laughing and seem-

ing high on *anasha*. A tall black man approached Misha and patted him on the shoulder. "Hey, Mikhail! What's up?"

"Nothing," Misha replied curtly. "Listen, I'm in a hurry."

"Hurry? Forget it. Come on and have a drink with us."

Chechen reached for his gun and suddenly realized he had left
it on the floor of Misha's room. Misha was trying to resist the student's offer in a meek way but they kept urging him to drink and
finally he said, "Okay, but I'll drink right here. Gimme the bottle."

"Right here? Man you're strange today. Okay guys, give him the
bottle."

Misha took the bottle with his left hand.

"Hey man, what's with your right arm? Holding onto your
balls?"

Misha wanted to shout they'd all lose their balls if they didn't
let him go but instead he gulped down half the bottle. His head
went dizzy and he felt a pleasant warmth and even the lever in his
pocket seemed easier to hold down. For a moment he felt so spirited he nearly let it go off. Horror-stricken, he pressed it back again,
his aching fingers obeying him poorly.

"What's with your hand, anyway?" the tall man asked.

"Fingers aching."

"Next time don't stick them in the wrong place!" The whole
company laughed as Misha burst out the double doors of the
building and into the street, Chechen right behind him.

Misha was walking at a fast pace, almost running from the dor-
mitory, Chechen trailing him by a few feet.

"Hey, Mikhail, where are we going?"

"There's a pond nearby."

"A pond?"

"Yes, there's no other way. And don't think you can fall out of
range, The fragments fly three hundred feet."

They reached the pond in a few minutes, a safe distance from
the nearest buildings and screened from them by the trees. The
surface of the artificial pond was covered with a thin sheet of

melting ice. Misha pulled his hand with the grenade in it out of the coat pocket into which it had been jammed. He could hardly move his fingers, they were immobilized with cramps. He put his left hand over the grenade, securing the lever and almost tore it away from the cramped hand. Misha gave a last look around and awkwardly tossed the steel ball into the air. Chechen watched breathlessly as the grenade lazily climbed in to the air above the pond and then fell abruptly through the ice and vanished.

"Let's get out of here," Misha said turning his back on the pond and rubbing his right hand briskly.

A loud explosion came from under the pond. A large hump of water mushroomed above the surface scattering ice and falling back with a loud splash.

Back in Misha's room Chechen took his gun from the floor and put it back into the holster under his arm. Then they sat on the blanket quietly smoking. Chechen finally asked, "Listen Mikhail, where did you get the bloody dollars?"

"I didn't know they were fake. I swear on my father's grave."

Chechen was suddenly serious, all business. "Now listen, I know that some of Tofik's crew in New York and Germany were able to get these laser copiers, or pieces of them, one at a time, into Moscow. It is my job to find them and destroy them. I've looked all over the Chechen Brigade—nothing. Suddenly you turn up with what I'm looking for. Where did it come from?"

"Reso paid my last monthly salary with it."

"Reso?" There was surprise in his voice. "Reso is the trump six to Givi and Tofik. What are you doing with their shooters?"

"It was Pavel's idea and you'd better not mention it to anyone if you don't want to get into big trouble. Reso is a boss with Givi and was paying us with fake bucks. You better tell Pavel immediately."

"I will. Where does Reso live?"

"He and two of Givi's sixes Zhurab and Chacha share a big luxury suite, number 539 North at the Hotel Russia."

Chechen inspected the fake hundred dollar bill. "It's printed on a Xerox laser copier and the image is good. Where do they keep the machine?"

"I think they are getting ready to do it right in the hotel."

"I've got to stop that. Zekki will be furious if he thinks someone is spoiling the market for his good stuff." Chechen stepped over to the box in which Misha kept his grenades. "Aren't you afraid to keep this fruit in your room?"

"I'm selling them gradually. I brought two dozen back from Afghanistan. Now I've got eleven left."

"Sell me a few."

"How many?"

"Say . . . five, maybe six."

"Ten thousand," Misha quoted decisively.

"Are you kidding?"

"A good American or Belgian handgun goes for one hundred thousand. One orange can make more trouble than ten Colts. So the price is reasonable."

"I'll take one if you'll let me pay you later."

"No problem. Before you throw it be sure you have a place to duck. The fragments can kill at two hundred feet."

"I will take great care," Chechen answered.

Pavel was sitting in the Caspian Restaurant munching black caviar on toast and drinking iced vodka when Chechen finally found him and beckoned him out. Reluctantly Pavel left his repast and met Chechen at the door. They walked along the sidewalk to where Pavel's Volga was parked and climbed into the back seat. Chechen thrust the hundred dollar bill at Pavel who studied the banknote. "They are putting our business in danger," Chechen was saying. "Sooner or later the *ments* will spot the forgery and be on the alert."

"So what do you want to do?" Pavel asked.

"Let me get rid of the bastards. And what does Misha do in Tofik's gang? I thought he worked for us!"

"None of your business. Never mention it to anyone. As for what to do, we do nothing."

"You mean we let them get away with it?" Chechen asked incredulously.

"If fat Givi is doing it, others are. We just sink to the bottom and wait until we can produce the real stuff. There was no need for you to drag me away from my dinner. Get out of the car and keep quiet."

Chechen stood on the dark street watching the rear lights of Pavel's Volga disappear down the street. First a stab in the ass, the hand grenade ordeal, a threat to the scheme he had worked on with Zekki in New York, and now Pavel's poorly concealed contempt. Fury burned inside him and just one thought filled his head. Hotel Russia, Suite 539 North. He felt the steel "orange" in his pocket.

It was a ten minute brisk walk to the Russia Hotel and as Chechen walked through the North entrance he saw the familiar, sharp-featured face of Givi's trump six, Reso. He shrank back into the crowded North lobby but Reso's wild eyes seemed to bore into him. Chechen knew Reso recognized him even though it had been many months since the gunman had last seen him. Fortunately Reso must have had an urgent appointment because ordinarily, seeing a member of a rival gang walking into the lobby of the same hotel in which some of his men were staying, he would have stopped and investigated.

Chechen took an elevator to the fifth floor and started to walk past the watch woman at the desk. He gestured down the hall from where the sounds of revelry emanated from a suite.

"I'm expected," he muttered.

The desk lady nodded. A party was going strong and from another elevator in the bank two men with brightly made up girls wearing gaudy evening gowns emerged and waved to the desk as they started down the hall. Chechen followed the party goers. He passed a waiter leaving the suite after delivering drinks and food and watched the two couples join the gathering as greetings were shouted to them.

Chechen stood in the doorway staring at the party in progress with unblinking black emotionless eyes, his hands in the pockets of the lambskin coat. Several of Givi's men were sitting around a long, low table drinking with sensuously attired girls. A large packing case with German markings stood just inside the door. Chechen assumed it contained the laser copier that was printing the U.S. dollar images.

Chechen pulled the ring and threw the faceted steel ball onto the table among the bottles and glasses. One of the girls screamed. Chechen dove through the door into the hall and scrambled away from the outer wall of the doomed suite. Just then a hurricane of fire and steel shards shredded the suite, tearing away heads and limbs of all those present, shattering the large carton, bursting out windows and frames, destroying the TV set and even ripping through the walls into the corridor, the spent splinters slightly wounding Chechen in the side of his face.

Choking in the smoke, he ran to the elevator, his deafened ears oblivious to the wail of the fire alarm or the shrieks of the warden woman whose blanched face flashed in front of him. An elevator door opened and he pushed himself through it, paying no attention to the people inside who stared numbly at his wild dark face with streaks of drying blood and black marks of ashes on cheeks and forehead. On the ground floor Chechen was surprised to see Reso pushing his way into the lobby. The trump six for some reason must have returned, Chechen thought, as Reso spotted him and shoved his way through the wild melee to get at the man he now knew must be the cause of whatever had happened at the hotel.

Chechen crouched, his head below shoulder level in the hysterical throng. He eluded Reso and forced his way out to the street, waving down a taxi and jumping inside. He shouted an address cramming bank notes in the driver's breast pocket.

Sinking back in the seat he covered his face with his dirty palms. His only thought now was going to the bottom and staying there for a long time.

CHAPTER EIGHTEEN

❖ ❖

After the murder of Potma, the other thiefs considered how best to handle Bugai, Potma's massive and vicious frayer. He and his crew, now without their thief-in-the-law to guide them, posed a threat to thief's discipline in the camp. Maxim sent his frayer to make an offer of partnership to Bugai even promising him the title of thief, a great honor since Maxim was an old and respected thief.

The offer was also indicative of how powerful and feared a man Bugai was, a legend among frayers. Close to seven feet tall, powerful as a bull, he was inherently violent and aggressive. He was caught and convicted of raping and killing three girls and then half a dozen boys, who put up a more satisfying fight. The court tried to sentence him to death but the law restricted execution of culprits under the age of eighteen. Sentenced to fifteen years of labor camp Bugai knew no remorse. Five years later he was transferred to Tulun Camp from a teenage colony and assigned to a barrack supervised by Potma. "Break him right away!" the commandant ordered.

In a matter of an hour, four of Potma's sixes were badly injured in the attempt and two others fled from the barracks to escape the rampaging giant.

The incident became known all over the camp causing much laughter and dirty jokes. The administration of the camp found it funny too. The two sixes lost their positions and soon turned into cockerels or goats—passive homosexual partners, the most despised and suffering category of prisoners. Maxim imposed one condition on his offer of protection and future thiefdom to Bugai. At the right moment he and his men would help Maxim kill the Jap. Bugai agreed immediately.

A few days after the thiefs' questioning in Karamushev's office the inner guards let Maxim into Jap's apartment. It was late at night, after lights out. Jap had put out a bottle of Armenian cognac, a delicious assortment of sandwiches and two crystal wine glasses on the low table in anticipation of the visit. He was sitting on the floor behind the table in a well-ironed blue shirt and his black jeans.

Maxim appeared in his camp costume, thick, waist-reaching cotton stuffed bodywarmer, dark loose working breeches and *valenki*—felt Russian winter boots, most common footwear of prisoners in northern camps.

Entering the cell he removed them, exposing thick wool socks—a luxury only a thief could afford. "I hear you are leaving your cell and returning to the barracks," the Jap said casually. "Are you planning some sort of action?"

Maxim shook his head. "I think the men need me close at hand for a while." He sat on the floor, poured himself a full glass of cognac and gulped it down.

"Have a snack," Jap offered.

Maxim poured himself another cognac and downed it, then he took a slice of ham, put it on a piece of bread and started to lazily chew it.

"We have to talk, Jap. Serious matter. For all of us."

"Without Tofik and Josik?"

"That's right. Trouble is brewing. You and I are in danger."

Jap gazed at him calmly. "Who called for that last *skchod* and set Potma up to try to steal my authority?"

"Tofik. He is after you—after both of us. He plotted with Potma and Josik to do away with us."

"I don't understand. What wrong have I done Tofik? I do not know what affairs you may have shared with him, but me?"

Maxim thrust his face forward over the table closer to Jap's. "After you piked Potma, Josik was afraid to join with Tofik against you and me. Yesterday night the Jew came to my cell and revealed to me the whole affair. Tofik plans to kill you because he suspects your Chechen guy in New York murdered his Georgians in the Kiev restaurant. At least a dozen people recognized Chechen and knew you gave the orders from here. Now his counterfeiting plan is ruined for another half a year."

Jap was prepared for the accusation and assumed a hurt look. "Tofik is wrong to think I could or would reach out from Tulun Camp to New York and have his people killed."

"I agree, Jap. I told Tofik he had it all wrong. But on top of that he just got word that for sure your Chechen killed four of his men and two women in their Hotel Russia suite with a hand grenade. And today a message reached him that he lost another man in New York, he thinks it was Edward, his most valuable under-boss."

Jap made no display of his shock at Chechen's unsanctioned violence. Pavel would never have permitted such an incident. He was also surprised to hear of the hit in New York. This was one more painful indication of how he was losing control of his *organizatsyia*. "If such things happened it was not on my orders."

"Well, Tofik thinks you did it."

"What else did Josik say?"

"He is frightened and wants to stay away from the whole thing."

"He can't manage that. I'll offer him a choice."

"Yeah. Besides we'll need his men."

"What do you mean by that, Maxim?" Jap asked.

"Tofik paid Karamushev a million rubles to persuade the camp chief and his associate to take the troops away from the camp for a few hours. Tofik's sixes will start a fight and stab us both."

"Why you?" Jap asked.

"Tofik wants me dead because my people in Odessa took over all the gambling business on the Black Sea coast. Several Georgian gangs will pay Tofik handsomely to do away with me."

Maxim drank another glass of cognac, belched mightily, and went on with the plan. "Later the troops will return and wipe out what's left of our crews. Camp authorities will be awarded a citation for crushing a mutiny of criminals led by two authoritative thiefs—you and me."

Just then there was a knock on the door of the cell. Karamushev, always respectful, waited for Jap's invitation to respond and then he entered.

"Commandant, my dear man," Jap said, "this is a bright surprise." He turned toward the cell containing the sauna. "Maria!"

Maria, unabashedly half-naked, appeared from the door to the bath cell carrying two bottles of cognac.

"Nice to see you, girl," boomed the commandant taking off his boots. "Be a sport, bring another glass for an old man. Hell of an icy frost outside. I could use a good drink."

Jap nodded at Maria. "And bring us some of that ham."

"Thank you, Jap. You really respect old people. That caring warms the spirit better than drinks."

Maria appeared by the commandant's side and poured a glass from the bottle and left it beside him. He helped himself to some ham. "Now this is something," he praised as he threw down another glass of vodka from the bottle especially reserved for him by the Jap and the generous snacks Maria prepared for him. "Only Ukrainians know how to prepare good tasty fat." Jap and Maxim laughed appreciatively as the commandant guzzled drinks from his bottle and discussed his opinion of the American singer he had seen on one of Jap's video tapes, Madonna.

"If she has tits on her then our girls have real knockers!"

After more drinks and sandwiches Jap brought the conversation around to its point. "You are a rich man now," he said to the apparently drunk commandant. "You say Tofik contributed a million rubles?"

"I thought that to Tofik's million I can add a small present from both of you," Karamushev boomed. "Tofik devised a clever plan to strike you and Maxim with my troops away. I propose that you will be the first to strike with your men and a bit later we would assist you with our troops."

"How can you prove we will be safe?" Maxim asked bluntly, eyes glinting viciously.

Karamushev poured himself another glass from the vodka bottle, downed it as if it were water, and ate several tomatoes one after another.

Then to Maxim he said, "Well young man, you should always trust your elders. Two-thirds of the money from you and Jap we shall receive only after the whole affair will be settled. Yes?"

"How much do you want?" Jap asked.

Karamushev shrugged his shoulders. "Not much. Another million. And if you split it that is really nothing to you."

"I discovered the plot," Maxim claimed. "I will give four hundred thousand. The rest is Jap's."

The Jap nodded. "Agreed." Then to the commandant, "Your information and friendship is more valuable than money. When does Tofik attack?"

"The date is set for Monday. Four days from now. You prepare to attack on Sunday, one day before they plan to hit. That gives you tomorrow and Saturday, two days, to prepare."

"Whose side will Potma's sixes take?" Jap asked. "I can bet that Tofik is already recruiting them. This Bugai is a son of a bitch."

"With commandant's gunmen protecting you? No problem," Maxim replied.

As they continued eating and drinking they discussed the details and decided that the money would be delivered to Kara-mushev by courier on Saturday. When it came to paying the com-mandant's bribes, communications to the source of a thief's money were quick and clear. The commandant rose unsteadily to his feet. An empty vodka bottle marked where he had been sitting.

"Well, guys," he belched, "I guess we haven't forgotten any-thing. I still have affairs. If problems come up—contact me imme-diately. Nice talking to you. But—as they say—'frost and cold is no bliss, time is ripe to take a piss.' See you." He left the cell and a short time later Maxim downed the last glass of cognac and rose, too. "Many things to do in the barracks. I don't think I'll sleep before this is all over."

"It is never over," Jap said quietly.

"You are right. Shall I drop the word to your men, too?"

Jap shook his head. Maxim as well as the other thiefs never stopped trying to undermine the Jap's authority, even with his own frayer and crew. "I will drop the word myself."

They embraced and kissed. Maxim left, the cell door banging shut behind him. Jap returned to his place and poured himself some cognac. The sauna door opened cautiously and Karamushev appeared on the threshold, absolutely sober, as if he hadn't had a drink all evening. "You put on a fine act, Chief. I knew that having a back door to the sauna would come in handy some day."

Karamushev's blue eyes were fixed on the Jap. "You are in hell of a trouble, Jap," the commandant said seriously. "They are after you. I have never seen such a show as Maxim put on just now."

"Except for your own," Jap chuckled.

A conspiratorial grin flitted across the commandant's lips. "Maxim and Tofik paid me half a million rubles for your head, another half a million to get the soldiers away so they can kill Fofa and your crew. I have to shoot you by the end of the operation according to the plan."

Jap nodded thoughtfully, saying nothing.

"All this because of some murders in New York—America would you believe?" Karamushev mused. "And then this grenade launching at the Hotel Russia against Tofik's men. That, I can understand, would make them angry."

"I wish I knew about the Moscow grenade attack," Jap mused helplessly. "How did you hear about it?"

"I allowed Tofik a visitor from Moscow." The commandant smiled. "I would do the same for you but with somebody in the prosecutor's office after you, checking on your visitors, it is hard. I will do my best for you but do not be surprised if I cannot do everything you need. A new young administrator has just come into the camp chief's office. Like all of them he hopes to become the Minister of Interior someday. I will have to be careful if I plan to retire peacefully."

"And very, very rich," Jap added.

"I will try to help you but I must do the best I can for myself and my family. I will at least leave two good men with machine-guns to protect you here."

"Chief, after all this drama tonight there is no doubt in my mind that Tofik and Maxim will attack on Saturday. I never believed that Maxim was suddenly my friend and ally."

Karamushev nodded. "You figured that right, Jap."

"That only gives us two days to prepare."

"By tomorrow Maxim and Tofik will already be congratulating themselves that you will not live to see Sunday morning. I promised to remove the guards on Saturday long enough for them to destroy you and your crew."

"How about arms, at least pikes and picks for my crew?"

"They'll have to take care of themselves. But I'll make it easy for some of your sixes to get into the tool shop."

"And if you will permit me a phone call to the keeper of my bank in Irkutsk tomorrow morning—"

"Of course, Jap," Karamushev instantly acceded.

"I'll have your lemon ready tomorrow night."

Karamushev gave Jap a long searching look. "You know and I know that an investigation into a camp uprising is the one thing that can for sure keep you from being transferred from Tulun until Martinov secures your release."

Jap nodded. "There'll be another lemon for you next week if Tofik and Maxim do not survive this riot."

The jail chief nodded. "Watch out for yourself, Jap."

"Do not worry Commandant. They are suckers, and suckers always lose. Always. Sit down and have a real drink, a real talk about such details as getting the pikes, picks, and crowbars for my men. And we talk money, perhaps diamonds and the way some old officers become rich."

The prospect of battle seemed to excite Jap. "Maria! Where the hell are you? Bring us a bottle of real vodka . . . and of course ham. The commandant likes ham."

CHAPTER NINETEEN

F ofa was escorted to the lair of the Underground King by one of Karamushev's guards. The frayer listened attentively to the Jap's instructions. He was a very reasonable and well-balanced man, the most intelligent of the five frayers in the camp.

Back in the barracks Fofa informed his sixes and common *kents* that the rival crews were going to attack Saturday morning. The regular guards would not be in the camp to defend them. Therefore the Jap was now passing on his orders through Fofa to his men to prepare weapons.

He stood facing the three wooden tiers of shelves on which the prisoners slept and lounged when in their barracks. They listened to him from their perches.

"So guys . . . it looks like a few of us may not live. Maxim and Tofik want to wipe out the Jap and our gang."

"Hey Fofa," someone called out. "What about the *zirhicks*?"

"That's the point," Fofa called back. "Jap was told that Maxim and Tofik made a bargain with the commandant to keep the guards in their barracks."

No one spoke as Fofa continued. "They outnumber us three to one. Four to one if Josik joins them. We cannot fight them outside the barracks. Jap told me he made a deal with the commandant and when *zirhicks* return they will be on our side and machine-gun down everyone outside. Now, all of you with weapons put them here on the floor. Let's see what we have."

The usual weapons concealed by prisoners were "pikes," the bodkin, a sharpened rod or screwdriver good only for stabbing, and the crafted knife with cutting blade and stabbing point. They varied in length, sometimes prisoner artisans fashioned swords two feet long. The artisan in a prison camp was a highly respected and privileged person. As the Russian saying goes, "naked people are inventive."

Unfortunately the weapons which lay in front of Fofa were just common rough pikes, about twenty sharpened screwdrivers, a big razor sharp kitchen knife, and ten wide, sharpened iron bands of various length with blunt ends wrapped in thick tape and ropes to provide a firmer grip. For the defense of 50 guys against at least 150 attackers this was totally inadequate. Fofa was nevertheless surprised at how much there was to be found. The last barrack search was just a week ago and not a single one of these pikes had been found.

"Well guys, it is not enough. We have to get into the store with the heavy tools, next to the canteen." He looked around the circle of prisoner-troops. "We must pick our best guys for this. They will go and fetch the weapons for the rest of us."

Fofa's eyes rested on Volodya, a young blonde prisoner with a wary, haunted look in his blue eyes. He was reputed to be only twenty-one or twenty-two though the deeply etched lines around his jaw, temples, and cheeks made him appear at least in his mid-thirties. He was sitting on his nearby third tier berth. Here was a tried and tested man the frayer knew.

His prison history was a barracks legend. Volodya fell behind the bars when he was seventeen, falsely accused of rape. In the teenage colony he was beaten savagely and at eighteen he was transferred to a camp in northern Kazachstan where one of the first so called "breaking dungeons" was organized. Here Volodya led a bloody battle against the bitches who had tried to break him, almost killing him with beatings, rapes, and starvation. He and his men killed every bitch in the camp impaling their heads on pikes. It was therefore natural for Jap's frayer, Fofa, to pick Volodya for the key mission in this war to the finish.

Fofa handed Volodya a liter bottle of vodka. "Give this to the guard at the passage. If he won't take it—stab him. Do not stay long in the store. Just take everything we need and return."

"I'll need six men," Volodya replied.

"Choose any six you like," the frayer agreed.

The six men, pikes under bodywarmers, ear-cover hats on their heads, made their way outside through the opened gate, looking around cautiously. It was almost five o'clock in the morning and absolutely dark. The camp seemed to be deserted, only sentinels at their posts. Dark figures of the six prisoners were discernible against the white snow. When they approached the guard post at the passage through the fence the sentinel, an eighteen-year-old boy, raised his machine gun, a bayonet fixed on its barrel.

"Stop there!" he ordered.

"Hey, *Zirhick*, do not shoot," Volodya replied. "We need to talk. I have no weapons, the guys will stay here. May I come closer?"

"Okay. Five steps. No jokes or I'll shoot your brains away."

Volodya took five steps towards the sentinel. Despite the frost he felt sweat running down his spine. He took out the bottle of vodka. "Easy deal man. We need to pass, we'll be back in five minutes sharp . . . this stuff is yours."

The sentinel considered the bottle. His relief was coming in about fifteen minutes. Even if the prisoners do something wrong it won't be discovered in less than an hour and then it would be the responsibility of the next guard. And he would return to the soldiers' barracks, fry potatoes with his squad and chase it down with vodka, then go to sleep.

"Sounds fine," he said. "Hand it over."

"Open the gate first."

The sentinel opened the gate and let them through into the working *zona*. Volodya gave him the bottle.

"Move your asses!" the trooper shouted. "The change of posts is in fifteen minutes."

The six men rushed to the the store building. A light burned inside. Volodya peered through the frosty window. Armen, a fat, hairy, privileged prisoner, or *fool*, from the Caucasus was sitting at his table.

Volodya touched the door. It was not locked and grasping the hilt of his sharpened screwdriver in the sleeve of his bodywarmer he walked in, his friend Boris and the four others hanging back, just out of sight.

Armen lifted his head. "Hey, what are you doing here?"

"I came to visit you. We need to talk."

"What kind of fucking talk at night? Who let you through? Get your ass out of here!"

"Hey, man. Do not make waves. I tell you . . ."

"Get the hell out of here! I would kick your ass if I was not afraid your asshole would swallow my boot!"

"Listen, Armen. Take it easy."

"What! May you shit barbed wire!"

"As you did?"

"Fucking shit! I'll call the guards!"

"Hey, Armen, what is that behind you?"

The simple trick worked. Armen turned his thick neck, looking backward. Volodya swung his pike and thrust it down into Armen's chest from above the left clavicle and immediately withdrew it, raising the pike for a second blow. Armen turned, seizing the wound with his hand.

"*Sooka*!" he yelled for a guard, trying to jump up, but his fat

184

belly caught the under edge of the table holding him long enough so the second thrust went into the corner between his nose and left eye; the pike pierced the thin bone of the eye socket and sank into the head destroying the base of the brain. Blood gushed from his nostrils in two thick rivulets and he collapsed to the floor with a loud thud, dead on the spot.

Volodya let out a thin whistle. His most trusted friend, Boris, and the other four rushed inside, shutting the door after them. They carried two big sacks and several pillow cases. Screw drivers, hammers, files and bodkins went into the pillow cases. Crowbars, spades, picks and axes were stuffed into the sacks. In three minutes they almost emptied the store leaving just several dozen old broken spades.

Under a great weight of tools over their shoulders they ran back to the passage in the fence with surprising agility.

The sentinel opened his mouth in astonishment. "Hey guys, what are you up to?" he exclaimed letting them through the gate.

"We're starting work early today," Boris called back. At the barracks the gates were flung open for them. The six marauders fell to the concrete floor, dropping their loads and gasping for air. The prisoners immediately began selecting their weapons.

As Jap had ordered, Volodya and his raiders brought back more implements than they could use so that less would remain for the enemy.

"What about Armen?" Fofa asked Volodya.

"Armen is sleeping. Everything went easy."

"Sleeping? Are you sure?"

The grim smile as he said "yes" convinced Fofa to ask no more questions.

Meanwhile the soldier who had taken the bottle of vodka faced his patrol officer on duty. "Where is my relief?"

"There will be no relief. Orders are we all return to barracks," was the reply.

"Yeah, but . . ."

185

"Shut up! This is none of your business."

The sentinel, glad to be off duty, followed his officer away from the post pressing the concealed bottle of vodka closer to his stomach.

Twenty minutes after the sentinels left their posts and the soldiers evacuated the main camp, Bugai led the late Potma's sixes from their barracks, knives under bodywarmers, and walked down the camp's main street. They stopped a short distance from the barracks where Fofa and his men were waiting. The trump six chosen for the initiation of talks marched up to the gate of the barracks and knocked loudly. At first there was no response. Then a sleepy voice called out, "What the hell do you want?"

"Get up guys," the six replied in a merry voice. "The brotherhood decided to go on strike. We want to know what your barracks thinks. Open the gate."

The gate opened. It was dark inside. Everyone seemed to be sleeping. As his eyes adjusted to the darkness he saw a crowd of the Jap's guys standing around, heavy tools in their hands. That was the last thing he saw. The smashing blow of a hammer to his forehead instantly killed him.

Bugai and four sixes waited outside for some time. He had just given them the order to go inside the store and get some tools when the door of the barracks opened and a prisoner walked out, holding a package in his hands. Dawn was just breaking. The man from the barracks covered half the distance to where Bugai was standing and threw the package at him, turning and rushing back to the gate which closed abruptly after him.

Bugai sent a man to retrieve the parcel which had been thrown into the snow. The dirty rag was unwrapped and in the dim light of dawn Bugai and his men found themselves looking at the severed head of his trump six, torn dorsal roots and severed muscles hanging loose, remnants of the spine sticking out between them.

There were gasps from the men closest to the grisly offering.

Before Bugai could react, the six he had dispatched to the store came running back, his breath coming in tearing gasps. "Bugai! We're in shit up to the ears! Armen has been killed, the store is empty!" The six slapped a blood-caked sharpened screwdriver into Bugai's hand. "I pulled it out of Armen's face."

Bugai stared at the death weapon and cursed. "Get everyone here! We'll overrun the bloody barracks!" he shouted. In a minute the whole of Potma's gang, run by Bugai, charged the gates sticking their tools into slits around the doors but the crowbars were stricken away from inside by hammers. They kept up the attack and were beginning to force the doors when Bugai heard cries from the left of his attacking horde. He turned from the portals behind which the Jap's men crouched, ready for a fight to the death when the doors fell, and saw a crowd of prisoners brandishing heavy tools of all description approaching his men.

Josik himself was leading his guys and sixes. Confused, the physical if not mental giant, Bugai, decided that it was Josik, not the Jap's men who had killed Armen and emptied the store. Rage flared inside him, red circles appeared in front of his eyes as he turned to face the attack from an unexpected source and direction.

Josik was meticulously following the strategy Jap had drawn out during yesterday's secret meeting. His men hated Bugai more than any six or frayer in the camp which made his plan easier to execute. A rumor had reached them, carefully spread by Josik, again at Jap's orders, that after this whole affair was settled Bugai would be made a thief-in-the-law by Maxim. That was too much for them and they demanded that Josik lead them against Bugai which was what Jap wanted.

Josik trotted down the main street in front of his "army," pike under his jacket. Bugai was already half-insane with fury as the two leaders faced each other, their men behind them. Josik took a step forward and suddenly reverted to type, the Leningrad jewelry dealer. Perhaps negotiations could end this war before it started.

Loudly, though his voice betrayed uncertainty, he cried out,

"Listen, frayer." He hoped the respectful term would bring reason to Bugai's inflamed mind. "We must talk."

"Talk?!" Bugai bellowed and stabbed Josik in the stomach with the pike Volodya had used on Armen an hour ago.

"Mama!" Josik cried, sinking to his knees into the snow. His sixes screamed in fury and rushed forward, swinging their weapons as the two gangs attacked each other with loud shrieks in a ferocious battle. Their numbers were approximately even, but Bugai's men were scattered. Josik's gang swarmed over them, their hammers, spades, and picks delivering lethal blows. The fight turned into a bloody hand-to-hand battle.

The monstrous Bugai struck down attackers with a huge and powerful left fist, a clawing pickaxe swinging in his right hand. In seconds he killed four men and maimed another three, his axe splitting heads apart as melons, ribs and shoulders flying into fragments.

Terrible screams of the wounded filled the air. But Bugai's men were suffering heavy losses, two sixes killed. Dead and wounded were lying in the snow, blood reddening its white surface.

CHAPTER TWENTY

⊰⊱ ⊰⊱

The Jap's men watched the carnage from their barracks. Finally Volodya approached Fofa. "I think we should help the men of Josik."

The frayer shook his head. "It's too early. Jap said to let Maxim and Tofik appear first."

Volodya glanced through the slit in the door. "Josik's men will be wiped out soon."

"Jap gave his orders. We wait." Almost half of Bugai's men lay dead or badly wounded on the snow. And it was at this moment that several of the late Potma's best sixes fell upon the massive frayer from behind. He was hated and feared by everyone and the time for vengeance was at hand. One of the pikes stabbed him in the buttocks, the other in the back. Bugai yelled, turned around and smashed one man's head with a hammer he had picked up and opened up the breast of another like a tin can with his pick-axe. The other three fell back, their pikes in front of them. Several more of Bugai's men fell as the enemies closed around him. That would have been the end of Bugai had not a huge gang of prison-

189

ers appeared from the barracks. Maxim and Tofik were leading them, axes swinging in their hands. They overran Josik's men from behind killing several of them immediately. Out-numbering Josik's men two to one, Maxim and Tofik were chopping rivals down with their axes, splitting heads on all sides.

From inside the barracks Fofa realized that the moment Jap had told him to make his move had arrived. "It's time to move on them," he shouted above the din of the battle raging outside, "or we'll lose the surprise of attack . . . Get ready guys." He threw down his cigarette butt. "Open the gates! Don't wet your pants! I'm with you! We'll put them in the shithole head first!"

The gates opened and the Jap's fifty men, well-armed from Volodya's foray on the store, charged out silently and fiercely, an unexpected savage tide sweeping down on the shocked fighters of Maxim and Tofik engaging Josik's gang. Several sixes had been placed at the back ranks to push forward reluctant prisoners. They were smashed on the spot. Jap's men plunged into the enemy crowd like a herd of enraged bulls, their heavy weapons inflicting gaping wounds and death in every direction, blood splattering into the faces of the fighters. The total mayhem moved against the barbed wire fence, some of the prisoners cut through the wire or crawled under it trying to escape slaughter, others just plunged into it, wounding themselves.

Maxim and Tofik were violently fighting the unexpected strength of the Jap's gang, both leaders covered with blood from the pike stabs they had received. Bugai managed to wound one of the Jap's sixes.

Raising him to his feet as if he weighed nothing Bugai yelled, "where's Jap? Where's bloody Jap?"

Maxim ran up to him. "Jap is in internal jail, you idiot! Take some guys and go there! He is not guarded, I made a deal with the boss! You can finish off this scum . . ."

"Shut up. I know what I'm doing!" snapped Bugai. He dragged the gasping six behind him, retrieved his pickaxe, and moved with a limping stride toward the jail building stepping over corpses, the pain in his stabbed buttock maddening him.

Both sides had suffered heavy losses, only half of the fighters continuing the struggle; many men were trying to crawl away to a safe spot. Volodya, almost exhausted by the violent battle, realized it was time to quit. He had a hunch the guards could be back any moment. Then three of Maxim's men almost caught up with him. They were hefting a pike, a pickaxe, and a crowbar. There was no chance against them and Volodya fled, the guys on his heels screaming curses after him.

Jumping over the bodies lying in his path, Volodya ran into a passage between the two barracks. His pursuers fell behind but he was already out of breath—running through the snow in felt boots was exhausting. He stumbled over a spade and tripped, his hammer fell aside and he was sitting in the snow, gasping for breath. The battle still raged nearby and his enemies were getting closer, clutching their weapons.

"Looks like it is coming to the end," he thought, surprised at his own indifference and lack of fear. But as he stared at them the men bent on killing him waved their hands in a strange way and dropped their lethal tools. Bloodied bits of fabric flew from their jackets and from the holes in their chests which appeared suddenly there came smoke, then blood gushed in streams. The three fell, throwing their legs up in the air. The felt boot of one of them flew off his foot and fell a yard or more away. Only then was Volodya aware of the sound of machine guns firing.

He burrowed into the snow. And just in time. Hell opened in the following seconds. The volleys of a hundred machine-guns crossed the battle space in all directions, the fusillade of bullets raising fountains of snow. Soldiers were poised in lines along the snow banks behind the wire fences all around the perimeter of the barracks zona. The sun had risen and in the morning light hundreds of prisoners outlined in the bright snow were easy targets.

The storm of bullets cut men down by the dozens, the lead

slugs puncturing the bodies, spattering brain matter from heads, tearing away hands and ears. Several groups of prisoners were closer to the firing lines and fell under withering crossfire. Body-warmers spit out lumps of cotton mixed with blood torn away by the bullets, smoking and catching fire.

The magazines had been loaded especially for this exercise— one regular cartridge, one white phosphorus incendiary round, and a tracer, in groups of three. The terrified prisoners stopped fighting with each other and fled in all possible directions, throwing weapons away as they ran. Some of the quick reacting men fell to the ground at the start of the shooting burrowing into the snow for safety. Others fled to the barracks gates and tried to haul them open. The ones who struggled with the doors fell backwards, bullets lacing them while some of those behind managed to slip inside the safety of the barracks walls. But even inside the prisoners were not safe. Some bullets tore through half-open gates or windows. Surviving prisoners crawled below the first tier of berths where they found a measure of security.

In several minutes the battleground was free of rioting prisoners. Those men who were near the inner wire fence fell there, some sprawled and hanging on the barbed wire.

Volodya managed to crawl inside his barracks from the snow bank where he had been lying. Fofa was one of the first to reach the barracks gates. He flung them open, diving inside as a hail of machine-gun rounds snapped at his heels. The howling crowd of prisoners from Jap's gang, covered with blood and wounds rushed after him inside, some falling to the floor hit by bullets just as they thought they were safe. The whole of the barracks was a dark bloody mess of twisting, shrieking bodies. Fofa was already closing the gates when several other prisoners came running toward the beckoning safety of the barracks as the doors started to swing closed against the lead fire storm. They were not the Jap's men for all were mixed together now to escape the vengeance of the guards.

"Do not close! Fucking wait!" they screamed. The crossfire from at least ten barrels caught them. Fountains of snow, splinters and sparks spurted into the air as they fell shrieking in front of the closed gates as if swept down by a giant brush. The front runner threw himself against the gate staining the splitting wood with blood before he fell backwards.

Fofa miraculously was untouched as men fell torn and bloody around him. Volodya too was spared by the fates as the machine-gun fire died away as abruptly as it had started. Silence fell over the area as soldiers raised their heads to see what was going on in the barracks *zona*. Corpses and work tools lay everywhere.

Then the first groans of the wounded could be heard growing louder, more pitiful. Shock was receding, fierce pain seizing the bullet-riddled prisoners. Many injured prisoners began to move tentatively, some tried crawling in the direction of the barracks. Wounds inflicted by bullets and heavy instruments were terrible, far beyond the aid of the camp's crude medical resources. Some men had their fingers and hands torn away, the lacerated skin hanging like rags. The worst were the gut-shot prisoners, insured of a horribly painful, inevitable death.

The moment for the prisoners who had pretended to be dead was ripe. Many jumped to their feet and ran to the barracks. Sporadic shooting broke out again as soldiers and officers amused themselves shooting at the running *kents*. If a volley hit a man on the run he would jump high yelling and then pitch forward on his head, legs somersaulting over him.

The two hundred soldiers and twenty-five officers had expended three magazines of thirty-six rounds each when they received new orders. The troops locked full magazines into their weapons, fixed bayonets, and entered the *zona* in single file holding their machine guns in front of them.

The surviving prisoners watched from the barracks windows and slits in the metal gates. They felt safe. Once in their barracks the soldiers had orders not to shoot them. But those lying in the snow at that moment were sentenced to death. Once again shots rang out in the frosty air. Then wary soldiers poked at bodies with their bayonets and if there was a response they fired. One of the prisoners hanging on the barbed wire groaned and started to move. A soldier came from behind and fired a whole volley into his body which exploded off the fence. Major Karamushev entered the *zona* with his squad near the barracks of Maxim and Tofik. Some things were still uncertain. As he neared the barracks, his guards after him, the gate creaked and the head of Maxim cautiously appeared. The soldiers raised their barrels but the jail commandant ordered them to lower their weapons. He waved at Maxim, inviting him to come out. The thief, limping badly, his bodywarmer torn in many places, cotton sticking out, approached the commandant. His prison garb was blood-stained and his left hand, smashed by a crowbar, hung useless. But he walked firmly toward the major, still thinking that the million rubles he and Tofik had turned over to the commandant that week was buying him immunity to danger from the camp administration. His right arm was concealed under the ripped bodywarmer.

"Hi, Commandant," Maxim greeted Karamushev. "Everything is okay? Sort of change in the plan? It seems like you came back a bit early? We did not bargain like that."

"What kind of a bargain are you talking about?" Karamushev unbuttoned his holster.

"Hey, Commandant . . . you got the money. This ain't right." Maxim stared at the holster, terror and hate glittering from his eyes. "It is a mistake. You can pay for that . . ."

"I never make mistakes, Maxim," the commandant returned in a cool, level tone pulling his pistol out.

"You . . . you can end on the pike for that," Maxim cried, an urgent note in his voice. He pressed the button on the hilt of the switchblade knife he was clutching and as he drew it from under the tattered bodywarmer, the long, thin, deadly sharpened blade sprang out. He started to leap but his wounded leg hindered the move. It was the last chance he had.

"I guess it is you who are mistaken," Karamushev uttered curtly as he shot Maxim twice in the stomach.

Maxim sank to his knees clutching his belly, his mouth wide open, the knife falling to the snow. "Ahh . . . .fucking shit . . ." he groaned, blood running from the corner of his mouth. Karamushev took a step closer to the kneeling thief and put the barrel to Maxim's forehead. Another shot cracked in the frosty air.

Maxim's body reeled backward from his knees, blood ran from the smashed head and melted the snow, making a big, dark red pit. Maxim's head sank into it, his unshaven chin pointing to the grey cloudy sky.

Karamushev looked up and saw Tofik coming toward him, his bodywarmer wide open, great belly sticking out, powerful hairy hands of a wrestler hanging free at his sides. His big owlish Georgian eyes looked out at the commandant solemnly, indifferently, as if he was staring at something behind Karamushev. Tofik's short cut, curly hair was almost white, his left temple blood smeared. Prisoners were watching them from the barracks windows, clutching the bars.

Karamushev waved his gun at Tofik impatiently. "On your knees scum," he growled. "Quicker!"

Tofik paid no attention to the commandant's words as he approached, watching him with big, dark, unblinking eyes. Loudly and with dignity he said, "You are scum yourself, Commandant; stinking scum. Know what? Stick that barrel up your ass— maybe you'll feel warmer, sort of frosty today."

With that he let loose a long full spit at the officer. It fell on one of Karamushev's boots. Tofik wiped his mouth with a hairy hand and turned his back on the commandant. He took several steps up the slope toward his barracks raising his arms for attention. Addressing the prisoners staring out of their barracks he shouted, "Brothers! Get the word outside! Jap bought and planned this whole bloody . . ." and that was as far as he got. Three machine-gun volleys tore his back from the right shoulder down to the left side, the bullets streaking through him, throwing lumps of flesh, fractured ribs and blood clots out of his powerful chest. His body-warmer smoked. His head fell backward, eyes staring at the sky; gray clouds and packs of crows already catching the scent of feeding rested in the last glimpse of his consciousness. He took one faltering step and fell face forward, dead before he hit the ground. One of the soldiers came closer and released another volley into the prostrate body. The torn bodywarmer caught fire from the phosphate rounds and started burning with pale, nearly invisible flames.

Suddenly a gasping soldier ran up to the commandant. "The doors in the jail are all smashed! Two guards are dead!"

Karamushev cursed loudly. "Everyone, after me!" He ran toward the jail building, the soldiers at his heels.

CHAPTER TWENTY-ONE

ugai limped towards the internal jail building, hauling Jap's
wounded six behind him, entering the main door just as
the soldiers outside began gunning down the last of the battle ravaged prisoners. Standing behind the thick metal gate he
heard the distinct rattle of machine-gun fire and realized that
something had gone wrong. It did not matter anymore, though. All
he wanted was to get the Jap.

"Can't you hear what's going on?" the six cried. "We better get
out before we're trapped and shot in here."

"Never mind that," Bugai roared. Bugai proceeded down the
stairs, the helpless six bouncing along behind him. He stopped at
a metal gate. Through the peephole he could see the stone stairs
descending to the innermost coldcell. He swung his pick at the
gate, methodically destroying the lock, and then threw his weight
against the door and forced his way through, barreling forward
until he reached a lowered portcullis at the bottom of the stairs.
The machine-gun fire was almost inaudible as he cranked the gate
of spears up and set the rachet.

The gargantuan Bugai slid under the spikes of the portcullis dragging the suffering six after him and found himself at the heavy oak door of Jap's sanctuary. Raising his pick he smashed the lock with a single blow, then he pushed the terrified six into the chamber.

"You go first," he ordered.

The six took only two steps before machine-gun fire streaked through the darkness of the hall. Green and red tracer bullets tore into him. He screamed as the impact of the rounds propelled him back out of the inner corridor to Bugai's feet.

"No guards, huh?" Bugai pressed his powerful body against the wall, his pickaxe clenched in both huge hands, knife in his teeth. Footsteps rang out in the cement hall and a guard, machine-gun in hand, sprang out of the corridor. Bugai swung almost immediately, catching him in the chest with his heavy pick. The flying body knocked a second guard off balance, blocking his weapon, and Bugai leapt forward thrusting his knife through the back-up guard's fur hat into his brow. The machine-gun chattered deafeningly for a moment, bullets bouncing off the the ceiling, as Bugai swung the pick into the guard's chest, killing him on the spot. Leaving the bloody heap of bodies behind him, ignoring their weapons—he preferred his knife— Bugai approached the Jap's cell. He tugged at the final door. It was open. He stumbled into the room, forgetting the pain where he had been stabbed in the buttock.

The comfortable cell was lit by a bulb hanging from the ceiling on its electric cord. The Jap was standing in the middle of the room, composed and silent, a gleaming *pchak* in his right hand. "Aha, fucking king, you are dead!" yelled Bugai poising himself for a charge.

"We will see." The Jap's face was calm.

Bugai lunged, slashing the space in front of him with wide, semicircular arcs of the knife. The Jap evaded the clumsy slashes and struck out himself, inflicting a long deep gash along the giant's right arm. Blood streamed from the wound as Bugai dropped the knife, yelled and sprang back.

He reached out and caught the Jap by the throat with his bleeding right arm. Jap felt himself being strangled. His vision blurred as he started to lose consciousness.

Then, as if in a dream, he saw Maria dash out of the sauna and reach into the glowing fireplace. She grabbed a burning log and lunged at Bugai from the side, jamming the fiery torch into his ear. His grip on Jap loosened and he bellowed like a wounded elephant as he dropped Jap and fell upon the woman, grasping her by the hair and giving her a hard blow in the face. But Maria remained on her feet; she was ready, clasping the knife Bugai had dropped. With a scream of rage she thrust the blade into his belly up to the knife's hilt. The bloody hulk stopped yelling and seized Maria by the throat. As Jap scrambled to his feet he heard something that sounded like a dry stick snapping. Snatching up his *pchak* from the floor he stabbed it into Bugai's neck.

Grabbing the massive head by the hair he cut one gash after the next into the bull neck. With skilled, deliberate slashes Jap proceeded to make an example that would forever preserve the legend of the Underground King in labor camp lore. Blood spurted upwards, Bugai's body convulsing, but not until Jap was clutching the severed head by the hair in his left hand did the knife chops cease. The head seemed almost alive, its features twisted as he threw it into the fireplace.

The bloody knife still in his hand, Jap knelt beside Maria's prostrate body. Her neck was broken and she was dying. Jap looked into her tear-filled eyes. She could not say a word as her lips fluttered and her eyes rolled back in her head. Jap looked numbly at her face. Not tears, but some kind of moisture appeared in his eyes, his heart still pounding wildly. He closed her eyes, his bloody fingers smearing her eyelids.

He was still sitting on the floor looking at her when Karamushev burst into the cell, gun in his hand, the guards after him. He stood shocked, bewildered at what he saw. Everything was smashed and broken. The commandant turned his head and met the staring eyes of the half-blackened skull among the smoldering logs in the fireplace.

CHAPTER TWENTY-TWO

Half an hour later Jap and the commandant were sitting comfortably in the unbloodied sauna cell. A half-empty bottle of vodka rested on the bench in front of them. Outside the guards were throwing the corpses onto open convoy trucks. Their orders were to burn all the dead in the crematorium.

"That fucking son of a bitch," Jap growled to Karamushev. "Poor Maria."

"I've seen a lot in my life but nothing like this."

"Where are the rest?"

"In hell . . . you may relax and be quiet. . . . It's okay now."

"I'm never quiet . . . maybe that's why I'm still alive . . . what's it like outside?"

"Heaps of corpses . . . total victory."

One hundred and ninety corpses lay in front of the barracks, staring into empty skies with frozen eyes. Another twenty-five dead were carried out of the barracks later. Thirty-eight men survived the massacre. Only one frayer, Fofa, was among them. Not a single six was left alive. Two thiefs had survived, the Jap and

Josik, who had been only wounded by Bugai's stab and lay in the snow quietly all through the shooting nestled between two corpses.

"Chief, I would like to go up to the sick room and see Josik before he is transported to the civilian hospital in Irkutsk."

Karamushev nodded, finished off the last of his drink and led Jap out of his cell.

In a bare cubicle designated as the infirmary on the first floor of the internal jail, Josik lay on a blood stained cot. Jap dragged a chair inside and sat down next to him.

"Well, you turned out to be much smarter than I thought," Jap said cheerfully. "Congratulations. You tricked those bloody fools in a most professional manner."

"Yeah, a professional with a hole in his belly. Hell, they scared the shit out of me!"

Josik let out a pained wheezing, both hands going to his wounded stomach. "When I am well and at-large again you will be the first thief I call—if you are also at-large," he added with a wink.

"You and Fofa who also survived and Volodya, we will all be together on the outside soon. But now, tell me. How did you make those two assholes, Maxim and Tofik, do such a wrong move as to ask Karamushev for assistance?"

"I told them you paid him five hundred thousand rubles to kill them in the cells. They pissed their pants and rushed to the commandant offering him twice as much to let them kill you. Later on he informed you and I guess doubled his income. Right?"

"Man, that was smart. Here," he held out a bottle. "I've brought you some cognac. You'll drink it after your belly is fixed in Irkutsk."

"And then come back here again," Josik lamented.

"When I'm out I'll try to get you a reduction in sentence to time served. We've got a big future."

"I feel like I've lost the best time in my life."

"That's not the way to look at it. The day you are released will be the first day of the rest of your life."

The barracks occupied by what was left of Jap's men was almost empty. Just twelve prisoners were resting on the boards. Several others, including Fofa, were in the civilian hospital. Only one hanging light bulb remained unbroken after the battle. It shed a dim yellow light on the cavernous brown interior. All labor in the camp had been curtailed because of the investigation and the prisoners lay on their berths staring indifferently into the dusk. Occasionally a few words of conversation drifted from one man to the next as they sat or lay smoking, exhausted and emotionally numb from their experiences. Even the possibility of additional sentences failed to scare them. The proverb "Jail—our native home" loomed large in their future.

Lazily, they discussed the jail building interrogations to which they were subjected every evening, confirming details of the evidence they were giving.

Directly under the single bulb Volodya was lying on his stomach, smoking a cigar he had rolled, heavily laced with *anasha*. He was naked to the waist as the camp artist, who had miraculously survived the massacre, was working on his back and shoulders creating an epic tattoo of a dragon seizing the winged devil by the throat. The legend depicted was of Japanese origin, exquisitely detailed as befitted the hero of two camp uprisings, and demanded endless patient hours and thousands of painful needle punctures. But Volodya felt nothing; the sweet and musky smoke rendered his head light and dizzy, as if he was flying somewhere above the dark nucleus of this slave hole among grey and white Siberian clouds.

Soon after the battle was so cruelly resolved Volodya had been brought by Karamushev to the underground king's cell. Jap had already heard about him from Fofa; they had a long talk. Volodya had never imagined that this notorious hardcore criminal, this king of thiefs, could be such a reasonable, quiet and wise man.

Jap appointed him a second frayer and gave him a certificate with his signature anointing him with the title of thief-in-the-law. This document was guaranteed to protect him more effectively than a gun in all camps and prisons. The crowning laurel was Jap's promise to get him out when the time was ripe and make Volodya part of the business empire he would be re-establishing.

Lying there, under the barracks bulb, smoking and feeling what seemed only feeble needle bites into his skin and the artist's breathing on his back, Volodya smiled in exhilaration. He was afraid of nothing anymore—he felt powerful, confident that he would break through all camps, jails and tortures. He would make it, he would be back and then he would become a major force in Jap's *organizatsyia*.

CHAPTER TWENTY-THREE

A t eleven o'clock in the evening Oksana had just finished cleaning her apartment after a small party for some institute friends when the doorbell rang. Apprehensively she crossed from the kitchen to the foyer. The memory of the three KGB officers who had raped her, first in their secret office in the Arbat and again in her apartment, was still strong even though she knew Pavel had disposed of the problem and she now had no enemies. Peering through the peephole she saw only a fish-eyed view of a lavish bouquet of flowers, red roses and white lilies. Cautiously she opened the door on the chain lock.

"I hope I am not disturbing you," came a soft male voice.

Oksana peered around the door at a vaguely familiar figure clad in a dark overcoat and fur hat. She opened the door and her visitor stepped inside, holding forth the flowers. He was a pleasant looking man with a friendly smile, but still she couldn't quite remember the face.

"May I come in?" he asked, standing just inside the threshold.

Then he handed the flowers to her and added, "I thought these might cheer up your apartment on a cold night."

"Thank you," she replied. "Yes, come in. But . . . what does this all mean? Do I know you? Are you one of Pavel's people?"

"Who, me?" He smiled and shook his head. "No. You have forgotten me but I have not forgotten you, nor have my colleagues. I am Major Boris Burenchuk, Militsia. Do you remember our last meeting at Petrovka 38?"

The apprehension returned but she held herself firm. "Oh yes. Of course. Come in. Will you take off your coat?"

Boris was wearing a brown three-piece suit and solid brown tie, very inconspicuous, like all plainclothes policemen. His eyes were soft and brown as well. She remembered that he had questioned her in a polite manner. "What do you want of me now? That was last October and here we are the end of March."

Oksana spent a few minutes separating the flowers into two smaller bouquets. Boris followed as she walked around the living room of the apartment placing them in vases. Oksana had tried to give a more feminine touch to her father's apartment by covering the dark furniture with brightly colored floral-designed slip covers.

"The flowers are beautiful," she said. "Thank you Major Burenchuk. I suppose there is a reason why the Militsia wishes to talk to me."

"Please, let's sit down. We have some matters to discuss." Boris looked about the room. "You have a cozy apartment."

Oksana gestured at the two chairs at her kitchen table. "Would you like some tea? Or maybe coffee?"

"Coffee, if you please. You had guests?"

"Yes."

"It's fun to have friends over, of course, but it is boring to do the cleaning afterwards; my wife is always unhappy about that side of entertaining at home."

Oksana heated a kettle and made two cups of instant coffee. Then, sitting down with him at the table, she asked, "What is the intrigue behind this strange and pleasant visit by an almost unknown man?"

"Very nicely put," Boris replied chewing on a leftover sandwich and putting cream and sugar into his coffee. "Intrigue is certainly present. We have to discuss a serious problem which concerns both of us—me in a professional way and you—personally."

"As I remember," she affected an apologetic smile, "I wasn't able to be much help when we met in your office."

"But perhaps now you know more and can help me." He reached into his suit coat pocket and pulled out a small red ID card. She glanced at the picture and read his name. "I know, presenting identification and all seems pompous. In reality lots of guys wipe their feet over me—District KGB, General Prosecutor, my own boss, Colonel Nechiaev and some hoods from organized crime too—such as Jap or even Pavel."

Oksana felt as if struck in the face. So that's it! And she was stupid enough to mention Pavel right at the door. Boris decided to lessen the impact and gently tapped Oksana on the knee.

"Now, now, do not be so shocked. I just want to talk and perhaps make a few things clear. I could have invited you over to my premises of course, but I thought about it and decided it would be more relaxing for you if we visited here. Want a cigarette?"

She nodded and he produced a pack of Marlboros. She accepted a cigarette which he lit for her. "I'm trying to stop smoking," he explained as he put the pack away without taking one himself. "Now—since I last talked with you about what the press are calling 'the Arbat massacre,' I interviewed the dean of the institute and his testimony was in total contradiction with what you told me. You had a bitter conflict with Marat and with the dean and were on the verge of being expelled for some obscure reason involving Marat when suddenly the KGB boy changed his mind and advised the dean to leave you in the institute."

Boris gave her a long quizzical look. "Maybe you can tell me why he changed his intentions so abruptly?"

"I do not know. I had no conflict with the dean and no conflict with Marat."

"I suppose we could ask the dean about it in your presence but this is a mere trifle in comparison with what followed." Again the sympathetic but questioning expression came to his face. "As you must know a small lie can give birth to a big suspicion. You see, Marat made the call to the dean literally five minutes before the explosion that burned him to cinders. We made a special check to discover this remarkable timing. The dean remembered the moment well. He had just turned off a football game on television. We never asked you any questions at that time since our investigation showed far more serious people were involved in the case." He paused a moment staring speculatively at her. "Since then we have monitored your activities."

"You chose an uninteresting time in my life to follow me," Oksana commented.

"Yes, the last few months have not been very adventurous from a romantic point of view," Boris agreed. "Quite frankly, by the time KGB opened up to us and we were able to learn the identities of the victims and then trace their associates, it appears that we missed a memorable visit you made to your home in Irkutsk."

Oksana felt confused and defensive. "Is it so strange I should visit my father?" she asked. "Even though he comes to the meetings of the Deputies in Moscow from time to time I enjoy going home where my mother and I were so close until she died during a bad Siberian winter."

"I am sorry about your mother. Your father should have sent her to the Crimea to spend the winter."

"She was devoted to him and wouldn't be away from him." Oksana sighed. "I am beginning to realize how much he depended upon her. He turned into a different man after she died. I visit him when I can."

"Oh, you went to your father's home all right but you also visited a very strange place for a young girl, Tulun labor camp. And confined there is a very interesting man who we fear will soon be released."

"Yes, I visited Slava Yakovlev. I know his wife. It was a social visit. I brought him some food and wine to make his prison life more comfortable."

"And news from the outside, no doubt. Also you probably conveyed instructions from Yakovlev to his frayer, Pavel."

"Are you accusing me of something?" Oksana asked belligerently.

Boris held up a hand as if to ward off her anger. "Let me go on. While you were at home your dad had several meetings with a man you mentioned just now when I came in—that is with Pavel. So, dad and a notorious thief-in-the-law had long discussions but finally came to terms and it all ended in a nice supper in Irkutsk's fashionable restaurant for Party officials. Then you returned to Moscow."

"You seem to have spent an inordinate amount of time investigating me when you could have been chasing criminals."

Boris smiled. "On the train to and from Irkutsk a very strange man accompanied you all the way. I understand that you may not know who he was but through research we found out that he is Mikhail Chichladze. You call him Misha. He fought bravely in Afghanistan killing, apart from Mojaheeds, also women and children by rather intricate tortures. He is still wanted by the International Commission on Human Rights. He worked for Pavel and has now become part of the criminal crew operated by Givi Gigauri, an underboss for the late Tofik, a thief-in-the-law recently killed in the Tulun uprising."

"But what does that have to do with me?" Oksana struggled to keep her voice from trembling.

"Perhaps nothing."

"If you are insinuating that Misha and I had any kind of relationship—"

Boris raised his hands. "No, no! Certainly not. In fact you have led a surprisingly celibate existence for a woman so young and beautiful. It is almost as though you had been seriously abused by a man, or men, and wanted no more to do with them. We interviewed another girl who had been expelled from the institute. She too had worked at the Russia Hotel. Marat tried unsuccessfully to coerce her into playing dirty games with him and his superiors."

"Marat was an animal." Her voice rose. "I am glad he is dead!"

"Our surveillance of the street phones near your apartment fixed conversations with Nadia Bolshokova, a professional prostitute and close associate of Pavel."

Oksana struggled to keep her tone level. "Why are you telling all this to me?"

"It seems that Jap, Vyacheslav Yakovlev, may be released from prison far ahead of schedule. In fact in the next month. Many powerful party officials have come together to work for his liberation. Among them is the First Secretary from Irkutsk, your father." Again Boris fixed her with his unblinking gaze. After a moment he continued. "I came to the conclusion that you are a reasonable girl and your connection to these gangsters is tenuous at most. I have no intention of frightening or harming you; in fact I could have put you behind the bars of an interrogation chamber some time ago."

"Should I be grateful?"

"Woman's prison is a rather nasty place for a young girl. I would never have allowed you to be held so much as an hour. Besides, if you were arrested your so-called friends would be alarmed and might even make attempts to get rid of you. After all you are not part of their crew, just an amateur."

"You want some more coffee?" Oksana asked brightly, postponing the issue.

"Yes." He smiled wryly. "My throat is dry after all this talk." Oksana composed herself as she went to the stove and turned up the heat under the kettle, standing with her back to the detective as she made two more cups of instant coffee. Then she returned to the table, sitting down with Boris. He took a long swallow of the coffee and reiterated his earlier statement. "I am not going to arrest you, or press charges against you, or anything of that sort. But I do want your help."

Oksana put her cup down and stared silently at Boris.

"You know what's going on with the crews of Jap and Pavel. From the moment Jap gets back you will know at least a little of his plans. Keep me informed."

Oksana stared incredulously at the Militsia major.

"I cannot tell you what I don't know."

"So the killer Chichladze, your Georgian bodyguard—"

"I have not laid eyes on him since my return from Irkutsk," Oksana shot back.

"So this Misha will continue to walk around the streets and even if we find him Jap and Pavel, or Givi, who he now apparently serves, will recruit other cutthroats—"

"I told you, Major," her voice rose, "I know nothing of this business. Now please leave me alone. I have worked very hard to become an interpreter. That is all that interests me."

"Whether or not you are interested, you are involved with Jap and Pavel at his side," Boris gently insisted.

"No!" Oksana protested.

"Someone must have passed on orders from Jap to bomb the suite of Givi's men at the Russia Hotel."

Oksana shook her head in shock at the implied accusation. In a quiet tone Boris continued. "You must have heard how Jap provoked a bloody riot at Tulun. About two hundred prisoners were killed . . ."

"I'm sorry to hear that, but what have I to do with such an incident?"

"Maybe during your visit with Jap he said something that if reported could have avoided that massacre."

"You are the Militsia; you catch the criminals—that's your job!"

"But we need the help of observant law-abiding citizens to do our job effectively," Boris replied.

"When I was going through hard times, when I wanted to die, nobody helped me but Nadia."

"And Pavel," Boris added. "I am not asking you anything super-human, just for information."

"You want to make of me some sort of Militsia spy?"

Boris realized she was right. That was just what he was trying to do. "I truly want to be your friend, Oksana." He could not disguise how physically attractive he found her. "But you must look at this situation realistically."

Oksana started to protest but Boris held up a hand. "I have found at least two other young women cruelly mistreated by these," the acid tinged words came out, "these 'warriors of the invisible frontier.'"

Oksana was staring at him wide-eyed, her hands trembling as Boris continued. "Perhaps someone went too far when Marat was forced to instruct the dean to take you back, just five minutes before the explosion. That gave us much to think about."

Seeing she was shaken, Boris tried to be gentle. "Remember, I can't prove your involvement in this affair. I won't even try to prove it or investigate it further. But I need your help in the days ahead with Yakovlev about to be set at-large. For instance, what will be his next criminal enterprise? There is much you could tell me that would make my work easier."

Oksana suddenly pulled herself erect. "Major Boris Burenchuk, I am an interpreter in English and German, not a criminal informant. I'm a grown woman. This is my last word." She smiled faintly. "More coffee?"

Boris stood up, looking at Oksana gloomily for a few seconds. "No thanks. I've had enough. The moment will come when you need my assistance." He reached into his pocket and pulled out a calling card, laying it on the table. "You can reach me twenty-four hours a day at this number. Don't be too late asking me for help. And as a matter of fact I may be in touch with you. We have American visitors from time to time who need interpreters."

"I will be most happy to help you in that way. And thank you for the flowers. They are beautiful."

A sad smile came to his face. "It is a pity we did not come to a meeting of the minds but I will try to see that you have no trouble with the Militsia."

"What about the surveillance?"

"This is our professional decision to make."

"Aha, that's nice. Are you any better than KGB?"

"Yes, I am sure you'll agree we are. One more thing . . ."

"Yes?"

"Do not be silly enough to inform your 'friends' about our conversation, do not even hint to them about it—or you'll see that I am right about them much sooner than you might expect. Your bodyguard, Misha, could end up your killer. Have a good night."

After Boris left, Oksana urgently wanted to take a handful of *kopecks* and go out into the street to a telephone booth, but she realized that she was probably under surveillance. Somehow she had to reach Nadia secretly the next morning.

She was realizing more and more that when you accept the help of people like Pavel, repayment is never completed. Slava Yakovlev was coming out of prison soon, and like it or not, she would find herself in the middle of the sort of intrigue she had never wanted to be part of in her life.

CHAPTER TWENTY-FOUR

The Moscow Militsia officers waited eagerly for the eulogy to the alcoholic, drug addicted, notorious despoiler of young girls who founded Chekka, their parent organization. Its offering would mean the end of the interminable speech by General Major Nickolai Myrikov, Chief of Moscow Militsia. At last, to their relief, it came. "And as our brilliant and brave founder, Felix Edmondovitch Dzerzshinsky used to say, 'I must go now to consult with the politicians.'"

Myrikov nodded to grey-thatched, bushy-browed, ruddy-complexioned General Alexi Bodaev, commander of the Militsia Criminal Brigade, sitting beside him as he pushed back his chair and stood up. "I leave this meeting in the capable hands of the Deputy Commander."

Gen. Bodaev also stood up. "We wish you success with the Justice Minister and prosecutor, Comrade General Major."

Myrikov looked around the ornate Grand Conference Room of the Interior Ministry building at Petrovka 38, a hopeless expression momentarily crossing his face. "For two months I have been

215

arguing against the release of Yakovlev." The police chief shook his head. "He seems to have many powerful friends in high places. If I cannot convince the minister he is unleashing a one-man crime wave on Moscow by allowing a reduction of Jap's sentence, we here will have very little rest in the coming years. Yes indeed, wish me luck."

Myrikov walked the length of the wide blue, red and gold Persian carpet stretching out under the majestic, highly polished mahogany conference table and onto the parquet floor. He approached the double doors that gave entrance and exit to the formal meeting room with its three crystal chandeliers evenly spaced and hanging from the ceiling.

The chief strode through the doors, which were closed after him as Bodaev took over direction of the meeting. His officers noticed his eyes lifting to the center chandelier directly over his head. It was as close as he ever came to acknowledging the fact that the KGB department of Militsia Control maintained close electronic surveillance of activities throughout Petrovka 38. Then he gestured at Boris Burenchuk, as usual dressed in a meticulously tailored brown suit and tasteful tie.

"Before I close the meeting have you anything to report on the Arbat case?"

Boris allowed himself a quick tight smile as his eyes lifted to the center chandelier. "I am still carrying out my assignment to identify the killers of the three KGB officers. Recently I met with Oksana Martinova at her apartment."

"I would like to talk to Martinova in her apartment," someone chuckled.

Boris frowned. "If we do anything at all to intimidate her, we will lose a woman who can help us," he cautioned.

Colonel Vladimir Nechiaev, the Sly Fox, looked up at the chandelier and smirked. "Yes, Major Burenchuk, we all appreciate the efforts you are making to catch the killer of those three brave KGB officers."

Bodaev nodded. "Any questions or remarks? Meeting dismissed."

Wordlessly the detectives followed Nechiaev from the conference room down the long hall to his inner office. "Is it secure in here, Taki?" Nechiaev asked.

"I guarantee it." The slender, youthful man with thick, neatly combed black hair smiled. The butt of an automatic handgun poked from the shoulder holster he wore under his right arm.

Major Yuri Navakoff, Americanski, stepped into the office closely followed by Col. Alexander Kamerov, General Bodaev's deputy. In contrast to his boss, under whom he held the title of deputy, Kamerov was heavy set and tall, with an air of geniality lighting up his wide, ruddy features. "I will report back to General Bodaev under secure circumstances what we discuss now." Sly Fox walked to a cabinet behind his desk and brought out a bottle of vodka. Taki found a set of glasses and put them out on the conference table which formed a T with the desk.

Nechiaev poured vodka into the glasses and held up his glass. The others followed his example. "Fuck KGB and all their corrupt hangmen."

"KGB mother fuckers," Americanski agreed.

"KGB eat shit," Kamerov said matter-of-factly.

"KGB eat pussy of whores." Taki brandished his electronic surveillance detector which insured the privacy of conversations held in the room.

Yuri Navakoff picked up his drink and downed it silently. Sly Fox poured shots of vodka into the glasses of the detectives gathered in his office as he explained to a newcomer from the Regional Militsia, the necessity of avoiding all sensitive talk in the grand meeting room, or any other part of Petrovka 38 that is not swept for electronic surveillance at least once a day.

"KGB reports against us whenever it can discover something it considers anti-Soviet we might do," Nechiaev warned the neophyte. "We know that Jap has many powerful associates among deputies, the PolitBureau, and even in KGB. After all, it was

Merkushev, Assistant Chairman of Supreme Court of Russian Federation, who pleaded successfully before the Presidium of Moscow City Court for Yakovlev's early release. Now that Jap is about to get out and assume leadership of his *organizatsyia* once again, we must take great care not to let KGB know of procedures on our part against him."

"You'd think they don't want us to catch the people that killed their officers," Yuri remarked.

"May I remind you it is the duty of KGB to keep us from uncovering incriminating evidence against any high-ranking Communist Party official," Kamerov replied. "Jap owns many People's Deputies and PolitBureau members."

"Including Nickolai Martinov, I gather," Sly Fox commented.

"What keeps those few of us honest who really care about the Militsia?" Yuri Navakoff, Americanski, asked in disgust.

"Fear of each other if one of us turned." The glint in Sly Fox's eyes reflected his statement.

The door from the anteroom opened slowly as Colonel Nechiaev looked up to see who was entering his office without a signal from his man on the reception desk. Boris Burenchuk stood there smiling, a paper bag under one arm. The public affairs officer had created a unique position for himself within the structure of the Militsia at Petrovka 38. He was too much of a politician and diplomat to be totally trusted by suspicious policemen, yet he alone of the Militsia officers enjoyed entree to each one of the many spheres of power and influence that revolved around Ministry of Interior police operations.

His very acceptance by the KGB officials who monitored operations at Petrovka 38 made him suspect among his peers. Yet it was Boris to whom they turned for help and advice in the sensitive situations that were constantly arising. Cross currents of intrigue and conspiracy characterized all internal security operations. It was Boris's ability to understand and manage these undercurrents that caused the particularly vexing case of the Arbat massacre to be entrusted into his care.

Also it was Boris Burenchuk who directed the news released to a voracious army of journalists springing up in the new attitude of openness championed by President Gorbachev in his Glasnost and Perestroika philosophy. It was Boris who decided which individuals would be recognized in the media and what would be said about them. Good press, in Moscow, as in the West, could enhance police careers, so he was valuable to all.

Since Boris was a good source of information to the Chief of Detectives concerning operations in other bureaus in the Ministry of Interior, Sly Fox had to assume that Boris might trade information regarding modus operandi of the detective division. In short, Major Burenchuk was an officer to be cultivated and at the same time treated with caution. On one matter in particular, the women of Moscow's demimonde, he was recognized as sophisticated beyond the most-seasoned officers at Petrovka 38. Trust a Uke, as they referred to his Ukrainian ethnicity, to have that sector under control.

The Chief of Detectives greeted Boris genially. "Ah, Boris, just in time for a shot of vodka."

Boris smiled and shook his head placing the paper bag on a table by the door. Unlike his colleagues he was a moderate drinker who preferred beer and wine, and even then in modest amounts, to hard liquor. His moderation compounded the suspicious attitude toward him on the part of some of his comrades.

"What can you do for us?" Nechiaev asked with a smile.

"What are we doing about Yakovlev, the Jap?" Boris shot back.

"You have a special interest in him?" Nechiaev asked.

"I am getting to know the beautiful daughter of one of his benefactors in the PolitBureau. I can tell you exactly what happened at the Arbat and who did it but we have the problem of proof. There is no doubt in my mind that Oksana was abused, probably gang raped, a favorite KGB custom. Through her prostitute friend,

Nadia, she met and traded to Pavel her father's influence on Jap's behalf for the killing of the three officers who did it to her."

"You know that is so but you will never prove it," Sly Fox declared. "With Jap we are dealing with a high order of criminal intelligence." He laughed harshly. "As our public prosecutor recently commented, there are no PolitBureau members in organized crime management, there is no room for incompetence in that society."

"I can learn much about Jap, given the time and freedom to operate on my own initiative," Boris offered. "Nickolai, father of Oksana Martinova, is now close to Jap and you can be sure that Oksana, who visited him in Tulun, will know what he is doing when he is released."

"Is Oksana another of your girlfriends?" Americanski asked.

"These women are my friends; we help each other." He turned a reproachful look on Yuri Navakoff. "But you know it is no more than that. This department has had me followed by various clumsy oxen. I always go home to my family when the day's work is done, or the night's work completed."

"What are you suggesting?" Nechiaev asked.

"If you want to find out more about Jap, Oksana can help me."

"Why would she help you?"

"Because she is scared and I will be her friend. She knows I am aware of her part in the Arbat massacre. And even though she also knows I can't prove it, she would not want me to try. She's an English interpreter. I will get her important interpreting jobs."

"Nickolai Martinov," Nechiaev mused. "Yes, one of the Polit-Bureau members who profited from the sale of Scud missiles to Iraq."

Sasha Kamerov chuckled mirthlessly. "So today we have hundreds of very rich party leaders."

"And there is nothing we can do about such corruption," Yuri commented hopelessly, holding out his empty glass. Sly Fox immediately filled all the glasses. Only Boris refused.

"*Nasarovia!*" Nechiaev tossed down his drink. Then to Boris he said, "What are you suggesting about Oksana Martinova?"

"She will tell me what Yakovlev is doing."

Yuri Navakoff grinned lewdly. "She can translate for me any night she is free."

Boris glared across the table. "I repeat what I said earlier. If we scare her, we lose her." He stood up pointing to the paper bag he had brought in. "When you run out of vodka be my guest."

CHAPTER TWENTY-FIVE

The Militsia and Internal Affairs investigating contingent at Tulun went into a state of shock when the release decree for Yakovlev, V.K. arrived at the prison. Fiercely they cursed the dumbheads in the Supreme Court, wondering how to conduct the investigation without the chief participant in the whole affair present. Jap, meantime, was standing at the entrance to the camp control post. The huge, black American car that some months before had brought Oksana Martinova to Tulun for her visit with Jap was now waiting to take him away.

Karamushev had already been relieved of his post in the Tulun Camp administration but was still in his uniform and running the internal jail until his replacement officer arrived. Now he was saying good-bye to Jap.

"Karamushev," Jap said quietly, "I want you to do me one last favor."

"What sort of favor?"

"Find the grave of Maria in the women's camp. Remove it and

223

place it outside of the camp. You are a rich man. I want you to put up a monument to her."

"A monument? To this slut?"

Jap's eyes flashed dangerously and his face contorted into a reflection of deadly umbrage. Karamushev hastily stepped back and changed his tone.

"What kind of a monument Vyacheslav Kyrillovitch?"

"Of course she was a slut," Jap muttered. "But Maria was a woman, a real woman. She made life bearable, even pleasant. And in the end she saved my life at the price of her own." He nodded to himself as though saying a final prayer, if indeed he was capable of such an act.

"Let it be a monument to a woman whose life was maimed by the bloody system," Jap declaimed. "A system which turned her into a slut, but could never wipe out her humanity. Do it for me, Karamushev, and send a photo to my Moscow address."

"Well . . . okay, sure. No big deal. I'll do that."

Jap gave a last look at the labor camp in which he had spent the past nine years. The noxious cloud no longer hovered above the smoke stack of the crematorium. After the uprising it had accomplished several years' worth of consumption in a matter of days, incinerating the bodies before the investigators from Moscow could reach distant Tulun. Although a surprising number of shapeless lead pellets were discovered in the tile and iron retorts, there was no effort made to prove they were melted bullets, aftermath of the massive indiscriminate shooting of over two hundred prisoners.

Standing beside the car's back door was Jap's frayer, Pavel, who Major Karamushev had met in the days before Brezhnev's son-in-law, Gen. Yuri Churbanov, had himself fallen behind the bars. Yuri had arranged unlimited visiting and communications privileges for Jap with Pavel and his other associates. That was all rescinded when Churbanov himself was incarcerated. Nobody, least of all Jap, had ever imagined his stay at Tulun would last nine years. Now, as he left the camp, Jap was dressed in a perfectly tailored, handsome fur coat and fine leather gloves. "Well, Jap," Karamushev was saying, "no hard feelings. We had almost ten years together and I can't say they were the worst in my life. I hope you have no complaints about mistreatment."

"Commandant, dear, you are a real man. And do not pay any attention to those jerks on the commission. Enjoy your money and laugh at them. Everything left in the cell is yours, TV sets, video players, any carpets which are not"—he cleared his throat—"contaminated if you know what I mean, there was all too much toward the end. Take it all, as a present apart from everything else, in memory of our friendship."

"Thank you, Jap. You are the only thief-in-the-law I ever admired. You know why? You do it all not for the sake of some bloody 'law', but to live beautifully. These other suckers—Maxim, Potma, Tofik—what did they live for? They lived like dogs and died like that, too. Only Tofik, perhaps—yeah, he was a man. He did not blink an eye under the barrel and spat in the end. Yeah . . . well, to hell with that."

Jap took a step toward the shiny black automobile waiting for him then he turned back another moment.

"One last matter, Commandant. I have heard a rumor that some of the survivors of my gang, Volodya and Fofa, may be transferred to Krasnogulag 86. Please don't let this happen."

"I'll try to oppose such a move but my powers are severely limited now."

"At least let me or Pavel know if this happens."

"I'll get word to you, Jap."

"Yes, let me know." With that Jap walked to the large sedan.

Karamushev looked after the car as it drove away, his eyes following the gleaming machine until it disappeared around a curve in the road, concealed by the tall fir trees surrounding Tulun camp. Now he too could leave this place of the damned forever and look forward to living wherever he liked, his wife had already picked out a place in the Crimea, as far from Siberia as a Russian could go.

Jap sat back comfortably in the spacious interior of the big American car. Pavel leaned forward and from a bar built into the back of the front seat he removed a decanter of cognac and two globe-shaped goblets. He filled them both, handed one to Jap, and replacing the bottle leaned back beside him.

"Magnificent car," Jap remarked. "Hard to believe such a machine exists in this part of the world."

Pavel smiled enigmatically. "You will meet the owner in about two hours, when we reach Irkutsk."

"Oksana's father?" Jap asked.

"Who else but the First Secretary? We will be guests at his apartment in Irkutsk until we return to Moscow."

"I look forward to meeting this benefactor you have discovered so I can thank him myself for all he has done."

"And he will do a great deal more as you will learn before our dinner with him tonight is over," Pavel chuckled.

For the two hours it took to reach Irkutsk, Pavel brought Jap up to date on all their enterprises. Jap was shocked to hear that Chechen, without orders, had killed four more of Givi's men, two of them sixes, at the Hotel Russia in Moscow.

"And where is Chechen now?"

"He has gone to the bottom until you decide his fate."

Jap thought about it and sipped his cognac. "So we have done in six of Tofik's men, and Tofik himself died in the uprising."

"For which you are personally blamed," Pavel added. "And it's seven of Tofik's men we killed. Victor sent a shooter to New York to kill Edward who was trying to undercut us with the North Koreans."

Jap shook his head. "No wonder they tried to kill me. What is Givi going to do about it when he knows I am back?"

"Givi and Victor should be having a peace meeting today. It is to the advantage of all of us to avoid war right now."

"Most important at this moment is, have you made all the preparations for the meeting with the managing director of Krasnov 86?"

"Nickolai Martinov set it up. Yevgeny Volkov will meet us tomorrow morning at the Dome nuclear facility."

"And the other?"

"It took us several days, but we located his family and have them covered," Pavel chortled.

"Good. We couldn't go near the Dome otherwise. Hamster is what Galina Brezhneva called Volkov because he's fat and furry. He would love to get the drop on me, as the Americans say."

An anticipatory gleam came to his eye. "I look forward to seeing Oksana again."

"Yes, but first Olga has planned a dinner for you with close friends. And Victor will be there. By then he should have made peace with Givi who wants it as much as we do. My best trump six, from the restaurant business, Hakim, will work all day to prepare this feast."

Jap laughed aloud. "So my old Kazakh friend, Jap the second, is still with us?"

Pavel also laughed. "Yes, the guests will not know who is the waiter and who the master."

"I should have sent Hakim to Tulun in my place," Jap muttered. "Nobody would know the difference from our pictures." He paused, then, "Tell me everything you can about Oksana's father. He did much to get my early release."

"For a huge part of your *obshak*." Pavel shrugged. "But useful as Nikolai Martinov has been to us up to now, he will be even more important when we start our main operation. So far he has collected a full lemon from us in cash and diamonds and—"

"It's the best use we have ever put our money to," Jap growled.

"I'm glad you feel that way. I leave it to you to discuss with him how much we must pay for the nukes."

"We should have a very interesting conversation with Nickolai tonight." Jap nodded and sat back, sipping from the glass of cognac held in his right hand.

CHAPTER TWENTY-SIX

⋘⋙

The morning after his release from Tulun Labor Camp Jap stood with Pavel and Nickolai Martinov at the edge of the former sports club turned helicopter pad in a remote residential area of Irkutsk. Waiting for the helicopter to transport them to their destination, Martinov started to explain about the Dome.

"Yeah, yeah," Jap mused aloud. "A nice place. The only threat that terrified the guys at Tulun was a transfer to Krasnogulag 86." The chuffing of rotor blades sounded in the distance.

Nickolai watched the helicopter settle in. "The residents of the secret city, Krasnov 86, at the base of the Dome, call the privileged administrators who live here in Irkutsk and come in from the heavens everyday the 'screw winged angels.'" Then, with a frown, he observed, "Yevgeny Ivanovitch did not send the executive dragonfly for us?"

As the green military helicopter landed and they were escorted to the middle of the field by a civilian aide, the rotor blades continued to turn lazily until the three men were seated in the passenger area behind the pilot and copilot. The turbine engine immediately went into high pitch, the rotors began whirling and the aircraft rose from the ground in a deafening shriek of power. The helicopter reached its altitude and headed northeast away from the city. The clear blue waters of Lake Baikal stretching out below to the horizon belied the insidious pollution of the chemical waste and bacterial effluent discharged from the cellulose plants and factories that had sprung up since World War II along the hundreds of miles of the lake's shoreline.

After almost an hour's flight, the rim of a vast wasteland of shattered rock appeared ahead of the helicopter. Intense blasting for ten years under the mountain created the secret underground factory five square kilometers in area and three kilometers from top to bottom below the mountain's surface. Hollowing out the mountain had also spawned an ecological disaster of over twenty square miles in which no vegetation of any kind, no animals or birds could survive. As many as one hundred thousand prisoners had perished in the construction of the secret uranium mines, plutonium processing plants, nuclear warhead and missile manufacturing facilities, all contained in the gigantic arcane Dome. Dozens of elevator shafts and sixty kilometers of passages connected the ten levels of weapons manufacturing facilities. A railroad wound from the outside, into and through the monstrous manmade cavern.

At first prisoners slaved and died, but later they were replaced by the twenty thousand highly paid skilled workers and their dependents who lived in the secret city of Krasnov 86, the lone habitable refuge in the midst of the accumulation of waste and rubble resulting from the Dome's construction. All were indulgently employed by the Dome, in and around which two thousand guards provided security. The Krasnogulag, situated in the midst of the rocky wilderness, supplied the labor camp prisoners consigned to the plutonium and uranium high radiation processing chambers.

The helicopter began its descent into the elevated center of crushed stone covering most of the visible landscape below. The chopping of the engine and blades, unfettered by any semblance of sound proofing material within the fuselage prevented conversation until once again the helicopter was on the ground and the blades above revolved in gentle arcs.

Jap, followed by Pavel and Martinov, stepped out of the helicopter. From the landing pad they looked out over the panorama of rock-strewn plain spreading in all directions. Guards along the rim of the pad secured the area and watched over other helicopters. The young aide who had accompanied them strode toward the terminal building perched on the rocky summit of the Dome.

After a telephone call he beckoned them to follow him into the cement and brick terminal where they faced a wall dominated by three sets of sliding double doors. One of the doors slid open and their escort gestured them in and pressed a red button. The doors closed and the elevator smoothly dropped into the depths of the granite mountain. Jap looked around silently. Three sides of the car were adorned with mirrors and polished redwood. It was definitely a car that would stop at the office of an important director in the economic and manufacturing Soviet hierarchy.

Yevgeny Ivanovitch Volkov sat at his desk on the top level of the Dome waiting for the arrival of his visitors. Two kilometers below him was stored one of the Soviet Union's largest reserves of nuclear material. The exact size of the volatile cache was known only to him and a few of his subordinates.

Volkov's office was not large but it was well-equipped. A telephone console was capable of putting him in instant communication with any of his assistants and units. There was a direct line to the Minister of Defense in the Kremlin. He also maintained direct lines to the various presidents of the important republics within the Soviet Union who supplied him with fissionable material.

One of his office walls was actually the sliding door of the elevator to the helicopter pad on the surface of the mountain above.

All his life he had been an obedient, albeit well-rewarded, performer of orders given by political superiors. Soon, he felt, the opportunity would arrive for making the enormous personal profits he had dreamed of since his days in the court of Princess Galina Brezhneva. That was the purpose of this meeting. An internal phone buzzed. He picked up the receiver. It was his director of helicopter operations announcing the arrival of the First Secretary of the Region and his associates.

"Bring them down," Volkov ordered. He had been shocked to hear he would be meeting a businessman, one V.K. Yakovlev. But it was not an uncommon name and probably the man wasn't actually the Jap. But now, looking at the visitors on the closed circuit television screen as they walked into the elevator bank, Volkov recognized the slightly oriental features of Jap himself. The director had heard that Yakovlev had been sent to the labor camps but paid no attention until this moment. What happened in Moscow, if it reached his attention at all, usually came in a garbled state. Now he realized that Jap had indeed fallen behind the bars, was presently at-large, and under the protection of Martinov. This would be an interesting meeting indeed. Volkov resolved to make a controlled effort not to let his hatred of the notorious criminal warp his business judgement.

The door slid open and Nickolai Martinov, followed by Jap and Pavel, stepped into the brightly illuminated office of the director of the Dome complex. Volkov was standing behind his desk, a cunning look on his face with its thick heavy cheeks and short crooked nose. Small eyes almost hidden behind swollen lids, his greasy thin black hair combed straight back, he indeed resembled his mentor, Leonid Brezhnev. "Nickolai," he greeted the Irkutsk First Secretary, "a pleasure to see you again." Then to their escort, "Secretary, thank you for bringing my guests to me. Now you can please leave us alone and see that we are not disturbed." The secretary melted back into the elevator which closed immediately.

"Yevgeny, meet my associates from Moscow. This is—"

"No need to introduce our dear guests," the director interrupted. "I know the Jap," he said and then to Jap, "How long is it since we last met?"

"It's a small world, Director," Jap replied. "And it has been a long time."

"What's wrong, Yevgeny?" Martinov was startled at the cold look on the director's face.

"I told you, Nickolai, you must find the right people for this delicate business! Do you know who you have brought to me?"

"Come now, Director," Jap said airily, "look where you are. In the end you came out the winner. And I can tell you that between Nickolai and my associate," he gestured at Pavel, "you will make millions in hard currency American dollars. Surely that is more interesting than nursing a grudge from another time, another era that no longer exists."

"You know each other?" Martinov was surprised at the electric recognition factor between two men he thought he was introducing for the first time. Jap laughed easily. "I guess Hamster and I both owe such success as we've known in life to Leonid Brezhnev. And you can say the same, Nickolai."

"Hamster?" Martinov questioned, a puzzled look on his face.

"That's what Galina called him because he was fat and furry." Jap ignored the look of annoyance on Volkov's face. "So how's life treating you, Director?" Jap produced a cigarette. He pulled a chair in front of the table and sat in it, Pavel following his example.

"What brings you to our secret dome?" Volkov's tone was sharp.

"Business." Jap lit his cigarette. "Would you mind giving me the ashtray over there?"

Volkov slid the ashtray toward Jap. "Help yourself. What kind of business, may I inquire?" the director asked, knowing that Martinov must have discussed the possibilities with Jap at length.

"Things are changing. Great opportunities are ahead of us." Jap's whole demeanor brimmed with enthusiasm and optimism.

"After all, what small amount did you get when you made it possible for Gorby the Purse and his supporters on the PolitBureau to sell three thousand unregistered SK-14 missiles, Scuds as they're known, and the launchers and the tonka fuel for them, to Saddam Hussein?" Jap smiled at the look of surprise that came over Volkov's face as he glanced at Martinov.

Drily the director of the Dome managed to say, "You seem to be well-informed considering where you have been recently."

Jap ignored the statement. "I anticipated our past disagreements could be a problem today. But in an hour my associates and I are leaving your Dome with a made deal and an understanding about our future transactions, which will make you almost as rich as Gorby himself."

"I am listening, Jap," Volkov replied.

"When the Communist Party falls, as it must, and we are running things, my associates and I will become your biggest customers. We will buy the missiles, the nuclear warheads, the plutonium 239, and the enriched uranium from you directly and resell it internationally. This is not something you can do personally, nor can the PolitBureau or even the president. We will be the businessmen who make these deals."

"Do you think I will die from the necessity of bargaining with you? For my stuff, when the time comes, I will always find customers."

"And we can easily buy what we want in Ukraine. A hundred or more Russian-hating Ukes have missiles and warheads under their control."

Volkov flashed a cunning smile. "True. But none of the Ukrainians know the firing code to the missiles in their charge."

Jap shrugged. "Well, right now I am prepared to buy three buttons of plutonium 239 from you and take them back to Moscow as proof to certain foreign businessmen that at the right moment we will be able to deliver whatever we promise."

Volkov stared at Jap aghast. "Sell plutonium to you? One button, ten grams, combined with merely conventional explosive—plastic, TNT, even dynamite—is enough to make half a mile, say in the center of a city, radiation poisonous for a year."

"For the right amount of money? Of course you'll sell. What about the SK-14s?"

"That was on direct secret orders from the president. I'm the boss here and you made a serious mistake in coming."

Jap shrugged. "I do not think so, Hamster." He leaned forward and flicked his cigarette at the ashtray.

Volkov glared across his desk. "I was in doubt what to do with you when you first came in here. I could call the guards. They'll take you out and shoot your heads off for attempting to penetrate a secret state enterprise. I will question them on the incident, scold them for being too quick, and then sign their vacation papers for five days."

"Strange," Jap turned to Pavel. "Why just five days? In the camps they get a ten day vacation for shit like that."

"I see. You do not believe me?" Volkov was grinning.

Jap shook his head. "If in three hours I am not back in Irkutsk, measures I have taken will be performed."

A cold chill came over Volkov. For a few moments he had made the mistake of forgetting all he knew about the Jap. "What measures?" There was an unmistakable quaver in the voice.

With his cigarette Jap pointed at the phone on the director's desk. "Telephone your wife, ask how the kids are."

Volkov seized the receiver and dialed his home number in Irkutsk with a trembling finger.

"Yes? Who is speaking?" he barked. "I want to talk to my wife!" There was a short wait. Then Volkov yelled into the phone, "Fuck you, not possible. Permission? What kind of a fucking permission?" A pause and he screamed, "Jap's?!"

Jap screwed his cigarette butt into an ashtray. "Listen, Director, don't get distracted by family affairs; we have more serious matters to discuss."

"You asshole!" the director screamed. "You'll pay dearly for that!"

For the first time Martinov made his presence felt. "Jap, release the family or no deal." His voice was hoarse. "What in hell happened between you two?"

"Do you want to tell him Hamster?"

"This man is a murderer and a gaming cheat!" Volkov cried.

Seeing that Martinov, his main supporter, was upset, Jap explained in quiet tones. "Yevgeny Ivanovitch was one of Galina Brezhneva's favorites. I guess she liked all that hair that covered his plump body. Her husband Yuri and I were associates." He smiled pleasantly across the desk. "Where was her *katran* located in those days, Hamster? Near Gorky Street as I recall." To Martinov he explained, "*Katran* was what we called a gambling spot." He chuckled. "And of course Galina offered the added incentive of very young whores as well."

"What's that got to do with our business today?" Martinov's voice rose in volume.

"Do you want to tell the First Secretary the story?" his voice became mocking, "Comrade Director? Or shall I?"

Volkov glared across the desk in silence so Jap continued. "It shouldn't have any bearing on our business today but I guess it does. You see there was this night fifteen years ago in Moscow when I arranged to meet Yuri Churbanov at his wife's *katran* for a night of dice play. He assured me I would win but he wasn't there. I saw our friend Hamster at the dice table and standing behind him was the most exotic young Tartar girl I had ever seen. I only later discovered she was his mistress."

"Shit on you—cheat!" Volkov growled.

Jap sighed deeply. "Well, to make a long story short, I lost most of my bankroll to our friend across the desk," he gestured at the scowling Volkov. "And then Yuri arrived and observed my predicament. Within minutes my luck changed and I won all my money back. Yuri defeated his shrewish wife, Galina in magnetic manipulating of the dice, and Hamster lost all his money to me."

"Cheated," Volkov growled again, staring at his telephone.

"It sounds as though it was General Churbanov who did the cheating," Martinov observed. "An old habit of his. But Yevgeny Ivanovitch, after fifteen years you would let the matter of a dice game get in the way of a million, no billion dollar—that's dollars I say, not rubles—business venture?"

"Well, Nickolai," Jap contributed, "there was one more facet to this incident that might have contributed to Hamster's chagrin which appears to linger on long after the basically meaningless event." Jap smiled depreciatingly at Volkov. "After I saw the pictures of your charming wife and children our people snapped this past week, I really can't understand you holding this grudge."

Martinov observed that the Dome's director was sputtering close to the breaking point. "All right, Jap, finish up and let's get down to business."

"You asked me what happened and I'm telling you. Anyway," Jap went on, "being a sportsman I gave Hamster the opportunity to win it all back on one turn of the dice. I put up the money and suggested he put up the Tartar girl for one night with me." Jap laughed aloud and gestured across the desk. "He stared at me— just as he is doing now. But when the girl agreed, quite readily I might say, we made the wager and—I won the girl. And when one night wasn't enough—for either of us, Volkov went mad. But the upshot of it all was that Galina made her father appoint Yevgeny Ivanovitch as director of Krasnov 86."

Martinov nodded and gave Jap a stern look. "Right now you will release the director's family. I won't let anything happen to you here. How did this—this hostage situation—happen?"

"My brilliant frayer, Pavel, has been in Irkutsk for a week with some of our best sixes." Jap pointed at Volkov. The director's face was red, he was cursing and snorting like a bull. "I doubt he'll listen to you. He is the boss here."

"But I am the First Secretary of the entire region," Martinov announced.

The director shook his fist at Jap. "You won't see the daylight! Ever!" he shouted.

Jap gave Martinov a wan smile. "You see why I took precautions?"

It was almost half an hour before Martinov and Jap calmed Volkov down. In forty minutes the four men were sitting around the table in their shirt sleeves, coats removed, tense, smoking heavily and spiritedly bargaining.

"Now for the three buttons of plutonium I will pay you thirty thousand rubles."

"Impossible," Volkov cried.

"You are shouting loudly enough for your wife to hear you in Irkutsk," Jap said quietly.

The director suddenly remembered Jap held the upper hand. His family was hostage.

"And time is growing short," Jap continued. "One hundred thousand for the three buttons."

"Two hundred thousand for the three buttons, thirty grams," Volkov demanded.

"You've got it," Jap agreed.

He gestured at Pavel who opened the briefcase he was carrying. Stacks of crisp new hundred ruble notes were packed neatly inside. "Two hundred thousand. Exactly." Jap spoke in a caressing voice.

Volkov stared at the money and then picked up his phone. In moments he had dispatched his first assistant to go down to the fissionable material storage chambers and bring back three properly sheathed ten gram buttons of plutonium 239. "How did you know the exact price you would end up paying?" he asked.

"It was the price I decided upon," Jap said. "I was sure that after we had talked you would be reasonable."

Once again Volkov felt the icy fingers of fear in his gut. The Jap was back and if anything, more ruthless than before.

"Now let's discuss the missiles and warheads we will market for you, and also the plutonium 239 and enriched uranium." Jap gave Volkov an owlish look across the desk. "By the way, how would you like your payments made? We have excellent connections in Zurich for issuing letters of credit."

"From you? Cash, Jap," Volkov said harshly.

"In American hundred dollar bills, yes?"

"That will be acceptable. Paid here at my office on delivery."

"Of course. The plutonium buttons will bring forth many orders in the future. How much would you need for the new, solid state fuel SS-25 missile, the Sickle I believe you call it."

"It is impossible to anticipate the future but I would estimate five million dollars!" The director's voice shook as he named the price. "We're talking about the real thing, special new release. It will deliver a fifteen megaton warhead over twelve thousand miles."

"For that price the warhead is included, I assume," Jap pressed.

Martinov jumped into the negotiations. "Nobody, not even Saddam, will pay over five million dollars for the delivery system without the warhead."

"Of course. The warheads come attached. And the codes. That will be your trump card." There was a triumphant ring to Volkov's voice. "Only when the last payment is made do you release the firing code to the buyer."

Volkov was silent for some moments and then he shrugged. "But how can we talk about what may be happening one or two years in the future?" His voice was calm now. "There is a problem I haven't told you about yet. I have a deputy, Dr. Zilko, who I suspect reports directly over my head to Moscow. As a matter of fact I had to give him the executive helicopter today for a visit to another secret city. Somehow when the time comes he will have to be neutralized. But . . ."

"I'm sure we can take care of that problem," Pavel broke in.

"We will decide what can be done when the right circumstances arise. In any case we can't come to a final price now."

Jap nodded. "Yes, you are right about the moment for final negotiations on this business. When the new face of Soviet and Russian politics shows itself, and I know that will have to happen in less than a year, we will decide what is equitable. Also you, Hamster, will have to help us work out the method of transporting the rockets, warheads, and nuclear materials to the buyers."

"I'm afraid, Jap, it must be your responsibility to provide an AN-22 turboprop military cargo airplane. It is the only aircraft in our inventory capable of transporting the SS-25 Sickle missile complete with its launcher distances up to six thousand miles."

"You do not have access to such an aircraft?"

Volkov shook his head sadly. "In its infinite wisdom the Kremlin separated responsibility for delivery and storage into two different ministries. If I had both capabilities I could sell, and deliver as well, throughout the world."

"Just tell me where we will land this AN-22 cargo plane," Jap replied confidently.

"There is a landing strip just beyond the main tunnel at the base of the dome. It is over two miles long and will take any aircraft ever built. The launcher carrying the SS-25 can be driven out of the dome, onto the airstrip and up the ramp into the belly of the AN-22."

"I'll have the plane available," Jap promised.

Volkov's assistant reappeared and gingerly set a box small enough to fit in the palm of a man's hand on the desk. He virtually scuttled back into the elevator. After the door slid shut the director gestured at the box. "Pick it up, Jap."

Jap reached for the lead container feeling its satisfying weight in his hand.

"Remember, do not open it except under safe circumstances which include a glove cabinet."

"I have to take your word that this is what you say it is," Jap intoned as he held the heavy box in his hand. "But as you suggest, experts will examine it." A wry smile twisted his narrow lips.

The director shrugged as he walked to the safe, opened it, and emptied the briefcase full of rubles into it. "And I will have to take your word on the amount of rubles in that pile. But we all have much business to transact in the future."

With that Volkov handed the empty attache case back to Pavel, who placed the lead container in it and snapped the lid shut. Then the director returned to the cabinet and took out a bottle of vodka in one hand and between the fingers of the other hand he pinched the stems of four wine glasses carrying them across the office and placing them on the desk.

"There is one more request I have to make," Jap announced. He pulled from his pocket a folded piece of paper and handed it to Volkov. "Here are the names and serial numbers of two prisoners at Tulun Labor Camp." He handed the director the information on Fofa and Volodya. "If they are transferred to Krasnogulag 86 I would appreciate it if you would notify me and see to their immediate release."

"I have no authority to . . ."

"If anyone asks, they died, as do all of your slaves, of radiation poisoning, even sooner than usual after exposure."

"But . . ." Volkov began to sputter.

"Those men are worth fifty thousand rubles each to me, free and unexposed to radiation."

Volkov understood the arrangement and possible consequences if Jap's proposal was ignored. He nodded in concurrence. "Shall we drink to this transaction?" he suggested, pouring vodka into the glasses. They finished off their vodka in a single swallow.

"I hope you know what you are handling, Jap," Volkov cautioned gesturing at the black attaché case. "Plutonium must be kept in an inert atmosphere. It will ignite spontaneously in air and the tiniest amount near the skin will result in instant cancer."

"The buttons will only be conveyed to safe and experienced hands," Jap replied.

Volkov refilled the glasses.

Jap held his up. "And we all are concerned for the safety of you, my dear Yevgeny, and your family. To assure your security my sixes will be permanently assigned to the beautiful city of Irkutsk beside Lake Baikal, pearl of Siberia and although you will never see them or be aware of their presence they will always be close—for your protection."

Volkov drank down his vodka without a murmur although he trembled inwardly. Even the vodka failed to quell the stomach spasms. Just the name Jap terrified potential targets of his extortion procedures.

"Now perhaps you will send us back to Irkutsk in one of your helicopters," Jap suggested. "I must catch the overnight flight back to Moscow. We have much to accomplish before we see you next. Not the least of which is acquisition of an AN-22 cargo plane."

Volkov's glance fell on the cabinet in which he had just placed two hundred thousand rubles. With a grin he said, "Of course, Jap. One more vodka before you leave?"

Jap shook his head. "It is most important that I am back in Irkutsk within the next," he glanced at his watch, "one hour. Remember?"

"Of course," Volkov asserted. He picked up his phone and gave the order for the helicopter flight.

"Call your wife in an hour, she will be happy to hear from you. And tell her she will have no such problem again since my people will be constantly watching out for her protection. Neither of you will ever see them but they will be there."

Volkov nodded seriously, walked across the office, and pushed the elevator signal.

"Well, my friend," Jap said to Nickolai, "we have successfully concluded the first chapter of our business at the Dome. I look forward to a most profitable relationship."

Volkov finally seemed to be catching the spirit of the occasion. He had already put the equivalent of a life's salary for a skilled worker into his safe.

Jap walked through the elevator doors after Martinov, turned and nodded to Volkov. "To the early maturity of circumstances favorable to our future business."

Pavel followed, calling over his shoulder, "And don't worry about your deputy. He is now my problem."

CHAPTER TWENTY-SEVEN

This was the part of his work Vladimir Nechiaev never got used to. He lifted the police blanket and stared down at the corpse of Victor Kalina, Jap's illegitimate son who bore his mother's name. The body lay where it had been found, face up in front of the elevator in the lobby of Victor's apartment building on Solyanka Street. A single bullet had been fired into his face at close range. The murder had been reported by an anonymous resident of the building and the local Militsia had arrived within minutes. Recognizing the connection to Jap, they immediately called Nechiaev who rushed to the scene of the crime.

"I knew that Jap's return would bring us trouble and he hasn't even landed in Moscow yet," Nechiaev lamented as he dropped the blanket back over the corpse. "This is only the beginning."

The Militsia had finished fingerprinting the area and removing all possible evidence, and Nechiaev was double-checking the crime scene when Taki came bursting through the doors of the apartment building and summoned his boss to the car radiophone.

It was General Bodaev. "Come to Leningrad Highway and Pravda Street!" he barked. "There's been a massacre on the side street outside Olga Yakovleva's apartment house. That's Jap's wife."

"Oh fuck!" Nechiaev called back. "What kind of deep shit storm are we in?"

"I'll be waiting for you," Bodaev called over the radio phone. Nechiaev jumped into the front seat of his car beside the driver. "Bring the body to our morgue," he called out to one of the detectives as the car started off.

Pravda Street was a gruesome scene. Three bullet-shredded corpses lay on the sidewalk, and a burned out car with another charred corpse on the floor rested at the side of the road. Cartridge shells were strewn everywhere around the bloodstained sidewalk along with weapons which had fallen from the hands of the gunmen. Two Militsiamen found a still smoking grenade launcher and piles of machine-gun cartridge shells on the third floor of the opposite building.

Nechiaev arrived just as investigators were taking last snapshots of the place. Bodaev walked around the ambush scene and returned to his chief of detectives. "Find anything at Kalina's place?"

Nechiaev shook his head. "Professional job except no silencer. Someone heard the shot and reported it. Just one shot, no shell, no witnesses. It was early morning. The gun was waiting for the killer in a postbox; we found it open and an oil spot inside." His eyes narrowed as he took in the scene of slaughter. "Anything of interest here?"

"Let me show you." Bodaev led his chief of detectives to a bullet-torn sprawled body lying in the doorway of the century-old mansion converted to an apartment building. "Recognize him?" Nechiaev stared at the bloody corpse. There was enough of the face left to recognize. "Impossible!" Nechiaev exclaimed. "It looks like—"

"No it isn't. That's Hakim, a Kazakh and Jap's double." He pointed at another bullet-mutilated body. "He was barely alive when we got here and managed to tell us what happened. Givi's sixes led by Reso had Olga's apartment staked out waiting for Jap. Hakim and three others preparing a homecoming feast at Olga's apartment walked into the ambush." Bodaev shook his head. "First Victor murdered, now this! I'm sure by this time they realize they didn't get the real Jap. We should be at the airport to meet him."

Nechiaev glanced at his watch. "Actually Jap and Pavel should be a couple of hours out now. Where are the Criminal Brigade Reserves?"

"Don't you know?" Bodaev exclaimed. "Part of the reserve unit is guarding Yeltsin and Gorbachev, there is a squad stuck in Tulun still investigating the uprising, and Jap? He is in the air on his way here at this moment. One fucking mafioso makes two hundred Militsiamen run back and forth like rabbits! I'll take care of things here. We'll search the apartment. You get to the airport and set up a security net. We cannot afford another killing."

At Sheremetievo I, the domestic airport, Nechiaev spent the next two hours stationing plainclothes agents and marksmen in a security net. Video cameras and airport guards covered the area. "You'd think a general secretary was arriving," Navakoff commented.

"He is a general secretary in his own way," Nechiaev replied, "and his deputy, Pavel travels with him." He shook his head in disgust. "To think, we have to guard them!"

As Nechiaev and Navakoff were walking through the terminal Taki ran up to them.

"General Bodaev called on the radio. Jap's wife Olga returned to her apartment and after we told her what had happened, she left to meet her husband. We arrested one of Jap's men who was in the apartment on a weapons charge."

No sooner had the Militsiaman delivered Bodaev's communique than the walkie-talkie Nechiaev was carrying crackled with the news that Jap's wife had arrived in a Mercedes with driver and bodyguard at the main entrance to the airport terminal building.

Moments later they saw a handsome, tall woman with close cropped blonde hair and a long fur coat walk into the terminal. Nechiaev was alert, scanning the area, looking from face to face for a possible assassin, but contrary to his expectations Jap's flight disembarked quietly.

Jap came through the portal into the terminal, Olga on one side of him, Pavel on the other. It looked as though they were leading Jap who appeared to be somewhat numb. Olga must have told him that Victor was dead and given him the details of the ambush at her apartment, Nechiaev surmised. Quietly he ordered all posts to let Jap and his people go through.

"Watch them to the car and follow it," he spoke into his radio. But to Nechiaev's great astonishment Jap, Pavel and Olga did not get into the Mercedes. Instead, without even bothering to claim their baggage, they boarded the airport bus which took off in the direction of Moscow. The driver and bodyguard in the Mercedes, with no orders, remained parked in place. "They've changed mode of transportation," Nechiaev called over his radio. "Follow the bus."

Bodaev radioed orders for Nechiaev to proceed to Olga's apartment where perhaps he might find Jap and his wife and Pavel. A Militsia group was still stationed outside the apartment which had been searched and the doors sealed. Nechiaev had been waiting over an hour when Olga appeared. She was alone. She seemed bewildered.

"I'm sorry to bother you at this difficult time," Nechiaev said. "But I'm afraid we had to search your apartment and must keep men stationed here. I know it is inconvenient, but it is for your own safety. And your husband's. Do you know his whereabouts?"

The answer shocked him. "My husband went to Petrovka 38. He wants to talk to you and your authorities."

Nechiaev dashed from the apartment and plunged into his car.

As Taki sped along the Leningrad highway towards the center of the city Sly Fox took the receiver of his car phone in hand and made a call to his office. Boris Burenchuk answered.

"Fox, you will never imagine who sits here waiting for you!"

"I know," Nechiaev replied wearily. "What's he doing?"

"Nothing. He's waiting in the corridor. I gave him a cigarette."

"Tell him I'll be there in five minutes."

CHAPTER TWENTY-EIGHT

⬦⬦

They sat on either side of Nechiaev's desk, Jap gazing absently out the window, his eyes narrow slits, his face still. It was the first time Nechiaev had ever met Jap face to face and the legendary thief-in-the-law was nothing like Nechiaev had expected. He looked, in fact, like any grieving father, crushed by the death of his son, and for a moment Nechiaev forgot the dead boy was a notorious gangster and his father possibly the most feared crime figure in all Russia.

"Want some coffee?" Nechiaev offered.

"Thanks. A small cup please."

"Cigarette?"

"Please."

Jap drew on his cigarette for a moment before reaching into his breast pocket and producing two folded papers, which he handed to Nechiaev. One was the certificate of release from prison signed by the investigation brigade chief in Tulun and Sly Fox returned it. Later Jap would exchange it for his passport which was in the Militsia office serving the district which he had last called home.

The second paper was an application to the Criminal Brigade of
Moscow City Militsia at Petrovka 38. It contained a request by citizen Yakovlev to investigate the homicide of citizen Victor Vyach-
slavavitch Yakovlev, his son. This was the first time Nechiaev had
ever heard Victor being called Yakovlev. It was touching, he
thought, that Jap was trying to legitimize his son in death as he
had failed to do in life.

Sly Fox put the application in a file on his desk. "Citizen
Yakovlev, my deepest condolences. Victor was young and this is a
genuine tragedy. But you know, of course, that you are one of the
few people who can be extremely helpful in stopping further
bloodshed on the streets of Moscow."

Jap ran a hand across his face. "Commandant I do not want
blood spilled."

"You know this Reso?"

"Yes. One of Tofik's men."

"He was seen near your wife's apartment this morning. We
think the criminal group of Givi Gigauri, formerly Tofik's gang,
intended to kill both you and your son. We covered you in the airport, but in the case of Victor, they obviously were the first to
strike."

Jap nodded. "I noticed your men at the airport. I thank you. I
appreciate your concern."

"Do you have any information about the events this morning?"

"They attacked my men near my wife's apartment. Probably
because they took one of them, Hakim, for me."

"Did Reso shoot him?"

"I do not know anything for sure. I have been back in Moscow a
few hours after almost ten years away. I haven't even been home
yet."

"We are talking strictly unofficially."

"That is why I am talking at all," Jap replied.

"You understand, now that I have told you the names of the
suspects, you will be charged if anything happens to them?"

"Yes, I do. I've told you, I am tired of bloodshed. I want them brought to court."

"Can you supply me any information about Givi's group?"

"Anything you want. I had many long conversations with Tofik before he was shot by the guards at Tulun."

"Are you not afraid that other thiefs-in-the-law will call you traitor?"

"No. As for our conversation, you will not tell anyone about it."

Nechiaev nodded, satisfied. "Okay. No paper records."

Jap lit another cigarette.

Pavel sat at the desk in the apartment he had prepared for Jap's homecoming. He glanced at his watch and then up at Misha who stood across the desk from him, his long black cloak hiding the custom shortened Kalishnikov machine gun. "You have had about two hours to obey the orders of Givi and Reso to find and kill your old employers," he said. He filled a glass in front of him with cognac and took a long swallow. "Givi will be anxiously awaiting your report. Let us not keep the fat pig waiting any longer."

Misha nodded. "When I left Givi, he was talking to his travel agent, buying tickets to Tblisi and Odessa for himself and his sixes in case I fail. Only Alexey stays in Moscow. I never saw Givi so full of fear."

"He should be." Pavel lifted the telephone from its cradle and dialed the number on the slip of paper Misha had handed him.

Misha bent forward over the desk hoping to hear Givi on the other end of the line. The guttural "*Da, Da Da Da,*" came from the receiver of the phone which Pavel held away from his ear.

"Givi, it's me, Pavel."

Givi's voice came over evenly, almost indifferently. "Nice to hear from you, old chap. What's up?"

Pavel's words snapped over the line. "No time for jokes, Givi. What kind of a maniac are you?"

"What are you talking about?"

"War is no way to run a business."

Givi's voice came across in a snarl. "Tell it to Jap and his guys with hand grenades."

"Shut up, Givi. This is no time to argue. Do you want this bloodshed to go on forever?"

"What are you talking about?"

"You know damn well what I'm talking about!"

"Listen, Pavel, you sound strange," the false note of concern in Givi's voice almost made Pavel lose his temper. "And how did you get this number?"

"From that bastard of yours, Misha."

Now the worry was real. "Where is Mikhail?"

Pavel let himself go as though standing at the footlights. "Aha, you want to talk to Mikhail. Well, if you address our Creator Himself, maybe He'll supply you a phone number in hell!"

"What do you mean?" Givi asked hesitantly.

"Mean?" Pavel shrieked into the phone. "I mean your bloody Mikhail shot Jap dead and is shot dead himself by the *ments*. I found your number in his pocket."

"Why *ments*?"

"Because, you bloody fool, Jap is guarded by Militsia since the instant of his arrival. They were on the alert from the moment your jerks killed Victor. They have the corpse of this other Georgian barbecue, Misha, whom you stole from me. At this moment they are preparing a major hunt after you and your crew; and if they don't get you, every crew in Moscow loyal to Victor and Jap will go after you . . ." He heard Givi slam down the phone and arrested his hysterical outburst with a grin at Misha.

"What will Givi do now?" Pavel asked.

"He will immediately become lost, you can be sure."

"We must cut him off before he can disappear into his native Georgia. He would later return to Moscow with all of Tofik's gang looking for revenge."

Outside the apartment building Pavel and Misha climbed into

the back seat of the waiting black van and the driver sped off into the night.

"I hope you are right about the Kosmos Hotel," Pavel said. "I would not like to see Givi get away. It would send the signal that Jap cannot win the war Givi started."

"Givi keeps everything in his suite at the Kosmos," Misha answered. "He can't go anywhere without first going to his suite."

An hour later Givi, wedged uncomfortably into the front seat of a yellow taxi, shouted to Reso and two other sixes in the back seat to wake up as they approached the Kosmos Hotel. He pulled a bundle of thirty ruble notes from his jacket pocket and complimented the driver on the speed he had maintained from the cab station at the edge of Moscow to the hotel.

As the cab approached the hotel, a lone man walked toward Givi's taxi from behind. He had just stepped out of the dark van which had been parked for some time across from the hotel's front doors.

"Hey Givi, who's that behind us?" Reso cried out hoarsely.

Givi cast a quick glance into the side mirror and froze in terror. He stared into Misha's reflected face illuminated in the bright mercury lights along the hotel's sidewalk, black eyes gleaming viciously, face contorted, lips tightly pressed together.

Misha swung the barrel of the machine gun under his cloak to the level of the back seat of the cab and squeezed the trigger. A long volley pierced the back of the cab, the rounds stitching a path across the vehicle from right to left ripping through the bodies of Reso and the other two sixes whose screams sent passersby diving onto the pavement.

Misha fixed the barrel on the huge outline of fat Givi beside the driver and squeezed off another fusillade, every round aimed into the massive shadow of Givi's back. Several of the heavy caliber bullets tossed Reso's body between the front and back scats. Another burst shattered the gigantic gangster, his blood gushing onto the windshield which in a split second was smashed into glass confetti by the rounds ripping through the gross body. Givi's head fell backwards, mouth wide open, left hand still clenching the bills.

People around were screaming and jumping aside, the crowd at the bus stop fell backwards, trampling over the pedestrians who were emerging from the metro, curses and shrieks filling the air.

Misha lowered his smoking weapon and took a fast appraisal of the scene. The square behind him had almost instantly emptied. Returning to the van was impossible as terrified pedestrians ran aimlessly in all directions between him and what was to have been the escape vehicle. Misha turned and fled in the darkness toward a group of five-story houses. No one followed. The bullet-pocked taxi remained standing at the curb.

In the course of two hours with Jap, Nechiaev learned more about the "vegetable mafia" Givi Gigauri operated than he had during a two-year investigation. It was data that could have won the prosecutor a conviction the previous year when Givi had been on trial. Jap finished his discourse and lit another cigarette. The ashtray between them was full of butts, the air in the office blue from smoke. At that moment the door opened and General Bodaev walked in.

Jap turned his head and met the general's blue-eyed stare.

"Good evening, Citizen Yakovlev. This is an odd place to find you."

"Good evening, Commandant. Well, life is life."

"Please accept my condolences on the loss of your son. We could not foresee this tragedy and, of course, you people are hard to follow."

"That was not your fault, General."

"What are your plans now if I may ask?"

"To live on. But first, do you think I can see his body?"

"Certainly. Colonel Nechiaev, please take Citizen Yakovlev to our morgue."

The morgue was a dim, narrow, low-ceilinged vault in the basement of Petrovka 38. It was illuminated by a dozen bulbs which gave uneven yellowish light. The floor tiling was ancient and cracked.

Silent, clean shaven and bald, the morgue assistant located the correct hatch, opened it, pulled out a metal shelf to half its length, and folded back a stained sheet, all in one swift, trained movement. Jap found himself looking down at Victor's naked torso. It was of a bluish color, his short cropped light hair disheveled. There was a bruise on his forehead and a neat black hole on the left side of his nose where the bullet had entered his head. No need to look at the jagged exit wound at the back of his skull. Victor had seen it coming. Jap reached out his hand and touched Victor's chin with the tips of his fingers, muttering something Sly Fox could not make out. After a few moments Jap turned to the detective. "When can I take him away?"

"Tomorrow, after the autopsy."

"Is that so necessary?"

"I'm sorry, but this is a crime and autopsies are a routine procedure."

"I understand." After a last lingering look Jap pulled the sheet back over his son's body and turned away as the slab was pushed back into the shelf.

Back in Bodaev's office Jap glanced down at his left wrist and looked up. "I think I will be going now," he said. "I am completely confused by these time zone changes I've been through today. Could you tell me what time it is now in Moscow?"

"Half past eleven," Bodaev said. "Where are you heading?"

"My wife's apartment."

"There is a Militsia patrol there. You shouldn't run into any trouble."

"Thank you again. I will return for the body tomorrow."

"Come about five o'clock then," Bodaev said.

"I'll be here, Commandant."

Nechiaev called to an officer on duty. "Please see Citizen Yakovlev through the front gate," he ordered.

As Jap left the room with his escort, Bodaev and Nechiaev listened to the footsteps recede down the hall to the iron stairwell. Bodaev lit a cigarette and blew out a cloud of smoke. "I can't help feeling that there is more than paternal grief behind this meeting," Bodaev muttered. "What did he tell you?"

"He supplied a lot of evidence about Givi's crew. It will take some time to check it out but we're on the way to making another case."

A tight smile crossed Bodaev's lips. "Misfortune to one can be advantage to another. A common enemy breeds strange alliances. The death of Victor brought Jap to frame his enemies to us. I want a detailed report, marked top secret. Even KGB do not have information like this."

The phone rang. Bodaev picked it up and listened. Suddenly his face reddened and contorted into an expression of fury. He slammed down the receiver and turned to Nechiaev. "Another gunfight. This time outside the Kosmos Hotel. There are casualties."

The usual crowd of curious bystanders was missing when at midnight Bodaev and Nechiaev arrived at the bloody scene of the third shooting of the day. Major Yuri Navakoff, as usual wearing his acid-streaked blue denims when on street duty, the American flag sewed to his left breast, met them at the hotel entrance and took them to the car. They examined the taxi with smashed windshield glass, its door open and bodies still sprawled on the seats.

"The four of them are dead," Navakoff said. "The driver is okay though his pants are messed up. Very professional execution."

Nechiaev glanced at the bodies and turned to Bodaev. "It's Givi and his men. Jap's work!"

"It's all clear now," Bodaev said as for the third time that day the forensic experts combed the murder scene and the photographers flashed their shots.

They strode back to their car. The front door was open and Bodaev plunged into the seat."Who would think?" Nechiaev began.

"I know," Bodaev interrupted wearily. "Thinking seems not to be the common quality of our Brigade, its chief included. Now you understand perhaps why Jap was confused about time zones and confirmed he was with us at eleven thirty."

Nechiaev shrugged sheepishly but said nothing. "I'm an old man," Bodaev murmured, his voice strong with indignation. "Before this week is over half of Moscow Militsia, all of KGB and all of general prosecutor's office will be dying from laughter." He shook his head sadly. "And why not? A notorious thief-in-the-law drinks coffee with the head of detectives of the Criminal Brigade, while his crew proceeds with gangster warfare in the streets of the city. And why shouldn't they laugh if the best our brigade can do is take photos of the dead bodies?"

"Jap was at Petrovka 38?" Navakoff asked incredulously.

"Yes," replied Nechiaev. "And thus made his alibi unshakable."

Suddenly Bodaev started to laugh. "Imagine, guys. Tomorrow morning our Prosecutor asks Jap, 'Where were you yesterday from eight o'clock to eleven at night?' And Jap answers, 'I was with Colonel Nechiaev and General Bodaev in their office helping an investigation. Ask them.'"

For a moment it was all too much for Bodaev, but he quickly continued his harangue. "And the colonel and the general nod their dumb heads and say, 'Yeah, yeah, Jap was with us, half the Criminal Brigade can confirm it, including us.' Sounds nice, no?"

"Stop it, General," Nechiaev barked. "This is not funny."

"Really? You think so? By the way Sly Fox, did you warn Jap that he should not avenge himself upon Gigauri and his men?"

"Yes, I did," Nechiaev answered dutifully.

"Good boy," Bodaev's tone was dour. "Now Jap will claim that he learned about Victor's assassins from you and therefore could not even plan such a mischief as shooting Givi." He breathed deeply, his face reddening. "You know boys, the way we're going we'll live to see the time when Jap gets an award for courageous struggle against organized crime."

The three were silent for some time. Meanwhile the emergency truck came after an hour of delay. The bodies of Givi and his three sixes were heaved onto stretchers and covered with sheets. Givi's body was so heavy that it took four men to haul it out of the front seat of the cab and heft it onto the gurney. His spread arms, by now going rigid, stuck out on both sides from under the cloth barely wide enough to cover him.

Bodaev watched the clean up procedure from his car. "Okay guys," he said at last, "forget it. He makes no mistakes who does nothing at all. Fox, do not be offended, it was my mistake too, forgive an old man for growling. Nervous stress you know. Jap is back one day and what happens? One homicide, two all out massacres. What do you suppose we have to look forward to?"

CHAPTER TWENTY-NINE

⊰⊱ ⊰⊱

T wo days later at noon on a sunny, late spring day Vaganko-
vo cemetery was the destination for a stately procession of
some fifty limousines. At the entrance to this, one of the
oldest cemeteries in Moscow, a place where burial space could
only be found for the most renowned Communist Party members
and the richest of private citizens, the cream of the criminal world
had gathered to pay final tribute to a member of their community,
Victor Vyaschslavavitch Yakovlev.

The open grave was covered with enormous wreaths and gar-
lands. It required considerable time for all of the bereaved to
reach the interment site. The ancient burial ground was vastly
over-crowded with graves and the mourners had to wend their
way in single file along the narrow passages through the jungle
of headstones.

The proceedings could easily have passed for some imaginative
Paris designer's odd fashion show. The men wore handsomely tailored suits of very dark to light colors made from the most expensive material. Golden watch chains crossed protuberant bellies.

Bejeweled gold rings shone from the thick hairy fingers of the bosses of Moscow crews, their frayers, consultants and financial advisors. Almost every man was accompanied by a wife or a mistress. The women wore dark and black suits and dresses under black mink fur coats. The majority of the mistresses were expensive prostitutes. The faces of the women were covered with black veils and almost every woman carried a bouquet of flowers. A number of shapely young women who (despite their black mourning attire and veils) looked remarkably sensuous stood alone dispersed throughout the crowd. They were some of Victor's myriad mistresses.

Celebrities of Moscow cinema and show business were introduced as if at an art or theatrical festival—they all were Victor's friends who were indebted to the deceased. Some ran businesses with Victor. Singer and actor Josef Kobzon was also present with his new mistress who was at least twenty years younger than her famous lover. Besides Kobzon there were several other People's Deputies present.

A funeral luncheon had been organized on the grassy lawn at the edge of the cemetery for 500 persons but there were many more guests that arrived to pay last respects to Victor and be part of the most important underworld event in recent years.

A separate delegation came from the Moscow stock market to mourn the death of an outstanding businessman. Victor, despite his youth, had money spread around all corners of profitable commerce. There were also representatives of the art and literary society, including several acclaimed Soviet writers, poets, and painters who had been encouraged by the generosity of the art lover Victor had become. A string quartet from the Moscow Symphony Orchestra played solemn music for the occasion.

Jap was amazed and proud to savor the success Victor had gained in his short life as reflected by the distinguished mourners gathered at the funeral. And then the slender figure of a veiled young woman in a full length black dress appeared beside him. "Oh, Slava, I am sorry, so sorry."

Her voice was familiar and his heart tightened in his breast as she lifted her black veil. He stared into the lovely face that had been in his thoughts constantly.

"Oksana." His voice choked for the first time that day. "How thoughtful you are to come."

"Since I heard about this tragedy all I have been able to think about was what you told me that day in Tulun. I know how much Victor meant to you and your plans for his future."

The palm of his hand touched her shoulder and the charged current passing between them released a tremor within him. "Someday very soon I will tell you how much your being here means to me. But I must not betray all my true feelings today." As Oksana stepped aside for another mourner to express condolences Jap's spirit came alight; with her appearance the day had become as uplifting for him as it was tragic.

Many speeches were said over Victor's expensive coffin. The speakers droned on, praising Victor for a list of virtues and merits no living person ever had or ever would possess. The praises would have continued until late at night but Jap stopped it all with a single gesture at the end of two graveside hours. The coffin was lowered and Jap opened his palm and let fall lumps of clay which hit the lid of the coffin.

Victor's mother pushed back her veil and was the second to drop a clump of earth on the casket. Then, without a word to Jap, she pulled down her veil and disappeared into the throng of mourners.

Jap turned his back abruptly on the grave and with Olga holding his arm led the way through the maze of gravestones to the elaborate dinner tables.

An hour later, as the funeral repast proceeded with numerous solemn toasts, Jap faced the leaders of the Moscow criminal crews at a separate table. The funeral provided the needed cover for such a meeting. They sat at a long table in two opposite rows. They were all here, the return of the Jap and the immediate war clash signaled a new era in procedure. None of the bosses and frayers wanted an attempt to appropriate their interests initiated by another thief-in-the-law. Jap was well aware that the efficient massacre of Givi and three of his top men, only hours after his return from ten years in prison, had thrown severe trepidations into the others. Still, he also knew that at this moment few of them were willing to acknowledge Jap as the highest authority over all of them.

Jap decided to make his edge apparent without any show of arrogance or acquisitiveness. He stood up at the head of the table, hands in his pockets, black funeral cloak flying in the wind, his face expressionless as he stared straight ahead looking at no particular person, almost as if all of them were absent. His voice was hushed, let them strain their ears to hear.

"Thank you all for coming," he began. "As Horace wrote in his Odes, 'Pale Death with impartial tread beats at the poor man's cottage door and at the palaces of kings'." Then abruptly, "No more shooting. No blood. It will not bring my son back. This shouldn't have happened but he was young," there was the slightest catch in his voice, "and I was denied the opportunity to teach him what I have learned in this life of ours."

Jap paused and looked around the table at which were seated the highest order of Moscow's criminal society separated from the other mourners distinguished in more legitimate fields. "Tell all Gigauri's people, Jap will touch no one. Everyone can return to his business. But I am taking over Givi's trade with Central Asia."

This was just what he had resolved not to do but with circumstances so drastically changed, for discipline's sake it was a necessary and, of course, highly profitable move.

"That is fair and just," he went on. The gathered throng murmured a chorus of agreement. "All conflicts in the future will be solved peacefully at first hand." A hard glint lit up the black pupils of Jap's eyes behind the slanted slits of his lids.

"He who breaks the peace will go down the drain very quickly. That's Jap's word. We are businessmen not bandits. Remember that well. Another major conference will take place in a few months on a serious matter. Be ready. Everyone will be informed in due course."

Now he did give them all a pleasant smile his eyes widening, revealing himself. "So, have some fun now . . . drink to the memory of the deceased soul. Tell Givi's relatives they can bury him anywhere they want. Here or in Georgia. I do not mind. And make him and his men a splendid funeral. He was a real man, just like Tofik was. So let us join our ladies and remember Victor as we enjoy this dinner in his honor."

Jap turned to walk away leaving a silent, thoughtful group of crime figures behind. Looking to his right Jap spotted a tall Georgian in black dress approaching him. It was Alexey, Givi's frayer and heir apparent to whatever was left of Tofik's organization. The throng of gangsters at the table froze. Jap took a step toward his foe. Alexey approached him quietly, his face a mask of indifference. They stood face to face a few moments.

"I came to see you, Jap. I am sorry about what happened. It's," he shrugged searching for the right word; there was none. "Business."

Jap nodded, not uttering a word.

"I came alone and I say no condolence, that would be too hypocritical. But I've brought you a present. Over there." He waved his hand at the far fence of the cemetery. Jap turned back to the table. "Pavel, come with us."

Pavel rose from his seat and the three of them walked to the entrance making their way among the gravesites and monuments. The bosses at the table watched them go.

At the entrance was parked a black Volga sedan. No musclemen in sight, only a driver behind the wheel and some figure in the back seat.

"Alexey," Pavel's voice was harsh, "if this is some joke, it's the last one in your biography."

Alexey chuckled, walked up to the back door and flung it open. Pavel and Jap saw a skinny teenage boy, pimples all over his face, his nose running, hands tied behind his back. He was making an uneasy retreat from the door as if trying to get away from the daylight, squinting up at Jap and Pavel.

"What the hell is that?" Pavel asked abruptly, grimacing at the sight.

Alexey lit a cigarette. "A boyfriend of Zaza, one of Givi's perverted sixes. This little rat shot Victor."

Jap was dumbfounded. He stepped closer to the back door of the sedan, peering inside to see the boy's face better. Suddenly he reached out with both big hands, grabbed the boy by the collar and dragged him out of the car.

"Speak," he growled. "And tell the truth or you'll regret it."

Outside the boy fell back against the car, a torrent of words pouring forth. "I ain't do nothing! Zaza was a motherfucker, used to fuck me ass and mouth, hurt me you know. One day he says go to the spot, see this guy, he gave me a photo. He gave me key to a postbox said there will be a gun in it and shoot the guy."

"Did you know the man you shot?"

"Only saw him that day at Givi's house. Zaza push me in Reso's car and we follow him two hours to apartment in Moscow. His driver and another guy carry him out of the car and into the building."

"Victor got into a drinking contest with Givi," Alexey explained.

Jap nodded and gave the boy a look of such serenity that had the youth known how to read a thief-in-the-law he would have realized he was dead. "And what did you do?"

"Waited all night for guy to come out, finally he come out in the morning and walk two or three miles to his apartment where Zaza put the gun in the mail box."

Jap did not believe a single word of excuse. Anytime he wanted to this runaway kid could have given Zaza the slip. Zaza would have found himself another boy the next day. Zaza promised him money and gave him some after the killing. Victor was not the semi-human rodent's first victim. Zaza would not have picked a novice for such an important assassination. This pimple-faced ferret must have a long list of victims to his credit despite his tender age. He epitomized an abominable new tradition in the criminal world, training teenagers for killings. These callow youths were in fact much more cruel, ruthless and indifferent than adult assassins.

Jap shuddered briefly, reliving a moment in his past when a callow avenger blew away Mamatadgi's brains with a stolen pistol. Was fate at last punishing him? His own son shot through the head by a young brainless sadist?

"I appreciate your gesture, Alexey," Jap said. "There is no more point in spilling blood among us. I forgive you."

As they embraced each other Jap asked, "Alexey, what are you going to do now?"

"Return to Georgia. Nothing else for me to do here."

"You can remain if you want. But you must contribute to Victor's funeral."

"How much?"

"Half a lemon. Not much."

"It's a deal."

They stepped apart and Alexey gave Jap a cigarette and lit it for him. At that moment they heard a shrill cry behind them and turned their heads. The boy, hands tied behind him, tried to escape by dashing out of the car but Pavel caught him with a foot to the shank and the boy toppled to the ground screaming. Pavel pressed his foot to the youngster's throat and turned to Jap.

"What do we do next?"

Jap drew in a lung full of smoke and slowly exhaled it as he stared at the shining horizon beyond the cemetery. "Alexey is right," he said. "This is a rat. So you take it and bury it in the hot asphalt. Alive. The way Victor looked into the bullet that killed him."

"Ah, now I recognize good old Jap," Alexey said smiling.

"In some things we should always be conservative," Pavel agreed.

"It is a different beginning now, without Victor." A vision of Oksana, her veil lifted, fleeted across Jap's mind. "There is no more revenge to extract, no room for bitterness."

The boy twisted and jerked under the pressure of Pavel's foot on his throat. Jap looked down at the boy thoughtfully a moment. He turned to Pavel. "On second thought let him go. The *ments* will have him in the camps soon enough."

ROBIN MOORE

BOOK
TWO

❧ ❧

THE MILITSIA

CHAPTER THIRTY

⊰❧ ❧⊱

D irector Yevgeny Volkov sat in his office at top level of the underground Dome in the secret nuclear city, Krasnov 86. He was waiting for a report from the football-field size testing pad several miles to the east. A group of engineers from the rocket assembly factory and a detachment of the rocket regiment were supervising the test fueling of the last SS-19 missiles to come out of the plant. The steel white cigar over sixty feet long lay on the massive platform of the rocket carrier surrounded by a herd of fueling trucks. All together they carried thirty-six thousand pounds of fuel and oxidizer for the rocket's tanks. The fueling could be performed only on even ground in quiet surroundings from one truck at a time. The onerous testing required twice as much time as an actual blast-off because, after filling the rocket with fuel, the crew had to pump it back out again into the tanker trucks—the rocket could not safely be transported with tons of fuel inside. Among the rocket troopers the procedure was known under two names—"sexual job" and "jerking off."

Out at the test site eight soldiers dressed in rubber suits were fueling the missile's tanks. The vapors of the fuel were extremely poisonous; personnel working with the fuel for over a year developed many disorders, from constant headaches and extreme nervousness to impotence.

The soldiers on this last fueling of a liquid-state ICBM were novices. The colonel in charge of the rocket brigade became annoyed at how long it was taking to fill the tanks. They would still have to be pumped out again, leaving just enough fuel to be ignited and burn for a minute before it was all consumed.

"Increase the pressure of the pump," the colonel ordered. "We are way behind schedule."

The captain, an old hand on the job, started to explain to the colonel that the hose was an old one and frayed. The previous commander of the regiment had simply stolen the new one for his personal purposes when he was transferred. The colonel impatiently waved him off so the captain strode over to the truck and gave orders to increase pressure.

From a safe distance the colonel began signing waybills for receipt of the fuel when he heard a gasp from the technician. Looking up, the blood drained from his face. A thick brown cloud was rising over the rocket. One of the soldiers had already collapsed from the deadly fumes, his rubber hood and mask providing feeble protection. The fuel was spurting from the ruptured hose in a stream as thick as a man's arm and was immediately evaporating in the air turning it into poisonous gas.

The captain yelled out, "Turn off the valve!"

But instead the driver of the fuel tanker tried to pull the truck away. Panicked, he threw the vehicle into reverse and scraped the fuel truck beside him striking out a long leaping spark.

A fireball brighter than the sun rose above the testing pad. The blast turned the trucks over like toy cars and blew them to hot flying scrap metal. All the buildings and the several hundred feet of wire fence were knocked down by a fiery wall. Burning fragments of the rocket hull and of the trucks flew in all directions. The rumble shook buildings three miles away; one and one-half square miles of ground was seared. Eighteen tons of fuel and oxidizer blew almost simultaneously turning everything around them, including the regiment of rocket soldiers, into a black mushroom of dust reaching high into the morning sunlight.

Deputy Chief Engineer Plotnikov burst out of the elevator into Volkov's office shrieking the news. "Another one . . . The whole fucking rocket!"

"Oh shit! What happened?" Volkov shouted.

"Nobody knows. The flames are still too thick for the firemen to approach."

"Oh well." Volkov was annoyed, but not too greatly disturbed. "Accidents are possible in any business, especially ours."

"I'll never get used to it," Plotnikov moaned.

"Understandable. Well, go find the details and brief me."

It was mid-afternoon before Plotnikov and the engineers assembled enough information to warrant a direct telephone report to Moscow where it was the morning of 21 August 1991. Volkov decided to inform Minister of Defense Yazov directly before calling the Central Committee supervisor. The director did not want the ministers to learn of the catastrophe from any other source. Direct phone contact with Moscow was unusual. Here at the secret Siberian city of Krasnov 86, near Irkutsk, the less contact with the outside world the better it suited the security conscious Defense and Interior Ministries.

It was always a problem to get into direct contact with the top men in Moscow, but even so, Volkov was surprised at how long it took for the Defense Minister to answer his personal number in the Kremlin. If Minister Yazov was away from his desk the duty officer should have answered immediately. Just as Volkov was deciding to wait a few hours and call back, the phone in Moscow was picked up.

"Who's fucking calling?" Yazov's strangely brusk voice barked over the wire.

"Comrade Marshall, this is Director Volkov of the Krasnov 86 complex . . ."

"Aha! A-t-tention . . . Are you on my side, pal?"

"What? Ah . . . er, of course I am, Comrade Marshall . . ."

"Good! This is good! Pity you cannot drink with me . . ."

Only now did Volkov realize that the minister was drunk. Something was seriously wrong. It was only nine in the morning in Moscow.

"Comrade Marshall, I wanted to inform you, that unfortunately . . ."

"No! I do not want to hear anything fucking unfortunate! Only fortunate!" He yelled into the receiver with so much force that the director jumped up in his armchair four thousand miles away.

"Volkov!"

"Yes, Comrade Marshall. . ."

"Yes, yes," mocked the minister. "Haven't you blown up yourself and the Dome with all your fucking stuff yet? Haven't you?"

"No. But as a matter of fact . . ."

"Shut up! Shut up . . . You will! Remember what good old Yazov has said."

Volkov started to lose patience. "Comrade . . ."

"Fuck you! Do you think I do not know what fucking disorder goes on all over the place? Buggers!" he snarled all of a sudden. "You've sold the fucking country. Thieves. All of you are thieves!"

"Comrade," Volkov pleaded.

"Shut up! You report to whoever you want! By tomorrow I will either run our empire or I'll be arrested, you hear that?"

"Arrested?!"

"Well not yet but I will be if we don't succeed. Already Akhromeev is hanging in his study. The idiot tried once but the rope broke. Second time the loop got him. Nice, eh? Talk your unfortunate incident over with yourself! And remember, you are loyal to me and the Committee in this emergency."

The phone went dead.

It was six more hours before Volkov fully realized that the tide of power in the Soviet Union had turned forever and the Communist Party had destroyed itself. After numerous calls to to the Central Committee in Moscow where everyone was in shock, dismay and panic, and to the White House where Yeltsin and his loyal followers were jubilant and celebrating, the result of the attempted hard-line coup was clear. Volkov's former supervisors were as demolished and destroyed as the technicians and rocket soldiers on the smoking testing pad.

Volkov's reaction was quick and decisive. "Plotnikov," he called across the office to his deputy. "How many rockets have been destroyed?"

"Just one, but it was the biggest liquid fuel hot launch ICBM we have, the SS-19."

"Yes, yes. I see. No survivors?"

"No."

"What a tragedy. Listen, Alexis. Just in case," he mused. "I want your official report, and all the paperwork, to indicate that not one but four rockets were destroyed; Yes four!" he repeated decisively. "Three of them our solid fuel SS-25 newest missiles, the finest ICBM in the Soviet Union or the United States."

Plotnikov nodded in wonderment. "Hmm. Yes, but how . . .? I mean Doctor Zilko will see the report and know in an instant that we are concealing three of our newest delivery systems."

Volkov nodded soberly, stood up and paced across his office. After some reflection he turned suddenly on his subordinate. "Plotnikov, would you like to become number two in command here at Krasnov 86? It would mean a big raise in your salary and you would report directly to me."

A shocked look came over his face. "But Doctor Zilko . . .?"

Volkov cut him off curtly. "Zilko has argued with me for two years about even the most unimportant matters. As chief of the security laboratory of the secret city of Krasnov 86, he must be held responsible for this disaster. How many men were burned alive in this catastrophe as a result of his negligence?"

"We haven't had a final report yet but it seems as though everything within two miles of the liquid fuel explosion on the ground has been destroyed. The entire rocket regiment from the colonel to the lowest ranking soldiers must have evaporated. That would be at least a hundred trained men. But Dr. Zilko cannot be blamed."

"Shut up, will you please? Your director knows what he is doing. I will personally have Zilko arrested and escorted out of the Dome. His security clearance is cancelled. If he does not want to be the subject of an inquiry which could result in his disgrace and possible execution at an early age, Zilko will not try to return to his office."

Volkov clapped his new second in command on the shoulder. "You will take over Zilko's office as of now. Your raise will be reflected in your next check."

"I will do my best, Comrade Director. But for four years I have only been the chief ventilation engineer."

"I know. But now you will be obliged to become an expert on the missiles and warheads."

"What will Zilko do?" Plotnikov asked.

"I will suggest that he go to the First Secretary, Nickolai Martinov, and request a political job. I will even recommend him for a non-technical position away from the secret city. He will be able to take care of his family, unless he makes a fuss."

Volkov continued pacing around his office. "Four! Correct?"

"Four what, Comrade Director?"

"Four of our SS-25 Sickle ICBMs destroyed. And while you're at it add a mobile launcher to the destruction list." Triumphantly he prowled about his office. "So we face the brave new world with no bosses over us at Krasnov 86! Submit to me your damage reports as the new deputy director, Plotnikov."

As Plotnikov stepped into the elevator Volkov reached for the telephone. The moment was at hand that he and First Secretary Nickolai Martinov, yes and the Jap, had anticipated.

CHAPTER THIRTY-ONE

T he Hall of Colleagues at Petrovka 38 overflowed as more than a hundred and fifty Militsia agents, men and women, crowded into the auditorium. The commotion of anxious questions, arguments, hushed whispers, tense speculations rose to a crescendo. A troubled General-Major Alexi Bodaev with his Criminal Brigade around him occupied the front rows.

Ignoring conventional salutations, General-Lieutenant Nickolai Myrikov began to speak and the hall slowly fell silent. "This is a most important and difficult day," he began, trying to explain the right wing coup in progress.

"We have no official word as to the whereabouts or the state of health of Mikhail Gorbachev at this time," he continued. "But it is the duty of the Militsia, without fear or favor, to continue defending the citizens of Moscow against the growing violence of the criminal element."

Having said nothing that could offend either side, and for the first time making no mention of Felix Edmondovitch Dzerzhinskiy, General Myrikov walked from the podium, still maintaining neutrality and, he hoped, the tenure of his powerful position no matter which side prevailed.

Bodaev was worried. After Myrikov's statement, he had called a meeting of the men under his immediate command.

"There is no way of knowing how this conflict will resolve itself," General Bodaev said. "We can only follow General Myrikov's orders to stay neutral and do the work expected of the Militsia." He turned to Nechiaev. "What has been discovered as a result of the counterfeit hundred dollar bill turned in to us last week?"

"I think that somehow Jap is behind this," Nechiaev speculated. "Our New York colleague, Peter Nikhilov, is in Moscow on private business. Before leaving New York he discovered that high quality counterfeiting presses and paper have been sent here in a container full of clothing from a big New York warehouse. One of Jap's people in New York is involved."

The snatches of news from radio station Moscow Echo told of the crowds gathering around the White House, Russia's parliament building on the Moscow river toward which tanks were proceeding. After the inconclusive meeting, the officers of the Criminal Brigade returned to their offices. They were staunch democrats, dedicated to the ideals of Boris Yeltsin, for whom they had all voted, and President Gorbachev, whom they supported. Major Yuri Navakoff, Americanski (he had been wearing an American flag sewn on his denim jacket since his visit to New York with the police boxing team) was the first of the Militsia officers of the Criminal Brigade to quit the Communist Party as the tanks rolled toward the White House. Soon the entire corps of Militsia detectives disdainfully tossed their red membership cards through the open door of party headquarters at Petrovka 38. It was a daring move yet the officers, as one, felt they had to make the most strident protest possible against the coup.

Since early morning, CNN had been reporting live, beaming to the world the only television network coverage of the coup. The Soviet television stations were controlled by the coup plotters and only the ballet "Swan Lake" was to be seen on Soviet TV, repeated every three hours. Somehow the hard-liners had overlooked closing down CNN and by the time they realized the coup was being televised over the international network they had already lost the support of the high level national television executives who had the authority and the means to cut off CNN's satellite link.

Monday afternoon in the Urkaine Hotel, facing the White House across the Moscow River, a group of Pan American stewardesses, using all the mascara they could gather, imprinted on a bedsheet "AMERICA 4 YELTSIN" and proudly hung it outside their 12th floor window to the cheers of the gathering crowds on both sides of the river.

Well into Tuesday, troops, armored personnel carriers, and more tanks rumbled into Moscow on the orders of Vice President Yanayev and his fellow plotters as CNN kept telecasting the events. Soviet television stations continued to carry only "Swan Lake" as massive protests against the coup erupted in Leningrad, already being called St. Petersburg again. But the military pressure exerted by the hard-liners was by no means over.

The rain began in the afternoon and continued steadily through most of the night. There was no doubt in the minds of every Militsiaman standing firmly before the White House, in full view of cameras and, of course, the KGB agents who supported the hard-liners, that if the coup succeeded they would be purged to a man, imprisoned, exiled, and likely executed in the old style Bolshevik manner by their ultimate boss, Boris Pugo.

Nobody followed the progress of the coup with more intense interest than Vyacheslav Yakovlev. Standing next to Jap in their spacious new secure Moscow apartment was Zekki Dekka, Red Rolf, and Pavel. Pavel boasted, "You see, I was right when I paid such a bribe to be able to receive the American CNN channel in Moscow outside of the hotels."

"What are they saying Zekki?" Jap asked.

Zekki Dekka translated the commentary of the wide-eyed blonde woman reporting the action from Atlanta in the United States. The American, Red Rolf, was staring transfixed at the events taking place a few miles away around the Russian Parliament Building. He was tall and thin, his red hair turning gray at the sideburns, and his gray suit giving him an anonymous appearance in a Russian crowd.

"What does this mean to our operation?" Rolf asked.

With Zekki translating Jap answered. "It means you came to Moscow with your printing plant at the right moment. Chaos is the friend of the thief-in-the-law, utter anarchy is the thief's lover. We must do anything possible to keep the barricades standing. One thing I can see, the ruble as we knew it is dead."

"And the dollar stands firm," Zekki added. "Jap, you are brilliant."

"How is production coming?" Jap asked.

"We have the intaglio printing process working now," Zekki answered. "We should soon be turning out a plate of thirty-two one hundred dollar bills in record time."

"What about security?"

"Jap, we've gone over all this," Zekki replied wearily. "We have four Chechens on guard twenty-four hours a day."

"You had five. And already one of them is in Butyrka Prison," Pavel added. "The big jerk just had to go into Moscow to see some girlfriend and stock up on Caucasus hemp. Once in the city, of course, he reverted to type and tried to extort a storekeeper. The *ments* picked him up."

"We heard in New York he was behind bars," Zekki exclaimed in disgust. "What's wrong with him? He did a perfect job in Brighton Beach and goes berserk at home."

"We must work fast," Jap exhorted. "Chechen knows where we operate."

"Chechen won't talk," Pavel said confidently. "He knows we have his family located. Our lawyer sees him regularly and tells him not to worry as long as we are behind him."

Jap turned his attention back to the TV. The commentary was unnecessary, the picture told the story.

"Pavel," he suddenly called, "we must act. Tonight is critical. If the people ignore the eleven o'clock curfew set by the putschists and continue to resist at the White House until tomorrow the Bolsheviks will be defeated."

"What do you propose?"

"Get the word out to all the thiefs. We must send our people to the barricades." He walked to the window and looked out. "It's raining and spirits falter. Bring food and drink, vodka, to the demonstrators. Bring them umbrellas. And we must give them money. If we pass out half a million rubles or even more to the resistors and they break the back of this coup it will be the best spent money we have ever put out."

By Tuesday evening the thieves had organized, and an underground army of several hundred criminals was spending hundreds of thousands of their extorted rubles on food, coffee, vodka, cigarettes, and any other comforts they could find, and distributing the goods to the demonstrators. The criminals bought out McDonald's, Pizza Hut, and other food emporiums and carried their offerings to the stalwarts standing, arms locked, around the Parliament Building.

Characteristically, the criminals were taking no chances. Delivering comfort and encouragement was as far as they went, always alert to getting out of the line of fire if an assault really was launched. But they did an effective job of morale building and spent their rubles lavishly.

For some time there was genial banter between the Militsia and their traditional quarry as everyone speculated on what would be the outcome of this fateful rainy night turning into the morning of Wednesday, August 21st.

"If the Communist Party wins, your boss, Pugo, will have you all shot or sent to Siberia for life," Dimitri, an old Moscow mafia hit man handing out cakes, taunted Yuri Navakoff.

"And if Pugo and his gang win," Navakoff laughed back, "they will wipe out all you criminals who don't pay half the money you extort to the PolitBureau and party *apparatchiks*."

"But at least we won't have you young, underpaid heroes to deal with."

Yuri frowned at the sore point the racketeer had brought up. They were all suffering on their bare subsistence salaries. "So why are you out here spending enough money to pay the salaries of the entire Militsia for a year?" came his rejoinder.

"Perhaps we prefer outwitting the Militsia to the old Bolshevik regime," Dimitri answered as he turned to go beyond the barricades and purchase more sustenance for the masses of resistors.

As others of the criminal brotherhood handed out refreshments around the barricades, Navikoff spotted a familiar form in traditional acid-splashed faded denim wearing a seaman's cap approaching him through a lane in the steel pipes and crashed trucks. The barricades were, of course, far more symbolic than practical. The tanks could make short work of them. Even the KGB Black Berets on foot, the Militsia officers knew, if they obeyed Pugo's orders, could quickly push through, blasting their countrymen into compliance with the junta's decrees.

"Peter Nikhilov!" Yuri exclaimed. "Why do you want to risk your life out here on the barricades?"

"Russian history in the making!" Peter said. "If only my father could have lived to see this day, when the Russian people stand up against the Stalinists."

Yuri shrugged. "The orders to crush us might be obeyed by some hard line unit and then we could all be killed."

Peter surveyed the scene beyond the barricades, noting the motley collection of boats blockading the Moscow River preventing any military river traffic from approaching the White House. "We are witnessing the end of communism."

"You'd better be right," Yuri answered. "We all quit the Party. If the communists win, we die."

"Hey, Yuri," Peter tapped his heart. "I have a Russian soul in this American body. There's no way real Russians are going to shoot each other."

"I hope you're right. But I know the Black Berets of the KGB better than you."

"Listen to me," Peter demanded. "I found out something tonight. I came here to be part of history and I saw Zekki Dekka passing out coffee and cakes."

"Who is that?"

"He was with the Chechen murderers I faxed you about."

Suddenly loud cheers rang out through the rainy dawn as the tanks on the other side of the bridge started to turn on their treads and begin rumbling and clanking away from the central area of Moscow. As triumphant shouts echoed along the barricades, Peter took his Russian colleague's arm and turned him around pointing at a stout, bespectacled middle-aged man wearing a slouch hat drawn down on his head against the rain and a shapeless rain coat. He was carrying an open umbrella in one hand and offering cakes to the hungry throngs as he walked among them.

"As I said," Peter remarked drily, "it's a good thing I wanted to be part of history or I would never have been out here and spotted old Zekki Dekka."

"He is the master counterfeiter?"

Peter nodded. "And when this coup attempt is over tomorrow you had better keep a close eye on him."

"If we're still in business."

"You will be. It is our belief that Zekki brought to Moscow the

283

finest etched hundred dollar plates and treasury bill quality paper ever seen outside the U.S. Department of Printing and Engraving."

Yuri hooked his left hand around the American's right arm and started to lead him away from where they were standing. "Peter, you'd better tell Colonel Nechiaev what you just told me."

Yuri pulled Peter with him to where Nechiaev was standing with Boris Burenchuk observing the phenomenon of the racketeers and Militsia united against the common enemy of hard line communists.

"Colonel," Yuri broke in, "quick, look over my right shoulder at that man holding an umbrella over his head. You know all the criminals from Leningrad to Rostov-on-Don and Odessa. Have you seen him?"

Nechiaev focused on the figure Yuri had pointed out and shook his head. "I have never seen him."

Peter repeated his story.

"So what is he doing outside prison?" Boris asked.

Peter smiled and shrugged. "He was considered to be a potential asset by a certain agency of the U.S. Government. They arranged his release."

"There are a number of regional Militsiamen out here," Nechiaev observed. "Tell them to follow this Zekki when he leaves and find out where he's staying and who he's associating with."

"I wouldn't be surprised if Zekki leads you to Yaponchik," Peter commented.

Nechiaev turned back to Major Navakoff. "Yuri, the surveillance of this man is in your hands."

Zekki, in the company of Dimitri and another of Jap's sixes, left the barricades convinced that the coup was rapidly falling apart. Two of the off-duty plainclothes Militsiamen, who had joined their colleagues in protesting the coup, volunteered to go back on duty. They followed the Russian racketeers and their foreign ally through the exuberant throngs of Muscovites.

At Jap's apartment, he was jubilantly congratulating his cohorts when the telephone rang. Jap looked at it suspiciously. "Who has this number?" he asked.

"Practically nobody," Pavel replied, picking it up. "*Da,*" he answered. A wide grin came over his face and he looked at the American and then to Zekki. "Tell Mr. Rolf it is his toy, Nadia, on the line." Pavel listened at length and wrote down a number on the pad beside his phone. "Yes, Nadia, you and Zekki and the American will return to the plant in Zilisi. Maybe as soon as tomorrow. Thank you, and thank Oksana for us."

"What was that?" Jap asked as Pavel hung up.

"Oksana called Nadia from a phone booth to say her father had called her."

"I can believe he might have been worried about his daughter," Jap acknowledged.

"Nickolai wants to talk to you right away at his private number and he wants you to meet him in Irkutsk as soon as possible."

"Get Nickolai on the phone now," Jap commanded.

For the next hour Pavel alternately hung up the phone in disgust and then tried again to put the call through. "It seems everyone is trying to call outside Moscow," he muttered.

Suddenly Pavel looked up from the telephone. "Hey, Jap, I think I'm getting through." His voice lowered. "Nickolai, I have been trying to reach you for an hour. Take down this number in case we are cut off." Pavel spoke the number distinctly into the telephone. "Here's Jap."

Triumphantly Pavel handed the telephone to his boss.

"Nickolai," Jap began heartily, "I have been thinking about you these past three days. With no central government left you are king of the region."

Jap laughed at the response. "Of course you were always king. Things are moving faster than an ICBM falling on target, and speaking of that, it is my guess that the plans we discussed in Irkutsk with Hamster are ready to be put into action."

There was a pause, then Jap said, "This phone is as secure as my experts could make it and besides, the usual spies are in such serious trouble that at the moment they are out of business."

The others in the room could sense that a serious conversation was taking place by the long periods of Jap's listening and his grunted cryptic remarks.

After another pause Jap's voice was again cordial, even jovial. "I look forward to seeing you very soon, Nickolai. Yes, of course. I'll personally see Oksana and bring you a letter from her. Sorry to get you up in the middle of the night. Yes, indeed it was worth it. Goodbye."

Jap hung up and turned to the others, a triumphant smile on his face. "The past few days have set off a landslide of opportunity. It's the whole new world I have been expecting these past years finally come to pass." Jap spun around. "Zekki, you will contact your Iraqi friend, Azziz, and tell him we are ready to do business and he must start preparing his government's letters of credit. Also get in touch with that North Korean, Kim Tong Park. Tell him we'll be able to fill his order sooner than we thought. You and the American will get back to Zilisi and make the plant turn out product as fast as you can. We must take full advantage of the anarchy ahead of us before others can move in on our business."

Zekki translated for Red Rolf who was caught up in the excitement although unsure what was causing it. Zekki laughed at his response. "Red Rolf asks that we send Nadia back with him."

"It's already done," Jap agreed. "Anything to make our people happy and increase production."

CHAPTER THIRTY-TWO

everal days after the abortive coup passed through its death
throes and the Communist Party was declared no longer in
existence, Peter Nikhilov attended a meeting of senior
detectives in General Bodaev's large office with windows overlooking the grassy courtyard on Petrovka 38. Peter wasted no time
with niceties. "Where did your men lose Zekki Dekka?" he asked.

"In those crazy streets that run off the Arbat," Yuri Navakoff
replied.

Nechiaev smiled craftily. "Don't we know their haunts? Just
bring any one of them in and we'll soon have everything we need
to know." He turned to Peter. "What more can you tell us about
this Zekki?"

"He was a master steel engraver who took his skill to America."

Nechiaev made a suggestion. "Perhaps if we can bring Jap in
and question him we might find out something."

Boris Burenchuk broke his silence. "No, that would be a mistake and destroy the plan I have been developing."

Bodaev looked at Boris in surprise. "Plan? What plan?"

Boris shrugged and pointed to the ceiling. Bodaev nodded.

A crooked smile came over Peter's face. "Just before I left the Brooklyn DA's office to come to Moscow an informant told me that Zekki Dekka's gunman known as Chechen travelling under the name Josef Zilinski is in jail here."

"Would this Chechen or Zilinski know where Zekki is now?" Bodaev asked eagerly.

"Zekki took care of him in New York," Peter replied.

"Look up the arrest records," the Sly Fox ordered. "Find Zilinski."

"Good luck, Vladimir." Peter's tone was flat. "He has four or five identities going for him."

"We'll find him," Nechiaev declared confidently.

"We must," General Bodaev insisted.

"I suggest, General, that we meet here after lunch," Nechiaev responded. "We can pull all our records on every arrest made in the past six months and try to identify him."

Peter Nikhilov took Boris Burenchuk to dine at a restaurant where it had always been safe to talk and now, with the disruption of KGB and dismantling of the Communist Party, was guaranteed secure by Boris. "When will you be ready to meet Oksana?" Boris asked.

"Give me another couple of days to finish some business. Then I will slip into the cover we devised."

"What is this business of yours?"

"It has no bearing on what we are trying to do," Peter replied.

"Forgive my cynicism," Boris remarked, "but why are you willing to help us in this investigation of Jap?"

"For one thing I still have a job with the Brooklyn prosecutor and whatever Jap is doing in Russia will come to roost in my territory, Brighton Beach and Brooklyn. This is as much my problem as it is yours."

"I'm glad you feel that way," Boris said seriously.

"So for you I become an American of Russian ancestry who is anxious to do business in the land of his heritage. I can't speak Russian and I need an interpreter. I was formerly an American law officer and I became friendly with the Militsia. Now I am in the field of arms dealing. Since the Russian mentality considers policemen automatically corrupt, Oksana's associates should figure they can do business with me."

"And I envy you, Peter," Boris said with a smile. "Oksana will be a most beautiful companion as well as an interpreter. You'll meet her tomorrow evening."

"I just hope she still likes me when we spring the trap." His eyes roamed the well provisioned table. "Now that is settled, let's eat," Peter replied reaching for the caviar.

At five p.m. Peter and the Militsia officers of the Special Crimes Unit were still examining the files on men who had been arrested in Moscow over the past few months and were being held in Butyrka.

They had no idea what name Chechen would have been using and there was neither an arrest recorded nor a prisoner being held named Josef Zilinski. Peter reached in his pocket and pulled out his chronolog.

"What's that?" Boris asked.

"Tells the time everywhere on the globe. It's ten a.m. in Brooklyn. Can I use a phone?"

"Are you sure you'll recognize this Zilinski if you see him again?" Nechiaev asked as Bodaev reached for the telephone on a table behind him and set it on the desk. "What did he say when you talked to him at the airport in New York?"

Peter shrugged. "He was hanging spaghetti on my ears. I'd guess he's in his mid-thirties and he could certainly be one of those oriental looking Jews as easily as a Chechen from the Caucasus. I wanted to detain him but the immigrant rights groups would have had my ass."

Nechiaev smiled his sly look. "We had a similar problem until the coup failed. We couldn't touch a member of the People's deputies, the entire PolitBureau had immunity from police arrest or investigation. Now they're fair game," he added with relish.

As Bodaev started to dial, Nechiaev said to Peter, "I must warn you that there is no such thing as a secure call to or from this building. Even with the KGB out of business since the coup failed, we suffer the presence of implants, moles to use your American term, who monitor our decrepit telephone system."

"There's nothing I can learn from New York that the bad guys don't already know," Peter chuckled.

"But they'll know that now we know," Nechiaev remarked.

"Are you that compromised here at Petrovka 38?" Peter asked.

"Just between us in this room, my Americanski friend," Bodaev said sadly, "there hasn't been a month that we haven't discovered someone in the Militsia taking money for information."

"Hey, don't feel like you have an exclusive on the problem," Peter said sympathetically. "We also catch cops selling information."

General Bodaev reached an operator, gave permission for the connection to New York and then Peter began the torturous process of putting through an overseas call.

After fifteen minutes the gravel-toned Brooklyn accented voice of Doug LeVien, the District Attorney's head of investigations, came over the phone. Peter assured his part-time boss he would be back from Russia on schedule and then broached the subject of Zekki Dekka and "Chechen."

"So Zekki is there?" A note of excitement carried over the wire from Brooklyn to Moscow. "Now look, something just came up. The Bureau of Engraving and Printing finally admitted the missing plate for printing the face side of one hundred dollar bills was stolen, not just misplaced. Two employees, both naturalized immigrants, have not been seen since the plate disappeared.

"Jesus! It's probably already over here!" Peter exclaimed.

"Why would they want to send it to Russia?"

"I can't explain it now," Peter called over the phone, "but that plate is worth literally a thousand times more in Moscow than in the U.S. Now do me a favor, find out everything we have on Zekki Dekka and his sidekick, the guy the emigrés call Chechen, his last known alias was Zilinski, and anything else you've got on counterfeiters in Brighton Beach. I'll call you late afternoon your time, from an overseas pay station in one of the hotels."

Peter hung up and glanced at Bodaev. "I know you checked your arrest records and the prison records and found no trace of Zilinski which is what I expected. But perhaps if I went into the prison and observed the inmates, I could recognize this mad Chechen and we could question him."

Bodaev looked from Peter to his men seated around him and then back to the American. "At this point I am ready to try anything. We've got to keep up to date on Jap's activities. But there's three to four thousand men in Butyrka. How can you see them all?"

"There must be a way," Peter replied. "And besides, we don't want to make this search appear to be a police lineup. I'm sure that 'Chechen' whatever his name is, has a way of getting word to the outside if he needs to."

"I can call Colonel Arkady Sergeiavitch Matlovov, the commandant of Butyrka Prison," Bodaev offered.

"And you are sure you'll recognize this Chechen wild man?" Nechiaev asked.

"I'll know him when I see him," Peter replied positively.

CHAPTER THIRTY-THREE

⋘ ⋙

The English speaking business and political crowd was fast filling TrenMos Cafe, named in honor of sister cities Trenton, New Jersey, and Moscow. The customers looked like the diners and drinkers at an expensive, upscale big city American restaurant. From six in the evening on, the bar was three-deep with drinkers consuming American cocktails and highballs.

For the most part the patrons were Westerners visiting Moscow on business and looking for a touch of home. The talk was about politics, proceedings at the American Embassy, or deals being made in hard currency. The restaurant is located in the Lenin District of Moscow which encompasses some of Moscow's best hotels, Red Square, the Bolshoi Theater, and important government offices. Its ceiling is hung with flags of the individual states in the U.S. and the walls are covered with pictures of celebrities who have visited the restaurant.

Boris Burenchuk helped Oksana from the Mercedes he had borrowed for the evening from Petrovka 38. It was the first time

Oksana had visited TrenMos although she had heard of it frequently from tourists at the hotel.

The American owner, Jeffrey Zeiger, greeted Boris at the entrance and admired Oksana openly. They chatted in English for a few moments and then the host seated them at a quiet table for two against a wall. "These flowers were especially ordered by Boris," he said. "I hope you enjoy them."

Oksana smiled warmly at Boris. "They are beautiful." She was wearing a stylish black halter-top dress with an amethyst pendant punctuating cleavage that caught enthralled attention from the businessmen standing at the bar.

Oksana's eyes swept the room, taking in all the wall and ceiling decorations, the piano in front of the picture window looking out on Lenin Prospekt, and off to her right the patrons sitting and standing at the bar. She tried to keep her eyes off the large gray envelope that Boris had casually placed on the table between them.

Boris ordered Russian champagne and when it was poured and the bottle placed in the cooler beside the table he toasted Oksana. "Here's to you. And to a good future, for both of us."

They sat back in their comfortable leather-backed chairs and sipped champagne. It was very odd for Oksana to be in the famous restaurant with her polite companion, and she felt ill at ease. Her wide eyes remained fixed on Boris, watching, waiting. Obviously this police officer had serious reasons in mind for asking her to dine with him. This was not some sperm-blinded young KGB hoodlum. And the envelope on the table beside him was there for a purpose.

She didn't have to wait very long before Boris, in his roundabout way, began to broach the subject.

"I'm sure your friend Yakovlev told you about the interesting evening we had with him the night of Victor's death a couple of months ago."

"I haven't talked to him," she replied coolly.

"He gave us some valuable information on food racketeering. It would have helped us convict Givi, but unfortunately Givi was dead by the time we finished taking the evidence from Jap."

"Major Burenchuk, this is all very confusing to me," Oksana said with a helpless smile. "There is nothing I can tell you about Slava Yakovlev."

"Well you know he is interested in doing business in America and you will probably be his interpreter. Since he seems to enjoy the company of the Militsia Crime Brigade I thought you might pass on to Jap that he has not reported to his parole officer in a month and we would like to know where he is."

"I haven't seen him."

Boris handed her the menu. "I'm sure you'll find something you like here. Since you speak English so fluently you should also learn to enjoy the kind of food they eat in America."

He sat back and gestured about the room. "How do you like it?"

"This place? Well, I like our own restaurants better. They're cozier. By now we would have caviar, meat, chicken and ham on the table to eat while we decide upon the main course." Her glance fell uneasily on the envelope but Boris made no move to open it.

"I hope you enjoy this place," he said. "I have arranged for an American who needs an interpreter to meet us here. He would pay you well."

"You are worried about my welfare?"

"No. I just thought it might be a good opportunity for you." He smiled. "I am, however, worried about my welfare. There is still pressure on me to solve the Arbat case."

"You keep intimating I am involved in criminal matters," Oksana bristled.

"Please, Oksana, I merely suggest that we can help each other. And I certainly cannot deny that it is a pleasure to be in your company. Also you actually know this," he paused, "businessman, this Yakovlev, in whom we have an interest."

"The one time I saw Slava he said he was a capitalist, not a criminal. He believes that soon everyone in Russia will be in business for themselves or working for private concerns the way it is in Europe and America. He also said that communism would wither away." She laughed mirthlessly. "He was wrong. It blew away. In only three days."

"That's the only time you've seen him?" Boris asked pointedly.

She nodded. There was no way he could know of their discreet meetings. As Oksana put her drink down her eyes shifted to the envelope once again. Boris caught the glance and a tight smile passed across his lips. "Oh yes, I have something you might like to keep."

He reached for the envelope and pulled out a glossy photograph. With difficulty Oksana refrained from any expression of surprise as she stared at the grainy telescopic photograph of herself, with her veil lifted, talking to Jap at Victor's funeral, her eyes soft with compassion. An unmistakable almost embarrassing expression of fondness shone from Jap's face, the black pupils of his eyes resting on her from wide, barely slanted eyelids.

Boris let her stare at the photograph a moment and then slid it back inside the envelope. "A touching picture." There was a note of sincerity in his voice. "Your visit to him at Tulun and then your appearance at his son's funeral obviously had a much deeper effect upon Jap than you perhaps realized."

Oksana could think of nothing to do or say and wondered if the Militsia had somehow managed to circumvent the Jap's tight security at their other meetings. "Keep it," Peter offered. "Everyone agrees it's the most moving shot taken at the funeral."

Then suddenly to her surprise and relief a nice looking man in a very American suit, with dark hair and regular features that somehow had a vaguely Russian cast to them patted Boris on the back and in English said, "Boris, It was nice of you to pick an American saloon for our meeting. I understand that your young lady speaks English." He turned to Oksana. "I'm Peter, Peter Nikhilov."

Boris stood up, clapped Peter's shoulder, and shook his hand, gesturing at a chair the waiter, as if on cue, brought to the table.

The chagrin Oksana had felt disappeared in the warmth apparent between the two men, barely able to talk to each other without an interpreter. She felt strangely affected to see the harmony between this American and Russian.

"So I am in luck to find my good friend Boris sitting with a beautiful woman who can also interpret."

"How do you know Boris?" Oksana asked.

"I met him at the boxing matches in New York. We were both public affairs officers promoting the spirit of cooperation and friendship between New York and Moscow police. Actually I was no longer on the force but a volunteer for the job."

Oksana told Boris, who nodded enthusiastically, what Peter had said.

"What brings you to Moscow, Peter?" she asked.

"I'm a businessman. Even though I don't speak Russian my associates asked me to come because I got to know the Moscow cops so well in New York. Also I am of Russian heritage." A waiter placed a stem glass in front of Peter and poured champagne into it.

"You see," he went on, "in my business you need cooperation with the police. Hell, I used to give plenty of cooperation to folks who needed it when I was a New York cop."

Oksana understood police cooperation and gave him a knowing smile. Peter laughed. "Yeah. Maybe not what you think though. Everything was pretty straight."

Oksana, already enjoying the company of this slightly brash American, gave Boris the gist of what they were saying. He nodded and smiled.

"What kind of business are you in, Mr. Nikhilov?"

"Please, call me Peter. So what do ex-cops do? We go into security or arms dealing, or both. By sheer luck the commies put on this broken coup just as I arrived. Everything's for sale. I had AK-47s offered me all day, everything but a guided missile and I'll bet I could get one of those, too, complete with warhead."

"What would you do with it?" Oksana asked.

"Sell it, for double, triple to an East German group I work with. Like I said, I'm a businessman."

"You sound a lot like a friend of mine."

"Yeah? Tell him I'm buying, for good old American dollars. Say, do you by any chance *sprechen zie Deutsch*?"

Oksana grinned at the attempt. "Of course I speak German. I spent four years training to be a professional interpreter."

"Well Oksana, you are the answer to this American's prayer. May I engage you to interpret for me?" He winked at Boris. "Tell him what I said."

To Boris she said in Russian, "I cannot work for this man. I am busy at the moment and I do not want to get into business dealings."

Boris glanced openly at the envelope on the table. "Is Yakovlev keeping you so busy you wouldn't be able to help out a friend of ours?"

"Why is Slava so important to the Militsia?" The irritation tinging Oksana's tone caused Peter to blink.

Oksana put her hand over his for a moment and then said in English to Peter, "We do have our little disagreements, nothing serious." Peter nodded and smiled back.

"Don't you like him?" Boris asked. "He's a very nice man, and unmarried."

"What's that got to do with it?" Oksana glanced at Peter a moment. He was pleasant looking, not classically handsome but a comfortable type.

"Oksana, you will be doing us a great favor by staying with Peter as his interpreter and guide to Russia. He will pay you very well and we shall be grateful at being able to help out a friend."

Peter was amused at Oksana's translation of the exchange which came out that the Militsia would do its best to help him in his endeavors. He was perceptive enough to realize that now was not the time to press the issue. "Well, Oksana, tell Boris this evening is on me. How would you like to try an American dinner?"

"I suppose if I speak the language I should learn to eat the food. What do you suggest?" she asked, obviously relieved that the subject had changed.

"Are you hungry?"

"Haven't had time to eat all day."

"In that case you can't beat a New York cut sirloin steak. Tell my friend it's time to look at the menu."

They decided on their entrees and after ordering dinner Oksana sipped her champagne and advised Peter on the best sights to see in Russia. "You'll want to see the Bolshoi, of course, and then there's the Kremlin tour and . . ."

"I really want to see Siberia and Lake Baikal," Peter interrupted. "I'd like to see as much as possible of the homeland my parents knew. Do you know this area at all? My mother is from this region."

"Where are your parents now?" Oksana asked genuinely interested.

"My mother is still in Brooklyn. My father was killed just a couple of years after I was born. We were living in Germany and the Americans sent him back to Russia under the Yalta agreement. Stalin killed him. Until now I never had any desire to see or hear about the Soviet Union."

Oksana quickly calculated that Peter was in his mid-forties although he looked very youthful. "Our history books have only recently begun to tell us the truth about that era," Oksana said.

"Well, now that I'm here, I really want to know about my family homeland. And my associates in New York and Germany are paying all of my travel expenses. I would appreciate any guidance you could give me."

She couldn't help but feel some empathy for the American, and responded, "Well, I will try to help you." An American trying to capture some of his Russian heritage was not uncommon, she had discovered from her experiences as an interpreter, and like many Russians, it made her feel proud that Americans had this cultural interest in Russia. And the fact that his specific interest just happened to be the region of her own origin made her more sympathetic to his cause, because that was a rare request. Not many Americans wanted to visit Siberia.

Oksana began to enjoy the company of the American. But she suddenly realized it was getting late. Finishing coffee and cognac she said to Boris, "I would like to get home. I am due on the morning shift at the hotel, and then I have afternoon classes at the institute."

"Yes. It is fortunate that Marat called the dean and ordered him to reinstate you just before he was killed," Boris said pointedly in brisk Russian. "My driver will drop me back at Petrovka 38 where my car is parked. Then he'll take you both home. You might want to invite Peter up to your place before he is driven back to his hotel. The driver is on duty all night so don't worry about keeping him from home." Oksana blushed and bristled at this last, but said nothing. As they stood up Boris reached for the envelope Oksana had left at her place. "There is a second print in there you can give to Yakovlev if you like." She shrugged, tucking it under her arm.

Outside, Boris helped Oksana into the car and then took his seat up front with the driver as Peter slid into the backseat beside her.

"Say, you upper level cops go in style here in Moscow," Peter observed.

"Oksana, there's a bottle of cognac here if you want it," Boris prompted.

"I have what we will need," she replied.

The Mercedes stopped on Petrovka Street in front of the monolithic Militsia headquarters building and Boris slipped out waving back to Oksana and Peter. "*Do svidaniya.*"

"So long," Peter replied. Peter and Oksana rode silently back to her apartment. When the car stopped, Peter helped her out onto the sidewalk.

"You are welcome to come up for what you Americans call a nightcap if you like," she said nonchalantly.

The words were forming themselves in Peter's mind to say something like "just because Boris set this up doesn't mean you have to invite me to your apartment" when he quickly realized that she had not translated Boris's words on the subject. Pretending he didn't know Russian was going to be a hazardous game. He simply replied, "Sure."

They took the elevator up to her apartment and she unlocked the door. He followed her in, through the strings of beads that separated the foyer from the living room.

Oksana poured them each a cognac and she sat opposite him on the sofa.

"I was most serious when I asked you to be my interpreter and guide here," Peter said after taking a long sip of the cognac. "Whatever the going rate is for a full-time interpreter, I'll double it. I want to see this empire, I want to go to Siberia, and I think I can start some exciting business ventures in this new Russia. I want to learn our language. I could do all this with your help."

"I am still in my last semester at the Language Institute," Oksana replied.

"Couldn't you get a leave of absence to work with me? It would be fun for you as well."

"I will have to think about it, Peter." She laughed. "And we will have to pronounce your name properly. No more 'nickel off the price.' I had a terrible time translating that for Boris this evening."

"I promise faithfully to be Nik-HI-Lov evermore," Peter said in anticipation. "Can we be together tomorrow? For dinner?"

"No." Oksana saw the disappointment on his face. "I do not know if I can do it tomorrow but call me," she amended. "Please, let me think about this. In any case, not dinner at an American place. I will show you a real Russian restaurant."

He nodded. "Fair enough. How do I reach you?"

"Call Boris."

"I need a translator to talk to him. How about if I come up here and you can call Boris?"

"But if you are here already," a clever smile came across her lips, "we don't have to call him."

"Good." He smiled. "What time shall I be here?"

"I get back from the institute at six o'clock. Give me an hour. And now, Mr. Nikhilov, I must get some sleep."

"Fine. Seven o'clock. Right here." He stood up and they walked to the door together. She opened it. "Goodnight, Oksana," he said.

"*Do svidaniya*, Peter."

Oksana stood at the door of her apartment and watched Peter walk down the hall to the elevator. He turned, smiled and waved as the elevator door clanged open, and he backed in. She sighed happily. This was a good man, she thought, charming, and of course, an American.

CHAPTER THIRTY-FOUR

Boris Burenchuk was waiting in an unmarked car with a plainclothes Militsiaman driver at the curb outside of the hotel. Peter had left his comfortable apartment to make his cover as a visiting American businessman staying at a Moscow hotel more secure. Now he climbed into the car beside Boris and they were driven through the confusing tangle of signless streets for what seemed many miles of drab, massive cityscape before finally reaching their destination and parking in front of a warehouse. Boris was expected at the prison and he and Peter were escorted across a Byzantine-looking cobblestone courtyard surrounding the prison, a brick and stone structure four stories high punctured with even rows of windows, which ran between stone towers at each corner of the square monolith.

Inside the prison's reception room Boris introduced himself and Peter to a young officer whose slanted eyes and high cheek bones gave him an oriental look. "I am Captain Malik Mukhamedov. The commandant is expecting you," he announced leading them into a cheerful wood paneled office. Colonel Arkady Matlovov was standing behind his desk as they entered, a pleasant smile on his gaunt face.

"General Bodaev told me who you are looking for and I gather time is pressing," he began. "We have many ethnic Chechens in this facility, and as any Militsiaman knows they seem genetically directed toward violence even when it is unnecessary."

Peter smiled wanly. "I'll recognize him." The commandant led them out to the hallway. When they reached a heavy metal door Arkady produced an iron key as ancient as the structure itself.

"Has there ever been an escape from Butyrka?" Peter asked.

"I have never heard of one occurring in the past one hundred years," Arkady replied. "Despite our antiquated appearance, we are quite secure here."

They walked up an iron staircase to a second level tile-floored hallway running the length of the square prison structure. "These are the same tiles Catherine the Great put down when she built this prison." Then he gestured at the row of steel doors down both sides of the corridor. In each door was a small, square hatch midway from the floor to the top of the door. "We open this when the *calanda*, the meal, is served to the inmates."

Arkady pointed to the top of an iron door in the wall. There was a two-inch-wide crack between the top of the iron door and the cement door jam. With his finger, he traced the course of a thread which extended across the ceiling of the corridor and into the crack at the top of the facing cell.

"Placing that thread is what they call racing horses," Arkady explained. "They make a paper tube and tie a thread to a small pea which they blow through the tube across the corridor to another cell. The inmates secure the thread in their cell and then they can send messages on small bits of paper which travel along the thread from one cell to the other."

Arkady gestured at the thread and a guard reached up with a stick and pulled down the fragile communication device. Shouted obscenities instantaneously echoed from within both cells.

"Rustler! Horse thief!" the inmates cried—English words they had learned from American Western movies and TV shows.

Arkady, looking at the fallen thread, said seriously, "You see they have many ways of passing messages to each other. I can't guarantee how long we could keep word of your inquisition of a prisoner from getting to the outside."

Boris, Peter, the commandant and two guards ascended two more flights of iron stairs. "I have tried to separate the Chechens and bring them together in the exercise pens," Arkady said as they stood at the end of the walkway on the roof of the prison watching the prisoners pace about their small yards, swinging their arms and breathing deeply in the relative September warmth. "There are twenty pens on each side, forty in all, four hundred odd inmates out here now. Look them over," Arkady invited. "I'll walk down with you so they will look up. Most of them wave to me. If you see your man describe him to me and we'll separate him from his cellmates." As they began to walk along the uneven plank catwalk, Peter stared down at every face below him first right then left.

The inmates seemed sincerely happy to see the commandant and waved up at him. Cries of "Arkady Sergeiavitch!" and "My dear Commandant," rang out. Peter was truly surprised to see what appeared to be the honest affection the prisoners, criminals all, expressed at the sight of their prison warden. He was well aware of the hatred usually harbored by prisoners for Militsiamen and jail officials. The attention of every prisoner was fixed on the commandant walking ahead of him so none of the inmates below noticed Peter as he peered down intently scanning the men below. Then with only two cages remaining on each side of the walkway left to be examined, Peter's heart jumped as he very clearly and distinctly recognized the Mongolian-like face of the man he had last seen grimacing at him as he boarded the Lufthansa flight at JFK airport after the Brighton Beach murders.

Turning his back on the prisoner, Peter identified him to

Arkady. Back inside the commandant's comfortable wood-paneled office, Arkady turned to his assistant. "Bring me the name of the prisoner the American identified. And try to discover whether he knows he has been recognized. Something tells me he knew he was the subject of our inspection tour."

"I think I turned my back in time," Peter said.

"Maybe," Arkady replied doubtfully. Then to Malik he snapped, "Separate the man from the others, put him in solitary and bring me his dossier."

As the captain left the room Boris spoke up. "I'll notify our chief of detectives, Vladimir Nechiaev, that Peter has identified the man the emigrés called Chechen in New York."

Arkady chuckled. "So you will turn my prisoner over to the tender mercies of the Sly Fox? He will beg to come back to one of my cells."

The commandant's dark eyes gleamed as he went on. "Now, we will have a drink. Would you like to wash your hands? You never know what gets on you up there."

Following Arkady's lead, Peter and Boris banged down their drinks in the traditional Russian swallow. Hereditary Muscovite though he was, Peter had never been able to comfortably perform this feat of alcoholic indulgence but he got it down and kept it down. Boris gave him a sympathetic glance before himself suffering this amenity of the Russian drinking code.

"As a cop I've been around a lot of prisons," Peter remarked. "But I never saw one where the inmates had the admiration and affection for the commandant that these prisoners seem to have for you. Unless, of course," he added, "it's all an act they are putting on."

"Perhaps a little of both. But they are human beings and should be treated as such. They, of course, live under crowded conditions and I can sympathize with them and do my best to make life as bearable as possible. I tell them we are all partners here, the difference between them and those of us on the other side of the door is that we go home at night. But when we get home we are almost as crowded as they are."

The commandant refilled the three glasses. "I do not live much better than my inmates," Arkady continued. "At my apartment six of us live in two rooms."

"When can we interview our man?" Peter asked.

"Interview?" Arkady guffawed. "I will set up a place for the Fox to interrogate him. And when you are finished he will stay in solitary until you solve this case."

"Thank you, Commandant." The office door swung open and Arkady's assistant, Malik, reappeared holding a thin brown file folder which he placed on the desk in front of the commandant. "We have very little on him. The Militsia, now they know the name under which he was arrested, should be able to tell you more. He violently resisted arrest for extorting a shopkeeper on Arbat street. He was carrying a party card but couldn't remember the name on it. The card proved to be a counterfeit."

"He must have some high criminal connections," Malik observed as he shuffled through the documents in the file. A very expensive Moscow Mafia lawyer has been to see him."

Arkady nodded wisely. "Once we separate him from the general population and his lawyer can't find him, his people will be alerted that he is a suspect in a major criminal enterprise."

"How often does his lawyer come to see him?" Peter asked.

Malik consulted the files. "Twice in the past two months. He could be back next week again."

Boris smacked his right fist into the palm of his left hand.

"We have very little time."

"Sly Fox is going to have to work fast on this one," Peter said. "Zekki could be moving his printing operations right now." A grim smile appeared on Arkady's lips. "If this Chechen is the answer I will soften him up for you very fast. This I do not like and do not allow to be practiced in my prison but if we are under dire circumstances, I will have him ready to talk very openly to the Sly Fox." He turned to Malik. "The exercise period is about over. Separate the prisoner immediately and put him in Catherine's Pit. Report back to me when it is done." Arkady reached for the bottle of vodka and poured them all another shot. "I could put this Chechen in with two or three bitches. In time they would have raped and tortured everything he knows out of him. That was my predecessor's style. I do not believe in physical torture unless absolutely necessary."

"And the pit?" Peter asked.

Arkady chuckled at the obvious curiosity written on both his visitors' faces. "When Catherine the Great built this prison in 1786 to hold both political and criminal captives she knew that certain incorrigibles would be thrown in here and she ordered dungeons prepared in which the prisoner could neither stand nor lie but had to curl up on the stone floor in the pitch darkness and live with his excrement if he was fed, or die of starvation, in blackness and silence. For a hundred years men died in these unbelievably horrible conditions. Then the use of the pit was outlawed although it remained in the bowels of this structure. Once in a while, despite the ban issued by Czar Nicholas and sustained by the Soviet government, a modern day incorrigible has been placed for perhaps a day or two in the pit. It still seems to work. Generally, they come out babbling about the doomed spirits that are still there. They will do anything to avoid a repeat visit."

Peter nodded in satisfaction. "That sure beats any short-term means of persuasion we have in America. Ghosts, eh?"

"We're resourceful here in Russia," Boris said. "Ghosts don't demand much payment."

"In twenty-four hours Chechen will be ready to tell you everything he knows rather than go back in," Arkady said pouring them all another shot of vodka.

Twenty minutes and two vodkas later Malik returned with the news Chechen was experiencing the anomalous torment of the pit.

"Did he say anything to the others in his cell when you took him away?" Peter asked.

"He said for them to pass the word out," Malik replied.

"In that case, we will have to keep them separate from the population and deny them the opportunity to see their lawyers," Arkady said decisively. "That can prove quite awkward and provoke high level complaints."

"Between the pit and Sly Fox, we'll get Chechen talking," Boris commented.

"The last time we threw an inmate in there we heard him screaming to get out after a few hours," Malik laughed. "I truly believe that a psychic could identify many specters still imprisoned in the pit."

"Good. We'll come back tomorrow afternoon," Boris promised.

CHAPTER THIRTY-FIVE

⊰⊱ ⊰⊱

Within hours of the time Chechen was separated from the general population of Butyrka the internal telegraph system had spread the information to enough prisoners so that an inmate visited by his lawyer was able to propel the intelligence outside the walls. Before the day was over, Pavel learned that Chechen was the subject of special attention at Butyrka. Jap made an instant decision to move the money plant. The next morning he and Pavel drove the two hours north and east of Moscow to personally issue the shut down orders. They were followed by a car full of Jap's gunmen.

The town of Zilisi was falling into decrepitude with the loss of much of its industry. It was famous for its churches, long since plundered of their icons and crumbling into ruin.

They drove by the biggest and most modern building in town, the Communist Party Headquarters, a three-story new brick building now locked up and sealed, its assets—or those that could be found, confiscated.

"It is indeed a pity to close up shop out here," Pavel lamented. "We don't know that Chechen was even questioned."

"He was separated from the main population. That's enough for me. Besides, none of the party bosses we had in our pocket are good anymore," Jap observed. "That's what happens in coups. Now, anyone might poke his nose in our business out here."

The car passed the schoolhouse where the children were just beginning to gather and continued on toward the three story apartment building at the edge of the field that was part of the collective farm surrounding the town. They drove up to the double door entrance in the side of the building and stopped.

Dimitri and his Chechen guards, machine guns slung over their shoulders, recognized the boss and bowed their heads. He and Pavel walked inside and turned to their right following a hall formed between racks of men's and women's suits, jackets, dresses and shirts. Bales of casual clothing were stacked along the walls. Pavel and Jap strode through a deserted office and on into the printing plant formed by tearing out the walls of four apartments and transforming them into a single busy working hall.

Zekki Dekka was standing at a table examining each U.S. Treasury hundred dollar bank note the plant was turning out. Once the newly produced bills had been processed and inspected, they were stored in a vault that only Zekki could open. He looked up, amazed to see Jap actually on the site of criminal activity. "What on earth brings you out here?"

"Get ready to move, Zekki," Jap snapped. "That's why."

"Move, Boss? But why? We've got a smooth operation running."

"I want all the essential elements out of Zilisi in two days. Keep working today but I want us out of here tomorrow night."

"What's the trouble?"

"I'll tell you later. What's the count as of now?"

"When we closed shop yesterday we had exactly eight million two hundred thousand dollars in processed bills in the vault."

"I thought we were doing better," Jap remarked.

"It took more time than I expected to get started. We run off the face side, thirty-two at a time from the plate Red Rolf grabbed in Washington. Perfect. But the reverse side we've got to do intaglio one at a time. There were problems with the green ink, there always are. Now we've finally got it down to just over a quarter of a million dollars a day."

"Marvelous, Zekki, but we're still moving."

Zekki shrugged. "Well, the rest of today and tomorrow morning we'll have another quarter million or better, counting what's still being processed in the aging room. Would you like to see it?" he asked eagerly.

Jap sighed. Master craftsmen had to be shown appreciation for their efforts over and above mere money. He followed Zekki up a flight of stairs to a musky smelling loft.

Four men in jeans, loose fitting pullover dark shirts, a week's growth of black stubble covering their faces, and wearing soft woolen slippers trampled, their knees rising waist high, through an ankle-deep pile of crisp hundred dollar bills. Misha, his machine gun ominously displayed, a scowl on his black bristle covered face, walked among them as they paraded through the spurious currency. They handed it back and forth to each other, jamming it into their pockets and pulling it out again, holding it to their noses and sniffing greedily.

"You are keeping them honest I see, Misha," Jap greeted his gunman cheerfully.

"They wouldn't dare even think about anything funny," Misha growled.

"By the way, Jap, we're running low on cocaine." Zekki chuckled. "The paper in the bills is absorbing more coke than I thought. And of course it keeps the tramplers happy."

Jap smiled approvingly. "That's one thing I never would have thought of."

"Smell of coke proves the currency has been through dealers. Everybody knows that you don't give a coke dealer counterfeit if you want to live." Zekki sighed regretfully as they descended the stairs to the main room. "So where do we go?"

"A deserted factory at the north edge of Moscow. We can set up again there."

A door opened at the far end of the printing factory and the American, Red Rolf, walked in and over to where Jap and Zekki were standing. "Zekki, did you tell Jap we're finally printing full speed ahead?"

Zekki shrugged expressively. "The boss says we move."

"That's ridiculous."

At that moment the tall, slender, elegant looking figure of Nadia Bolshokova appeared in the door. She was dressed as though for a fashionable cocktail party wearing a clinging knee-length dress with a slit up one thigh and a snug bosom which showed off stirring cleavage to best advantage.

"Slava!" she exclaimed, "Pavel! We had no idea you were coming today."

"You dress like that for the workers?" Pavel asked.

"For the past few days I've been looking at all the clothing that arrived in the container with the presses. Nobody but me seems interested. We could make a fortune selling all these garments through Gums."

"The fewer questions that anyone connected with this operation have to answer the better," Pavel replied. "But help yourself."

"I'll take the currency with me now," Jap announced. "Finish processing the bills upstairs and bring them and the rest of your product when you come back to Moscow."

"Come on with me into the office where the vault is," Zekki replied.

"Zekki, this is crazy," Red Rolf protested.

"What Jap says goes," Zekki called back. "We print all day today and tomorrow we move."

"I want to bring as much of that lovely clothing as I can with me," Nadia said. "The American and I had such a nice apartment here and I hate to leave all the food and champagne."

"Quite frankly I think Jap is overreacting to certain circumstances," Pavel agreed. "But he is the boss. He told Misha to stay until the last person is out of here just in case there is some sort of a problem."

Then Pavel grinned understandingly. "You and the American have a cozy little spot out here, don't you? Jap broke one of the thief's main rules for you. Never let an outsider, particularly a woman, see an operation in progress. But he wanted the American to be happy and he thought we'd be running this wilderness print shop for at least another month."

"It has been enjoyable, and profitable," Nadia said. "The American is most grateful for my special favors and very generous."

"Good, keep him happy. Is Zekki working hard?"

Nadia laughed raucously. "He just found a little fifteen-year-old girl and gave her parents, in this ruined town, five hundred rubles, a fortune to them. So they let her stay with him at night after her school."

Nadia shook her head and clucked her tongue. "Zekki thinks sixteen is middle-aged, old age starts at eighteen."

"Just as long as nobody knows what's happening in the plant."

"They think we're making clothing. Zekki also gave the girl's father a new suit and the mother a very nice dress. He will be heartbroken to leave her."

"Let him bring her along."At that moment Zekki returned with a suitcase and put it on the floor beside Jap who opened it, smiling at the sight of the stacks of neatly bundled hundred dollar bills. Then he glanced up. "Let's have a snack and a drink before Pavel and I go back to Moscow," he suggested.

Carrying the suitcase full of counterfeit bills, Jap walked into the end room, a parlor, followed by the others. Misha, who had been assigned to protect the money printing operation followed. Jap beckoned another gunman to keep the tramplers honest.

"Misha," Jap said. "I will feel very secure here if you are standing outside the door keeping watch."

Flattered, the gunman stepped out through the back door. The forward bumper of a gleaming black sedan protruded from the open end of the one-story garage beyond the apartment building where an armed driver was posted.

In the cozy surroundings of the parlor at the end of the building, with bright colored clothing hanging on the walls, Nadia spread cold cuts, smoked sturgeon, thick ham, pineapple slices and two types of Russian dark bread on the table in the middle of the room. She placed a bottle of American bourbon and a bottle of cognac on the table and then retired from the room closing the door behind her.

Jap gestured to Pavel, Zekki, and Red Rolf to help themselves. "We are well on the way to achieving our goal. Now it is time for me to bring you into the details of the plan, the big *delo*. You may think I am being overly cautious . . ."

"We are all with you, Jap," Pavel's voice rang out. "You owe us no explanation." He took a long swallow of his cognac as his sentiments were echoed by Zekki and Red Rolf.

"I appreciate your confidence. Have you contacted Azziz?"

"He's in Moscow, at the Iraqi embassy. I talked to him yesterday and so did Red Rolf."

"That is good because we are going to do a lot of business with him."

"Then it's just as well we are going to be in Moscow," Zekki said. "Red and I told Azziz we could get him whatever he wants."

"Red mercury is what he is looking for, to send back to Baghdad," Red Rolf added.

Jap laughed. "Red mercury? What is he, a fool? That's what the con men are trying to sell for making a *small* atom bomb. I have a few grams of plutonium 239 for him to show his people what we can deliver."

Red Rolf's eyes widened when Zekki translated. "You actually have plutonium in your possession?"

Jap's eyes glittered. "If I don't, there is going to be one factory manager and his family dead. Yes, we can get anything we want but we've got to turn out the money."

"I'll personally give the plutonium to Azziz," Red volunteered. "Azziz and I handled some of the arms sales to Iraq in 1988 when we were rooting for them to destroy Iran."

"And you will tell Azziz that we can supply his big man nuclear warheads and delivery systems that will reach from Baghdad to New York," Jap exclaimed. "I know they would love to have that."

Red Rolf let out a whistle. "I'll get a minimum fifteen million dollars if I could deliver a late model solid state fuel burning ICBM like the Sickle complete with its mobile launcher."

"That's about the number I had in mind," Jap agreed. "And when Iraq has one, every crazy dictator from North Korea to North Africa will want to buy an ICBM or at least a few kilograms of plutonium 239"—almost in awe Jap lowered his voice—"at a million dollars a kilo, the world's most expensive substance."

"Also we can buy gold, platinum, diamonds and emeralds with what we're printing," Zekki contributed enthusiastically.

"And get caught?" Jap snapped.

"There is risk of course," Zekki conceded, "but . . ."

"I never take unnecessary risks and never leave traces," Jap's tone was sharp. "We will not buy gold and gems with our counterfeit. This project is too big and that could draw attention to us before we pull this off."

Zekki, Red Rolf, and Pavel nodded in agreement as Jap continued. "We may use as many as one hundred people in my *delo* but only the four of us in this room will know the origin of the capital we put out to accomplish our goal." He paused, then, "You, Zekki, because you are the genius behind the dollars, and you will create the forged letters of credit."

Jap turned to the American. "You, Red Rolf, because you instigated this scheme in America during the time of Brezhnev and this year provided us with the plates to produce perfect hundred dollar bills."

Zekki translated adding, "And he got me out of prison."

"Also Azziz was originally my contact," Red Rolf spoke up seeking full credit for his contribution to Jap's *delo*.

"That is true," Zekki confirmed. "And I forged many loan instruments for Azziz when he was buying arms."

Jap put a hand on Pavel's shoulder. "Pavel, of course, will coordinate everything."

"No one ever doubted you, Jap," Pavel exclaimed.

"Now keep this in mind," Jap's voice was emphatic. "People have died recently because they were putting out counterfeit money and perhaps drawing attention to our operation before my *delo* was ready. Although I did not approve Chechen's grenade attack at the Russia Hotel it seems to have discouraged others from passing fake hundred dollar bills from laser color copiers."

"Not one of our bills has been passed," Zekki declared. "And we must not take the slightest chance on compromise."

Jap stood up, the suitcase of counterfeit currency in his hand as he turned to Pavel. "As soon as we get the new plant established and Zekki works out an agreement with Azziz, we fly back to Irkutsk and visit Hamster again." Lovingly, he patted the suitcase full of hundred dollar bills.

CHAPTER THIRTY-SIX

C aptain Malik Mukhamedov and two guards dragged Chechen from the black hole of Catherine's Pit in which he had spent twenty-four hours. In the darkened cavern under Butyrka Prison, Chechen was pushed into a chair under a high intensity beam of light. Vladimir Nechiaev and Peter Nikhilov stepped out of the dark recesses of the cavern and stood over the pale-faced, stout prisoner as he dug his fists into his eyes to shut out the searing blaze.

From the dark shadows the voice of the commandant rang out. "Now, Chechen, or whatever your real name is, you have spent some time in a place where we could put you indefinitely with the suffering spirits who died before you."

Chechen made a feeble attempt at defiance. "I want to see my lawyer. My boss is a People's deputy." Arkady laughed scathingly. "The Communist Party and its entire apparatus no longer exists. Your boss will soon also occupy a cell here. There is no person in Moscow who can help you except for this American." Chechen found himself staring into Peter Nikhilov's face.

319

"So it was you!" Chechen gasped in English. "I tell them in cell I think I see New York cop up there. What you doing here?"

"Still looking for the killer of the two Georgians in Brighton Beach," Peter answered in Russian. "Is there anything you want to tell me?"

Chechen sat in silence for more than half a minute before Peter turned to Arkady. "Put him back in the hole. He's no good to me."

Arkady, carrying out the charade, gestured at Malik. "Throw him back and forget him."

"No! No don't. Not there," Chechen shrieked in Russian, fear tinging his shrill tone. "What do you want of me? I will try to help."

"So who are you?" Peter shot back. "Josef Zilinski? Or have you used so many names you can't remember your real one?"

"My name is not important. What is it you want?"

"Where is Zekki Dekka?"

"I don't know where he is," Chechen growled. "Give me water."

Peter shrugged. "Since you know nothing you are of no use to me. Too bad you can't help me find Zekki Dekka. I could arrange for you to leave Russia and go back to Brooklyn. I could even forget about those two Georgians that were so mysteriously murdered at the Kiev Restaurant."

Chechen remained silent. Peter turned to Arkady. "Well Commandant, he's no use to me. He still thinks I have to treat him like some privileged visitor to America."

Malik reached for Chechen's shoulder as though to take him back to the hole.

"No," Chechen cried. "You will be in great trouble when my lawyer reports you to the deputies."

Malik laughed mirthlessly. "Don't you understand? There is no chamber, the Soviet Union no longer exists. You could have the chief of the KGB in your pocket but he is in Lubyanka Prison himself. There is no one to help you."

Chechen resisted being pulled to his feet. Malik raised his

knout, a slow smile spreading across his oriental features. "I can beat you to within an inch of your life before throwing you back into the hole, I can put you in with two bitches." Chechen trembled at the suggestion. "There is nobody you can complain to above the commandant who is standing right here."

"Give me water." The words came out of Chechen's throat in a dry whistle. At a gesture from Arkady a guard appeared with a tin cup.

"Start talking to the Americanski," Arkady ordered. "If we like what we hear you can have this cup of water."

"And not go back to the hole?" Chechen rasped.

"That depends upon your information."

At that moment Nechiaev moved into the dazzling circle of light that enveloped Chechen. The black pupils of his eyes stared down fixedly at the prisoner.

Chechen sensed the authority of the Moscow chief of detectives. "Zekki is with Dimitri," he began. "Water."

"Of course he is with Dimitri," the Sly Fox mocked. And then he brought his face close to the prisoner's. "But where is Dimitri?"

"He moves around. I don't know."

Nechiaev reached for the cup and dashed the water in Chechen's face. The prisoner licked the moisture from around his lips and then seemed to roll over like a whipped dog mumbling, "Zekki sent me from New York to tell Dimitri to find a quiet *dacha* somewhere in the country outside Moscow where he could get enough electricity to operate new machinery."

"Did Dimitri do that?" Nechiaev snapped.

"I do not know," Chechen shot back. Then, "Water. I am trying to talk."

The guard brought in another cup of water which Nechiaev took and held just out of Chechen's reach. "What machinery, what equipment for counterfeiting has come into Russia in the past three months?" he asked.

"I know nothing of this," Chechen replied reaching for the water.

Nechiaev allowed the stretching fingers to touch the metal cup, even to get a grip on it and pull it toward his parched lips. Then in a deft movement he released the cup of water and, just as the prisoner had brought it to his mouth, the Sly Fox batted it into Chechen's face, the water splashing over him. Eagerly he licked away what moisture his tongue could contact.

Peter Nikhilov re-entered the interrogation. "You were working closely with Zekki in Brighton Beach and Moscow. Surely there is more you can tell us."

The American detective's ability to speak idiomatic Russian was always a severe shock to the emigré criminals. "And what do you know about the hundred dollar plates that were stolen from the U.S. Treasury Bureau of Engraving and Printing?"

Peter simulated anger although inwardly the procedure was giving him a chuckle. He raised his voice to a shout. "Where they print the money!" On a hunch, he added in a menacing tone, "You were there with Zekki and the American, Red Rolf, in Washington when the plates disappeared."

Peter stared down at the surprised look on Chechen's features and read his mind. He was thinking that Jap would get him out if he didn't talk. Peter and the Sly Fox exchanged knowing glances. Now was the psychological moment to turn him around. Peter shook his head and walked towards the door.

"Chief, I have gone as far as I can as an active duty United States investigator. I appreciate your offer of allowing me to take this prisoner back to New York but it is no use. I suggest you turn him over to the bitches. Commandant, if you will show me out we will let the chief get on with his business."

The prisoner could not have missed the anticipatory points of light that gleamed from the black pupils of Nechiaev's eyes. Whether or not deserved, Nechiaev had earned a reputation in Moscow's criminal society as a sadistic torturer. "No!" Chechen shrieked. "The Society for Russian Immigrants to America give me the green card. You cop cannot leave me with Sly Fox. He a killer cop!"

Peter waved his right hand. "Goodbye, Chechen, Josef, whatever your name. You can't help me, I can't help you." He stepped out of the circle of light and started to leave the dismal chamber as Nechiaev moved in closer to the thoroughly shaken and terrified Chechen.

"Now," Nechiaev began, "with the American gone, we can finish our business—in the Russian manner." Chechen looked from the sharp-faced chief of detectives to the inscrutable far eastern visage of Malik and let out a strangled shriek. "Officer Nikhilov! Please come back. I will tell you everything! I want to go back to New York!"

Peter and Arkady grinned at each other. They both nodded and turned back toward the now-broken prisoner, Peter reaching into his pocket and pulled out a tiny tape recorder.

"First, give me your name, your real name," Peter began. "We know that half the documents you emigrés carry, from Moscow drivers licenses to passports and birth certificates, are counterfeit and forged. We will check out your records immediately."

A trapped look came over Chechen's face. "But you strip me naked, down to my true identity."

"You are, in fact, from the Chechen-Inglesia province of Russia. Yes?"

"My name is Dzhaba Camerdnadze," he began haltingly.

"Why are you back in Moscow?" The Sly Fox shook his head in disbelief. "Why did you walk away from all that American welfare and forgiveness of criminal activity? Why did you murder those two Georgians in Brighton Beach?"

Chechen looked back at him in silence.

"What do you know about the Russia Hotel grenade bombing?" Nechiaev suddenly asked.

"Nothing," Chechen gasped. "I will tell you how to find Zekki."

"Indeed you will," Nechiaev shouted. "But there is more—much more you will tell me."

Both Nechiaev and Peter decided to concentrate on the main piece of information they were seeking, the whereabouts of Zekki and Dimitri. "Where is this *dacha* in the country?" Peter demanded.

"It isn't a *dacha*. It is a three-story apartment building in the town of Zilisi."

"The town with the ruined churches?" Nechiaev asked, "where your people, the Mongols were stopped four hundred years ago? About one hundred and fifty kilometers north of here?"

"That is correct. I went up there with Dimitri twice. He thought it was a good, safe area to set up Zekki's machinery."

"How do we find this apartment building?"

Chechen seemed to be thinking hard. Finally he said, "It is near the school. I remember them saying that in September the school children walk by it to go to the fields and harvest the potatoes."

In a lightning-like thrust Peter snapped out, "How did you and Zekki steal the plate that makes hundred dollar bills in Washington?"

Chechen was so taken aback by the question he could only stare up in silence, mouth open, his sweat-drenched face bathed in the bright light.

"You heard the question." Nechiaev's voice was low. "How did you steal that plate?"

"I do not know. Zekki and the American with big government contacts did it. They had someone who worked in the money printing building with them. I do not know any more than this."

"Who else is in this scheme?" the Sly Fox shot out. "Give us names, descriptions."

"The American was tall, thin and had red hair. That's all I can remember. I came back to Moscow because I was afraid I would be accused of murder in New York. Zekki was in Moscow only a week before I was arrested and brought to this prison."

There was a long pause as Chechen collected his thoughts, hoping that what he had revealed would satisfy his interrogators.

They stared down at him pitilessly and he knew he must somehow supply more information.

"Well, what do you remember?" Nechiaev demanded.

"Zekki said the American spent many years planning to counterfeit first the ruble, then the U.S. dollar. Now this same red-haired American is working with Zekki and Dimitri and there is some kind of an Arab." The words poured out. "From Iraq. I met him with Zekki. He knows Saddam Hussein and even though they lost the war this Iraqi has money in all countries to spend on weapons. I don't know his name but he wears expensive Western clothes, has a mustache, and he even looks like Saddam."

There was a long silence as Peter and the Sly Fox exchanged glances. Then, in measured tones, Nechiaev said, "We will check out everything you have told us and visit Zilisi. In the meantime we will ask the commandant to find you a more comfortable solitary cell."

"What about going back to America?" Chechen asked plaintively.

"If your information helps us find Zekki and Dimitri and any others turning out fake money, I will see that you get back to Brooklyn." Peter grinned down at Chechen. "The murder suspicions against you will be investigated but I think you would be happier facing American justice than what the future holds for you here."

"I told you everything I know."

"Everything?" Peter asked. "You haven't mentioned Yaponchik."

At the sound of the name Chechen palsied, his hands shaking, fear wildly reflected in his eyes under the bright light. "I know nothing of him," Chechen finally breathed.

"Is he connected with Zekki?"

"I know nothing of him," Chechen repeated. "I worked only for Zekki."

"After we find Zekki I'll talk to you more about Jap." Nechiaev turned to Arkady. "Commandant, keep him in solitary."

Chechen let out a shriek. "Not back there again!"

"No," Arkady answered. "Until we find out if you are telling the truth you will have a comfortable cell all to yourself."

CHAPTER THIRTY-SEVEN

◁≫° ◁≫°

It was twenty-four hours from the time Nechiaev interrogated Chechen before the Criminal Brigade received approval to raid the suspected counterfeiting plant. Zilisi was a hundred kilometers north of the official metropolitan Militsia jurisdiction and the Ministry of Interior bureaucracy at Petrovka 38 was still in a state of disruption from the coup attempt and unable to make fast decisions.

Thus it was that on the morning of the third day after Peter Nikhilov had identified the suspect in the Brighton Beach murders, the Militsia Mercedes driven by Taki and carrying Nechiaev, Boris, and Peter arrived in the outskirts of Zilisi. They were followed by a second car driven by Yuri Navakoff accompanied by three other Militsiamen. They quickly located the school as other police vehicles converged on the target of the raid.

Captain Valerie Kutuzov had been assigned to lead the raid with his plainclothes Militsia officers attached to the regional headquarters closest to Zilisi. He and his men had driven directly to Zilisi and parked their two old and battered civilian cars near the school.

Nechiaev, Peter, and Boris stepped out of the Mercedes. Yuri parked behind them and started to take his favorite riot shotgun out of his car but Nechiaev stopped him. "We don't want to alarm them before we get in position. We'll have to handle this with our handguns if it comes to that."

Yuri sighed regretfully as he placed the weapon back under the front seat of his Volga sedan muttering, "I have never seen a Chechen submit to a peaceful arrest."

Peter and Nechiaev followed the sketchy directions given them by Chechen in Butyrka. The apartment building stood at the edge of fields that were part of the collective farmlands to the north and east of the town.

"If we are lucky we can stop this operation right here," Nechiaev said. He spotted Captain Kutuzov and his men inconspicuously keeping the front entrance under surveillance. By hand signals they communicated each other's presence. To the rear of the building, facing the fields beyond, was a narrow back door. Mops and brooms stood on either side of the door. The nose of a sleek, black limousine poked out the open double doors of a shed just a few meters from the rear of the building. The car, which appeared to be American-made, looked out of place in the rural Russian setting.

Two boys walked toward the entrance to the apartment building. "What are those two kids doing?" Navakoff asked. "They should be in school."

Boris stared at the boys. "They are dressed like Chechen kids, look at those fur hats." The Militsiamen watched as the boys entered the apartment house. "Lookouts," Yuri said. "They've seen us."

Kutuzov turned to the Moscow chief for signaled instructions. Yuri tapped Nechiaev on the shoulder. "Let me take over for him and make the arrest. He has no experience in fighting Chechens."

But it was too late. Kutuzov and two officers, following the chief's hand-signaled orders, darted toward the front entrance where they were met by two Chechen thugs. The two men lingered briefly in the dark recesses of the entrance, and then one of the Chechens abruptly tossed a hand grenade at the officers and retreated. Valerie and his men threw themselves to the ground waiting for the grenade to blow up and spew lethal shards of shrapnel in all directions. Miraculously the grenade failed to explode.

Without a second thought Kutuzov led his two men, guns drawn, through the entrance of the apartment house. Inside, they came across racks of shirts, coats, dresses, pants stretched the length of two rooms along with bundles of miscellaneous garments from T-shirts to jumpsuits. The regional Militsia leader turned and shouted out the door, "What is this, a branch of Gums department store?"

Boris and Nechiaev ran across the bricks and weeds toward Kutuzov. Taki and Yuri Navakoff headed for the shed in which the American car was parked. Peter, on orders from Nechiaev, stayed behind, observing everything.

Nechiaev moved closer to the apartment building entrance as Valerie Kutuzov and his men, hemmed in by the stores of clothing, were met in the hall by a grinning Chechen holding a grenade from which the pin had already been pulled. Nechiaev entered the hallway just in time to see the Chechen roll the deadly device along the floor between the bales of wearing apparel as though it were a bowling ball.

"Get down behind something!" Sly Fox shouted as he threw himself back outside the door and hugged the ground. But there was nowhere for the regionals to find shelter as they desperately forced themselves into the folds of the raiments lining the walls. The second grenade exploded in a hail of deadly steel slivers and pellets.

Seconds later Nechiaev leapt back through the door. Kutuzov

had taken the full force of the blast. His body was lying in a torn and bloody heap among the shredded toggery. Also entangled in the slashed garments lay his two severely wounded officers. A red tide of their life's blood was seeping along the floor of the hall. The bomb thrower, himself, had been mortally wounded. Nechiaev shouted for help.

Yuri Navakoff and Taki stopped in their tracks as three men in business suits dashed from the rear of the building and made for the limousine, their shooters spraying the area where the Militsiamen were crouching with covering automatic rifle fire. Peter was torn between cutting off the escape route and going to the aid of Nechiaev.

A sound of AK-47 fire burst above their heads and Yuri and Taki were pinned down by the Chechen gunmen. Peter tried to get a good look at three fleeing men. He thought that Zekki Dekka was one of them and another one certainly looked like a Chechen. Probably the driver, he thought.

Then, glancing back toward the garage, Peter caught a brief glimpse of a red-headed man who was dressed in typical American grey slacks and a dark blazer. He dashed out the back door and jumped into the black sedan as it roared out of the shed and sped toward the highway that ran along the edge of town. The Chechen shooters stayed behind, firing at the police raiders, sacrificing themselves in order to gain freedom for the bosses.

Yuri handed Taki his 9mm automatic handgun and, crouching low, started to run back toward his car, Taki covering him as best he could, emptying first his own pistol and then Yuri's at the Chechen gunmen. Yuri reached his car, grabbed for the riot gun and his AK-47 and slinging a bag full magazines over his shoulder he rounded the corner of the building and opened fire at the Chechens still spraying bullets in Taki's direction.

Peter ran for the building entrance and inside the hallway gasped at the sight. Blood was spattered all over the clothing hanging in racks in the hall. The young Militsia captain was obviously dead, bloody rents torn in his jacket and pants, his face almost unrecognizable from the grenade's steel shards.

"There's nothing we can do for Valerie," Nechiaev rasped in despair as he pulled a coat from the rack behind him and spread it over the body. The fierce crackle of Yuri's weapons outside were a heartening sound. The Chechen shooters were firing only sporadically at the Militsiamen now. They had accomplished their mission. Their bosses had escaped.

Nechiaev gestured toward the rear of the building. "Peter, see what you can find that will give us some clues as to what is really going on here."

Peter nodded to the chief and left the bloody hallway, stepping through the door into the late morning sunshine. Taki and Yuri, crouched low to the ground, advanced on the shed which the getaway automobile had hurriedly exited.

As the Militsiamen proceeded cautiously toward the garage the Chechens threw their rifles out the door of the shed and straggled out, hands high.

Peter walked into the back door of the ground floor apartment and started to search the richly furnished quarters. Obviously this was a country refuge for the highest ranking criminals involved in what Peter now knew must be Jap's counterfeiting operation.

He pulled open the door to a refrigerator. The racks were piled high with champagne and vodka bottles as well as jars of red and black caviar. This room at the end of the building with its own back entrance leading to the garage was obviously the lounge and no signs of machinery or documents or even a work table were to be seen.

He walked through the door into the next room and in an instant realized it was a recently stripped factory of some sort. It was actually three or four rooms with the walls knocked out to make it one large manufacturing space.

Then a flash of movement caught the corner of his eye, and he turned to see a woman's leg protrude from the folds of fabric that hung over a recessed closet in the wall.

He strode to the draperies and jerked them aside revealing a scantily clad, heavily bosomed, black haired mature woman staring at him with wide dark eyes. Suddenly she made a dash past him, but she did not go far, bumping into Sly Fox as he came through the doorway. The impact knocked the gun out of his hand but he seized the struggling female who was screaming and cursing like a taxi driver. Nechiaev pinioned her flailing arms behind her back and pressed her to the wall with one hand as he snatched his pistol from the floor with the other.

"Come on, honey, you are under arrest."

"You miserable junkyard dog, fucking *ment*, lemme go! I'll have bruises all over my wrists from your grubby paws."

"Careful, honey, behave yourself. And watch your tongue— you'll upset my guest, who like most Americans is naive and sentimental. He still sees something saintly about all women." He turned to Peter. "Peter, anything of interest here?"

Peter tried not to stare at the full breasts barely contained in the mature woman's bra. She was clad only in the most revealing of intimates, her wide dark eyes fierce and flashing in all directions.

"Who is this?" Peter asked. "Let her go, Vladimir."

Nechiaev released his grip and the woman dashed into the closet, wrapped a robe around herself and then stared out at both men defiantly.

Vladimir laughed sardonically. "You are looking at the famous Mademoiselle Bolshokova, a lady most agreeable in many respects and highly esteemed in certain circles devoid of law abiding citizens." He turned on her with a guttural growl. "You are in deep shit, dear, you know that?"

"I am in shit all my life you wretch of a dung eater. The closer I am to you the deeper I am in it!" she spat out massaging her wrists.

"Any more of your foul mouth and I will really make you sorry, babe. There are two dead officers out there. I can charge you with accessory to murder."

"Two? Fuck you! I have nothing to do with that!"

"That may be so but you are looking at the likely prospect of sucking cocks in jail free of charge to the end of your life."

A derogatory smirk came over the irate courtesan's face. "With your salary of a bit over 500 rubles—if you'll forgive me for mentioning it, it is you who are sucking cocks free of charge." She drew herself up haughtily. "As for me, I perform fellatio—each time for what you are paid a month."

Sly Fox's face reddened. Angrily he hissed, "All right, Cobra. You are begging for real trouble—you're under arrest." He seized her by the shoulder.

"Wait," Peter intervened. "She's hardly dressed."

"Which is how she spends most of her time." He started to push her from the room.

"Wait, wait, wait. I would like to ask her some questions."

As Nechiaev was about to bluster a reply Boris Burenchuk came into the room. "Come, Fox, there is quite a sight here. You won't believe it." He glanced at the girl. "Nadia, nice to see you again, my dear."

Nechiaev released his hold on her. "Watch her," he said to Peter as he followed Boris out of the room. Nadia straightened an overturned chair and lowered herself into it. When she looked up at Peter he saw the folds of flesh around the mouth. She looked fatigued. "Have you got a cigarette?"

He handed her a pack of Marlboros and a lighter. "So you are Nadia?"

"That's right." She took a cigarette out of the pack and lit it.

"Keep them," he said taking back his lighter.

"Who are you and what do you want?" she asked inhaling deeply.

"I am looking for a friend who I was told might be here. Zekki Dekka."

"Who told you that?" she challenged.

"A mutual friend of ours. A Chechen with many false names."

"So Jap was right," she exclaimed aloud to herself. "He did talk."

"What is Jap's connection with this place?" Peter asked.

Nadia stared back at him silently, drawing on her cigarette. She realized her quick answer had been a foolish breach of any chance she had to get herself in the clear.

"We could help each other," Peter suggested.

Just as quickly, she realized that she was, indeed, looking at her only chance of saving her own life: the American. America. Nadia shrugged. When she spoke, her voice now had the resolve of self preservation. "Jap and Zekki and others are going to Siberia to buy something special with the dollars they printed here. Maybe diamonds or gold or platinum."

"Who else was here? Two men ran out and jumped in the car, leaving you."

"You see, I know enough to help you. If I tell you everything will you get me to America? If you don't, I'm dead."

"I'll do what I can."

Nadia continued. "There was an American named Rolf."

"And you were entertaining him?"

"I was not brought here to give business consultations. Who are you to ask all this shit? American CIA?"

Peter smiled, he liked the nerve of this girl. "Sort of."

"I have fucked KGB, Militsia, prosecutors and bankers, but not a single CIA. Want to make a date?"

"Not now. And anyway you've been fucking a CIA operative, or a former one turned rogue."

Nadia looked surprised. "I thought he was an American mafia."

"Same thing. Why was it important to keep Red Rolf out here?" Peter asked.

"He started a money printing idea long ago with Jap. And he is the contact with some Iraqi named Azziz who he knows for several years."

"How did you get chosen to entertain the American?" Peter asked.

"My friend, Oksana, is their interpreter."

"Oksana Martinova?" Peter asked. Suddenly abashed, he realized he might have blown his cover with Oksana as a non-Russian-speaking American.

Nadia bobbed her head. "Of course. You know her?"

"How in the world did you ever even meet the daughter of a Party First Secretary?"

"It was set up. Pavel arranged it with Sunray, a dwarf goon who threatened her in a restroom and I just happened to come in and save her and her friend. Later she got into real trouble, purely by coincidence, but much to Jap's advantage. Then, as her friend, I arranged for Pavel to get her out of the mess."

"Why did you set her up? Why did you need her?"

"Her father had the power to get Jap out of prison, just as you have the power to get me to America."

"This is very important. I told you, I'll do everything I can."

"One other favor. I truly am a friend of Oksana's. Please tell her that for me, and tell her I'm sorry for dragging her into this."

"I will. Now, where has all that phony money that was here gone to?"

"Zekki was in a hurry. Jap and Pavel, that's Jap's number two man, told him to get everything out of here. I dropped in to pick out some clothes before the bastards dump them. And here you are—two dead *ments*, and Sly Fox gives me the chance to go to prison. Shit. I hate lesbians."

Nechiaev returned, looking serious. "So, chilled out a bit?" he said to Nadia. She gave him an icy look.

"Hey, Fox," Peter put a hand on her shoulder. "She can really help us. She knows plenty. Treat her right for me. Okay?"

"Do you think it pleases me to drag her to Petrovka 38? She

alone can cause more trouble than three arrested thugs." He turned to her. "Get dressed. You will, unfortunately for us, be our guest for a while. But yes, Peter, I'll do as you ask." Peter gave Nadia an encouraging look and followed Nechiaev out of the room into the main hall and up a flight of what appeared to be recently built steps.

The loft was empty, discolored shadows on old wallpaper showed where furniture had once stood. Four men on hands and knees faced the wall. A Militsiaman covered them with his assault rifle. All four wore handmade woolen socks. A carpet of crumpled hundred dollar bills covered the floor. A loud whistle of amazement escaped Peter's lips as he kicked through the currency.

"How much do you think there is here?" Nechiaev asked.

Peter stared at the counterfeit money, picking up a handful of the hundred dollar bills and examining them. "Excellent quality," he murmured. "I learned when I was chasing the cocaine cartel that one standard shoe box packed tightly with hundred dollar bank notes comes to a million dollars. I'd guess there's almost enough to half fill a shoe box here." He passed the bills from one hand to the other. "These guys are turning out virtually authentic used Ben Franklins."

"We shot one of these Chechen money agers when he pulled a gun on us just now," Nechiaev chuckled. "One bullet from my Makarov ricocheted off the three packs of banknotes in his breast pocket. Thirty thousand dollars can even protect you in a firefight against the Militsia thanks to these weak, ineffective guns that we are issued."

"You'd better get all this not-so-funny money collected and out of here," Peter advised. "Scour this place. We don't want even a single banknote left behind. And don't let any news accounts circulate until you find out where the rest of it is."

"It will be our secret for as long as we can keep it so," Nechiaev agreed. "We'll also keep our prisoners from here segregated." Outside the entrance to the apartment building the Chechen prisoners were handcuffed together as the chief of detectives and his men from Petrovka 38 stood by. An ambulance was taking the dead and wounded officers to the nearest hospital.

Peter escorted Nadia, now dressed in a smart business woman's tweed suit, out of the apartment. It was impossible to miss the intensity with which the two Chechen shooters stared at Nadia as she was led to the Mercedes. Obviously they had seen much of her. She had been staying with the men whose escape they had made possible at the cost of their own freedom and possibly their lives.

The searching looks on their hard Tartar faces, as though they were expecting some imminent event, alerted Peter to the possibility of further danger. Nadia's information could severely damage the overall counterfeiting operation. And her coming out of there without handcuffs on or a beating alarmed the Chechens even more.

Nadia saw the two glaring at her and then looked around as if searching for someone else. "Did you get all of the gunmen?"

"All that were guarding this place," Nechiaev answered.

Suddenly she shot a question at one of the Chechens. "Where's Misha?"

"Who is that?" Peter asked.

"The best killer Jap has."

"We'll send out some regionals to find him, unless he was in the car when Zekki and Red got away."

"No. He had his motorcycle."

Peter clearly recognized the fear in Nadia's face as her eyes searched the fields and scrub bushes beyond the apartment building.

Instantly, Nechiaev turned to Yuri Navakoff cradling his rifle in his arms, his trademark huge American revolver in his belt. "Look for another killer somewhere around."

Yuri had hardly strode out of the compound when the crack of a high powered rifle rang out in the distance. Nadia was slammed back against the Mercedes. Slowly she slumped to the ground, a red splotch appearing on her blouse above her heart.

"Oh Jesus!" Peter exclaimed, dropping to his knees beside her. Nadia's face went as white as the blouse she was wearing. He felt for her pulse for some moments, then shook his head looking up at a startled Nechiaev. In the distance they heard a motorcycle roaring away. Peter looked back at her and held her hand. Her eyes were fading fast. "I'll tell Oksana," he said. She blinked once and was dead.

Taki jumped into the driver's seat of the Mercedes, backed away from Nadia's inert body, and drove off, bumping across the rubble around the apartment house in the direction from which the shot had been fired. His left hand holding his pistol in firing position was extended out the window.

Peter was still on his knees holding Nadia but it was apparent that the marksman had been a crack shot from one hundred meters. He contemplated the sniper-type execution as Nechiaev and the other officers from Petrovka 38 surveyed the scene of the deadly encounter.

Peter took a last look around the refuse and clothing-strewn premises. "I'm sure that the killer was left in place to do just what he did if the Militsia arrived before they cleared out," Peter said. "It's really tragic, such a pretty woman, whore or not, caught in the middle of all this bullshit."

Nechiaev smacked a fist into the palm of his hand, frustration etching lines in his sharp-featured face. "How we could have left her an open target I don't know. I dread telling General Bodaev what happened."

CHAPTER THIRTY-EIGHT

❧ ❧

Boris and Peter stood outside Oksana's apartment. Boris carried a bottle of cognac and Peter held a bouquet of red roses. Peter had insisted on the personal visit. Someone had to break the news to Oksana that her friend Nadia was dead, killed by one of Jap's gunmen. Peter couldn't do it because if he said he had been in Zilisi with the Militsia he would appear to be one of them. This also seemed a good time to strengthen the relationship between her and Peter.

They heard the two locks click open and then the door swung inward on the chain. Oksana peeked out at them, saw Boris, and closed the door again unfastening the chain and then let them into her small foyer. They followed her through the strings of beads hanging from the ceiling.

"It's good to see you again, Oksana," Peter said handing her the roses.

Boris walked across to the kitchen and found three glasses which he filled from the bottle and took them to the sitting room.

"I was wondering when you would call me." Oksana took the

roses. "How did you get along without your interpreter?"

"My joint-venture partner speaks English."

"You both seem so gloomy. What's wrong?"

Boris handed her and Peter a glass of the cognac before answering. "*Nasarovia*," he said. They drank to the toast.

Then, "Oksana, something very tragic has happened."

A fearful expression crossed her face. "What Boris? Tell me."

"Your friend Nadia," he began.

"What about Nadia?" Oksana put her glass down.

"She was killed today. I am sorry.""

"Oh, no," she gasped. "Not Nadia. What happened?"

"Do you know where she was?" Boris asked.

An immutable look abruptly shrouded Oksana's features.

Boris smiled grimly. "I'm not here to question you. Nadia was entertaining the American, Red Rolf, out in Zilisi. Zekki Dekka was also there. You know what they were doing?" He held up his hand as she started to protest. "Please just listen to me Oksana. This is not an investigation, I'm just trying to tell you what happened."

"I don't know what Boris is saying, Oksana," Peter said.

"I'll try to put it all into English for you when Boris and I are finished," Oksana replied. "That is my job. No?"

"Fine," Peter said, and went to the kitchen and returned with the cognac, refilling the glasses.

Boris continued. "We questioned Chechen in prison and he told us where to find Zekki. When we arrived at Zilisi this morning we were fired upon. Zekki and Rolf escaped in a car under cover of intense fire by the Chechens who were guarding the place. Two of our men were killed in a grenade attack."

"And Nadia?" Oksana asked in a low tone.

"We found her in an apartment she and the American shared. He was part of this counterfeiting operation. Eventually she was most forthcoming and we took her from the apartment to our car outside and continued questioning her. But suddenly a shot was fired from some distance away." His voice trailed off. "She died instantly."

Oksana's lips trembled and she clasped a hand over her mouth. "Do you know who shot her?" she asked.

Boris nodded slowly. "One of Yakovlev's gunman. Just before she was murdered she kept asking about a man she was very much afraid of named Misha. Familiar?"

Oksana sat frozen on the sofa. She reached out for the glass of cognac which Peter had refilled and took a long swallow.

"Why did he kill her?" she asked.

"Undoubtedly so she couldn't talk to us." Boris stood by the window while Oksana translated for Peter.

"Will you be all right, Oksana?" Peter asked when she was finished.

"Yes. Boris is now playing Militsia detective on the trail. I seem to be caught in a constant battle of wits with them. They are trying to use me to find Slava Yakovlev. I have no idea where he is or what he's doing."

Boris walked back to the vestibule by the front door where considerable articles of clothing were hanging and examined the garments a few moments as Oksana watched him nervously. "This is all American made," he mused. "From Gum?"

Oksana shook her head. "They were presents from Nadia."

"Do you know where she got them?"

"I didn't ask her where her gifts came from," Oksana answered haughtily.

"The factory and apartment where Nadia died was full of such clothing. Oksana," Boris went on gently, "all those clothes we saw in Zilisi today, they came in a container which also was delivering everything Jap and his people need to make counterfeit money."

Oksana shrugged but didn't answer.

"There's one more thing." A regretful look came over Boris's face. "Nadia told us about you, something even you don't know. You were set up from the very beginning. That business in the restroom with the dwarf and the knife—Pavel set it up so Nadia could save you and become your friend. Jap needed you to get to your father. Nadia, just before she was shot, asked us to tell you she was sorry."

Oksana was devastated. Boris added, "The dwarf is called Sunray."

"Sunray . . . ." She repeated the word slowly, thinking back to that evening, reliving the events, no, not that evening, it was a different night, she had heard that, when? Suddenly she had it. Pavel, to Nadia, at the restaurant where she first met him: 'You are like a sun ray on a cold day?' Was that it? Something like that. It stuck out. It had been such an odd thing for Pavel to say. It was a code.

Peter, recognizing her distress sat down on the sofa beside her and put his arm around her shoulders. Looking up he asked Boris in English, "Can we leave her alone? This is all very stressful for her."

Oksana translated the words and after Boris answered she said to Peter, "Boris is asking us to have dinner with himself and Colonel Nechiaev."

"It's up to you, Oksana."

"I'd rather not. I've got enough to think about right now."

"Perhaps just the two of us?" When she nodded he said, "I'll leave it to you how to tell Boris."

"I will tell him that we are going to talk about my translating for you and then I will put you in a taxi for the Russia Hotel. That's where you are staying, yes?"

"That's correct."

Boris shrugged at her plan, nodded his head to Peter and walked to the front door, followed by Oksana and Peter. He took another look at the clothing hanging in the hallway and then put his hand on the door knob.

"*Do svidaniya*, Boris," she said.

"I'm sorry," Boris said. He opened the door and walked out.

Oksana double locked the door behind him and turned, facing the room. She took a deep breath, and let it out slowly, staring at the ceiling. Then, as if coming back to life, she said, "If you are hungry I will cook us some supper."Peter said nothing. They both went to the sofa and sat down, each taking another drink of cognac. Then she translated that last from Boris. "Nadia saved my life once when I tried to kill myself. Now I know why. God! That Slava is something else. Well, at least the KGB got theirs. I guess I have gotten something out of all of this," she said, trying desperately to find something positive to think about.

"So the jig is up," Peter said. "It's all out on the table now."

"Actually, it's kind of a relief. I don't know. I never understood what life in my country was really all about until Nadia and Pavel and now Slava," she walked over to the window and looked out at the night, "took over my education you might say."

Another long silence ensued. Then, "I have to wonder if Boris is right. He said they care nothing for me, they will use me and if they think I am a threat to them they will kill me."

Peter placed a protective arm across her shoulder. "When will you see Jap and his people again?"

"When Pavel calls, I guess. He always had Nadia contact me but now . . ."

There was no doubt in Peter's mind that Oksana was in a dangerous situation. He studied the beautiful, troubled young woman as she confronted her fears. Frequently when he took on an undercover masquerade he came to believe he was truly the character he was portraying. As the American ex-cop now looking for business opportunities accompanied by a gorgeous young interpreter he could bumble about pretending to be looking for excitement. But the reality of his position, if it was ever discovered that he was accumulating evidence to convict Jap of serious criminal offenses, would put the girl—and himself—in dire jeopardy. Of course, she already was. He had seen Nadia killed before his very eyes. There was no doubt in his mind what would happen to both of them if the truth of his mission ever came out.

"I am not really hungry," Oksana said. "But I'll fix you something. You like sausage?"

Peter shook his head. "I guess I lost my appetite too. You don't think you are in danger do you?" Peter asked apprehensively.

"I don't think Slava would let anything happen to me." But she looked worried as she turned to him from the window. "He needs my father's help." She crossed the room and reached for the bottle, pouring them both a shot of cognac.

"Oksana, you will be my interpreter?"

She nodded slowly.

"That makes me happy, and confident that I will succeed in business here," Peter said. "I hope you will be happy that we are going to be together much of the time."

"That will be fine. I hope we will be very busy."

"I'll take care of that. There will also be quite a bit of travel."

"Poor Nadia," Oksana almost sobbed going back into it again. "She was my only friend, in spite of what Boris said. All the girls from the institute were afraid to be with me after the KGB affair."

"Let it go, Oksana. Get on with life. I'll do what I can to help you sort this out."

He gazed into her wide brown eyes, and continued. "You make me feel much more secure about trying to do business here. We'll do well together. It's strange, this attraction I feel to the land my family all came from. I might add that I really didn't understand myself until I visited here a few years ago. That was my education. It was like seeing myself in other people, certain tendencies, mannerisms, cynicism. There's nothing more cynical than a Russian."

"I'll help you in every way I can although it sounds like you're doing just fine."

"There's a whole world out there, Oksana. This is a transition period. A time of great change, for Russia, for me, and for you. It is as if the continents themselves were moving. The key is finding the right people to do business with." A wry smile came over Peter's face. "In fact it just might be that Yakovlev and I could do some business together."

"What sort of business?" Oksana asked, obviously getting the drift, but wary.

"Well, an associate and I were buying aluminum here and selling it for a big profit in Finland. Now I have a buyer in Germany for unlimited amounts of red mercury. If Yakovlev has any connections with nuclear plants he can probably buy it cheap."

"What is red mercury?" Oksana asked.

"An ingredient required to produce small nuclear weapons."

Oksana shook her head. "I have never heard of it. But I will ask Slava when next I talk to him."

Everything seemed just grand at the moment. Peter was now becoming a true friend with Oksana. And he really did like her. She was a good person, beyond the business which brought them together.

"I can't help but just kiss you right now," he said and very delicately leaned over and kissed her on the cheek.

Oksana didn't move. "Why did you do that?"

"Because I really like you."

He kissed her again on the lips and she returned it, their arms gradually surrounding each other.

Neither wanted to be the first to disengage but finally Oksana pulled away with a sigh. Peter immediately dropped his arms and picked up the two almost depleted glasses of cognac, handing one to her. She did not refuse it. "I'm afraid I've overdone the cognac. But it is good and helped me get through some painful revelations this evening."

"You had a lot to digest," Peter agreed. He touched the rim of her glass with his. "From now on, we'll face the future together."

"At least until you go back to America." Oksana lifted the glass to her lips.

"And take you with me if you will come." His eyes met hers

and he nodded to reinforce his sincerity.

They finished what was left in their glasses and she set hers down on the coffee table. "I have always wanted to visit America."

"Good. Then it's settled. Tomorrow we go to the embassy and get your visa in the works."

The words were magic. They brought a glow to her face. Peter looked down at the empty glasses on the table. "Another touch?" he asked.

Oksana laughed. "Oh, Peter, my cup is running over now." She either slipped or purposefully fell against him and he held her in a strong embrace as his lips found hers again. The kiss was long and increasingly ardent.

Without saying another word, they moved together across the parlor, past the kitchen and dining alcove and into the bedroom. Oksana fell back onto her bed, looking up at him. She patted the space beside her and moved back toward the wall to give him more room.

Peter pried the loafers off his feet, pulled off his jacket, and lay down beside her.

"Oh Peter," she moaned, "my head is going around and around."

"I'll stay with you until you feel better," he said.

"I feel fine now, happy—and I shouldn't be. My poor Nadia."

"Let's just be together for now. We can put life in order tomorrow."

Without a word, Oksana turned on her side, her lips to his, her right arm over his shoulder, drawing herself tightly to him. They were both aware of the urgency in the embrace and kisses. Finally Peter breathed, "Oksana, let's get these clothes off our backs."

"Yes, Peter. Now."

He helped her to sit in an upright position and reaching under her blouse as she slipped out of it he unhooked her bra and slid it away revealing firm, beautifully formed slightly upturned breasts. He held them, thumbs caressing the hardening nipples and placed his face between them. Oksana put both her hands on the back of his head, holding him to her for some moments before reaching for the waistband of her skirt and pushing it downward. Peter unbuckled his belt and was soon bare from the waist down. He unbuttoned his shirt and pulled it off.

Now their bodies were pressed together, unhindered by any clothing although he hadn't taken the time and assumed the awkward position to remove his socks. For a moment he thought of the little man in the black socks copulating in old-fashioned porno pictures, but there was no stopping their lovemaking now and Oksana cried out in delight as he entered her.

For both of them their first release of desire, suppressed for the past hour, was simultaneous and tumultuous. "Oh Oksana, *Yalo blu vas*," Peter cried, realizing too late he had lapsed into Russian.

"So. You speak a little Russian," she said instantly.

"I had to learn to say 'I love you' in your language," Peter said, covering his lapse. "I was hoping I would need it."

"What else do you know?" she asked, unconvinced because he had said it so perfectly. It had the ring of a native tongue.

"*Spiceba*," Peter replied with a grin, slightly mispronouncing it as if reading her mind.

"*Spiceba*," she said perfectly, correcting him, "I thank you too. It was beautiful."

"And I never want to say another Russian phrase to you."

"What's that, Peter?"

"I never want to say '*do svidaniya*' to you, Oksana."

She laughed. "Nor do I, Peter."

He had covered his mistake but he would have to always be alert not to betray that he had grown up speaking Russian.

Twice more before morning Peter and Oksana made love, less urgently now, but delighting in the sensuous pleasure they could give to each other. It was late morning when they finally sipped coffee and ate some sugar buns Oksana had purchased the day before at the bakery around the corner.

The blast of the telephone startled both of them out of their lethargy. "I trust you have no engagements for the foreseeable future," Peter said severely.

Oksana made a face at him and then picked up the instrument. "*Da.*" She listened a moment and then gave a quick glance at Peter and replied in Russian. "I will call my father and ask him to set up the appointment at Krasnov 86 as soon as possible." There was a long pause. "I will call you back when I know. Meantime, I have an interpreting job which will last for some time. Yes, the American." Another pause. "Well, money's part of it. But this is my career. I like my work and I like him."

She listened a moment and then indignantly replied, "No he is not one of them. The *ments* are making American money from him in some way. In fact, you may even be able to do some business with him. I will tell you about it later."

As Oksana hung up Peter asked, "What was that all about?" acting like he hadn't understood a word of it.

"Slava wants my father to help him do business in Siberia."

"I don't suppose he said anything about Nadia?" Peter asked.

Oksana shook her head. "I'm sure they hope it will be a long time before I find out."

"When do you meet again? Did he say?"

"No."

"Well," Peter said. "What can you show me today that will help me do some business here?"

Oksana gave him a wide, knowing smile. "How can you think of business at a time like this? Well, I suppose we could take the tour they're giving for twenty dollars American through the secret KGB offices at Lubyanka. Everything, all secrets, are for sale now if you have hard currency."

"That's a great idea. Let's do it. You can tell them that there's more than twenty dollars American cash if they'll give me some good secrets." Then he paused. "It wouldn't awaken any bad memories for you?"

Oksana shook her head. "No."

"I will take you to a fancy lunch and we'll spend the afternoon bargaining for KGB secrets."

"Which," she added with a mischievous grin, "you can resell to the American newsmen in Moscow." Then, "Peter," a serious expression on her face, "maybe you would like to bring your things from the hotel to my apartment?"

"I would love that, Oksana. Thank you."

CHAPTER THIRTY-NINE

⋖⋗ ⋖⋗

Misha was the last of the fugitives from the money plant raid in Zilisi to arrive at the deserted factory building in the rundown eastern outskirts of Moscow. Zekki and Red Rolf were already directing their crew in setting up the printing plant once again. The highly paid workers hadn't been told how narrowly they had escaped the Militsia raid.

Pavel entered the new plant and summoned Zekki, Misha, and Red into the bare room Jap was using as his control post. They hadn't seen the boss since he ordered them to abandon Zilisi and all were chagrined that anyone had questioned Jap's wisdom in making the fast move out of the smoothly operating money factory.

"Was anybody left?" Jap shot out the question.

"Just some Chechen guards still alive," Misha answered. "I don't think Dimitri got away."

"What about Nadia?" Red asked. "We had to leave her or Zekki and I would have been caught."

"She got away," Misha lied.

Jap stared at his gunman a moment and realized he had indeed done his job. Nadia would do no talking.

While Jap was noted for his explosive moments of wrath, it was with remarkable equanimity that he faced potential disaster. Zekki and Red Rolf were forced to admit that they had fled from the money plant in Zilisi leaving a quarter of a million dollars behind in the final stages of processing. It was that or be captured in possession of the counterfeit money which would have been an even more grievous calamity.

Jap's reaction to the setback was a tribute to his fast thinking and self restraint. Instead of castigation, he made quick decisions. "This forces us to move much faster," he announced. "We have made the last permissible mistake. Another error"—he looked at each of his minions separately—"will be fatal—to everyone concerned. We now have very little time to consummate the *delo*. We will return to Krasnov 86 as soon as I can make arrangements for the AN-22 cargo plane we need." After a long pause Jap turned to Pavel. "But at this moment we must remove one danger point in our operation."

"We have the right guys who take our money in Butyrka," Pavel said anticipating Jap's problem.

As Jap had foreseen, Colonel Nechiaev wasted no time organizing a second intensive interrogation of Chechen, this time to take place at Petrovka 38. General Bodaev called the commandant of Butyrka and asked Arkady Matlovov to deliver Chechen by convoy the next morning at 7:30.

Chechen was awakened in his solitary cell at five in the morning and shoved into the corridor where the guards handcuffed him. He was hustled to a waiting cubicle and ordered to lie on the stone floor, two guards standing above him with assault rifles trained on his back. For almost two hours he lay face down and finally, at seven, the prison van arrived. He was prodded to his feet, led into the courtyard, and thrown through the rear door into the van. Not a visit to the toilet or so much as a sip of water was allowed him. The convoy officer, appearing to be sleepy and yawning, sat on the bench in front of him. Two silent guards were posted by the van's rear entrance. The compartment was shut off from the driver's cab by a metal wall.

Driving from Butyrka to Petrovka 38 along the uncrowded early morning streets, they reached the cross section of the Garden Ring and Samoteka Square. Chechen stared at the tops of the boulevard poplars through the small barred window and hissed with fury at the discomfort of a full bladder tortured by every vibration of the van. Just then the convoy officer sitting directly across the interior of the van from him reached into his pocket and started to pull something out. Strange, Chechen thought, prison guards were not permitted to smoke on duty. He stared down at his feet in misery and felt a push on his chest. He looked up to see the officer in front of him stretching a hand to him, a gun clenched in it, the butt within easy reach.

"Jap," thought Chechen. "He's finally taking care of me."

The officer was staring at him with unblinking, colorless eyes. The guards sat like unseeing logs one on each side of the back door. The van was making the turn into Petrovka from the Garden Ring and came to a standstill at the red traffic light.

"Take it," the guard officer rasped. "Everything is set."

The pressure in his bladder erased any caution Chechen might have known. He took the pistol with both manacled hands.

"Shoot through the roof," the officer said urgently. "Then get out. There's a yellow taxi right behind the van. Your guys are there. Dive in. They'll take off the cuffs. Good luck!" The guard unbolted the back door.

With the finger of one shackled hand Chechen squeezed the trigger. The bullet split through the corner of the roof, the sound in the small compartment deafening the guards. He let off another shot. One of the guards at the back door swung it open, and without another thought Chechen jumped from the rear of the van, the sudden morning light revealing the taxi just behind, dark figures looming in the seats. In one leap Chechen reached the taxi but before he could grab the door handle, dropping the gun, the cab suddenly rushed forward, circled the van and speeded up the highway.

"Bastards!" Chechen shouted after the cab. "Fuck your asses! Fuck you!"

He spun around, his bladder releasing its full contents down his pantleg, feverishly figuring which way to dash. Then he saw three rifle barrels pointed at him from out of the prison van. In an instant he realized Jap had set him up to die. Before he could reach for the fallen pistol fire spat from the back of the van, tearing his chest, splitting his head and heaving him backwards against the cars of horror-stricken drivers.

Nechiaev and Peter Nikhilov found themselves interviewing the prison convoy officer at 7:30 a.m. instead of interrogating Chechen. The death of another prime suspect, indeed the last one, was infuriating but Nechiaev maintained a calm exterior. With the Jap at large he was forced to anticipate the inexorable resistance to law enforcement that was occurring.

Nechiaev spent little time listening to the convoy officer's excuses. Somehow, the captain insisted, the prisoner had managed to hide a gun and the guards were forced to let him out of the van. But they succeeded in shooting him dead and should be commended rather than condemned.

Nechiaev dismissed the officer and turned to Peter. "The funny thing here is that the wretched captain will build himself a country house with Jap's money. But he or one of the other guards in the prison van will be caught again supplying drugs to the prisoners or something else and the rats all implicate each other to save themselves. A guard gives evidence supported by several prisoners. The captain is stripped of rank, brought to court and sentenced. In the camp, the former captain of the guards receives special attention of thiefs and their gangs. It would be a miracle if he gets out alive."

"Wouldn't the Jap help him?" Peter asked.

"Jap?" Nechiaev laughed derisively. "He will be the first to order him finished off. The captain can give evidence."

Peter nodded his understanding. "So the captain and the guards are potential corpses."

"Almost dead already. So why bother to arrest them and go through all the trouble with the Interior Ministry?"

"Have you checked Chechen's belongings in prison?" Peter asked.

"First thing we did after you spotted him," Nechiaev replied. "Nothing interesting."

"Can I have a second look at them?"

"Why?"

"You know what the proctologist says—one finger is good, but three fingers are better."

Nechiaev smiled and reached for his telephone. "I will give a call to Matlovov. Boris will drive you."

Late in the morning, Arkady Matlovov took Peter to the prison storage chamber, a large hall lined with thousands of metal boxes. A guard had already placed the box of Chechen's belongings on one of the high tables that ran down the middle of the room and opened the lid. Peter ran his fingers through the clothes and found a wallet at the bottom of the box. It was empty except for a small notebook. Peter rifled through the empty pages and then a card fell out. He picked up the business card of Azziz Al Faradi, Iraqi representative to the United Nations. For a moment, Peter's thoughts went to Hugh McDonald whose organization had been watching the Iraq Mission to the United Nations. Here was another link in the chain between Iraq's efforts to rebuild its nuclear capability and the Russian *organizatsiya*.

On the blank side of the card, Peter noticed what appeared to be a scrawled phone number. Z/D 291-37-17. He quickly shoved the card up his sleeve and turned to look at the commandant yawning in the corner. Matlovov was required to be present at this virtually unauthorized search by a foreign police officer.

"I am finished," Peter said. "Thank you so much."

Elated, he followed Matlovov back to the prison entrance, giving no hint of his discovery. The number had to be Zekki's phone in Moscow. Zekki had given the card to Chechen so obviously, the card was given to Zekki by this Azziz Al Faradi. On the way back to Petrovka 38 in the car he asked Boris, "is it possible to find the address of a place by the phone number?"

"Easily."

At Militsia headquarters Boris took the number Peter gave him and in a short time handed an address to Peter who glanced at it and requested a ride to the National Hotel.

It was mid-afternoon, morning in New Jersey, when he put through the call to Hugh McDonald. "Hugh, your old company comrade, Red Rolf, seems to be working closely with Zekki Dekka and Jap. He's also tied in with the Chechen, who we are sure killed the two Georgian thugs in Brighton Beach. Find out everything you can on Azziz Al Faradi, representative of Iraq to the UN. I believe he may be in Moscow."

"I'll see what we can turn up."

"Chechen, he was using the name Zilinski in New York, was murdered this morning. Almost certainly he was killed by Jap's people to shut him up."

"You're keeping real busy, aren't you?"

"Yes, between you and my Russki friends, I've become a full-time cop again."

"I'm sure your efforts are appreciated by all concerned. Call me back in a few hours. I'll try to get it together for you."

Hanging up from the call to Hugh, Peter set out to find the address Boris had given him. It was near the center of Moscow on the long, curved, narrow Vorovsky Street with its numerous nineteenth century architectural structures and embassies interspersed with high buildings. He walked into the spacious lobby of a ten-story apartment house made of light-colored brick. It was quiet in the mid-afternoon. Peter took the elevator to the eighth floor, walking down the hall to a black leather-covered front door. He pressed the doorbell several times over the next five minutes and finally heard the slapping of bare feet on the floor and then the lock clicked and the door swung inward.

A sleepy young girl in a loose fitting gown stared up at him from the apartment's dim interior. She looked to be only in her mid-teens but her well developed figure gave her a voluptuous quality distinctly disturbing in such a barely pubescent creature. Her brown hair in disarray, wide cheekbones, snubbed nose and large round eyes blinking incredulously at him, gave rise to an irresistible desire to pinch her warm tender skin.

"Good afternoon, lovey," Peter greeted her. "Where is Zekki?"

"Hello," she said shyly. "Who are you?"

"I am Pavel, his friend."

"Oh, come in then. I'll make us coffee."

Peter walked into the apartment and took off his raincoat. "Zekki went away yesterday. He did not say anything. He never does." She pouted. "He left me bored and alone. And I cannot invite friends in for the evening because you never know when he returns. He brought me here from Zilisi."

"Don't your parents mind you living with him?" Peter asked.

"He gave them money and clothes. I tried to pick out some of his foreign clothes for myself." She smiled engagingly as she slapped her buttock. "With my fanny it is hard to fit. I am going to lose some weight but Zekki likes me the way I am."

"How old are you?" Peter asked curiously.

"Old enough," she replied. "Fifteen. Why are you standing there? Since you've wakened me anyway, come into the kitchen while I take a shower and get dressed. Which coffee do you like best?" She turned on the stove. "Make enough for me."

She slipped into the bathroom and closed the door behind her. He could hardly believe the patter of information she had poured out unbidden. With this plump naive child-woman, obviously bored from being left alone, there was no need for sophisticated questioning. She would tell everything herself. He heard the shower water splashing in the tub and started looking around the compact one-bedroom apartment.

In the living room he sidled to the desk and studied the papers scattered over its surface. Pulling open the drawer, he found an envelope addressed to Azziz Al Faradi. It was unsealed, as though more material were to be added. Peter sifted through the documents and then came to several pages divided down the middle with Arabic writing on the right hand side and opposite it, the text written in Russian. He scanned the pages and was just beginning to form an idea of what Zekki and Jap's people were trying to do when the water stopped in the bathroom. He quickly collected the pages and slipped them into the inside breast pocket of his jacket.

Returning to the kitchen Peter poured hot water into a cup, dropped a spoon full of instant coffee into it and opened the refrigerator. It was full of uncorked liquor bottles. A rare Armenian cognac caught his eye.

His newly nubile hostess emerged from the bathroom, fresh after the shower, looking even more plump and pink than before. Her full figure was draped with a white silk gown. This was just what he expected of a perverted old lecher like Zekki.

"What is your name, honey?" he asked.

"Helen. What do you want with your coffee?"

"A drop of cognac, perhaps?"

Helen made herself a cup of coffee and placed the bottle of cognac in front of Peter at the kitchen table as they sat down.

"How long do you expect Zekki will be away?" Peter asked.

"I don't know. He said he was going to Siberia but I believe he was just kidding me."

"And you miss him," Peter said.

"I would not say I like Zekki very much, but he has money and is never cross. It is much better than some Russian drunkard who would beat the shit out of you and chase you around the apartment with a kitchen knife. My first boyfriend could be very mean to me. Zekki takes me to restaurants. My friend Nadia who has been with the American friend of Zekki taught me a lot about men." She looked at Peter covetously. "I just wish I could find a nice young man and do with him what Nadia taught me."

Peter regarded the girl almost with pity as he thought of the beautiful and elegant Oksana. "So Zekki keeps you all for himself?" Peter prompted.

"Well there is this Arab, Azziz, who came over just before Zekki went away. Zekki seems to want to please him. I was afraid to look at him and see how bad he wanted me. But I could not do anything with him. Arabs are weird and spread diseases."

"You mean Azziz the diplomat? He is weird for sure."

"Nadia told me the bastard was from the United Nations and he gave me flowers and chocolates and even wanted to present me a diamond necklace. I am afraid Zekki will give me to this dirty Arab. It's as though Zekki wants something big from Azziz and will even trade me for it."

"Listen, lovey, this is all very fascinating, but Zekki should have told you he has a package for me."

"Oh, sorry . . . No, he said nothing, just took his overnight bag and left."

Helen squirmed in her chair, putting one leg over the other as her gown slid half-open. Her full chubby legs tightly encased in black stockings made a tempting sight. "Are you leaving already?" she asked petulantly.

"You are irresistible, honey, but I have work to do. Thank you for the coffee and cognac."

As he reached the door she called out, "Maybe you come back later?"

He smiled at her. "I sure will. Don't go away."

During the taxi ride to the Intourist Hotel on Gorky Street just off Red Square, Peter read the papers he had taken from Zekki's apartment. Although he could not read Arabic on the right hand side of the page, he assumed the Russian language on the left was an accurate translation. Suddenly everything was clear to him. He pushed through the crowd around the hotel entrance and strode past the security guards and through the lobby to the overseas telephone booths. He ran his Visa card through the slot in the telephone and soon had his call completed. "Azziz has been in our sights regularly," Hugh told him, "from the moment he leaves the Iraqi UN mission until he returns. Somehow he slipped away and we haven't seen him for over a week."

"He's right here in Moscow, Hugh. And he's about to conclude the purchase of at least one SS-25 solid fuel missile, known as the Sickle with a five hundred and fifty kiloton nuclear warhead. According to the specs I've just acquired, this rocket mounted on its mobile launcher is fifty-seven feet long."

"Great Scott!" Hugh exclaimed over the phone. "At NEST we knew what he was up to, nothing less than getting Saddam ready to fight another war, this time with nukes.

"This Sickle has a cold launch mode," Peter went on over the phone. "In other words it can be fired off from anywhere; it is transported with a range of eleven thousand kilometers, seven or eight thousand miles."

Hugh's whistle of shock and amazement came across the line clearly. "With that missile, Saddam could threaten anywhere in the world. Any idea where the ICBM is coming from?"

"Somewhere in Siberia is all I can figure from what I've been able to turn up. As I see it they don't want Azziz to know the source and be able to deal directly with the supplier."

"And Red Rolf is somehow involved," Hugh muttered. "The counterfeiting sounded like him and I discovered that just before he left the agency under a cloud in 1989, he was assigned to arm-ing Iraq with the capacity of destroying Iran's military machine and government. He worked closely with Azziz."

"Far as I can make out, the real boss behind all this is the Jap, Yakovlev."

"We have nothing on him. You have no details on delivery of this ICBM to Saddam?"

"Nothing except the price and that it will be delivered somewhere in Iraq by the sellers."

"What's the price?"

"Twenty-five million for one delivered with its mobile launcher."

"If Iraq has one, Iran will be next in line and then—My God!" Hugh exclaimed, "there'll be no end to it."

"They're also peddling uranium at one hundred thousand dollars a kilo and plutonium 239 at half a million a kilo."

"Oh my God, Peter! May I ask how you got this information?"

"Long story but I believe it is accurate intelligence."

"With the Soviet Union in collapse and precious little central authority, what can we do?"

"With the help of my interpreter, I'll try to stop nukes getting to the rag heads," Peter promised.

"Interpreter? Peter, what the hell do you need an interpreter in Russia for?"

"My cover is an American businessman looking for get rich quick deals who can't speak Russian. Besides, you should see her. I'll check in tomorrow. So long! There's an impatient gentleman waiting to use the phone."

Peter opened the door to the phone booth, bowed to the businessman shifting his weight from one foot to the other and then immediately headed for the hotel's copy center on the mezzanine. Calmly, as though he were copying business memos, he xeroxed Zekki's nuclear delivery agreement with Azziz along with the other papers he had taken from Zekki's apartment. Then, he walked down the stairs to the lobby, out the front door and pushed his way through the crowd, stepping into a cab. He gave the driver Zekki's address.

A sullen-faced Helen opened the door to her apartment when he knocked but the moment she saw him a smile spread across her rosebud lips. Her *zoftig* young body was packed into a straining blouse and short skirt. "You don't know how happy I am to see you back," she cried happily. "I was afraid it was Azziz."

"The Iraqi? What does he want? Besides the obvious, of course," Peter chuckled.

"Something Zekki left for him. I told him there was nothing."

"What did he say?"

"He said that was impossible. He had just talked to Zekki some place in Siberia."

"You didn't mention I was here?"

She shook her head vigorously. "If I tell him, he will tell Zekki and Zekki would accuse me of being naughty with you."

"Well why don't you make me a cup of coffee, put some cognac in it and we'll talk."

His eyes followed the provocative plump form as Helen walked into the kitchen. Then he pulled open the single drawer of the mahogany desk with a green leather inlaid top and placed the envelope addressed to Azziz in it along with the other papers he had taken. Sliding the drawer closed, he straightened up and walked into the kitchen where Helen was heating a kettle of water.

She turned away from the stove and he felt her full breasts pressing against his chest. He put a hand on each of her shoulders and bent over, giving her a chaste kiss on the forehead. "Did you search carefully for the envelope Azziz wants?"

"I think so."

"Look again," Peter urged. Helen shrugged and walked over to the desk. "Maybe Zekki put it in the drawer," Peter suggested.

Helen opened the desk drawer and reached inside. Suddenly she laughed as she pulled out the envelope. "Now how did I miss it before?"

"Look, Helen, I do not want to be here when Azziz comes by. I'll just wait outside."

"You'll come back when he leaves?" she asked anxiously.

"Or at least I'll call." Peter gave her a friendly kiss on her pursed lips and then strode to the door, opened it, and stepped out.

He had hardly reached the elevator, when he heard it rising in the shaft. He moved away and pretended to be inserting a key in an apartment front door when the door clanged open. Cautiously, Peter stole a look at the man in the black suit and red tie who indeed looked like Saddam Hussein. Azziz walked down the hall and knocked on the door to Zekki's apartment which was immediately opened. Peter watched the Arab step inside and pull the door closed behind him.

CHAPTER FORTY

⊰⊱ ⊰⊱

Jap stood uneasily in the low-ceilinged, long, narrow underground vault. At its far end several cardboard head and torso targets attached to wooden poles were brightly illuminated. He watched as Max picked up the weapon, caressed its polished stock and smiled at Jap and Pavel. "Makes absolutely no noise, quieter than the most efficient silencer," Max said. "It's range exceeds an average pistol. Try it."

Pavel reached out for the crossbow. "Wet operations are my department," he said. "Of course this isn't why we are meeting. But as long as we're here—" He tried to insert the magazine containing the arrows. Max reached across and helped him place the set correctly. The crossbow was ready for discharge.

Max was younger, by at least fifteen years, than Jap. He wore a dark suit and was stoutly built. His hair was cropped short over a straight, low forehead which in the middle, with practically no indentation, slid down to become a flat nose. Small, piercing eyes were deeply set in the shade of the eyebrows. The narrow, small mouth seemed to have no lips. The whole lower part of his face was covered by thick unshaven bristle. The form of his ears and certain characteristic face features reminded Jap that Max had been a professional boxer when he was younger.

"The bowstring sets automatically," Max explained as Pavel took aim and squeezed the trigger. The arrow pierced the target at its center as the bowstring whirred again and another arrow clicked into shooting position. Pavel shot at another target and hit it in the head.

"A month since the coup failed and they are selling their weapons," Pavel remarked.

"KGB rushing into the private sector already?" Jap asked smiling.

"Many of us are," Max replied philosophically.

Jap took the crossbow from Pavel, aimed, and squeezed. The bolt flew true to the center of the torso.

"Well, Max," Jap said, "I didn't go to all the trouble of locating you for the purpose of buying medieval weaponry, lethal though I can see it is." He placed the crossbow on the table in front of him. "It has been a fascinating demonstration. You have created a great weapons system. Now, can we get down to the business that brings me to your KGB lair?"

"Of course, Jap. It's just that I recall you in the old days being interested in any instrument designed to kill or maim."

Jap chuckled. "That was when you did your killing for our side, before the KGB recognized your talent and appropriated you."

"I was lucky," Max conceded. "They offered me two alternatives. Join them here in the A Department or be disposed of by the A Department. Becoming part of the State apparatus was the only logical choice."

"If you can't beat them, join them," Jap agreed.

Max picked up the crossbow, took aim and squeezed off the three remaining arrows in the set. They stuck out of the forehead of the target in a tight cluster. Then wordlessly he put the weapon down. "If you follow me I'll take you up to one of our interrogation rooms where we can talk."

The prospect of going to a KGB Special Section interrogation room, even since the agency's abrupt forced reform after the failed coup, was chilling but Jap and Pavel followed Max out of the shooting gallery and up two flights of stairs and through curiously empty hallways.

"Since the events of August nineteen to twenty-one, most of our personnel have migrated to more hospitable surroundings," Max explained. "Only a few of us have remained on duty since many of our superiors were imprisoned or fired when the coup failed."

Max led Jap and Pavel into a bare room which looked out on the open courtyard of this bastion of State Security. There was a table in the middle of the room on which rested a handsome polished wood box over a foot long, six or eight inches wide. Also on the table was a thick manila envelope and beside it a file folder. Max pulled a chair out from behind the table and gestured to the two other straight back chairs facing him.

Outside it was a warm, sunny late-September Moscow morning. Jap and Pavel sat down to find themselves looking into the glare from the window. Max, sitting opposite them, smiled and opened the file folder in front of him.

"So, Jap, I always wondered about your background. When, to my great surprise, you contacted me last week I applied for the State Security files on you." He tapped the file folder in front of him. "You did not come here to see how a young six like me, who once buried an enemy under the pavement for you, has made out in life with the KGB."

"That is true of course, Max," Jap agreed. "It is a rule of the thief-in-the-law that we never contact anyone in State Security. But in the light of extraordinary events, everything has changed. Old rules no longer apply. And there is something that a surviving officer of recent KGB purges can do for me. A service for which I am prepared to pay handsomely, in rubles or dollars, or a combination of the two."

"It may just happen that we shall actually exchange services," Max said. "And since you are here, let us review the life reflected in these files. Information is, after all, our most precious commodity."

He stared down at the open file folder in front of him. "Yakovlev, Vyacheslav Kyrillovich. Born in 1936 in Dzezkazagan, to mixed Russian-Kazakh parents who moved to Samarkand in 1945."

"The biography is unnecessary," Pavel interrupted but Max went on imperturbably.

"Notorious drug dealer, Ali Mamatadgi, nicknamed Jackal, found dead from two gunshot wounds. Slava and his mother show up in Moscow. In secondary school he turns in poor grades, becomes boxing champion in all-Moscow junior competition. Refusal to serve in army on the pretext of boxing trauma. The trauma, however does not interfere with further boxing. Gennady Korkov, nicknamed Mongol, spots the young and daring athlete. Soon Slava becomes chief of a gang which includes several prostitutes."

The recitation continued despite Jap's obvious annoyance. "Heated irons were put to the bellies of drug dealers and rich racketeers fingered by the girls causing them to give much money to Jap's *obshak*." Max suddenly looked up from the file. "Aha, here we are. Jeweler Nathan Savich, found dead in his apartment, tied up, melted metal rod in his anus." The voice turned acid. "The Jewish community is alarmed. That was a big mistake. After all, Khrushchev's son is married to a Jewish girl. Gang members are arrested one after another. Mongol himself falls behind bars."

"All very interesting," Pavel interrupted, "but we have business to discuss."

Max chuckled. "Somehow Slava reasons with the outraged sons of Israel. He invests money in their businesses. Life is generous to him. He invests into people too. Party officials, Militsiamen, KGB officers and famous people—eye surgeon Fedorov for example, are in his debt."

Max paused. "An investment that really paid off was in Otari Quantrishvili: five hundred thousand rubles."

"Five hundred twenty thousand was the exact figure," Jap interrupted coolly. "Now can we get on with our business?"

Max ignored the request. "I'll correct it here. Yes, five hundred twenty thousand." He made a notation on the dossier. "Otari, gambling partner of Galina Brezhneva, recommends Jap for special jobs to Militsia General Yuri Churbanov, Galina's second husband. Jap produces and Yuri brings him to First Deputy of the Minister of Internal Affairs General-Lieutenant Nickolai Shelokov."

Pavel broke into the conversation. "That's all in the past, Max. We know that you know or can find out everything about everybody in the world. But your agency has lost its power. You can no longer kill openly."

Max was silent for several moments. "All right," he finally said. "We need some cleaning done but at this moment our hands must remain clean—or seem so. You will do the cleansing."

"Who do you want us to kill?" Jap asked warily.

"Certain dangerous former Party Secretaries and the like. What is it you want from me?"

"I need an airplane. An AN-22 cargo transport to be exact."

"Impossible," Max retorted. "What will you do with it?"

"I do not question your choice of who we must eliminate. I expect the same consideration from you."

Max nodded, conceding the point. "We want a smooth job that will appear to be suicide."

"We will be ready," Jap replied eager to get away from the oppressive atmosphere of this surviving department of the purged KGB. "But I need the AN-22. We came to you because you can get anything you really want."

The bargaining went on another half hour before Jap and Pavel stood up to leave the KGB Special A Division offices.

Max picked up the manila envelope on the table and held it out to Jap. "Inside, are keys and instructions how to get in and out of the apartment of the target that has been assigned to the chief of Department A from the highest authorities. Meantime, I will look into acquiring the AN-22 cargo plane you want."

Then he picked up the wood box and handed it to Pavel. "Since you are in charge of your *organizatsiya's* wet operations, I am presenting you with this crossbow similiar to the one you tried out down in the shooting gallery. It is easily assembled and may be useful to you someday."

Pavel bowed his head as he accepted the box. "I am most appreciative of this gift, Max, and I assure you that your A Department will be well-satisfied with our operation." Jap expressed his appreciation for the gift and Max escorted them from the building.

Edmond Kruchina was a badly frightened communist as he contemplated how his life had collapsed in one mad month, his once unassailable position, Manager of Affairs of the Communist Party Central Committee, shattered. He had sent his wife and children out to the country *dacha* that morning.

In Party buildings on the Old Square his minions had feverishly fed revealing documents into the paper shredding machines until the army and Militsia loyal to the democrats had sealed shut the once mighty corridors of power. Now, the secrets of where the party's misappropriated billions in gold and foreign currency had been deposited were securely locked in his head and among his personal papers.

Kruchina had swilled down nearly a full bottle of cognac and felt the need to escape the fog of doom hanging in his luxury apartment. He decided to take a stroll on Leninsky Prospekt in the night air. After half an hour walking the street, peering into shop windows and talking to the Militsiaman on duty, he felt better and let himself back into the warm, dark, dry apartment.

His frame of mind had improved. One trip to Switzerland and he could lay his hands on millions. But then as he entered his study he felt that something was utterly wrong. Slowly, he became aware of the man sitting in the dark shadow of the big room with eyes of an oriental slant that glistened viciously.

Kruchina stepped back involuntarily and tripped over the edge of the thick Persian carpet but was prevented from falling by strong hands seizing him from behind. A thick handkerchief soaked with chloroform was abruptly clamped to his face. Jap pushed open the French windows and Kruchina felt neither the rain on his skin nor the gusts of night wind, nor the crushing blow against cold wet metal far below.

Pavel finished snapping photographs of the documents arrayed on Kruchina's desk.

"Hey, Jap," Pavel called, "some interesting papers here!"

"Just get the pictures and get out!" Jap's voice was urgent. "KGB can show up any minute. They want these dossiers and won't sleep until they have them."

In minutes from the time they threw Kruchina out the window of his apartment, Jap and Pavel were out of the building climbing into the car parked on a side street behind the apartment building.

Despite the late hour, a crowd was already gathering around the corpse on the prospekt. It was a grisly sight. Kruchina's body hit the roof of the car parked below and broke through it. Blood was all over the interior of the vehicle into which the head had plunged. The major part of the body, legs held upright by the jagged rent in the roof, was sticking out of the top of the car looking like a ridiculous giant doll.

In the car, rapidly leaving Leninsky Prospekt, Jap again asked Pavel, "Are you sure all the chloroform will evaporate?"

"Dog sure. Not a trace in 15 minutes, not even in the lungs. A suicide. The guy was drunk, they'll find alcohol."

"Good. Now it is up to Max to produce the plane for us."

Pavel tapped the camera. "These pictures of Kruchina's documents will help convince him not to waste our time."

CHAPTER FORTY·ONE

❧ ❧

T hroughout the end of September and into October of 1991 Jap observed the crumbling Soviet Union fall into a state of near anarchy. It was a time of confusion and sharply rising inflation. But for Jap it was the propitious moment in history he had anticipated and for which he had planned during his final year in Tulun Camp. Politicians, some of them recipients of Jap's largesse, and ranking managers of high priority industrial establishments, descended upon Moscow from all parts of the former Soviet Union in an effort to clarify their positions.

Former Minister of Defense Yazov was in prison. The military establishment and its suppliers were in a serious state of disarray. And while the fate of the one-time super power was being discussed in the Kremlin, foreigners and tourists were turned out of the hotels surrounding Red Square to make room for the largest gathering of Soviet politicians and industrialists in Moscow's history.

Nickolai Martinov and Yevgeny Volkov made the trip to Moscow from Irkutsk together. Volkov stayed at the Russia Hotel.

Oksana regretfully had to ask Peter to find a place to stay while her father was occupying the apartment with her in Moscow. For two days Martinov and Volkov had been unable to locate ministers or even deputies to whom they were obliged to report. With the dissolution of the Soviet Union and central authority, Volkov found himself the equivalent of owner of the Dome at the secret city of Krasnov 86 and Martinov was the *de facto* ruler of the Irkutsk region of Siberia.

At this moment, with the nation's most influential political figures and directors of industry gathered in Moscow to shape the nation's future, the ambitious mayor, Gavriil Popov, chose to host an elaborate reception for the dignitaries visiting Russia's capital city from all over the former Soviet Union.

The twenty-floor building of the Council of Economic Assistance, next to the Russian Parliament Building or White House and across the Moscow River from the Hotel Ukraine, had been appropriated by the mayor to become the new City Hall immediately after the coup failed. The first three floors and a large underground facility with adjacent cinema theater and garage, provided a spacious setting for the festivities. Generous funds from the city treasury were made available to pay for one of the most sumptuous galas Moscow had seen since the Brezhnev years.

Celebrities of the stage and screen joined with the newly risen democratic political stars of Boris Yeltsin's administration to give the affair a lustrous quality unmatched during the fast-fading Gorbachev era.

The Democrats' command over the country's vast industrial complex depended upon the fealty of the temporarily masterless managers and it was vital for Boris Yeltsin and his followers to win these people to his side thus kicking one more support out from under the Communist Party. The celebration was an event in a chain of measures planned by the Democrats in their campaign to firmly seize total power in the new Russia.

Oksana invited Peter Nikhilov to escort her to the party. Her father, the top political leader in the Irkutsk region, had recently disavowed all connections with the Communist Party and was an honored guest of the Democrats. Oksana was radiant as she took in all the excitement of the festive affair. Her clinging dark blue silk dress, revealing bare shoulders, its length slit from ankle to mid-thigh, attracted appreciative glances from all sides of the hall. The American businessman, Peter Nikhilov found himself the source of considerable envy on the part of many of the men present. Although Oksana and Peter could not share her apartment while Nickolai was in town, she had given her American lover considerable information on the political and business scene that now confronted the suddenly liberated Russians.

Over three hundred people had arrived and the party was growing steadily as the doormen began collecting hundred ruble bills instead of the limited number of tickets sent out to the Peoples' Deputies, industrialists, and Yeltsin's Democrats.

The guests were not used to this Western-style party but as hard liquor and champagne flowed and delicacies were lavishly displayed, spirits rose and tongues moved freely, laughter sounded and heated discussions broke out. The mayor moved among the guests joking, laughing, making sweeping promises and listening attentively to everyone. Political and business deals were made, the deputies happily receiving commitments to supplement meager pay scales.

Peter and Oksana made their way into the discotheque, laughing at the antics of the musicians and the girls in shimmering violet tights dancing for the guests to thunderous rock music. Then they walked back through the passage to the brightly lighted reception hall and Oksana was greeted by the mayor who hurried across the crowded room as soon as he saw her.

Peter spotted Azziz almost as soon as the Arab entered the hall. He was talking animatedly with a heavy set, faintly orange haired, puffy faced man wearing a formless brown suit and clumsily knotted tie.

"Do you know those two?" Peter whispered to Oksana, nodding towards Azziz.

"I don't know the Saddam look-alike but the other man is Vladimir Zhirinovsky. He started some kind of a political party a year ago. Slava says he's a fascist supported by the new business-men who contribute money to his brand of nationalism and economic expansion."

"I wonder what he's doing with Azziz," Peter mused.

"Azziz? I've heard Pavel mention the name," Oksana said.

Then her hand, holding his arm, suddenly tightened. Peter followed her glance and recognized Jap from the pictures he had been shown at Petrovka 38.

"That is your friend Yakovlev, right?" he asked.

"Yes. Trust him to be where all the politicians and factory managers are."

"Is he involved with the Iraqi and that politician?" Peter asked.

"I only know, as everybody does, that Zhirinovsky went to Iraq and met Saddam," Oksana replied. "His funny little political party still supports Saddam and during the Desert Storm War when we were supposed to be on the side of the Americans he said we should send Saddam weapons, even nuclear warheads for the SCUDS."

"Let's hope that this Zhirinovsky never gets anywhere in politics," Peter said. He noted that the budding politician clapped a hand warmly on Jap's arm as they talked. As they watched, an oriental man walked up to Jap and shook his hand vigorously. "That's Kim Tong Park with the North Korean Embassy." She laughed merrily. "I wonder if Kim knows he and the American, Rolf, are blood brothers so to speak. Nadia told me that Pavel gave her to Kim for a week before Red Rolf came to town." The party presented Peter with a clear focus on the intrigue into which he was being drawn. Now, like it or not, he was an investigator again.

"I see my father looking over at us," Oksana observed.

"Who is the fat guy with him?" Peter asked.

"He is not fat, he is simply big. That's Yevgney Volkov, my father's friend. He's the man you said you wanted to meet. Remember? I told you he is the manager of a big mining complex and factory in my father's domain."

"Oh? Your father, an elected official has got a domain?"

Oksana laughed. "That's what he calls it."

Peter stared at the heavy man with interest. "Have you mentioned to him that I am in Russia to buy certain defense material for clients in Germany?"

"I told him you wanted to buy red mercury," she replied.

"What was his reply?"

"He laughed and said something like 'what? another player in the red mercury game.'"

"That is the reaction I hoped for."

"If you want to talk to him, now would be a good time." Oksana laughed disparagingly. "Everybody in this room has got something to sell for hard currency. Americans and Germans seem to be the main targets."

Oksana led Peter over to where her father and Volkov were talking to a stocky, brown haired man in a trimly tailored light suit. "That is Pavel, Slava Yakovlev's business associate," Oksana said. "He is also interested in defense materials." She made the introductions and Peter felt a stir of excitement as he realized he was getting close to his quarry. He had seen pictures and read dossiers on all of them at Petrovka 38. He wondered if Helen had told Zekki that a man who called himself Pavel had been to see her. Probably not, since that would lead to more questions.

Oksana introduced Peter to Volkov and as he shook the big fleshy hand the factory manager gazed at him suspiciously. "So you are Russian, huh? How come you do not speak Russian?"

Oksana translated and Peter chuckled and turned to Volkov. "How come you do not speak English?"

"Oooh, evasive son of a bitch, slippery as an eel." Oksana chose not to translate as Volkov belched and reached out for another glass of champagne and a slice of ham and then assumed a business-like posture. "Oksana has told me of your interest in one of our commodities. Even though this is a celebration, perhaps we can discuss the price you are willing to pay for the red mercury we produce."

Oksana translated and Peter, surprised at the openness of trading in what should have been forbidden merchandise, merely nodded.

"I would also need to know the dates you will accept delivery at our plant and make payment," Volkov said. "I assume you have the means of transporting this material to your buyer."

"My buyer and I have arranged transportation from Moscow to Germany," Peter answered through Oksana after she translated for him. "I am sure we can work out a way to get the material from the plant to Moscow. I am prepared to pay five thousand dollars a kilo."

Volkov's face reflected dismay at the price suggested by Peter. "Mr. Nikhilov," he said after a long pause, "the estimated price in the West for a kilo of enriched uranium is one hundred thousand dollars and according to those same estimates a kilo of plutonium 239 runs five to ten times that amount."

"But I'm talking about red mercury which, like heavy water, is only a component used to detonate fissionable materials," Peter persisted. "It is not, in itself, a weapons grade product."

Volkov nodded to Pavel and Nickolai. "He seems to know what, in theory anyway, red mercury is purported to be." Then for translation he went on, "It requires about one kilo of red mercury to trigger one kilo of weapons grade plutonium."

He turned to Peter. "Mr. Nikhilov, I don't know who your buyers are but if they are serious people why wouldn't they also buy the finished product? I can sell them, through you of course, weapons grade plutonium 239."

"I will certainly contact my clients," Peter replied. "From what I know about them I feel they would be extremely interested in buying plutonium directly."

"When will you know for sure?" Volkov persisted. "We leave Moscow in a day or two at the most."

"I'll have an answer tomorrow."

As Oksana was translating, Volkov turned to Pavel and Nickolai. "You know, if the American really has a buyer with the money ready, I could sell him the real thing. A tactical nuclear warhead contains three to five kilos of plutonium 239. The warhead of a strategic missile such as the SS-25 is packed with three or four times that much plutonium. At the Dome we have at least a billion dollars worth of plutonium in storage."

"Don't translate that, Oksana," Pavel ordered.

"No, do not," Volkov added. "Let's find out more about the American's customers."

"It will, of course, be necessary for me to provide them an accurate measurement of gamma radiation outputs from the source, a 'fingerprint' if you will, of the warhead from which the plutonium 239 will be extracted."

Volkov laughed raucously and exchanged his champagne for a glass of cognac from which he took a long swallow. "And you come to me speaking of red mercury."

Peter shrugged. "You have to start somewhere. I never thought it would be possible to make a deal for plutonium in five minutes at a party like this." He waved his hand around the room full of celebrants.

"Since the failed coup in August, anything is possible and in fact probable," Volkov replied. "Who would have thought that the Communist Party would be outlawed and Russia, overnight, become a free trade country with factory managers no longer able to find anyone they must report to?"

At a nod from Volkov, Oksana translated his statement into English. Peter listened and then said, "I would like to see those warheads so I can report to my people that they are actually available."

"Certainly," Volkov replied. "I will give you a tour myself. But tell me, these clients of yours actually asked you to purchase red mercury for them?"

"I am sure that if they had thought it possible, they would have asked me to buy plutonium 239."

Pavel realized Volkov and Martinov could very well deal directly with Nikhilov and hastily intervened. "All of this business will have to be done through the *organizatsiya*. Our chief is taking over the brokerage of all nuclear material sold from the Dome." He gestured toward his boss talking intently to the Arab and North Korean. "If the American has buyers, we will handle the sales. But let us not worry him with that detail now."

As he pretended not to understand the language, Peter absorbed the atmosphere of Mayor Popov's gala. The enormity of the national attitude became abundantly clear. Everything in Russia, missiles and nuclear weapons included, was on the auction block for hard currency. And it appeared that there were dealers from every country in the world here to buy.

At that moment a suave young man came up to Oksana and said something quietly to her. She looked across the room and nodded.

"What's that all about?" Peter asked.

"Slava wants me. I see he has his American friend with him now, as well as the Arab. They need a translator."

"The red headed American is Red Rolf I presume?" Peter said.

Oksana nodded. "You might as well meet Slava. It looks like you will be doing business with him and Pavel."

Oksana started to walk across the room toward Jap with Peter when Pavel stopped them. "I don't think it is wise to take this American to the boss," he said.

"Why not? Let the two Americans get to know each other."

"We don't know as much as we should about this one whose arm you are holding," Pavel said.

"He's a businessman, like you."

Pavel shook his head but said nothing more as Peter's eyes went from one to the other, assuming a confused air as he followed Oksana to where Jap was standing.

After introductions Jap gave him a look of interest which made Peter wonder how much Oksana had told the crime lord about their relationship. There was something of a proprietary attitude about Jap as he took her arm and drew her close, speaking softly, as though Peter might indeed understand Russian.

Peter turned to Rolf. "So what business are you in?" he asked.

"I'm an economic consultant and this is a good time to make money in Russia."

"What do you do about the language?"

"There's always an interpreter around." He glanced at Oksana. "She's the best." He sighed. "Someday I'm going to have to really learn Russian, that is if I can make any money in Moscow." He looked at Peter curiously. "What do you do?"

"Like you I'm in business. Do you know what they're saying?" He nodded his head toward Jap and Oksana.

"Not exactly, but I get the idea that Yakovlev thinks you are moving into his territory with Oksana."

"Are you in some business with the Jap?" Peter asked.

Rolf's eyebrow raised at the nickname. "With Slava? Not really. I met him through a mutual friend. He invited me to this party and said there would be many business deals cut tonight."

Peter glanced at Oksana and Jap and wished that he could take her by the arm and the two of them leave the party and go home together. The game was getting dangerous. If Jap had any inkling how much he had learned about his counterfeiting business and now the selling of nuclear weapons, Peter knew he would not live through this night.

Salvation came from an unlikely source. Nickolai walked over to them and asked for his daughter to join him. A group of American and German businessmen needed Oksana's services as a translator. Jap bowed to Nickolai's wishes and released Oksana, almost as though she were his property.

With relief Peter nodded goodbye to Jap and Rolf and walked back across the ballroom. "I think we ought to get out of here as soon as we can," Peter said to Oksana.

"But it's a marvelous party and I can't leave my father. Besides, where can we go?"

"I have a place, a small apartment I borrowed from a Russian partner when your father came to town."

"Stay a while longer. Later, if I see a chance for us to leave, we'll go," she promised.

Suddenly, to Peter's chagrin, he saw a familiar face and figure appear in the crowd near the Jap. The striped pants, black jacket with silver pipe trim, the silk vest and wing collar and the suspiciously wig-like hair, could only belong to Zekki Dekka.The young Helen was at his side wearing a tight black dress as he walked towards Jap and his companions.

Hurriedly Peter made his excuses to a perplexed Oksana, telling her that business partners were waiting to hear from him in America by phone. Nickolai Martinov and his daughter were surprised at Peter's abrupt departure but Oksana was caught up in the excitement of the evening. And she and Peter would be together again in a few days. Peter left the party and took a taxi to the Intourist Hotel on Gorky Street. It was full of stimulated people at the bar and in the two-story high court restaurant at the middle of the hotel. The casino was open and crowded with people waiting to get in. This pulsating atmosphere was one of the reasons that the most secure telephones for overseas calls were the international booths at the first class hotels. And particularly now, with the KGB in total upheaval and the Militsia too busy and shorthanded to listen to calls made by tourists in the hotels, this was the safest way to communicate with foreign countries.

"Hugh," Peter said, "your old colleague Red Rolf . . . "

"He's no colleague anymore!" Hugh cried. "He's a rogue opera-tor like Ed Wilson and—"

"Will you shut the fuck up and listen? I'm on a pay phone in Moscow. I'm trying to help you with your NEST situation."

"Sorry. Go ahead Peter."

"Red and Zekki Dekka are working with Jap's *organizatsyia* to sell missiles, nuke warheads, and plutonium 239 to buyers every-where from North Korea to North Africa.

"Where are they getting it?" Hugh barked over the wire.

"From one Yevgeny Volkov, the plant director of some complex near Irkutsk in Siberia that manufactures and stores missiles and enriched uranium and plutonium 239."

"When are they planning to move that stuff?"

"Who knows. There's some slob of a Russian politico named Vladimir Zhirinovsky mixed up in this. I gather he's a personal friend of Saddam. Anyway, I got Volkov to agree to sell me some plutonium. You can't believe the panic-selling for hard currency going on over here."

"You're really putting it together, Peter." Hugh's tone of admi-ration clearly carried over the line.

"Thanks. I'm doing my job but I need help if we're going to keep missiles and plutonium from getting into the hands of terror-ist states. And they seem to be lining up a deal with North Korea."

"We can't do anything in Russia officially," Hugh shot back.

"What about the U.S. Embassy here? Surely the spooks assigned locally can do something."

"Nothing!" Hugh shouted back. "Our policy is total hands off in Moscow until the situation clears up. The agency is under orders from the White House to keep out."

"Meanwhile you've got a nuclear bazaar about to go into busi-ness supplied by some plant in Siberia. Next thing you know every rag-head terrorist out of the Middle East will be sneaking plutonium cocktails into our country."

"You're a resourceful guy. Figure a way to stop it."

"Little me!?" He shouted over the phone. "To quote my favorite author, Hemingway, 'a man alone ain't got no bloody fuckin' chance.'" Peter stifled himself, looking through the glass of the booth to see if he had attracted attention. "Look, Hugh, I've got the plan, the agreement between Jap's guy, Zekki, and Azziz. I can get the location of this plant, I think I can even get into it. It's up to you and NEST to call in the Sneaky Petes at this point."

"If you can get yourself inside, you can do something important for the world. You've got your chronolog."

"I've also got the girl I'm going to bring home and marry. I'd like to survive to do just that."

"Peter, get a good night's sleep and call me back tomorrow. I'll see what I can do on this end."

"You do that. So long, Hugh."

BOOK THREE

THE SECRET CITY

CHAPTER FORTY-TWO

M ax found himself obliged to deliver the largest cargo airplane in the Soviet military inventory, the AN-22, if he wanted Jap to do another job for him. And the order for the assassination by suicide of Gregori Siderov, Kruchina's predecessor in the job of Communist Party manager, had been issued.

Aircraft division N42/824 which handled all military cargo flights in the area of Moscow and St. Petersburg was commanded by Colonel Vadim Hastovetz. For several days Max developed the leverage he would need to control the base commander. From KGB tapes and files he recreated the scene which clearly reflected the state of unaccountably and near anarchy springing up throughout the entire military establishment and in particular the Air Transport Division in which he was interested.

Hastovetz, a burly man in his mid-forties, displayed the manners of a petty warlord ruling a large retinue. Despite his wide moon-like face, crimson from hard liquor, and the typical appearance of a Ukrainian peasant, he was in reality clever and shrewd.

Max looked into the KGB files on the disappearance of the Division's helicopter pad covering and was able to recreate a scene which gave him insight into dealing with Hastovetz.

Col. Hastovetz's glare at the captain in front of him was a mixture of hatred, contempt, and compassion. The captain was lean and thin, his open blue watery eyes fixed obediently on his commander. The mode of the conversation conformed with the colonel's strict adherence to the army code of conduct. Shit upon subordinates, kick ass of equals, and climb upwards so you won't be shit upon yourself.

"Comrade Captain, fuck you three thousand times," the colonel sputtered. "What has happened to the fucking aluminum surface cover of the helicopter pad?"

"Comrade Colonel . . . I mean . . . I swear I didn't mean to . . . the bloody dentist poured me a lot of his best, and as you know . . ."

"How dare you, swine, to drink in working hours? You were on fucking duty!"

"But the alcohol was so pure, so refined, as clear as the tears of the Holy Virgin." The explanation from one hard drinking officer to his even more conspicuously consuming superior sounded reasonable.

The captain paused to garner further understanding and continued. "It was not that technical poisonous stuff they used to drain from the engines which tastes horrible and causes nausea and devilish headache the next morning." He continued to solicit the colonel's pity explaining that the bad alcohol made his wife go mad and all two hundred pounds of her turned on him and she had taken to throwing the laundry iron at him. How could he refuse the dentist's offer? Two liters of pure alcohol—a true way to pacifying family conflicts. So he agreed to let the dentist fasten a cable to the strips of gleaming metal that covered the helicopter pad and drag them off and into the van he used as his travelling dental clinic. The metal helipad cover was just what the dentist needed for the roof of the new house he was building.

"Comrade Colonel, you know my family life," the captain pled. "Just to keep things quiet . . ."

"How often do I have to tell you?" the colonel yelled. "A wife is not a relative, just a broad you are sleeping with!"

"Yes, sir!"

"Shut up pig! Now what can I do when assholes from headquarters want to come and their helicopter cannot land? All of us could be court martialed!"

"We'll mend—"

"Mend?" the colonel screamed. "You can't even mend your daughter's cunt. Excuse me! Soldiers fuck her wherever they stop her. I beg your pardon! In broad daylight! No shame, really!"

The captain accepted the colonel's railing. It was true. But in military compounds where officers' apartments and barracks were close together that sort of event was very common in all conceivable variations.

"If the helicopter pad is not ready in two days"—he paused threateningly—"do whatever is necessary; rob the next regiment, find the bloody dentist and take back the roof off his house. If the helipad isn't ready I'll have you flying, like a fucking helicopter. I swear! I'll stick the propeller in your ass and you'll fly! Like Soyuz-Apollo! Is that fucking clear?"

"Yessir!"

"Dismissed!" the colonel roared.

Hastovetz had not really been too hard on the captain. After all, he himself was often drinking in the sauna with the chief dentist when he came to the regiment well supplied with pure medical alcohol. And often his dental assistant, a woman about thirty, joined them, to "rub the commander's back." Hastovetz picked up the phone to call the chief dentist. If the captain was given two liters of pure medical alcohol, he as colonel was entitled to ten liters as a pacification gift.

And thus it was that a week after the helipad covering incident the regiment's KGB officer, Captain Yuri Makezenko, appeared in the office of Colonel Hastovetz bringing with him a younger man in a civilian light gray suit, white shirt and dark necktie. He was clean-shaven, his hair cropped short, with black deep set eyes which seemed to pierce to the soul of the colonel, casting an uneasy cold pall over him. This was Max.

The colonel cleared his throat. "Can I see your documents? The regiment has to be security conscious," he added almost apologetically. Even the junior KGB officers remaining in office after the failed coup frequently exerted more power than a general.

Without a word the visitor proffered a small red ID card identifying him as a member of the General KGB Board of St. Petersburg. Hastovetz nodded. "What can I do for you?"

"The board considers it necessary to recommend that Aircraft Division N42/824 sell an Antonov AN-22 Antheus turboprop to a certain joint venture with which we are working. I'll put you in touch with their representatives. It all should be handled this week. Today is Monday."

Hastovetz was somewhat bewildered by the strange request but did not show it. "We can't sell you a new AN-22," he equivocated.

"They do not need a plane right from the plant."

"Why don't your chiefs contact ours in Headquarters?"

"I can't explain that to you. I act on strict orders myself. I have waiting outside an aviation expert from the joint venture."

Hastovetz regarded the young KGB officer in the neat civilian suit uneasily. "Well, I can show you one of our old AN-22s in its hanger."

"That would be greatly appreciated—by myself and my superiors."

Hastovetz picked up his phone. "I'll ask the Division chief engineering officer, Colonel Panin, to meet us." The expert from Jap's *organizatsyia* drove with Max and Col. Hastovetz to a hanger a mile away from the headquarters building and found themselves looking at the biggest cargo airplane Max had ever seen. The Division engineer, summoned by the colonel, was always anxious to remain on good terms with the KGB and began to extoll the airship's virtues.

It was almost as though the Division was anxious to make a sale, Max thought. He had anticipated this might be the case. Since the coup failed, and with it the economy, loyalty in this new and hungry society was strictly pledged to the accumulation of money. Colonel Panin reeled off the specifications of the transport plane.

"The Antonov AN-22 Antheus can transport a payload of eighty tons at four hundred sixty miles an hour for eight thousand miles," he began but Max held up a restraining hand. The engineer and the expert from the *organizatsiya* climbed up a ladder to the side hatch and from the cargo hold ascended two flights of aluminum stairs to the flight deck where they stood discussing the great airship for half an hour.

Max wondered why Jap needed such a cargo plane and Hastovetz could not restrain his curiosity asking Max many questions, foremost of which was, "How much are they going to pay?"

Max shrugged his shoulders. "How much do you want?"

"Two million rubles at least?"

"That is too much," Max snapped although he wondered to himself why he should bargain on Jap's behalf.

"As the commander I would be criticized if I settled for a lesser price."

Indifferently Max shrugged again. "We'll find another commander."

The reply aroused a cautionary instinct in the colonel, whose own military style was to demoralize and unnerve those about him.

The chief engineer, along with Jap's specialist, finally climbed out of the plane's belly after a thorough inspection. Questioned by Max the visiting expert said, "In principle it is okay. It's seen a lot of service but this system is reliable in general. Besides, with old planes you know what to expect. New ones are unpredictable sometimes."

"Then let's go back to my office and settle this right now," Hastovetz took control. At headquarters Hastovetz invited Max into his office, saying to the others, "Comrades, excuse us. Leave us alone. We must discuss a very serious state assignment . . . if you please."

In his private quarters the colonel's head projected forward boldly. Under bushy eyebrows, his small, running blueish eyes glistened shrewdly. "Always nice to see our dear colleagues from Chekka."

"Chekka has long passed into eternity," Max said. "And soon it will not even be KGB." Having rejected the commander's pleasantry he sat down across the table from him. "Shall we get down to business?"

"Well, sonny . . . How much can you give for the airship?"

"I don't believe I have the honor to be your relative, Colonel. How much do you expect us to pay for this ancient flying saucer?"

Hastovetz giggled, avarice dancing in his facial expression. "You know, sonny, I may check what your real assignment is."

Max pinched the bridge of his nose for a moment with thumb and forefinger. "You seem not to realize, Colonel, to whom you are talking. That could have drastic consequences."

"Ah, sonny, Let's not frighten an old colonel." He leaned forward. "Now what do you need the plane for?"

Max sighed and from his coat pocket produced a packet of papers and began to read in matter-of-fact tones.

Hastovetz listened for a few moments and laughed. "So you looked up my service record. Standard procedure."

"What is significant is as commander of the Aircraft Regiment in Bosigovo, the suicide of a Private Berisik resulted from sexual abuse by four Azerbaijani privates. Our KGB files indicate the relatives of these rapists paid the commander, Colonel Hastovetz, 100,000 rubles to suppress the affair and destroy the evidence in the case."

He looked up at the colonel's face, suddenly gray and frozen. "In 1987, shortly before leaving Borisovo, Colonel Hastovetz illegally sold to two citizens of Georgia two armored vehicles for a price of one million rubles, also selling these individuals one hundred AK-47 assault rifles, ten crates of hand grenades"—Max smiled grimly at the mortified colonel—"and also appropriated from the regiment for his personal use two military trucks, one sold later to a certain Armenian citizen, Aram Grigoryan, for one hundred thousand rubles. Yes, and here is . . ."

"Enough!" Hastovetz cut him off hoarsely and reached for the carafe of water on the table.

"Maybe you want to look at my ID now?"

"No." The colonel was gulping water from the glass, shark's teeth clicking against its rim. "What do you want?"

"I told you. An AN-22 turbojet. Judging by available documents you are an experienced trader so I chose you."

In a resigned tone Hastovetz replied, "Consider it sold." Then, "Can you destroy the records?"

"These are copies but I will give them to you as a reminder that everyone makes mistakes they have to pay for. Sometimes much later." Then briskly, "Well, the price will be, say, a million rubles. The aircraft is old."

The colonel nodded assent. "And how are you going to pay?"

Max smiled. "You do not understand, Colonel. I am not a Georgian mafioso, I am the representative of a legal organization, the 'armed unit of the former and future Communist Party' so to speak."

"So what's the deal?"

"I offer you a legal operation, not a theft to which you are so accustomed. You sell the plane to the joint venture because it is old and obsolete. You have the right. You sign the documents. We transfer money to the bank account of the Division, eight hundred thousand rubles. Two hundred thousand rubles will go to you personally. In cash. You can keep them under your pillow, you can divide them among your officers, whatever. Joint Venture representatives will arrive tomorrow at nine o'clock. They will bring the documents and the money. You sign the papers, hand over the plane. It must be ready for a flight and fully fueled. Our navigator and pilots will take it off."

"And the two hundred thousand? Not listed anywhere?"

"Not a line. Enjoy yourself."

Hastovetz quickly recovered from the shock. The shark tooth smile returned. "Well, sonny . . . you have persuaded me. Working with our heroic fighters of the 'invisible frontier' is a real pleasure."

Max rose from his seat and started to put the papers back into his pocket. "If you still want these copies they are yours after the plane takes off tomorrow."

CHAPTER FORTY-THREE

➤➥

The Hotel Moscow's Spanish Bar was almost empty when Jap strolled in. It was before noon and the Cuban musical group performing Spanish songs had yet to make its entry. He saw Max seated alone reading the morning newspaper. A cup of black coffee steamed in front of him. The window beside his table overlooked Manege Square, the Kremlin wall looming beyond.

As Jap approached, Max looked up and folded the newspaper, placing it beside a manila file folder on the table. Jap took off his white raincoat and placed it over his right arm; his creamy light suit had not a wrinkle in it. He nodded to Max and sat down opposite him. Max seemed unchanged—same dark clothes, same bristle and penetrating gaze of the cold gray eyes.

"Nice to see you, Max," Jap greeted him and looked up at the voluptuous blonde waitress who materialized beside him. "Coffee, black, no sugar or cream," he ordered.

As the waitress left Max slid a newspaper clipping out of the folder. Jap glanced down at the headline which read, "Strange suicide of high Party official."

"Very slick job, we were all impressed," Max said. Then his lips twisted into a wry smile. "And what do you think of the statement about the suicide by Kruchina's predecessor and neighbor, Gregori Siderov?"

Max read aloud from the clipping. "That was the act of a courageous man; though I personally would have never done such a thing."

Jap tapped the folder with his forefinger. "My next job?"

"Yes. Siderov."

Jap's eyes dropped to the folder which Max had pushed across the table to him. "Was he as involved as Kruchina in moving the party's gold around the financial centers of Europe?"

"What do you mean?" Max snapped.

"In order to make life a little more secure, I photographed Kruchina's most interesting documents. And knowing your mission to protect certain of the highest former Party bosses, I could see why he had to kill himself."

Max froze and silence settled over them for some moments. Finally, studying Jap's inscrutable face, he said, "You are playing with fire, Jap."

"Both of us are."

"I want those photocopies."

"I do not refuse. But in our world only quick death is free of charge."

"What do you want?"

"I want my Antonov AN-22 turboprop now. Time is against me and killing party officials before they can implicate their superiors is not in my sphere of operations."

"Your plane is ready for delivery. One million rubles."

A wide, pleased smile came over Jap's face, even his slanted eyes betrayed satisfaction. "A good price. When can I have it flown away?"

"Directly after the next job is accomplished." He paused meaningfully. "And those photographs of Kruchina's documents are delivered."

Jap leaned back. "Job will be done soon. But the documents will be turned over after the plane is delivered."

"How do I know you will not keep copies?"

"How do I know I will not be assassinated after all the assignments are completed?"

Max stared directly ahead in silence for some moments. Finally he said, "It's a deal. And no more photographs of documents."

"Agreed." Jap picked up the folder. "I expect to hear from you immediately after I carry out the assignment."

As Jap stood up, the folder in his hand, Max gestured at it. "Everything you need, diagrams, keys, are there. We will be watching."

An hour later Jap and Pavel were studying Max's assignment, which presented many difficulties. Siderov usually was surrounded by family. "This is a job for Sunray," Jap suddenly exclaimed.

"The little freak has been useful to us before," Pavel agreed.

"We have a serious time problem," Jap said. "If the *ments* release to the press what they captured in Zilisi, Hamster will never trust our hundred dollar bills. I want Sunray to do this job tonight and we take delivery of the AN-22 aircraft in the next two days." Jap rubbed his palms together. "Azziz tells me that the Iraqi letters of credit will be ready in Zurich in a week."

Gregori Siderov, a burly man with a huge protuberant belly gained from years of high living, enjoyed gazing at the framed photographs of himself with his family and friends hanging on the walls of his spacious study. He especially savored the ones that showed his family on the grounds of the *dacha* on the Black Sea Coast. The windows of his Moscow studio, two stories in height, overlooked the grassy stretch of lawn separating the privileged apartment building for high Party officials from the pavement of Leninski Prospekt.

Common people in their massive structures divided into small living spaces would never be permitted to join two apartments into one and certainly not to construct a pool in one of the rooms complete with a fountain. Even the thought of bringing from America a prefabricated bathroom with shower, bathtub and toilet and planting it into a Soviet-constructed building would be considered heresy for the masses.

Soviet party officials were not expected to pay so much as a kopeck towards the cost of the brigade of workers who rebuilt their apartments. Special passages had been constructed so that an extended family such as Siderov's, with his son's wife and children sharing his State-bestowed largesse, would not be separated.

Sunray, a powerful dwarf only three feet in height, was a secret weapon known only to certain thiefs-in-the-law who paid him well for executing what he liked best in the world, difficult assassinations. Jap showed him diagrams of Siderov's apartment and gave him the exact measurements of the furniture inside the grandiose study where Siderov spent much of his time. Sunray studied the scale plan of the study, noting there was a real wood-burning brick fireplace with chimney in the room.

Siderov's son, Kyril, his wife and two young children, Igor and Helen, lived in their own apartment attached to Siderov's large quarters.

"You understand it is of the utmost importance that nothing happens that would give investigators a chance to suspect this was not suicide," Jap said urgently. "The note I am giving you to leave on the desk was forged by an expert."

Sunray nodded. He was a professional and in an hour had absorbed detailed information on the interior and exterior of the apartment and the movements of the guards at the front entrance.

That night Jap and Pavel drove Sunray to a point around the

block from the apartment house on Leninski Prospekt. Uneasily they watched him slither out of the car and lost him in the darkness as he approached the facade of the stone and brick luxury apartment building.

Silently he scaled the wall to the ninth floor. As predicted, he was in total darkness, the moon heavily shrouded by cloud cover. For Sunray, climbing the brick wall with its many ridges and cornices was like going up a ladder. The height had no effect on him; he had trained himself to be virtually immune to acrophobia. On his back was strapped a cotton sack containing a gun, a long Sai dagger and a smaller knife with a wide blade. The note handed to him by Jap just before he left the car was contained in a small rubber tube placed inside his mouth under his right cheek.

Sunray handily reached the tall French windows of Siderov's study and inserted the knife in the slit between the two window casements. Just as the plan Jap had shown him indicated, he was able to swiftly and silently swing the decorative though boltless windows slowly open. The armed guards at the ground floor entrance gave a false sense of security to the empowered tenants. He slid through the narrow opening in the double casement and pulled the windows shut after him. He crawled into the dark room picking out the fireplace and the giant sofa against the wall beyond. Feeling furry carpeting below his palms he scuttled under the sofa like a tarantula into its pit.

When Siderov came from his bedroom to breakfast the next morning, his wife Lora, grandson Igor and granddaughter Helen were sitting at the table. The breakfast was lavish, as usual, but Siderov hardly ate a thing, content to sip hot tea. Lora pretended not to notice. In the months since the failed coup attempt his appetite had steadily worsened. They chatted over family matters and he felt a little better. His granddaughter was cute and kept him cheerful. Her fresh little face, tender and lilting, blew away the dark night visions. By the end of breakfast he was smiling and repaired to his study to read over his correspondence and notices.

Standing over his desk, shuffling through the papers, a sudden dire presentment swept over him and he turned to confront a long, thin wicked blade pressing into his stomach, pointed by a muscled hand. The unbelievable creature wielding this dreadful impaling instrument was small, smaller than a ten-year-old child, but ferociously broad shouldered and tough. His big head with short-cropped black Mongolian hair was split by a vicious grin, slant eyes in a flat yellowish face gleamed with evil intent. Long front teeth protruded from under the upper lip like those of a rabbit. The little bastard was also holding a gun in his left hand, his short deformed squatty body supported on two curved, short but very stable legs.

Siderov felt his tongue sticking to the palate, unable to produce a sound. Instinct told him that an apparition that ugly will use his blade without hesitation. Then his thoughts went to Lora and Igor and beautiful little Helen and he felt close to fainting. The goblin conjured up the vision of a deepwater crab he had pulled out of the Black Sea once on the end of his fishing line.

"Not a sound!" Sunray hissed, "or I'll run you through." Involuntarily, Siderov raised his hands. He was five times bigger and ten, maybe twenty times heavier, but he knew he was helpless in front of this dirty insect. From what dark crevice had it crawled?

"I do not mean harm." The gnome's voice was thin and reedy. "I just want to show you something. Look at the window!"

Siderov obeyed. He felt nausea and pain in the stomach. His heart was pounding. Even the bright sunshine outside the window was ominous. The point of the blade was pricking his skin at the kidney.

"Go! Go to the window and open it."

In a surreal world he couldn't control Siderov walked cautiously as if afraid he would fall into a pit. Then he began to find hope in this terrifying situation. The bastard needs something else or he would have struck at once. Fuck! How did this little demon get into the apartment? What's wrong with the fucking guards below letting such a hideous scum into the building?

"Go on, open it!" the creature growled in its high-pitched voice, sticking Siderov in the rib.

He pulled back the frames of the French windows, opening them and staring out numbly at the familiar view of Moscow roofs before him. He had seen the vista every day of his life in the city and never paid it much attention. Now suddenly the sight took on new meaning. He desperately wanted to keep on enjoying this scene every morning for many years to come.

"Get off the slippers. Quick!" came the bleak croak from behind.

"Slippers? What for?" He stepped out of them, feeling warm parquette under his bare feet. What next? People below. Why not shout? Impossible.

"Now look down. There's something I want you to see and tell me what it is."

He bent forward, his head out of the window and looked down nine stories. A rush of terror seized him as the fresh air ruffled his face and the thin strands of hair on his head. A guard was posted in front of the entrance. Suddenly a bowel-voiding wrench twisted his stomach. Seeing nothing unusual below, he instantly understood what was about to happen. The last thing he felt was the hot wetness running down his leg and off his bare feet as he tried to back away. A powerful push propelled him out the window into the fresh morning air. The wind carried away his long wail, and the green grass of the lawn surrounding the building rushed up to meet his sprawling body, falling head down.

Sunray quickly stepped backwards, resheathing the dagger in a deft movement and slipping the gun into his pocket. He took the rubber tube from his mouth, pulled out the note and threw it onto the desk. Already he could hear the shouts from below as he started to leave the study and get out of the apartment. Then he heard pounding footsteps from outside the study door and shots from

the guard below, undoubtedly fired summoning help. The building would be surrounded before he could get away. He could
probably fight his way through Siderov's family but even if he
succeeded, even if he escaped, it would be obvious that Siderov
had been murdered and Jap would be merciless and give him only
a small percent of the money promised him.

So, reluctantly, he was obliged to put the alternative plan he
had devised into action.

At Petrovka 38 General Bodaev received the call minutes after
Siderov's impact with the ground below his window. He jumped
from his desk and strode down the hall to Nechiaev's office where
the daily meeting was in order. "First Kruchina, and now Siderov
ends up on the street," his voice rang out indignantly as though
both suicides were direct affronts to his authority.

Nechiaev jumped to his feet. "Get the regionals surrounding the
building. It may already be too late to stop this suicide maker." He
ran from his office, followed by Yuri Navakoff, down the stairs
and through the gate to where his car was parked outside. He did
not even wait for his driver as he and Yuri piled into the machine
and started off for Leninski Prospect.

At the front entrance to the luxury apartment building Nechiaev and Navakoff slid out of the car. They glanced fleetingly at the
obese barefoot body clad in a white shirt and dark slacks lying
face down on the grass. Impatiently they waited for the elevator
door to slide open. Even in this apartment building, a monument
to privilege, there was no operator. Nechiaev pressed the button to
take them to the ninth floor. He was beginning to experience a
sense of déjà vu except that this time, unlike the suicide of
Kruchina, he would be on the scene. He glanced at his watch, just
ten minutes after the victim had hit the ground. In Kruchina's case
by the time the Militsia had arrived, certain officers still in the
employ of the shrinking KGB had already ransacked the apartment
in a search, they said, for clues to the motive for this suicide.

Nechiaev strongly suspected that Kruchina had been murdered but any evidence that might have corroborated his presentment had been removed.

Siderov's son and his wife were inside the study, but horrified, standing well back from the window when Nechiaev arrived. Sharply, he inquired about the possibility that someone might have popped out of the study seconds after Siderov jumped, or was pushed, to his death. Both his son Kyril who had approached the study from his wing of the apartment and Siderov's wife Lora who had been outside the other entrance to the study reiterated that it was impossible that anyone could have come out of the room after the death leap without being seen. It had all happened in seconds—Siderov went out the window, the guards saw him hit the ground, and fired shots to get attention. Kyril and Lora, already close to the study, ran to the doors, opened them and rushed inside.

"Have any other investigators been here?" Nechiaev asked. Both Kyril and Lora shook their heads.

"Any note?"

Kyril gestured toward the table. Nechiaev strode to it and looked down at the scrap of paper. Without touching it he read the cryptic message, "Cremation only."

"Is that his handwriting?"

Both Kyril and Lora nodded. "Yes," they chorused.

Nechiaev strode toward the open French windows and immediately saw and smelled the evidence of the terror that had gripped Siderov as he went out the window. To his forensic investigator he pointed out the excrement on the floor beneath the window and the traces on the sill.

While the corpse was being photographed on the ground below, other pictures were taken in the study itself of the human waste the victim had undoubtedly excreted in the horror of the moment. After the pictures had been taken samples were collected in a test tube to be compared with what would be found on and around the victim's corpse.

Vainly, Nechiaev searched for any other clues. He did not believe that either Kruchina or now Siderov had taken their own lives yet there was no evidence to the contrary except the tell-tale excrement. A major difference though, was that Kruchina had been alone in his apartment when he jumped and Siderov's entire family had been present and seen nothing. Futilely, Nechiaev examined the study and the open French windows. He even looked up the fireplace but only a child could have ascended the narrow chimney. And it would have taken more than that to force Siderov out the window. It seemed impossible that anyone could have been in here with him when he went out the window. Yet Nechiaev vividly recalled Siderov's statement on Kruchina's apparent suicide leap. "That was the act of a courageous man, though I personally would have never done such a thing."

For the next half hour Nechiaev and Navakoff meticulously sifted through papers, account books, and letters, hoping to find some clue as to the reason Siderov might have killed himself. At that point two officers of the new, post-coup KGB arrived, presented their credentials, and questioned Nechiaev in a deferential manner. The KGB had changed drastically since a number of their leaders began occupying cells at Lubyanka Prison. The excrement, according to the two KGB officers, nevertheless, did not mean the victim had been forceably defenstrated. Frequently, they insisted, before an individual killed himself, especially when jumping from a great height, the anticipation of the fall caused sudden, explosive bowel movements. This was how they would defend the presence of excrement in the report of the suicide later, Nechiaev was certain. But their explanation was at odds with all of Nechiaev's considerable experience with homicide. He knew that the excrement was nearly prima facie evidence of murder, not suicide. The excrement resulted from fear of being pushed, not from a death wish jump. He was also aware, however, of the futility of arguing with even the post-coup remnants of the State Security Office.

Throughout the day Militsia and KGB officers came and went and other than the excrement on the floor and window they found nothing to change the diagnosis of suicide and finally, by nightfall, the family was left alone. Lora and Kyril shut off the study, scene of so much turmoil that day, and sadly went about having supper. Faithful to his father's last wishes Kyril had arranged for the body to be cremated after the obligatory autopsy had been completed.

It was late that dark night when Sunray slid down the upper reaches of the chimney and out the fireplace in Siderov's study. Only the years of bodily discipline had enabled the dwarf to remain all those hours in the tight confinement of the small chimney. He ached all over when finally he stood, soot blackened, on the parquet floor, flexing and stretching his muscles.

He crept across the room, silently parted the windows, and then pushed them open. Standing on the ledge he swung first one window closed and then stepped in front of it and closed the other one. A close examination the next day, he realized, would indicate that the windows had been opened and shut but the latch he had been able to open with his knife when he entered could not be pushed back into place the same way. From all he had heard from the chimney and learned from Jap before embarking on this assassination, the authorities had made up their minds it was a case of suicide and higher levels would insist they write their reports to reflect this view no matter what other evidence might turn up. He had earned his money.

Spiderlike, Sunray slithered and clawed down and across the facade of the apartment building to the wall facing the side street off Leninski Prospekt. Soon he was out on the sidewalk, around the corner from the guards, and walking as rapidly as his short legs would take him back into the maze of streets behind the prominent boulevard.

Just as planned, a black two-door Volga was waiting. As Sunray approached it the door swung open and he climbed into the front passenger seat and pulled the door shut after him. Quietly the automobile slipped away.

CHAPTER FORTY-FOUR

⋘° ⋘

Peter Nikhilov reached into his pocket and took out his chronolog, checking the time differential between New York, Moscow, and Irkutsk. In the Crime Brigade's conference room, dominated by a chart of Moscow and a map of the Soviet Union on one wall, Bodaev and Colonel Nechiaev sat at a table on either side of Peter Nikhilov as Boris Burenchuk stood with a pointer in his hand, the tip of it resting on Irkutsk and Lake Baikal.

"From what you have overheard this is the approximate location of Krasnov 86, one of our secret cities. We gather that Yevgeny Volkov, whom you were talking to at the mayor's party, is managing director," Boris was saying.

"Just brief us on everything, and together, we will come up with a plan of action," Bodaev added.

Peter placed a business card on the table in front of Bodaev. "I found this in Chechen's wallet when I searched his effects in Butyrka. It is the card of a diplomat assigned to the Iraqi mission to the United Nations in New York, Azziz Al Faradi. Azziz gave his card to Zekki Dekka. Later Zekki used it to write his Moscow phone number on the opposite side and gave it to Chechen."

"How did you know it was Zekki's number?" Nechiaev asked.

"Just a hunch at first. It had his initials in front of the number. I was with Zekki when he sent Chechen back to Moscow after the murder of the two Georgians in Brighton Beach."

"So you called the number and got Zekki?"

Peter grinned and shook his head. "Boris found the address for me and I visited Zekki's cozy nest. His little nymph let me in. She said he was in Siberia." He handed Bodaev some folded papers. "This is an agreement between Zekki and Azziz. It's in Russian and Arabic. Read it and tell me what you think Zekki is selling on behalf of some straw company to Iraq for twenty five million dollars." Bodaev snatched up the papers and began reading.

"Then two days later, Oksana took me to an interesting party."

"You mean at the Building of Economic Assistance?" Bodaev asked. "I had an invitation but did not go."

"You missed something. Azziz, Jap and his frayer, Pavel, Oksana's father, they were all there. With Oksana's help I got Director Volkov to offer to sell me plutonium for half the world price. Volkov works with Oksana's father and also Jap."

"Did you agree to buy?" Bodaev asked.

"I did. But before I could finalize anything Zekki and his girl-friend showed up and I had to split before my cover was blown."

Bodaev had been reading the agreement between Zekki and the Iraqi while listening to Peter. He let out a loud cry of shock. "Twenty five million dollars U.S. payable in Switzerland for one SS-25 Sickle ICBM with 550 kiloton warhead and its mobile launcher delivered to Iraq!"

He stubbed the cigarette butt into an ashtray and immediately lit another. Then he shook his head hopelessly. "Still, there is nothing we can do."

"What!?" Peter exclaimed.

"I cannot go to the prosecutor with your suspicions," Bodaev said regretfully. "As for the papers—Jap is smart. Zekki is, on the agreement, a foreign citizen. He has full right to strike bargains with another foreigner in New York, in Moscow, or on the North Pole. This Al Faradi has diplomatic immunity. I do not propose to jump to arrests. But," he held up the copy of the agreement Peter had produced, "this is the clue. It links counterfeiting to selling nuclear stuff, otherwise Zekki would not be part of it."

"Yevgeny Volkov has possession of enough nuclear material and missiles to sell for billions of dollars to terrorists from North Korea to North Africa," Peter muttered.

Nechiaev shrugged. "The witnesses we arrested became mutes after Chechen's death, they are even afraid of the guards, expecting a bullet between the shoulder blades at any minute. I would like to work them over but I already have serious trouble with Speaker of Parliament Chasbulatov. He is of Chechen origin and whispers to Yeltsin himself that Chechens are being detained illegally. Yeltsin kicks the Interior Minister, and he kicks the general and the organized crime unit."

"The Chechens at Zilisi were armed and shooting at us," Peter observed.

"The speaker describes our actions as outbursts of Russian nationalism against poor Moslem bastards," Nechiaev growled. "Next time I will simply give the order to shoot on the spot any armed Chechen. As Stalin used to say—'where there is a person, there is a problem; no persons—no problems.'"

Bodaev slapped the papers Peter had given him. "So, this Director Volkov offered you plutonium for a reasonable price knowing you are American?"

"Right," Peter replied. "And now it is up to me to come back to him."

"Suppose you agree to buy plutonium," Bodaev suggested, "and you go to Krasnov 86. You pay him half the money in advance and invite him to return to Moscow with the plutonium and receive the rest of the money. He will come. After he receives the money here, in our jurisdiction, we arrest him. Charges will be severe, even life threatening. He will testify against Jap and we put Jap back in the camps for the rest of his life."

Boris and Nechiaev nodded enthusiastically at the strategy.

A crooked grin came across Peter's lips. "There's the matter of a quarter million U.S. dollars to make the down payment. Do we borrow it from the State Treasury?"

"We have it," Nechiaev announced triumphantly. "We have the bucks we captured from Zilisi."

"This is entrapment," Peter protested facetiously. "We are paying Volkov to commit a crime he might not otherwise commit and then we indict him when he falls into our trap. In America the police, FBI, whoever, can be prosecuted and convicted themselves for entrapment."

Nechiaev laughed derisively. "I do not know what it is in America but here it is how we get our convictions. We are rewarded and promoted for this entrapment, as you call it."

Peter joined in the laughter. "Okay, okay. When in Rome do as the Romans do. When do I get the funny money?"

"We'll have to go through some formalities," Bodaev cautioned. "Like recording the fake serial numbers on the fake bills and the amount of confiscated counterfeit we use in this operation. Also we must make a report to the prosecutor's office."

"And take a chance on a leak?" Peter cried. "It's my life you are playing with. I shouldn't do this at all. I travel four thousand miles into Siberia, work my way into a secret city, buy plutonium, and get involved with Jap while he's buying missiles for Iraq. Why don't you just take the army out there, raid Krasnov 86, and grab the director and anyone else who looks like they're buying and selling nukes?"

A shocked expression came over Bodaev's face. Nechiaev swallowed, coughed and gestured at Boris, the diplomat, to explain.

"We do not know who might be behind Volkov," Boris said simply. "After all, when three thousand unregistered SK-14s were sold to Iraq, the entire PolitBureau and Gorbachev and other high officials participated in the profits. If we make a mistake by quietly arresting Volkov in Moscow it will be discreetly called to our attention and everybody will forget the incident."

"We are trying to investigate the second suicide of a chairman of the management of Communist Party affairs," Nechiaev went on shrilly. "Kruchina, and before him Siderov, handled all the party finances, including the sale of the SK-14s. We are convinced they were murdered, yet we are told from the top not to pursue that line of investigation." Nechiaev chuckled mirthlessly. "Now others who are worried about their own suicides are quietly talking to us."

Bodaev nodded somberly. "Peter is right. Nobody outside this room should know that we are turning over the counterfeit money to him. If questions arise later, well—we asked an American officer to check out some suspect currency for us."

"On that basis I will find out what I can about Volkov and the nuke sales—for you and for my own country," Peter said. "Acquiring and delivering nukes to oil-rich terrorist states could quickly become the world's most lucrative short-term business enterprise."

"I am sure that's what Jap is up to," Bodaev agreed.

"The possibilities of what terrorists with a nuclear capability could do in Western cities is frightening." Peter shook his head.

"When are you seeing Oksana again?" Nechiaev asked.

"Soon as I get out of here. She has something special to tell me. I get the feeling that she is going to say she has to leave Moscow with her father and Volkov tomorrow, and go back to Irkutsk for a visit. I'll just have to convince her to take me, too."

"I will have a heart-to-heart talk with her," Boris replied. "When I finish speaking to her she will not leave you alone in Moscow. We can pick her up for further questioning regarding the Arbat murders any time we choose."

"Seems to me her friends did Russia a favor wiping out those three thugs," Peter remarked and put the chronolog back in his pocket.

"Agreed. But we need to keep the leverage on her," Bodaev added. "She is our best means of tracking Jap's movements."

Peter stood up. "Well, if there is no further business, I've got to make a phone call and meet Oksana." He looked at Boris meaningfully. "Before you set up your little heart-to-heart with her, talk to me. It may not be necessary."

CHAPTER FORTY-FIVE

O ksana's depression at the death of Nadia had turned to fear as she accepted the fact that Slava Yakovlev had ordered Misha to murder the prostitute if she were taken by the Militsia, and the fact that she herself had been chosen and set up by the Jap via Nadia and Sunray.

Thusly, Oksana clearly demonstrated her trust of Peter when, after the mayor's party, she recounted to him the details of the rape by the KGB men and the revenge extracted by Pavel.

"And after all that, it was Pavel's gang that murdered Nadia," Peter finished the account, finally understanding the nightmares that seized her as she slept beside him. Only after they made love was she able to sleep soundly in his arms. Sometimes when they sat in a restaurant, as Oksana moodily smoked she would suddenly freeze, staring emptily across the room, the cigarette burning to her fingers. These momentary lapses from reality were a serious indication of her mental state. Peter did his best to lighten these moments, concerned that her condition might worsen. There was a lot of pressure on her to perform, and his success was totally dependent on her.

After his meeting at Petrovka 38, Peter asked Oksana if she knew how to use a gun.

She looked at him questioningly and he saw interest in her eyes as she replied, "I grew up with guns on the estate in Irkutsk."

"Do you have one?"

She shook her head. "What would I do carrying a lump of metal around with me? I'd be arrested."

"Better than being unpleasantly surprised. I could get you something really neat, small enough to fit snugly in your purse, big enough to save your life if you need it."

"I never thought I would need such a thing," Oksana mused. Then seriously, "It would make me feel more secure. Especially when I'm traveling."

"And we will be doing that. I am ready to make a deal with your father's friend Volkov." Peter paused, leaned toward her, kissed her lips and then added, "It could be very profitable. We can use a big stake when we get married."

"Married?!"

"Yes. I'm proposing to you, Oksana. Will you marry me?"

She turned her head upward and to the side for a moment, then looked back into his eyes, beaming and smiling, and said, "Yes, Peter Nikhilov. I accept!"

They sealed it with a long and passionate kiss. Peter said, "You know this means a new life together in America."

"I'm delighted, Peter." Then, "I think my father suspects what we are going to tell him when we visit Irkutsk. He asked a lot of questions about you."

"What did you tell him exactly?" Peter felt more than passing interest in Nickolai's curiosity about him since Martinov was to be a key player in his plan to thwart the sale of Russian nuclear weapons to terrorist states.

"He wondered why you were in Moscow. I told him that even

though you didn't speak Russian you were of our heritage and wanted to do business here."

Peter nodded approvingly. "Anything else?"

"Naturally he asked if you were a rich American. I said of course you were and I was happy to be your interpreter."

"Good. Now I am going to Dorogomilov market where I have heard the finest selection of guns in the world are on sale in the cellars below the vegetable stands and buy you an engagement present."

"Do you carry a gun, Peter?"

"Not in Moscow. My friends at Petrovka 38 have spared themselves the problem of getting me such a license." She seemed concerned with his answer.

"I have something I carry left over from my days as a reserve officer in our Special Forces, like your Spetznaz." He pulled out the large round metal pocket watch. "It's called a chronolog. Tells the time anywhere in the world."

"How interesting," she looked at it in his hand. "What's the time in Irkutsk?"

He glanced down. "Three in the morning," Peter replied.

"What is its little secret?" she asked.

"On our wedding day I'll tell you. I hope we never need it."

"Now you've got my curiosity aroused."

"So the sooner we get married the sooner you'll know my last secret." He smiled mysteriously.

"Oh!" she cried in exasperation. "You are terrible!"

"And you are terribly beautiful. Tomorrow I want you to arrange our flight to Irkutsk and my meeting with Volkov. Tell your father I will have about a quarter of a million dollars of my German and American clients' money on me in cash to pay Volkov for the product we discussed at the Mayor of Moscow's party."

"Everyone wondered where you ran off to," Oksana pouted.

"I made my deal with Volkov that night and I had to immediately get on the telephone to my clients in New York and Hamburg. If I hadn't done so I wouldn't have the cash in time for us to be on our way tomorrow."

Oksana's eyes shone with excitement. "I can hardly wait for us to tell daddy we're going to be married."

"When he sees the cash I am delivering to his friend, Volkov, I'm sure he'll give us his blessings."

"You think my father would sell his daughter to you?" Oksana asked in mock indignation.

"What do you think? From what I saw of old Nickolai he ain't giving anything away. Besides, he wouldn't want you marrying a pauper."

Oksana laughed merrily and hugged Peter. "He is an old rascal and I love you, Peter."

"*Ya lo blu vas,* too," Peter said slowly, and carefully. "See, I am learning the important Russian words and tomorrow you shall have your first engagement present."

CHAPTER FORTY·SIX

⋘ ⋙

In the large conference room adjacent to Director Yevgeny Volkov's office at the top of the Dome in the secret city of Krasnov 86, the Deputy Minister of Finance, the only minister with some degree of control over the operation, was receiving the first briefing Volkov had felt necessary to hold for a Moscow-based government official since the aborted coup. Officials of the Russian Federation were gradually attempting to assert their authority. Volkov had made the first approach to the new Deputy Finance Minister on his recent visit to Moscow and urged that an authoritative representative visit the Dome to discuss an important matter. The deputy himself, a hastily reconstituted former communist *apparatchik*, chose to visit the Dome when he caught Volkov's hint that there might be personal gain for him to garner.

Volkov had always avoided exposing his operational problems before members of the Chamber of Deputies or the bureaucrats from any of the ministries. However, to put unlimited millions of dollars in the personal accounts he envisioned opening for him-

417

self outside Russia he had to secure certain crucial certificates from the Ministry of Finance.

A carefully coached Alexis Plotnikov delivered the briefing to the Moscow representitive in the presence of other top managers and engineering personnel of Krasnov 86. Volkov's new deputy replaced the disgraced Dr. Zilko upon whose head was placed the blame for the accident which wiped out the rocket battalion and four missiles.

"Until August of 1991 when the attempted coup was put down we used to dismantle as many as three dozen outdated and dangerous weapons a month," Plotnikov declared. "But for the past month we can barely handle half a dozen. You ask 'why is this so?' The answer is the deficit of qualified personnel caused by the strike when the money from Moscow stopped coming in. Hundreds of skilled workers have left Krasnov 86. We must find new full-time specialists and increase the benefits to those still with us." All around the conference table heads solemnly nodded.

Volkov wanted to emphasize the most important point himself and took over the meeting. "Our problem comes down to money. Since the fall of the Communist Party the funds to pay our skilled workers are not forthcoming."

"Can you not just curtail production?" the deputy asked.

The group around the table collectively shook their heads. "It is a danger, national in scope, to allow old weapons to stand unattended," Volkov replied. "Dismantling the weapons, we destroy the parts that are classified, burn the explosives and recover the plutonium 239. Then we have to store it and that is a major problem. We are fast running out of space. One plutonium charge the size of a bowling ball encased in thin steel needs a separate pit one third the size of this room and must be separated from other charges by walls of granite or concrete reinforced with lead plates. This is vital to avoid a critical mass occurring in the case of any sort of accident. That would mean nothing short of a nuclear blast."

Again heads nodded in unison. Finally the deputy forced himself to ask, "What is the possibility of a nuclear accident?" He did not really want to hear the answer to that question.

"Explain, Plotnikov," Volkov ordered somberly.

"We have many missiles full of liquid fuel dating back to the early seventies and even the newer solid stage fuel is volatile."

"Then what particular accident are you talking about?" asked the treasury official.

"The day of the coup in August we had an explosion of fuel tanks," Plotnikov replied.

"I tried to report the destruction of four missiles to General Yazov himself but—" Volkov shrugged.

"I understand," the deputy minister replied cutting off further reference to the sordid coup affair.

"The danger in an explosion is the powerful shockwaves which travel at great speed through the rock of the mountain," Plotnikov continued. "We widened the tunnels to more quickly disperse such shock waves, but you can never tell."

Volkov saw that the financial officer was already confused and sought to heighten his fears. "Should detonation of the core explosives occur while stripping away the plutonium charges the spreading radiation could kill personnel by the hundreds."

Shivers and horrified looks on the part of the half dozen upper echelon supervisors at the meeting rippled around the conference table. "We have the situation now," Volkov continued in an ominous tone, "where due to lack of space, one warhead is being stripped of the core and six others await stripping on the tables in the same hall. People grow nervous."

Volkov's expressive shrug was accompanied by a dour look about the mouth and chin. "Lack of funds to pay them well leads to defections. This is not something we can just walk away from to save money. There are all kinds of exotic occurrences which could turn this place into a seething dome of nuclear radiation that would dwarf Chernoble. Earthquakes, meteorites, plane crashes, terrorist attacks. All these possibilities and more give us a high probability for disaster."

The somber nods of agreement served to further intimidate the Deputy Minister of Finance who visibly shuddered. "What do you propose?" he managed.

"I would like to take you for a tour below one of our nuclear facilities, the missile and fuel storage areas, and show you at first hand the process we use to extract plutonium 239 from the dismantled warheads."

Nervously the deputy cleared his throat and glanced at his watch. "As I told you my time here is severely limited. I am anxious to catch the afternoon plane back to Moscow. Just tell me what can be done about this problem."

Volkov nodded. "We cannot stop the constant flow of weapons that must be disassembled, but we can increase the number of workers and construct new pits outside the complex, very simple ones, but functional. All it takes is money."

The deputy frowned deeply. "You know perfectly well that financing of your programs has been cut."

Volkov smiled sympathetically as though at a backward student who cannot understand the lesson. "We do not ask for additional government funding. We only ask for permission to use the money we have."

"Sorry?"

Volkov inclined his head toward Plotnikov who produced a file folder and opening it announced:

"For the past two months the number of dismantled missiles amounted to fifty items. After the disassembly we have gold remaining from the electric circuitry in each weapon. The value of this gold is no less than fifty thousand dollars, in hard currency, per missile, total yield for two months being two million five hundred thousand dollars."

Volkov allowed the deputy to think about the figure for a moment. Then, "We send this gold to your department every six months. We now ask permission to sell it on the world market, using the income entirely for our operations, thus ensuring nuclear security at Krasnov 86."

"That sounds reasonable," the deputy allowed. "However, the minister . . ."

Volkov stood up and gestured to the Moscow bureaucrat. "Please, come into my private office. There are some files I would like to show you." The deputy followed Volkov out of the conference room and into the privacy of the adjoining office.

Quickly the director explained the situation. "Here at the plant we can transform the industrial gold taken from the rocket circuitry into bullion. I have the contacts to sell it in Switzerland for immediate hard currency. On the way back I can stop in Moscow, meet you, personally hand you, say ten percent of the cash realized. You can do as you like about turning it back to the Treasury, using it where you need it in your sole discretion. There will be no records and we will be able to finance all the Dome's operations without additional funding from your ministry."

Experienced communist that he was, the deputy made one comment. "I think fifteen percent would be a more reasonable figure."

"Yes, of course. Fifteen percent for you to distribute as you see fit. That should come to about one hundred and fifty thousand dollars every month to six weeks."

The figure was astronomical and inflation was increasing the value of the dollar every day. The amount of money the deputy could divert to his own account was almost incomprehensible.

Volkov placed a hand on the deputy minister's shoulder. "Come, let's go back to the meeting and conclude this business."

As they returned to the conference room Volkov was saying, "So you see, we're not talking about big money when you consider the consequences of ignoring a potential nuclear catastrophe."

In full view and hearing of his executives Volkov turned a crooked smile on the deputy. "What will the minister tell the world after an accident occurs here for lack of funds to retain the skilled workers we need and keep up necessary maintenance?" He paused meaningfully, then, "How does he explain it when radiation starts leaking into the global atmosphere—all because the Finance Ministry would not release this technical gold already paid for. It costs the Treasury no new money to take these safety measures . . ."

The deputy minister held up his hand. "Yes, yes, yes of course! I understand the situation now. I give you permission to use the gold you have, meanwhile I will discuss the situation with the minister and I am sure we shall come to a positive solution. I will sign a certificate permitting you to transport and sell your gold for hard currency. When the minister hears what the alternative could cost us I know he will agree."

"Secretary," Volkov called down the conference table to Plotnikov, "bring me the papers for the Deputy Minister of Finance."

Plotnikov leapt to his feet and walked around the table to where the deputy was standing, laying the papers before him. Silence pervaded the conference room as the deputy read the simple agreement which had been prepared along with the standard certificate for the director to sell the gold in foreign markets. Volkov produced a pen from his coat pocket and handed it to the deputy minister who ceremoniously signed his name and ministerial position, then looked up at the director. "This constitutes our defense against a nuclear accident here." All at the table smiled and nodded approval.

"My own mother could not have comforted me more!" the radiant director exclaimed.

"And now, Director Volkov," the deputy minister said, "if you will instruct the helicopter to take me to the Irkutsk airport I will be on my way back to Moscow."

"With a great accomplishment behind you, Deputy Minister. You can take credit for solving a devastating problem at no expense to the government."

"Yes, indeed. I hadn't thought of that. Thank you Director." Volkov stood up and led his official visitor back into his private office as the management and engineering team dispersed to their stations throughout the Dome. The director telephoned up to the heliport at the top of the Dome and ordered the flight. Then he walked across to his cabinet with the safe containing Jap's rubles still in it and took out a bottle of export grade Stolichnaya Vodka.

"Please allow me to present this token of our appreciation for your understanding, my dear Deputy. It may provide you some comfort on the long flight back to Moscow."

Gratefully the deputy took the bottle and stepped into the elevator. Volkov watched the doors close and the lights indicate the car was surface-bound before letting out an exclamation of triumph.

The final technical link in his plan to become one of the richest men in Russia had been accomplished. The certificate for selling gold gave him the right to travel to Switzerland and anywhere in Europe with diplomatic immunity, no customs inspection of his luggage anywhere. The money from the gold sales would indeed go into the Dome account and be used in its entirety for maintenance, after the Deputy Minister received his tribute.

Volkov visualized the huge amount of currency in neat stacks of hundred dollar bills he would soon have in his safe ready for the journey to Switzerland. Within a few days Jap would arrive to take delivery of the first SS-24 Sickle ICBM with its mobile launcher and at that time hand over the payment in dollars as the finest nuclear weapon manufactured in the world was loaded into the AN-22 Cargo plane Jap had somehow managed to acquire.

Added to the proceeds of Jap's purchase, he was expecting a call from Nickolai informing him that his daughter, Oksana, and the American would soon be arriving with more stacks of dollars. Volkov laughed to himself. Red Mercury, the American had said. But he would get true plutonium 239 for his clients with whom Volkov expected to deal directly in all future transactions.

The late fall weather at the top of the Dome was frosty and there was some snow, blown into drifts by frequent wind gusts. The sentinels at their guard posts around the helicopter pad wore body warmers and fur collars.

The Deputy Minister of Finance climbed into the waiting helicopter in the middle of the afternoon with the satisfied feeling of a job well done. He was already mentally writing his scenario for the minister next day, how he had solved an overwhelming financial problem at no cost to the government.

The helicopter quickly ascended into the air, polished metal gleaming in the sun. This was the special VIP chopper in which Volkov rode and which picked up the important government officials and special guests. It was insulated against noise and cold. The pilot set course for Irkutsk and radioed his flight plan to the airport control tower.

Another dark silhouette gliding in from far to the west appeared on the horizon almost simultaneously. Soon the hum of distant engines became a heavy throbbing beat. The guards looked up curiously, dancing from one foot to the other to keep their toes warm as the AN-22 cargo turboprop, green and brown in color, came in full view sending out roaring sound waves as it descended over the hills and sparse pine trees.

The giant airplane's wide, shock-absorbing undercarriage screamed as it made contact with the frozen concrete and laid strips of smoking rubber on the runway, far below the helipad situated at the top of the dome. It lurched forward at a slowly decreasing speed until finally the aircraft made a graceful turn and taxied back to the area of the airstrip closest to the tunnel entrance to the Dome, ten levels below Volkov's office.

CHAPTER FORTY-SEVEN

The Siberian landscape below was as cold and formidable as anything Peter Nikhilov had ever seen in his life. He asked himself the inevitable question, "What in the Hell am I doing here?"

The answer came back from deep within. "The last thing I dreamed of was saving humanity. I just wanted to get Volkov back to Moscow so Petrovka 38 could trap him and then get on with my business."

Oksana nestled up against him in the comfortable executive helicopter Volkov had sent to bring them to the Domo. Across from them sat the tall, skinny fur-swathed Plotnikov sent by Volkov to escort them to Krasnov 86 and beside him the bearish Nickolai Martinov. Peter still grinned inwardly as he thought back to what the sight of a quarter of a million dollars in cold cash had done to a greedy old rogue's judgement.

Martinov had been barely tolerant of his daughter's lover when he met the two of them in the decrepit wood and concrete terminal of the Irkutsk airport. They landed late in the morning of the day before, after flying all night from Moscow. As always Oksana was elated to be back in her home region. They had been driven by her father's chauffeur into the city thirty miles from Russia's majestic Lake Baikal.

The apartment of the former First Secretary was regal in size and decor. Nickolai's power in the region was as great as ever. He had immediately understood the prevailing mood among the victorious Democrats after the failed coup. With the banning of the Party he become an avowed anti-communist and called elections in which his minions elected him People's Deputy still ruling the region.

Since her father thought Peter could not understand Russian he was none too tactful in his remarks about his daughter's client who was also her lover. However, he did agree, after her spirited argument which Peter wished he could applaud without revealing he understood the language, that she and her fiancé would share a room together.

Time being of great importance, Peter knew that Jap was planning to buy missiles and nuclear material any day from Volkov and deliver them to Iraq, he set about ingratiating himself with his father-in-law-to-be. It didn't take a shrewd mind to figure out what would most impress Nickolai. So over cognac after a cheerful dinner, with Oksana translating, he laid out his plan to buy several kilos of plutonium 239 for his clients.

"And who will the final buyer be?" Nickolai asked.

"Does it matter?" Peter replied. "The profit to my clients, myself, and," he added with a significant wink, "those who help me, will be substantial."

Nickolai chuckled and patted Peter on the knee. This was the moment, Peter realized, to enmesh Nickolai in his plot to trap Jap and Volkov and put an end to any sale of nuclear devices to oil-rich terrorist states. He reached for his briefcase, which he had kept beside him since his arrival, attracting frequent speculative glances from Nickolai, placed it on his knees and snapped it open. After a moment he turned it around allowing his host a view of the neatly bundled and stacked hundred dollar bills. This was hard currency. It was the stuff on which today's world turned with far greater expediency than on diamonds and gold. Such commodities still had to be converted to legal tender of the realm. Nickolai had never seen such a display of American cash and audibly caught his breath.

"I brought a quarter million with me, which I will leave on deposit with Director Volkov against delivery of his products."

Nickolai stared at the cash, transfixed for some moments. Finally he said hoarsely, "Well my son, I think you will be speaking a language Hamster understands."

"Hamster?" Peter asked.

"A nickname by which Volkov is known to certain old friends."

"I see. Well perhaps you could count it with me and then tell Hamster that you are witness that I will not be arriving empty-handed when I come to view his product and negotiate sales prices."

"Yes, Son, I will certainly be happy to do that. And cash available in dollars gives me an opportunity to insist on Hamster allowing you to be given the full run of the Dome with an expert to guide you. I asked for Plotnikov who knows more than any of Hamster's deputies. Customers like you and Yakovlev deserve the best advice and," Nickolai gave Peter a deliberative stare, "it's worth your while paying for it."

"It is indeed," Peter agreed. "I appreciate your thoughtfulness. Just tell me how much and we'll take it out of there." He gestured at the briefcase.

It had been a high-spirited prospective father-in-law that bade a tired Peter and Oksana goodnight, giving them the master bedroom with the double bed.

As it turned out Plotnikov's advice wouldn't come cheaply. Nickolai had taken a ten thousand dollar bundle of bills out of the briefcase Peter recalled with a chuckle as the helicopter sped them toward their destination. Just how much Plotnikov would personally see of the money he could only guess.

"Almost there!" the pilot called out over his shoulder. The chopper sank gracefully to the ground and soon they were standing on the helicopter pad. The air operations division at the Dome was run with military precision by experienced personnel. Barracks for guards and officers and other buildings and hangers for the aircraft were arranged in precise rows. In contrast to the executive helicopter in which they had arrived, several other battered veteran army helicopters were arrayed along the edge of the landing pad. These provided transportation for the ordinary executives and visitors to the Dome, Peter surmised. He had heard Nickolai insist on the telephone, presumably talking to Volkov, that the deluxe helicopter be sent for them.

A security officer in thick black overalls and fur hat came up to them. He addressed Martinov in the old style. "Good morning Comrade Chairman. We have guests today, I see." He eyed Peter and Oksana curiously. "And yes, our new Deputy Director, Plotnikov, is with you. I received authorization from our Comrade Director to escort you through security check and into the elevator."

Martinov was secretly pleased at the reference to his communist glory days. Peter, his briefcase securely clutched in his left hand, Oksana beside him, followed Martinov and the security officer up to the entrance of a large cement structure which stood at the highest point of this stone-covered hill. Martinov and the officer went inside leaving Oksana and Peter stamping their feet in the cold outside.

The view from the top of the pad half a mile above the plain was a panorama of industrial buildings, mounds of earth and rock everywhere and a network of railway tracks glistened coldly under the morning sun like a thin, steel web. Trucks, locomotives and excavators looked like toys, the turrets of guard posts sprouting like mushrooms among them. Miles off to his right a vast area charred black caught his attention. Plotnikov, standing beside him, followed Peter's gaze. "Yes, that is the testing area for rocket engines."

Peter was still wondering how much Nickolai had given Plotnikov of the ten thousand counterfeit dollars when Oksana pointed off in another direction. "Look, there is an airplane down there. It's huge."

Peter looked down the slope off to their left, his view obscured by protruding rocks and tree tops. He saw what appeared to be the visible portion of a long airstrip. A gigantic airplane could just be made out at the near end of the runway. It was a military-type cargo plane bigger than any he had ever seen during his own days with U.S. Army Special Forces. The enormous aircraft made the fueling truck next to it look tiny.

"That is the AN-22 turboprop super cargo plane," Plotnikov explained. "It can carry an eighty ton load over ten thousand miles at a speed of four hundred fifty miles per hour."

"What is it doing here?" Peter asked.

Plotnikov shrugged. "It will probably take off with one or two SS-25 Sickle missiles for another storage facility. The safest way to move the ICBMs is by air. Even a slight ground collision could ignite the solid state fuel in a rocket, especially if it has been in storage over three or four years."

Peter was staring at the distant plane. "Where is it going?"

"Ah, that is information that is unknown, even at the highest administrative levels here at the Dome."

Martinov stepped out of the building with the officer and two armed guards. "We are cleared to go through security and then down into the Dome," he announced. "Sorry to have left you out in this freezing air."

"We saw much of interest," Oksana replied.

Martinov escorted Plotnikov, Peter and Oksana into the build-

ing, out of the frigid weather. It was full of armed guards and perhaps as many as fifty men in white jackets and pants, all wearing
Dome identification badges of various colors denoting the areas in
which they worked, were waiting for elevators.

"You go through a routine check for metal," Martinov instructed them. "Then you'll be taken down to Hamster's office where
Peter can attend to his business with the director."

"You are not coming, Father?"

"No, you are in the best of hands with Plotnikov and I have
an important business associate on the way I must meet at the
airport."

"Anyone I know?" Oksana asked.

Nickolai gave his daughter a mysterious smile. "You will soon
see." He left the building heading back to the helicopter.

As they approached the security barrier Oksana gave Peter a
stricken look. The small nickel-plated Parabellum Peter had
bought her in Moscow was in her purse. The pistol had partially
restored her sense of security.

"Do not worry, love," he said, understanding her fears. "You
just leave your purse at the guard station. Do not open it. They'll
be satisfied with that. After all, you are the daughter of Chief
Regional Administrator Martinov."

It worked the way Peter had anticipated. Oksana just gave her
purse to the young guard who placed it in a drawer for her to
reclaim when she left. Security control was similar to the check
before flights at all airports. Oksana passed through without trouble. The gate, however, reacted when Peter walked between the
metal detectors.

He reached into his pocket and pulled out the thick round
device which he showed to the security officer. "It's called a
chronolog," he explained, "and tells the time everywhere in the
world." Oksana translated. "Where would you like to know what
time it is?"

Several other guards gathered around to view the object. The security officer checked his own watch. "I know what time it is in Moscow. What time does your clock say it is?"

Peter glanced at the thick heavy round instrument. "Six in the morning," he replied.

"That's right. And in New York?"

"They're still drinking at the bars. It's eleven last night."

The security officer laughed. "No problem. Keep your time piece." Peter slipped it back in his pocket.

Oksana and Peter were led to an open elevator door and they were escorted inside by Plotnikov. The doors slid closed and the car with mirrored walls dropped down the shaft through the granite mountain crust to the administrative offices at the peak of the dome. It came to a smooth halt deep inside the mountain and the doors slid open revealing a spacious office. A large wooden desk featuring an array of telephones dominated the room, the figure of Yevgeny Volkov standing behind it, his arms folded above his belly.

"Welcome," Volkov greeted them cheerfully. "And in Plotnikov, here, you have the most knowledgeable guide possible to the Dome. He gestured at the chairs before his desk. Oksana unbuttoned her coat and took a seat, ready to translate for Peter as he removed a fur cape from over his American raincoat and sat down beside her. Plotnikov, unbidden to sit, stood behind them.

Volkov's fleshy face and small glistening eyes under bushy brows fixed them inscrutably across the desk. "Nickolai Martinov tells me you have important business to discuss and sends his daughter with you to insure accurate translation. I shall listen to you very attentively. But first, why did you disappear the night of the mayor's party in Moscow? I felt we were just getting down to business."

"Once you and I agreed in principle that I would buy and you would sell me plutonium 239 it was my responsibility to contact my clients in New York and Bonn and put our deal together," he paused meaningfully, "that meant arranging for a substantial amount of U.S. dollars to be available. Time was of the essence."

Volkov bobbed a pleased nod and his eyes went to the briefcase on Peter's lap.

"As you suggested," Peter went on, we are not really interested in red mercury—if there is such a thing. The term is, in my opinion, merely a code word for some substance which helps to create portable nuclear weapons." He smiled wanly at Volkov. "But it was the code word which peaked your attention I might add."

Volkov chuckled but did not reply, waiting for Peter to continue. "We are interested in fissionable material as a substance which can be used as a fuel for nuclear reactors."

"The technology for using weapon grade products in nuclear reactors has not been developed yet," Volkov stated flatly, studying his fingernails.

"Very nicely put," Peter approved. "But it will soon be developed, and will come as a great surprise to many. Those who possess enriched material will be totally independent from the fluctuations of the world oil market."

"Nickolai told me you were here on serious business. I am not interested in why you want to acquire weapons grade fissionable material. You can buy as much enriched uranium and plutonium 239 as you want from me. And for a very reasonable price."

"Which is?" Peter asked.

"Half a million dollars for a kilo of plutonium-239 and a hundred thousand for a kilo of enriched weapons grade uranium-235. Payments to be made in cash. Shipping the product out of the country is your concern."

"I noticed an AN-22 cargo plane on the airstrip below the mountain. I assume my clients would have access to the landing field. And of course they would have no need of so large a plane."

"Unless they had a more ambitious purchase in mind," Volkov said meditatively.

"For instance?" Peter encouraged.

"Plotnikov here just picked out one of our most recent Sickle SS-25 missiles, complete with warhead for sale to some foreign buyer through Oksana's friend, Vyacheslav Yakovlev."

"For how much?" Peter asked, feigning sudden interest.

"A mere twelve million dollars—complete with its mobile launcher."

Peter assumed his craftiest expression. "I understand that such a weapon can be bought in Ukraine."

"Very likely. But even those people who might perhaps sell you such a rocket could not give you the firing code. I can give you the code and you give it to the ultimate buyer—after his letters of credit have been paid. There is no other place, except another secret city like this one, that can make such a deal. And there is no other secret city as independent as we are out here in Siberia."

"So, as we say in America, you are the only game in town."

Volkov laughed aloud at the translation. "Indeed. For the time being at least I am the final authority at the Dome. I suppose some-day Moscow will get its governmental house in order and I will have to answer to some minister who will have to be paid an exor-bitant bribe but for now, Nickolai Martinov, the father of your beautiful interpreter, and I are the highest authority in the Irkutsk region."

Oksana blushed prettily as she translated Volkov's description of her.

"We could open a foreign bank account for you," Peter sug-gested.

"No bank accounts. Any account can be traced."

"But in Switzerland . . ."

"I visit abroad and especially Switzerland where I will soon be going on a matter of salaries for my key workers here at Krasnov 86. I will be on official business but I have learned that drawing from a personal account can leave me exposed. I only work with cash. And I do you a favor by charging only half the world market price, if you can buy it at all."

Peter nodded and smiled. "That sounds reasonable. To begin with, I need a sample of plutonium for my client. Can you prepare say, one hundred grams?"

"Do you understand how deadly it is? Under no conditions can it be exposed to open air. It burns in oxygen. And as for toxicity . . ."

"I am fully aware of its deadly properties." Peter paused and placed the briefcase on the desk. With a flourish he pressed both locks and the lid snapped open revealing the neat bundles of hundred dollar bills. "Half a million dollars for one kilogram of plutonium. Here is a quarter of a million. The other quarter million when my people take delivery of a kilo. As a matter of fact, after they have examined the sample they may want three to five kilograms."

Peter pushed the briefcase across the desk. "Count it. You will find two hundred and forty thousand dollars. The other ten thousand was paid out yesterday in consulting fees. This is to show you serious intent."

Volkov stared at the cash his jaw dropping. "You trust me that much?"

"It is the new attitude in dealing with nuclear material and missiles. In case we fail at some point you lose nothing. Purchasing plutonium from you saves my people from dealing with an unreliable supplier. There is no lack of money on their part."

"I hope I will meet these gentlemen."

"I can arrange that in Moscow. You mentioned that you could sell them a complete missile."

"Yes, I have many different types in storage, even submarine-launched missiles along with the Sickle SS-25s, our finest product. At thirty-five tons it is much easier to transport than any other rocket and its range is eight to nine thousand miles and can be launched from its mobile carrier anywhere."

"I have an idea," Peter said as though a sudden thought had struck him. "My clients will all be in Moscow next week. If you will bring the plutonium with you I will have you all meet and from now on you will be dealing with the principles—and I will return to America, with my interpreter."

Oksana gave Peter a surprised look but translated his words.

Volkov shook his head sadly. "I have no way to safely transport a kilo of plutonium from here to Moscow. The minister gives me sovereignty over the missiles and fissionable materials but not the means of transporting them, that is another ministry. Your people will have to find an airplane and come here for it."

"They can, of course, handle that," Peter replied. "You said you were going to Switzerland. Stop by in Moscow. My people will pay you for the kilo of plutonium. You could go on to Switzerland with that cash while they make preparations to take delivery. I can picture a very profitable business for you."

"And what do you get out of it?" Volkov asked.

"For setting all this up they will open an account for me in the Caribbean and make payments to me as your business together transpires."

For some moments Volkov stared at the cash on his desk as he pondered the offer which seemed almost too good to be true. Yet right there in front of him was the first payment and he would always be ahead of the buyers as he accepted cash for future deliveries made just outside his back door, so to speak.

Peter saw that the deal was basically irresistible to Volkov and decided to make it even sweeter. "And by then perhaps they would also be prepared to make a down payment on a Sickle SS-25. More cash for you to take to Switzerland." As Volkov hesitated Peter added, "Of course I would have to actually see the SS-25s you have in storage."

"I can arrange that right now," Volkov answered eagerly.

"And since Deputy Martinov arranged for Plotnikov to advise me, I would want him with me."

Volkov laughed happily. "Of course. It appears we are all in this business together and nobody knows the laboratories and storage chambers better than Plotnikov."

"So then, we have an arrangement that will make us all wealthy," Peter summarized.

And that's not counting the money from Jap, Volkov thought to himself. His only problem was what to do with all that money. Maybe he could even lure Oksana away from the American. He had a hard time taking his eyes off her as she translated for Peter.

Volkov opened a desk drawer, extracted three red and black badges and handed them to Peter, Oksana, and Plotnikov, instructing them to pin the identification tags to their jackets. Oksana handed hers to Peter. With the back of his hand caressing her left breast he carefully pinned the tag to the black blouse she was wearing. It was a small gesture of their proprietary interest in each other which was missed by no one.

"Well," Volkov said cheerfully, "I'll let Plotnikov give you a tour of the Dome. I'd do it myself but I am expecting some important messages." He led them to the sliding elevator door and pushed the button. "Plotnikov, take them down the inspection tube. Show our American friend the Sickle SS-25 missiles and then come back up, level by level."

The factory director jovially turned to Peter. "For years I would be afraid to fart without the permission of Gorby or some other idiot in PolitBureau. Now?" he shrugged. "We make our own rules."

"And choose your own buyers," Peter added, "for which I and my clients are most thankful."

The translation elicited a laugh from Volkov as the elevator door slid open and Volkov gestured his guests inside. As the doors slid closed Plotnikov said, "We go down nine levels, just above the enrichment laboratories. That's as far as we can safely go without penetrating the high radiation levels."

The elevator car jolted to a stop and the doors opened. They stepped out into a fluorescent-lighted mosaic-covered cavern which looked like the main level of the Lenin Square Metro station. And indeed, like a busy subway station, there seemed to be hundreds of white-garbed workers, heads covered with white turban-like wraps that gave them the appearance of medical workers scurrying around in this enormous manmade grotto. Plotnikov pointed out the rows of missiles, about sixty feet long Peter estimated, lying lengthwise on steel racks. "Just here alone are enough ICBMs to reach all the major cities of America at the same time. Even if three quarters of them were destroyed before reaching their objective—" he paused, a contemplative look on his face. "How interesting it would have been to see who would have won in such an exchange."

The gleam of ultraviolet rays poured down over the rows of rocket fuselages. Plotnikov chuckled at the puzzled look on Peter's face. "We discovered that a certain type of bacteria feeds on the cellulose of the solid fuel components, so we put in special lamps to keep the storage as sterile as possible. Critical temperature is sustained along with keeping the humidity at a low count. We also go to great lengths to guard against static electricity charges."

"Wouldn't it be safer to keep the warheads apart from the main hulls of the rockets?" Peter asked.

"That's the rule I tried to enforce but when we ran out of storage space the rule was no longer followed."

Oksana shuddered as she looked around the cavern. Plotnikov laughed. "Yes, it is true that this whole mountain, the secret city of Krasnov 86, could blow up at any time. But the pay and living conditions for the workers who live in these secret cities is the best in all the Soviet Union. We have the finest food and drink, no shopping lines, no shortages, excellent schools for the children." Plotnikov shrugged. "We all become fatalists. If it happens, so be it. Meantime we lead good lives."

"At what point is the warhead put on the missile?" Peter asked.

"Usually not until the delivery system is installed in its launching site. However, the entire weapon system, especially in the case of solid fuel rockets, is usually shipped intact."

"If by some accident the rocket blew up would that detonate its nuclear warhead?"

Plotnikov shook his head. "I could go into a long explanation of why not, but the answer is no. And there have been such accidents to prove the point."

"And the AN-22 cargo plane is long enough to hold an armed and fueled Sickle ICBM?" Peter asked.

Plotnikov nodded. "Easily. It was designed to transport our T-62 tank six to eight thousand miles. It will go out with its warhead attached. In Iraq, there are few if any people trained to assemble the weapon."

So he knows where Jap is selling the missile, Peter thought as he stood staring in awe at the ranks of six feet tall warheads. "What is Volkov going to do with all of these?" Peter finally asked. "I mean, Jap can't sell them all."

Plotnikov laughed. "That, of course, is Volkov's purpose in showing you what no one outside a tight circle of scientists, managers, and former Party Chairmen have ever seen. Follow me and I will show you the Sickle I chose for Jap to buy. And I will make certain that if you buy from Volkov you also get one of the most recently delivered SS-25 Sickles in the Dome."

They walked through the towering cavern so surprisingly decorated with mosaic art, white-robed workers swarming around the warheads and rockets, until they came to a rail track which ran through a tunnel-like entrance in the wall and into what Peter surmised was some sort of a delivery room for missiles about to be sent out of the Dome.

They watched as a Dome officer directed the transfer of the Sickle SS-25 onto the low, wide specially designed mobile missile launcher. It had seven pairs of wheels, each six feet high and over three feet wide, the bed of the truck being twelve feet wide—only a collision with a heavy tank could turn it over.

The weight of the carrier was an additional advantage. It crushed small obstacles, providing a ride as smooth as a Mercedes along a highway.

Two cranes lowered the sixty foot fuselage and attached the warhead onto the mobile launcher which was the same length, the warhead resting directly above the driver's cab.

"Next stop is the AN-22," Plotnikov said. "As soon as they get the order from Volkov to move it out."

"How long will it take to drive the missile out to the plane?" Peter asked.

"At least twenty minutes through the tunnel to the exterior. Maybe a total of an hour and a half from the time Volkov calls."

"And when does the cargo plane take off?"

"That depends upon Volkov and Yakovlev. My assignment was to be sure that he purchased the most recent model we had. In just a few years of storage the solid fuel can become critical to the point where if a crane dropped it the fuel might ignite."

A bell rang and the red telephone was picked up by the officer in charge. He listened, nodded, hung up the phone and shouted an order.

"He's saying, 'take it away,'" Oksana translated.

Looking like an army of huge white ants, workers swarmed over and around the missile.

As the driver of the mobile launcher approached the door to the cab Peter reached into his pocket for his chronolog. "Well, it is eight in the morning in Moscow. My clients will be looking forward to hearing from me," he remarked. "I will certainly recommend to them that they meet with Volkov as soon as possible and add some rockets to their inventory. By the way, Plotnikov, before they take it away can you show me where the plate is located that gives the birthdate of the rocket?"

"Director Volkov instructed me to help you in every way possible," Plotnikov agreed. He called out to the officer for a short delay and led Peter to the launcher. An iron step ladder was still standing beside the mammoth fourteen-wheeled flat bed truck.

Plotnikov signaled a worker to move the ladder to the rear of the rocket. "As a matter of fact I should give the code plate a last check anyway. The first Sickles, deployed in 1985, would be dangerously unstable now. The one I picked for Yakovlev was deployed in 1990. I don't think Volkov would switch missiles to get rid of an old one but . . ."

As Plotnikov mounted the stepladder, all eyes including Oksana's following him, Peter set the timer on the chronolog for three hours, plenty of time for the SS-25 to be loaded into the plane but well before it would be taking off. An explosion of the sixty-eight thousand pounds of solid fuel in a Sickle that far from the Dome, while causing minimum damage and loss of life within the secret city, would certainly destroy Jap's criminals and the AN-22. Such a blast would at least delay, and perhaps curtail any further sale of nuclear delivery weapons by rogue factory directors during this unsettled period of Russian governmental authority.

Peter pressed the chronolog's safety catch to the off position for the first time since he had appropriated it from the expedient devices store room at Fort Bragg when he was still a Green Beret Reserve Officer six years ago. The driver was just entering the cab of the mobile launcher as Peter locked three hours to detonation. That would surely give the Dome workers ample time to drive the launcher into the belly of the AN-22, get out and be safely back inside the granite walls before the explosion. And he was certain that the great cargo plane would not take off in less than three hours. An explosion in the air could conceivably destroy everything on the ground below it.

With the chronolog set Peter climbed the ladder beside Plotnikov and observed the plate attached to the SS-25 with letters and numbers indecipherable to him. Without Oksana to translate Plotnikov did not bother to explain the markings. Peter nodded and gestured Plotnikov to proceed him down the ladder. Just before following the scientist Peter located the black nickel-plated holes of the booster rockets, just the spot to start ignition that would fire the rocket's fuel. With his magnetic chronolog now clinging tightly to the inner surface of one of the boosters Peter descended the ladder and stood beside Plotnikov and Oksana.

On the way back to the elevator they passed the silent rows of sleeping rockets and warheads. Behind them Peter heard the sound of the mobile launcher's diesel engine starting up. A wry grin twisted his face as he thought of Jap hearing the news of the destruction of the twenty-five million dollar rocket.

But it would only be a temporary setback for Jap's *organizatsiya* and Volkov and Peter's old rogue of a prospective father-in-law. This troika of criminal intent would still find a way to sell off the inventory of the Dome for billions on the world terror market.

The Militsia officers at Petrovka 38 would have to take the initiative to work closely with whatever national law enforcement authorities were still operative in Russia and remained unreached by Jap or his cohorts. But, Peter mused bitterly, was there such team in the entire Russian nation these days?

CHAPTER FORTY-EIGHT

❖❖

A lthough Plotnikov offered him a tour of the various levels of the Dome approved by Volkov, Peter was accutely conscious of time. Under three hours remained until detonation. He was not positive his old keepsake chronolog, at least six years old, was still operative as a detonator. There was no telling how long it might have been in expediant devices storage at Special Forces headquarters before he had liberated it. Thus he had to convince Volkov to meet him later in Moscow where Petrovka 38 could trap him and then get away from the Dome with Oksana before the explosion on the runway.

At the elevator entrance a guard checked out their badges and then pressed the call button for them. The door slid open and Plotnikov led the way inside. The guard inserted his key in the lock that controlled access to Volkov's office and stepped back as the door closed and they were on their way up to the top level of the Dome.

Soon the door slid open again and they stepped out into Volkov's empty office. A small lead box which Peter assumed con-

443

tained the plutonim sample he had paid for with the counterfeit money rested on the desk. Vaguely Peter heard the sound of voices in the adjoining conference room. He walked to the desk and picked up the heavy box. "That is mine," he said. "I'll take it now."

Plotnikov shot a questioning glance at Oksana who translated for him. "As soon as the director gives me the order," Plotnikov replied.

"That's Slava's voice," Oksana exclaimed after listening to the conversation emanating from the conference room.

Peter had a hunch that something was about to go wrong. He didn't know what but he placed the lead box in his briefcase despite Plotnikov's protest. "Tell him I won't carry my case away without Volkov's permission," Peter said and Oksana translated. Plotnikov nodded.

Oksana started toward the open door to the next chamber but Plotnikov stepped around the desk and put a hand on her arm.

"The director said you were all to wait out here for him," he said.

Just then Volkov, a wide, pleased grin on his face, walked into his office from the conference room followed by Jap.

"Congratulations, Mr. Yakovlev," Peter said. "You own a like-new Sickle SS-25, the top of the line."

After Oksana's translation Jap replied, "I understand you also have customers for plutonium and the Dome's latest rockets." He watched Oksana as she put the words into English.

"That will be up to my clients and Director Volkov to work out. My job was to set up the possible sale."

"I'm sure Deputy Martinov informed you that you would be buying through us." Pavel's voice cut through the office as he walked in from the conference room. "Good afternoon, Oksana," he continued.

Oksana nodded to him and translated.

Peter listened. "Tell Pavel that's fine with me. It's all up to

Volkov and the principles and," he added hastily, "of course Deputy Martinov." He reached for his briefcase. "I have completed my assignment."

Plotnikov glanced questioningly at the grinning Volkov, flush with the money that Jap had obviously just paid him for the SS-25 Sickle missile now on its way to delivery. The director nodded. "Yes, it's his."

At that moment, to Peter's shock, Zekki Dekka came in from the next room babbling cheerfully about Swiss letters of credit and U.S. cash for the next shipment of two more Sickles to be made when the AN-22 cargo plane returned.

Zekki stared at the man who looked so like his nemesis in New York. Surely this couldn't actually be him. It was too unbelievable. No New York cop was smart and quick enough to penetrate this billion dollar crime scene in Siberia.

With his free hand Peter led Oksana toward the elevator. "My sweet, we are leaving. Tell the director to order the chopper. We will go back to your father's place in Irkutsk. I must call my clients in Moscow and Bonn on Director Volkov's behalf."

Before Oksana could get halfway through the translation Zekki, who had been staring at Peter open-mouthed, let out a cry which startled everyone in the room.

Jap shot a glance at him. "Hey! What are you doing!"

Peter retreated to the elevator, briefcase and fox fur cape in one hand, Oksana's arm in the other and pressed the button.

"Jap," Zekki cried, "do you know who this is?"

"Of course I do. An American. Don't yell, you'll scare the director."

"This is fucking Nikhilov!"

Now everyone was staring at Peter, even Oksana.

"So what?" an irritated Jap snapped.

"He is a cop!"

Jap cast a quick glance at Peter. Volkov's jaw fell open.

"You mean—*ment*?"

"No a fucking Russian-speaking cop from Brighton Beach, New York!"

"What do you mean?"

"That's a front, you asshole!" Peter snarled in English. Then in Russian to Jap, "Sure I was a cop in New York one or two days a week. The rest of the time I made money. Don't you use the *ments* to make money for the *organizatsiya*?"

The elevator arrived and the doors softly slid open. Peter put a foot in the door. "Oksana, come. We will not deal with such stupidity. I'll contact the director later."

"No!" Jap roared stepping toward the elevator. "What's going on? You stop right there."

In Russian Peter replied, "I have finished my business here. We are leaving. Unless you want me to explain to the director what Zekki does for you." Peter grinned at the puzzled look that came across Volkov's face.

Oksana gasped in surprise. Jap's face reflected an icy mixture of shock and anger. "So, he speaks our tongue," he said, immediately comprehending that rather than stop Peter, he must get him away from Volkov and out of the Dome.

"Of course he does," Zekki yelled. "He doesn't need an interpreter."

"We are not deaf, Zekki." Peter turned to Jap. "I do speak Russian, one of my little trade secrets."

"You deceived me," Oksana cried angrily. "I'll never be able to trust you again."

"Please, sweetheart." He pushed her toward the interior of the elevator. "We'll have to discuss it later . . ."

"What is the meaning of this?" Volkov demanded, giving Jap a hard stare.

Peter cocked his head at Jap. "You explain Zekki's bullshit—or I will."

Jap shot a withering glare at Zekki. "Zekki has about outlived his usefulness."

Volkov pounded his desk. "Are you saying this is some kind of trick? He paid me in hard currency."

"From Zilisi, Jap," Peter added.

Jap reflected on the situation for some moments. He and Pavel had been forced to leave their guns, even their knives, with Misha and the other bodyguards above before going through the metal detectors. There was no way he could kill Peter before he talked. Hastily he concocted an explanation. "We know the American has many arms contacts worldwide. If his police image in America is a front, well that doesn't concern us. Zekki does not comprehend the full situation. Let Nikhilov and the girl be on their way, Director." Jap threw a cautioning look at Zekki who finally understood and bowed his head knowingly.

Peter spoke up again. "I want to be sure there is a helicopter waiting to take us out of here and I want Oksana to call her father and tell him she is on her way home to him."

Volkov looked at Jap who nodded. The director picked up his phone and called the surface terminal giving the necessary instructions. A thoroughly confused Oksana submitted to being led into the elevator by Peter and the doors closed.

"Are you sure we should let him go, Jap?" Pavel asked gesturing at the closed elevator doors. "Or the girl either for that matter. It's a pity what has to be done. We saved her once."

"Right," Jap agreed. "We saved her and now we kill her and this American. He was sent by the *ments*. That's clear."

"What shall we do now?" Volkov was visibly shaken.

"You can call the helicopter directly from your desk here. Order the pilot to delay his next landing at the Dome."

Volkov quickly picked up his radio phone and made contact with the pilot of the helicopter on its way to land. "Captain Basil, this is the director," Volkov identified himself. "You will fly a holding pattern out of sight from the Dome until I call you to land," he ordered.

"Yes Comrade Director. I can only hold for half an hour before I am out of fuel and in the rocks."

"Stay in communication," Volkov replied. "I will maintain the helicopter frequency on the Dome radio phone for the rest of the day."

Peter and an angry, disillusioned Oksana stepped off the elevator in the terminal on top of the Dome. A guard returned Oksana's pocketbook to her as they passed through the security gates and she found herself staring at Misha, his long black ankle-length cape concealing, she knew, his machine gun. She nodded to Jap's gunman and followed Peter to a guard desk in a corner of the cold building.

"I take it that is one of Jap's men," Peter said nodding toward Misha.

"Yes," she replied simply.

"Now put through a call to your father from this telephone. Ask him to meet us at the helipad in Irkutsk. Make him understand you are in trouble. Blame it on me but tell him to meet us with armed guards. We'll decide what to do when we are all together."

The captain of the guards gestured at the chair across the desk from him and pushed the telephone towards her. She placed the receiver to her ear and started dialing.

In Volkov's office Jap, Pavel, and Zekki listened on a speaker as Oksana made telephone contact with her father.

"Daddy, I need help. I wish you were here."

"For many reasons I cannot personally be there at this time and witness what is going on. What is your trouble?"

"I am waiting with Peter for a helicopter to take us back to Irkutsk. Peter says you should meet us at the helicopter landing field with an armed escort."

"When are you actually taking off, Oksana?" The concern in Nickolai's voice was clear to all the listeners.

"I don't know, Daddy. We are waiting for the helicopter now."

"You will be met at the helipad. Try to call me just before you take off."

"I will try. I pray I'll see you soon."

They heard Oksana hang up and Jap turned to Volkov. "I wondered why Martinov did not come to this office with us. Surely he would want to see the money and get his share. He just didn't want to ever be accused of being part of a sale of nuclear material."

Then to Pavel Jap snapped orders. "Go up to the terminal and tell Misha that when the helicopter lands he will jump aboard. In the air the American and the girl will fall out. No bullet traces."

"Shit Jap," Volkov protested, "she's Nickolai's daughter."

"He will join her shortly. We do not need him anymore." He saw the expression on the director's face. "Your share is doubled without him." Jap laughed. "Stop worrying and go into your conference room and count the money on the table. But first, tell me what bargain you made with this Peter Nikhilov. The truth now, Hamster, if you have it in you."

"He wanted me to bring the plutonium he paid for in advance to Moscow. He was going to introduce me to his clients. I would be selling to them directly from now on."

Volkov's words came rapidly. "I have official certificates to go to Switzerland and sell gold salvaged from the electric systems of dismantled missiles. It would have been convenient to visit Moscow on the way."

"Convenient for the *ments*," Jap said scathingly.

"I of course refused to travel with the plutonium," Volkov added.

"But you would have had the dollars with you to put in Swiss banks."

"Yes," Volkov admitted.

"Yes, of course," Jap repeated. He breathed deeply. "Well this American will never see Moscow again so you can forget his clients. I will handle all sales of product from the Dome."

The intercom on Volkov's desk came alive again. "Comrade Director, Comrade Director. This is the mobile launcher. We are outside the Dome proceeding toward the airstrip."

"Call me again when you reach the plane."

Jap put an arm around Volkov's shoulder and led him through the door of his office to the conference room where the long table was piled high with stacks of hundred dollar bills.

Volkov gazed down appreciatively. "Where did you get this pile of greens?" he asked, a slight tremor of distrust still lingering from Zekki's confrontation with Peter.

"We sacked a bank in New York," chuckled Pavel.

All Volkov's past troubles and tribulations seemed unimportant now. Jap suddenly was no longer an intimidating Mongol but wise and friendly like a family mentor.

Jap and Pavel left Volkov groping through the tightly stacked bills, pulling paper binders from the middle of a package here and there to let the bank notes, all used and therefore the real thing, run through his fingers.

After a conference Jap said, "Go up to the terminal now and give Misha his instructions. And be prepared to activate alternative plan two." Then Jap called into the conference room, "Hamster you can radio the helicopter and order it to land and pick up the passengers for Irkutsk."

CHAPTER FORTY·NINE

⋖⋗⋖⋗

Peter watched the guard officer in charge pick up the phone when it rang and after listening a moment, furtively glance over at him and Oksana. Oksana was sitting gloomily in a chair, wrapped in her overcoat. Peter placed his briefcase beside Oksana and stepped out of the terminal into the frigid Siberian air. Though the sun hung high in the blue cloudless sky, it bestowed little heat on the ground.

Looking down toward the airstrip he noticed how precisely it was lined up with the tunnel leading from deep inside the mountain to the exact location of the huge cargo plane with elevated double tail fins. Still some distance from the AN-22, the Sickle on its carrier lazily rolled over the battered, crumbling concrete slabs of the airstrip, worn down by generations of planes and vehicles. He glanced at his wrist watch. In one hour and forty minutes his chronolog would detonate—if, after all these years, the shaped charge was still operative.

He whirled around as the chuffing of rotors in the air reached him. His eyes followed the helicopter as it descended and settled in on its landing skids. Almost instantly a tank truck drove up to it as the blades stopped turning and a maintenance worker jumped out, uncoiled a length of hose, and unscrewing the fuel cap on the aircraft, began filling it with gasoline.

Inside the lobby Oksana heard the metallic clink of the elevator doors opening and raised her head. Pavel walked into the lobby and over to Misha who was standing next to a fat fellow gunman. She noticed the urgency with which Pavel addressed them. Then he apparently became aware of her stare for he turned, smiled and walked over to her.

"Please give your father my respects. And take care, Oksana."

Peter stepped inside, nodded to Pavel, and picked up his brief-case. With his other hand he reached for Oksana's arm and guided her through the doorway. Once outside she shook his hand off her in exasperation and stalked toward the helicopter. It was not the executive plane they had come out on that morning with Nickolai. It was an old veteran of a chopper that clearly displayed its age and long years of service.

The sliding door on the left hand side of the helicopter was pulled open from the inside by the young co-pilot as they approached and a stepladder dropped to the ground. At the air-craft Oksana refused Peter's help, climbing into the fuselage and taking a seat on the canvas bench against the back of the two pilots' flight deck seats. Peter sat beside her and put a steadying hand on her knee. Abruptly Oksana rose to her feet and stepped over to the opposite bench, huddling in the far corner as far away from Peter as she could get.

"Oksana, keep the faith."

"You deceived me, made a fool of me," she called back.

"I just wanted to keep you close to me."

The pilot, considerably older than his assistant, turned around. "Control just called. We've got two more passengers."

Peter and Oksana were strapping the seat belts around their

waists when they suddenly became aware of two figures striding toward the helicopter from the terminal.

"It's Misha," Oksana cried. "And that fat fool they call Pop." Both of Jap's thugs leapt into the craft, Misha beside Oksana in front of Peter, his big black eyes watching him solemnly; the blubbery Pop pushed past Peter's knees and took the seat beside him facing Oksana.

Peter lit a cigarette and stuck it in his lips. Then he turned around in his seat to the first pilot.

"Can you make radio contact with the director?" Peter asked.

"Yes. He told us to land. Oh, he's on now." The pilot pulled the second earphone of his radio headset back over his ear and Peter could hear the pilot's side of the conversation. "Yes, four people. Three men and one woman. On our way back to Irkutsk." He turned to Peter sitting back to back with him. "Slide the door closed, please."

Peter leaned forward, face to face with Misha, as he grasped the handle and pulled the sliding door shut.

The turbo powered rotor whined and after a few moments roared as the chopper jumped up and then forward in a fast take-off, quickly rising to altitude. Peter noticed that as the machine steadily climbed it continued to circle the Dome area.

Secret city is right, Peter thought. No one will be looking for bodies here. They won't wait until we're halfway to Irkutsk.

Oksana seemed to sense what was ahead, giving Peter a frightened glance. Misha's eyes burned like two port holes into hell. As the chopper veered off the horizontal position the left flap of his coat fell open. Peter's eyes caught the blue black gleam of the machine-gun barrel. It was a shortened version of the AK-47. Misha caught Peter's glance and smiled evilly. He threw his coat back and tilted the weapon upward pressing the barrel against Peter's right side. The rush of cold air and deafening roar of the turbo engine driving the rotor blades made verbal communications impossible although there was no mistaking Misha's intentions. He kicked the side door back on its slides and nodded toward the open door, prodding Peter toward it with the machine-gun barrel. Peter's cigarette burned brightly, sparks flying from it.

"What the fuck's going on!?" the pilot yelled, turning around in his seat and staring behind him.

Misha cast a quick glance in the pilot's direction and Peter instantly took adavantage of his lapse of attention. He twisted his body escaping the barrel's line of fire and at the same time jammed the glowing cigarette into Misha's nostril.

Misha's yell rang out above the engine noise and a deafening, blinding bright volley exploded at Peter's side, burning the fox fur cape draped over his coat. The machine-gun rounds splintered the metal back of the pilot's seat and tore through his body, spewing blood on the suddenly bullet shattered windshield. Oksana screamed as the helicopter lurched tossing the men in a heap on the floor between the seats, Misha pitching on top of Peter who was quick enough to deliver a sharp knuckle blow to the throat.

Suddenly the helicopter shot upwards again and Misha abruptly fell backwards. He was clutching at Peter who kicked him fiercely in the stomach sending him back against the wallowing Pop. Fortunately the expert shooter had little skill in close hand-to-hand fighting.

The young co-pilot was hollering at the top of his lungs trying to control the stick and bring the chopper back to level flight. The fat thug, Pop, threw himself on Peter who from the corner of his eye caught the flash of a large blade in his assailant's right hand. He dove to his right and suddenly found his chest and head hanging out of the open side door, his legs and feet mercifully entangled inside the craft. He did not hear the young co-pilot scream as Pop smashed into the seat and his swinging arm drove the blade, missing Peter, into the boy's left thigh. The helicopter fell off to the right and saved Peter from becoming part of the panorama he had been staring into moments before as he fell back into the cabin.

The helicopter took another dive and Peter got a quick look at the butt end of the machine gun sticking out from between two seats. He snatched at it but Misha was quicker and retrieved the weapon. Peter tore the powder-burned fox fur from his back and threw it at the gunman, startling him for a moment, but then the eye of the barrel fixed on him. Miraculously it didn't spit fire. A quick side glance revealed to Peter Oksana pressing her nickel-plated parabellum pistol to the Georgian shooter's black short-cropped hairline. For some seconds Misha remained motionless and then turned his head only to receive the bullet straight through his forehead.

Smoke went through the back of his head, two dark-red rivulets ran from the nostrils, his body convulsed and then fell backwards. As the chopper shuddered and listed, Misha's body simply disappeared through the open side of the fuselage.

Peter sank between the seats gazing at Pop's back. The fat thug was embracing the seat on which he had been sitting, two blood soaked holes in the left side of his back. Oksana had shot him first, then Misha.

The ancient chopper's convolutions in the air astounded the small audience at the top of the Dome which stared, slack jawed, upward. Pavel and his men, joined by the officer of the guards stood frozen watching.

"What the fuck is going on up there?" the guard officer muttered. Pavel did not answer. The officer rushed back to his post to get on the radio just as something indistinguishable appeared from the helicopter and then was gone again.

Moments later a human form plunged from the side of the gyrating aircraft falling toward the ground. "They did it," Pavel muttered. The body finally hit the far edge of the helipad with a thump heard by everyone.

"Fuck," Pavel cried. "Bad shit. Quick guys, push it down the cliffs."

The men rushed forward, Pavel walking at a slow pace, waiting for the second body to fall. It was taking some time.

"Shit!" he muttered. "Are they raping her first up there?" He hated the idea of Oksana falling out and wanted it all to end as soon as possible.

The second body popped out of the chopper, plummeting toward the rocky plain far below. Pavel stared up for a moment and suddenly let out a string of obscenities. It had to be the body of fat Pop.

His guys were already waving their hands above the first body, a tall thin man, his black cloak torn away by the wind. Black eyes in the crushed head stared crookedly upward. The blood-coated face was unmistakably Misha's. At that moment the crunching thud of the second blob of a body hitting the rocks unnerved Pavel's little band of killers.

"Oh fuck!" growled the first thug. "Shit! What a gunman he was!"

"Bloody bitches," snarled another. "They will pay for that."

They turned to Pavel and were amazed to see him smiling, almost tenderly.

"Boss, what do we do next?"

Pavel could barely be heard murmuring, "Yes, yes man. This is my girl!" as he looked skyward to the helicopter still wildly circling the dome.

There was only one course of action available to him now. Jap had an amazing ability to plan for any contingency that might arise, Pavel thought as he reached for the powerful radio telephone clipped to his belt.

CHAPTER FIFTY

⫷⟫ ⟪⫸

The small, battered helicopter kept swinging in circles around the Dome. Cold air blasted into the cockpit through the bullet-shattered pilot's side windshield. Peter worked over the young co-pilot, finding the first aid kit under the pilot's seat. He had noticed the knife handle sticking out of the boy's thigh only after pushing Pop out of the helicopter and pulling the sliding door shut against the piercing wind. Oksana was clutching the back of the pilot's seat, long black hair whipped wildly about her head by the air streams, the silver pistol still tightly held in her right hand.

The cockpit was soaked with blood, the boy moaning. Peter had to struggle to get the pilot's dead body away from the controls and laid out between the facing passenger seats. Then he climbed onto the flight deck himself and tried to straighten out the course of the helicopter.

"Oksana," Peter called out sharply, "help me with the boy."

Her face appeared between them. "He's losing blood, Peter," she cried. "Do something, or we go down like a rock."

"Get the belt from the pilot's trousers."

Peter concentrated on leveling out the helicopter—tossed in the convection currents coming off the mountain—as Oksana pulled the belt off the dead man and twisted it around the boy's upper thigh. "Can you pull the knife out of his leg?" Oksana shouted.

Peter shook his head. "That would send pain waves through him that could make him flip the chopper and it might increase the bleeding."

Holding the control stick steady with his knees Peter looked through the first aid kit he had located under the pilot's seat. To his surprise and relief he found a handful of plastic one-shot syringes with capped needles. The label on them said "Promedol 1%," an effective morphine substitute. Immediately Peter pulled the cap off a needle and stabbed it into the boy's exposed upper wrist. In just moments the young co-pilot's contorted face began to relax and he leaned back against his seat.

"Steady now, lad," Peter directed the co-pilot. He reached into the breast pocket of his jacket and pulled out a stack of hundred dollar bills fastened with a paper tape in the middle. He had saved this much counterfeit in case he suddenly needed hard currency. He held them in front of the boys mouth.

"Open up and bite. Hold it down hard."

"Peter, what are you doing?" Oksana cried. "It's money!"

"To you, sweetheart. To you." Then he rasped in the co-pilot's ear, "Hold on, kid!"

The boy bit on the pack and Peter seized the hilt of the knife with both hands and yanked it out, falling backwards into the pilot's seat, the bloody scimitar in his hands. The co-pilot screamed, the chopper shuddered and fell off to the side. They nearly cut through the tops of the pine trees but missed by a few meters and the craft abruptly rose again. Once Peter had the helicopter on a level course, he pulled the cap off another syringe and administered a second shot of the pain killer.

"Now, how do I contact Director Volkov from here?" Peter asked.

"The radio phone. Put on the headset. It's plugged into the Dome frequency. The director said he would be monitoring us all afternoon. Just dial 321. God, am I thirsty."

The missile launcher carrying the Sickle lying on its mobile bed stood a hundred yards from the AN-22 cargo plane. The colonel in charge of loading operations looked through the papers presented to him by the captain of the accepting crew. They were in order. The officer put his signature on the papers and returned them, keeping one set of copies and striding back to his staff car which had followed the mobile launcher to the delivery point and would bring the driver and his assistant back to the dome.

"Call Director Volkov and tell him we are ready to move up to the plane and drive into the cargo hold," he ordered his second in command.

Jap was toying with a pack of banknotes, Plotnikov and Zekki were sitting in chairs against the wall, all of them waiting for Pavel to come down from the terminal. Then, when the missile was loaded they would radio the AN-22 to take off for the Caspian Sea and its final destination, Iraq. In his office Volkov had just given orders to the colonel to proceed with the loading when his radiophone on the helicopter frequency buzzed and he picked it up.

The helicopter was flying straight and level with the partially sedated co-pilot still able to keep it under control.

Peter now had time to be angry. He had thought that Jap, though a criminal, had some slight sense of personal integrity. He couldn't entirely condemn the master of Moscow's mafia for trying to dispose of an enemy he perceived to be both a cop and a

459

business rival. But ordering Oksana's death was so dastardly, it called for immediate and drastic retaliation.

Peter concentrated on his hastily concocted plan. With the headset covering his ears and the microphone at his lips he dialed 321 and almost immediately he heard Volkov's voice. "Come in" the director said.

In his calmest tones Peter began his message. "Director Volkov, are we on a closed circuit?"

"That is correct." There was a pause. "Basil," the director's voice was strained, "it doesn't sound like you."

"Now listen carefully, Director Volkov. Do not make a move that will draw Jap's suspicion. I know he is right there."

"That is correct."

"This is Peter Nikhilov in the helicopter. Much has happened in the last hour but I won't waste precious time. Casually press the emergency button on your desk. You will need guards. Continue to call me Basil."

"I read you, Basil."

Volkov was absolutely convinced he must follow the instructions given him by the American, speaking to him in perfect Russian, so calmly yet with such authority. Reaching for a stack of papers on the desk his hand contacted the emergency button as he pulled the files close to him.

"What is your position, Basil?

"Above the Dome. Listen carefully. The money Jap gave you is counterfeit."

The stunned look that crossed Volkov's face, eyes flying to full width, jaw clenched and rippling, instantly raised an alarm signal in Jap's mind. He moved close to the desk, trying to get some clue as to what this call was about. Instinctively he sensed trouble.

"Volkov." Peter's words came distinctly through the radio phone the director was holding to his ear. "I gave you counterfeit money captured by the Militsia in a raid on Jap's fake money plant. Check the serial numbers. They follow the numbers on the bills Jap gave you. There might even be some duplicates. You can save yourself by . . ."

Suddenly Peter heard Jap's reedy voice on the radio telephone. "Hello Basil. What is happening up there?" He had obviously decided something was wrong and snatched the headset from the director.

Peter made no answer but heard a commotion coming from Volkov's office and then the transmission cut off.

Four uniformed guards burst into Volkov's office, automatic weapons levelled. "What the hell are you doing, Hamster?" Jap cried. "What's this all about?"

"Everybody just sit still. I need to check on something. But first—" He dialed a number on his intercom.

At the same moment Jap unobtrusively held his own miniature transmitter to his lips and spoke a short phrase. "Plan Two. Immediately!"

"Plan Two is already underway," Pavel's voice came back.

The Sickle's mobile missile launcher had just reached the ramp leading up into the yawning hold of the AN-22 super cargo aircraft when the direct frequency with the director buzzed. The colonel picked up the phone on the dashboard of his car parked behind the huge truck about to drive into the giant transport plane.

"Colonel," he heard the director's voice shouting, "consider it a training exercise. Bring it back. Now! I want it back in storage as fast as you can move it. How long will it take?"

"Under an hour, Director."

"Get it back!"

Volkov slammed down the phone and rushed into the conference room. Jap made an attempt to follow him, but the director waved him away and the guards moved to stop him.

Volkov closed the door behind him and went over to the safe in which he had put the quarter of a million dollars Peter Nikhilov had given him earlier that day. He spread the packs of banknotes out on the conference table. It took less than five minutes to determine that the serial numbers on the hundred dollar bills he had received from the American followed in the same series as the stacked hundreds Jap had given him.

Perhaps, he thought hopefully, there was still some tiny hope, some sort of reasonable explanation. He couldn't bring himself to face the dreadful truth.

Feverishly, he rustled through the hundred dollar bills and then, like some invisible cudgel knocking him in the forehead, undeniable reality shattered his illusion of instant personal riches. He found himself holding two bills each with the same serial number, two twin one hundred dollar bills, one from Jap and one from the American. Even if one was real the other was surely a copy. No way in the world could he get around that fact.

He sank heavily into his leather chair, bills clutched in his hands, heart pounding violently. Suddenly it was all falling into place. Jap's overgenerous cash offers, the strange decision to let the American go . . . for that matter the American's blind trust with his quarter million dollars. How could two old veterans of business by bribery like himself and Martinov have been outsmarted? Then, yet another horrifying thought struck him. Maybe Martinov was in this with Jap. No wonder the old bandit hadn't wanted to be present today when payments were made, carefully removing himself from incriminating circumstances.

Damage control! He had to think fast. Maybe, if he played this game out he could outwit Jap and end up with real money. At some point the Iraqis would pay Jap in cash and letters of credit. Perhaps they actually had made a partial payment. Like an outraged boar wounded in the bushes, the director sprang to his feet and rushed back to the office, wads of hundred dollar bills grasped in both fists.

CHAPTER FIFTY-ONE

"**H**ow are you doing?" Peter cried out above the engine noise to the co-pilot sitting next to him.

The youth was feeling much better with the Promedol easing the pain in his left leg. "You are a pilot yourself?" he asked.

"Not really. I had five hours emergency training."

"It was enough for you to pull us out of trouble."

The helicopter rotors were beating rhythmically and after those terrible moments of tumbling in the air, Peter had set course for Irkutsk from the Dome which was still below them. He smiled at Oksana who was quietly putting her hair in order, ducking the wind that blew through the shattered pilot's side windshield. His heart quickened a moment when she smiled back warmly at him.

Peter looked at his wristwatch. In under half an hour the small, but powerful, shaped charge disguised as an oversize pocket watch was timed to detonate 65,000 pounds of solid-state fuel and the explosion would certainly destroy the cargo plane and everything near it—if his little expedient device was still effective.

"How long will it take to reach the city?" Peter asked.

"About forty minutes," the young flyer replied. "Why do you ask? You've already flown it once."

"Timing was different then. Let's hurry," Peter urged looking back in the direction of the AN-22 on the airstrip.

On the helipad, at the top of the Dome, Pavel was talking into his radio as he noticed, to his surprise, that way down below, on the airstrip, the mobile launcher with the Sickle missile resting on top of it was proceeding in reverse toward the tunnel into the Dome. He realized that something had happened in Volkov's office for Jap to have broken radio silence and declared an emergency.

Jap still had a few good shooters left on the helipad but Pavel did not think it wise to leave his post on the surface and take a chance on getting embroiled in something unexpected below.

Jap had wisely ordered two backup helicopters to be ready to go into action from locations halfway between Irkutsk and the secret city of Krasnov 86. They were Mi-24 D models designed to fly eight soldiers into combat. The four barrel 12.7mm nose machine gun and the two 57mm rocket launchers had been stripped long ago but each aircraft carried experienced gunmen.

Inside the terminal Pavel asked the guard captain what had happened. The captain looked at him strangely. "The director rang for emergency guards. I haven't heard anything since."

Something was surely amiss, particularly with the missile launcher retreating back toward the Dome. He decided to take a chance on calling Jap over their radio intercom and in a corner of the terminal building he pressed the send button.

"What's the problem, number one?"

"Stop Nikhilov at any cost. Hamster has gone mad and he's . . ."

The transmission abruptly came to a halt.

Pavel stepped out into the cold again and holding his coat tightly around his neck he walked toward the edge of the flat landing zone and peered down at the airstrip far below. He was shocked to see that the mobile missile launcher had borne its burden almost back inside the tunnel. Looking up, he observed the Dome helicopter streaking away from the secret city toward Irkutsk. The wild gyrations the helicopter had gone through when Misha and then Pop had fallen or been pushed out indicated that a tremendous struggle had taken place. Somehow the American had prevailed.

Pavel ordered one of the two emergency helicopters to circle the AN-22 cargo plane in case some effort were made by Dome guards to capture it. The second helicopter, with Fofa, Jap's old frayer from Tulun aboard, would intercept the Dome helicopter and shoot it down, making sure nobody survived.

The Dome helicopter was now on course for Irkutsk when the co-pilot pointed ahead of them and Peter noticed the big army helicopter in the distance coming from the direction of the city. They thought little about it except to make a slight course correction giving them a wider birth around the approaching machine. Then to Peter's surprise the helicopter ahead also adjusted its heading to maintain a collision course.

"Gain more altitude," Peter advised over the intercom and once again tried to dial the Director to no avail.

The co-pilot pulled back on the stick, adjusted the rotors and the chopper leapt skyward. To their surprise the oncoming aircraft also jumped upwards still on its reciprocal heading.

The combined speed of the two helicopters was rapidly bringing them together in the sky. Ominously the side door of the approaching aircraft slid open and the barrels of two hand-held machine guns could be seen protruding. Oksana's hand trembled and she dropped her comb.

"Turn, man!" Peter shouted. "Dive for speed and head back to the Dome."

Even as the co-pilot whipped the chopper around a volley of rounds reached out at them from the marauding aircraft. Peter barely had time to slide from the pilot's seat and grab Oksana, falling with her to the floor beside the dead body of Basil. A few bullets pierced the side of the chopper.

"Climb, man!" Peter shouted. "Back to the Dome! They are heavy and slow in maneuvers. Close to the mountain we stand a chance. In the open sky there is none!"

The Dome chopper was heading back full speed, climbing again. The army helicopter made a wide circle and sped in pursuit.

"Oh, shit!" the boy was crying. "Will there be an end to this shit today?"

"Dear God," Oksana whispered. "We are going to die."

Peter glanced at his watch. Only moments remained before the chronolog was set to detonate. He put his arm around Oksana.

The mobile missile launcher was slowly driving in reverse through the tunnel to the loading and delivery chamber. It was an inconvenient manner of proceeding with the drivers having to use mirrors and awkwardly stick their heads out the side windows but still much easier than trying to turn the cumbersome vehicle around on the runway.

Following Volkov's orders, the staff car had turned around and was leading the missile carrier back, the colonel bored and yawning. He couldn't understand why he had been ordered to return the missile to the Dome. In his five years of service at Krasnov 86, this was the first time they had ever taken a missile out, delivered it to a cargo plane, and then drawn it back again. They were about ten minutes from the receiving and delivery chamber deep within the granite confines of the Dome when the prolonged stay outside in the cold took its effect on the colonel. His need to urinate was suddenly overpowering.

Under the circumstances it was the easiest thing to do. They were close to the receiving area yet not visible to anybody. The floor had deep grooves along the walls. A special cleaning team daily washed out the numerous floors of tunnels, laboratories, chambers and passages. The water washed away the tiny layers of the radioactive dust which formed what could become a lethal sediment if not regularly flooded.

Dome personnel considered these prevention methods an invitation to use the tunnel floors as convenient latrines. It irritated the top administrators who had their private restrooms and when caught relieving themselves the Dome workers were fined severely. But nature inevitably took an upper hand in the contest with administration.

Without a second thought the colonel halted the carrier, stepped out of the staff car and walked to the groove. The driver of the mobile launcher joined him. Just as they were unzipping they heard a sharp explosive crack somewhere along the surface of the Sickle missile.

From his position on the helipad Pavel observed the sudden return to Dome airspace of the helicopter carrying Peter and Oksana. Not far behind them was one of Jap's two backup machines maneuvering to get into firing position. Pavel looked down at the AN-22 on the airstrip and saw an armored personnel carrier heading out toward it. Hamster must have become completely deranged, he thought, to send a squad of troops to Jap's cargo plane. What could have driven the director to such distraction? he wondered. In any case he had command of two helicopters filled with his armed sixes and controlled the situation, at least for the time being.

Over his radio, he ordered the second chopper to circle the mammoth cargo plane, the key piece of equipment in Jap's business inventory. The helicopters, with Fofa in command of the shooters, should easily be able to deal with the small aircraft desperately trying to evade annihilation.

Peter had never anticipated Jap being so resourceful. The army surplus helicopter with a squad of sharpshooters inside was a shocking surprise. The young co-pilot threw his craft into sharp dives each time the enemy lined up on him and then streaked upward as they caught up again.

Fofa and his gunmen had difficulties of their own. The big vessel was old and its armament had been dismantled. To shoot down the small dragon-fly they had to catch up with it and fire their submachine guns through the open sliding door. To be able to shoot from both sides of the chopper they slid open both the right and left doors and a ferocious windstorm rushed through the compartment tearing at the shooters, destrupting fine aiming and throwing the gunmen off balance.

Despite these problems, which none of the street gangsters had ever experienced before, they continued spraying machine-gun fire out the chopper doors. A volley caught the small helicopter again, heavy-caliber bullets puncturing the fuselage. The boy at the controls yelled and threw the craft into a deep left dive just as Peter pushed the body of Basil out the door to lighten the machine.

"We've got one!" the pilot called over his radio phone to Pavel.

"Get them all!" Pavel, standing on the landing zone looking up, called into his radio. He watched the big clumsy chopper full of gunmen pursue the smaller machine as it twisted toward the rocky mountain rising above the Dome's helicopter terminal building.

"We go down, circle the hill until they come upon us and then we go up again," the boy shouted. But the gangster pilot was no less inventive. Fofa's chopper took the opposite direction coming in on a wider circle in perfect position for firing close to the mountainside above the helicopter landing zone.

"God loves the Trinity!" Oksana cried into Peter's ear, near-death euphoria shining from her face. Peter hugged her to him as the boy jerked the chopper up again and away from the side of the hill, the fierce volley of incendiary rounds streaking just below them. The army helicopter did not give them a second chance to hide behind the slope as it swooped toward the smaller machine for the kill.

In the tunnel the colonel suddenly felt an overwhelming fear grip him and before he had his fly open his bladder emptied its contents in his pants as he stared at the bright glow inside the solid fuel rocket assembly. The huge tube was hermetically sealed yet he saw the terrifying rubescence breaking out along the seams of the container of seventeen tons of solid state rocket fuel. Along the side of the rocket housing the big red-hot spot was expanding at unbelievable speed, the outer layers of steel peeling off and coiling outwards, a metalic flower blossom opening.

A crimson faced, heavy breathing Volkov confronted Jap across his office desk, hundred dollar bills strewn over the floor where the director had angrily cast them. Jap stood in a relaxed manner, hands in his pockets, a raincoat over one shoulder. The mocking look further infuriated Volkov. Zekki sat on a chair in the far corner of the office, hands clenched between his knees, eyes darting between the green backs of his manufacture on the floor and the ruddy face of the pacing, infuriated director. Plotnikov was also concerned about his safety as he stared at the armed guards.

"Here's the deal," Volkov was hissing. "You do not take leave of my hospitality until the price for the missile is paid in real hard currency. Say two or three days."

"To come up with ten million dollars in so short a time is impossible," Jap snapped. "And if I am absent much longer they will start worrying."

"Who?"

Jap smiled amiably. "My people."

Volkov's smile was equally pleasant. "Your people are faraway. My guards are here. Do not try to intimidate me!"

Jap chuckled. "You are obviously a novice in the extortion business. You must first know whether the victim is capable of giving you what you want."

"I sit on the nukes. You sit on a hill of cash. Therefore we should be able to do some honest business."

"I would have to be free to contact my associates in Bonn, Zurich, Frankfurt, throughout Europe."

"I give you a free telephone." He pointed at the instrument.

Jap started to turn his back to the desk and Volkov was on the verge of barking out an order to the guards when to the astonishment of everyone the furniture in the office jumped like a kangaroo. The heavy desk performed a similar maneuver knocking the director down and smashing into the opposite wall with a crash. Zekki let out a shrill, woman-like scream as the floor raised up at least one foot and jerked aside. They were all thrown off their feet by the titanic shockwave that raced through the impregnable granite dome. The guards rolled on the trembling stone floor like tin toy soldiers as sections of ceiling plaster sifted down on them.

The solid composite propellant of the rocket on which Peter had placed his detonator consisted of oxidizer crystals, powdered aluminum, and synthetic rubber binder, which prevented the contact of aluminum grains with air. With the detonation, the small particles, released into the oxygen, burned fiercely.

Once ignited, this fuel never stops burning, producing the mass of hot gasses with a temperature close to 7400° F. Such a temperature produces a pressure of 930 atmospheres in the propulsion bay which drives the missile skyward. However, an uncontrolled explosion of the whole mass of the propellant instantly releases a pressure of 660,000 atmospheres.

Upon launching, the rocket rises at peak speed of 5.3 miles per second and reaches the height of 100 miles in half a minute. The fragments of a disintegrating missile would travel even faster.

The wall of fire filled the tunnel, evaporating the colonel and his men on the spot. Fire was hurled into the reception and delivery chamber turning it into a white hot furnace, metal sprinkling in molten white drops in all directions. The skulls of a hundred workers caught in the chamber exploded, the boiling moisture of brains tearing heads apart. In a fraction of a second the body of flames and melted debris flew into the circular tunnel around the base of the Dome, tramway rails coiled into flowing, white-hot spirals and fused with the ceiling, the cords and cables along the walls burned like straw, and the chain reactions of vicious short circuits all over the complex broke out.

The explosion of 35,000 pounds of solid propellant in the tunnel did not destroy the warhead of the missile; on the contrary, it was launched, in fact shot out of the giant tube in the granite mountain like a bullet from a gun barrel, a towering fireball like the tail of a comet accompanying it, incinerating the guards at the entrance in a fraction of a second as it tore to pieces the double steel thirty ton gates.

Oblique lightning exploded out of the hole at the foot of the dome, turning over fuel trucks like toys catching up with and obliterating the armored personnel carrier ferrying a contingent of guards out to the giant cargo plane. The small sun gone mad was actually the lacerated warhead, losing momentum, wobbling astray and pulling an orange cloud of flames after it leaving a fiery path through the AN-22. The melting aluminum mixture burned through the steel frame of the giant aircraft and red hot liquid metal drops bored into the fuel tanks.

A fresh wave of fire stormed out of the cockpit tossing the pilots high above the inferno in a cloud of shredded glass and fuselage. The entire mass of the plane jumped up on the spot like a living thing and disappeared in the fireball of a fuel explosion. Remnants of tail, wings, and motors were propelled high into the air and the helicopter, which had been circling the cargo plane, disappeared in a gigantic burst of flak.

In seconds that seemed like eternity, Pavel watched in horror the cataclysmic occurances taking place around the base of the Dome. In all his violent life he had never experienced such calamitous events as were erupting around him. Right in front of his eyes the helicopter he had sent to guard the AN-22 was obliterated. He was conscious of blasts in the depths of the Dome as the guards rushed about in terror, the captain trying to get through on the telephone to the director.

Somehow Pavel had to find Jap and get out. He looked up and saw his helicopter closing on the Dome aircraft, two shooters aiming their machine guns out the open door.

CHAPTER FIFTY-TWO

Peter held Oksana tightly in his arms as the big military helicopter Mi-24 D started its killer run at them from above and beyond the mountaintop they had been using to hop-skip away from the murderous attack. They had eluded the last sortie by diving close to the steep slope. The big cumbersome army transport chopper had been forced to turn aside, gain altitude and pull away from the rocky mountain. But now the marauding aircraft was heading for them again and this time there was little room for evasive tactics.

The co-pilot turned and yelled something to them, pointing towards the ground. Peter took his eyes from the enemy machine and looked down through the plexiglass panel in the closed sliding door. For a moment he forgot the blitzing aerial assault. A ball of fire flashed across the helicopter landing zone.

Then Peter's eyes caught the machine-gun muzzle flashes from the open door of the fast approaching aerial assassins. He tried to push Oksana down behind him.

Suddenly an updraft hurled both helicopters into the sky as though they were riding atop a high speed elevator.

The co-pilot cried out again and pulled the stick to his breast, further whipping the aircraft up and away. A cloud of black, oily ash was rising from below, fragments of buildings pursuing them upwards. But the Mi-24 D was not to be shaken off and once again swooped into its deadly pass at the already wounded smaller helicopter.

Pavel looked skyward through the smoke roaring up from the depths of the terminal and filling the air above the Dome. There was no time for any more aerial antics if he and Jap were to get out alive.

Holding the radio close to his mouth he shouted, "This is Pavel," on their chopper frequency. "Bring H One into Dome landing zone instantly."

"We're making a pass, Boss. We'll get them for sure this time," he heard the voice of Fofa come back.

"Fuck the pass. Now! That's an order direct from Jap. You can get that chopper later. Land fucking Now! You hear?!"

"Coming in, boss. They sure got God on their side that time."

"Fuck Him!" Pavel shouted. "You gotta get us outta here."

Pavel made an effort to call Jap on the radio but down in Volkov's quarters the time for talking was gone. Jap was conscious of Plotnikov at his side, his eyes rolling in abject terror, face whiter than the plaster coming off the ceiling, his mouth fishlike, opening and closing. He was clutching at Jap's sleeve.

Hamster had succeeded in cramming his huge body on all fours under his desk. Two guards were still unconscious from the heavy breakfront that had fallen on them. The officer of the guard was trying to get to his feet clutching at the wall.

Finally, shocked eardrums began responding to sounds.

"I knew it!" Plotnikov was yelling. "I knew this greedy pig

would roast himself here someday but I never intended to be roasted with him! Those are missiles!"

"Missiles?" Jap repeated.

"Just the beginning. If the storage goes up, it launches us to the moon!"

A rolling shriek penetrated even the most concussion-shocked eardrums. Zekki rushed and scrambled through the office to the elevator, tripped over something and fell, rose again and dashed into the elevator cab, hammering on the buttons. The doors, however, had been bent by the blast and did not close properly. The next moment he was joined in the car by the officer of the guard and another soldier who wrestled his way inside after Zekki.

Even the jaded, violence-prone Jap was shocked when the elevator was heaved upwards on a column of white hot gas, the mirrors cracking and spewing shards of glass into the office as the walls collapsed and the whole shapeless mass that had been the elevator cab plummeted back downward into the fiery pit below.

Jap seized Plotnikov by the collar. "How the fuck do we get out of here?! Talk to me!"

Plotnikov stammered incoherently for some seconds. "The Dome is one monsterous furnace below us, the entire power system is short circuited." His words came out tumbling over themselves. "In all the chambers and passages the personnel on this shift, over a thousand people are sealed off forever, roasted alive or burning up in stalled elevators. All emergency security systems and magnetic locks are burned out."

"Get us out of here!" Jap roared.

"There may be a way out," Plotnikov, terrorized by Jap's feral survival instinct, cried hoarsely. "I was the Dome's ventilation engineer until Volkov fired Dr. Zilko and put me in his place."

"Let's go then!"

"There is a ventilation corridor behind this office that leads to an air shaft from the surface. It's our only chance."

But their escape was barred by Volkov sitting on the floor under a thick coating of white dust like a flour covered chef. It would have been a laughable sight except for the machine gun he was awkwardly handling. At the top of his lungs he shouted, "Do not move, shitheads. Do not fucking move!"

"Director," Jap sighed. "Drop it. This isn't funny. The Dome is blowing up!"

The floor trembled again, the walls shook and a layer of plaster along with the heavy bronze chandelier which had resisted the first shock wave fell from the ceiling catching Volkov on the head and shoulders. The director grunted and toppled on his side. Another roar from down the elevator shaft became a thunderclap of white flames spewing upwards, sucking the air out of the office.

Jap picked up the machine gun and took an extra magazine from the bag of a soldier sprawled unconscious on the floor. Then, his contorted face and disheveled black hair lit by flashes of white fire and the red blinking alarm light, Jap followed Plotnikov through the conference room, a green storm of hundred dollar bills caught up in the air currents fluttering and swirling about them. They plunged into the smoky darkness of a back ventilating corridor. Jap and Plotnikov managed to run a few yards but the fumes were choking them.

They stopped, leaning against the wall as Jap dropped the AK-47, tore away his jacket, jerked off his shirt and wrapped it around his face and head. The crude respirator provided at least some relief as he retrieved his weapon. Plotnikov tried to follow Jap's example but found himself entangled in his own clothes.

Cursing loudly, Jap wrapped the shirt around the deputy's head and pulled the sleeves in such a tight knot at the back of the neck that he nearly strangled his gasping crying guide. Plotnikov clutched at the knot trying to loosen it.

"Come on, man," Jap shouted. "Move it or we are shish kebab!"

They raced through the smoke-filled red-lit corridors desperately trying to reach the ventiation shaft to the surface. Only Plotnikov's years as the ventilation engineer of the Dome could save them now. In several places the corridors had collapsed already and they had to climb over piles of rubble, wire and fragments, and spurts of water from the torn pipes mercifully showered them and made the fabric covering their faces more effective against the smoke. The roar and concussion of the explosions below gave wings to their feet as sweat ran in waves from their pores, red and yellow circles dancing in their eyes. Neither Jap nor his meek guide had ever felt death so close on their heels.

Twice they were knocked down by powerful quakes. One corridor into which Jap followed Plotnikov suddenly spewed a licking tongue of flame from a crack in the floor. They jumped aside pulling their soaked shirts close to their faces. But Jap knew a moment of elation. Fire could only break out where ventilation shafts fed in oxygen. They burst into a side room and found themselves in an abandoned laboratory.

Stumbling over chairs and equipment they ran through a chain of rooms that brought them into a parallel hall. Several blackened corpses scourged by fire lay on the floor, two were annealed to the metal wall. Turning the corner into a ventilating duct, they ran into four soot-covered people, unrecognizable except for their tattered guard uniforms.

They were furiously hammering on solid iron bars covering the opening into a vertical ventilation shaft. Jap sensed salvation as Plotnikov began mumbling and pointing at a lock on the grilled cover. Two of the men turned, shouting unintelligable expletives. A crack opened in the room behind them and fire again breathed out of the hall illuminating them all in an uneven light, black shadows outlining the figures of the other survivors.

In the flickering glow, Jap leveled the barrel of the AK-47 and squeezed off a fusilade of shots. Three men fell at once as if struck by a thunderbolt, the fourth balanced for a moment, his uniform smoking and then toppled onto the first three. Plotnikov's scream came out of his throat as a strange coarse wail.

Jap fired into the lock on the grating splitting it, and shoved the cover away, climbing in and gazing straight up the shaft. A tiny white spot was shining high above them, the iron bars of a crude wall ladder ascending endlessly toward the surface of the Dome. Jap slung the AK-47 on its strap over his shoulder and started climbing.

Sheer pandemonium reigned on the helicopter landing zone at the top of the Dome. Guards and workers were rushing aimlessly around as another powerful shock wave traveled from the rocket storage area up through the hollowed-out granite mountain. The helicopter maintenance crews were tearing tarpaulins from the two army helicopters in the hanger and military personnel were evacuating their barracks.

The senior guard officer left his desk and ran up to Pavel, who was standing outside the terminal.

"How are you going to get out of here?"

Pavel smiled wryly as he saw one of the army helicopters being wheeled out of the hangar. "How come you are splitting without the director's permission?"

The officer's face contorted, lips trembling. He jumped away from Pavel as if from an asp, and waving his arms he ran to one of the choppers fast filling up with soldiers and workers who had made it up to the roof of the Dome.

Pavel dashed inside the terminal and at the deserted guard captain's desk he tried to make telephone contact with the director's office below. Frantically he jiggled the receiver hook but there was no answer.

A foreboding roar sounded from behind the closed elevator doors and Pavel instinctively dropped the telephone and fled the terminal just as, in a tongue of fire, the sliding portals were torn from the shaft and blown across the building through the opposite wall, over the tarmac apron and through the hangar from which, just moments before, the second army helicopter had been removed. Then the roof of the terminal was blown off as fire filled the building and in seconds it disintegrated in a fiery geyser spurting into the sky.

Pavel and his two remaining musclemen, standing well out on the helipad stared at the conflagration in awe.

"Holy shit!" whispered one of the thugs, "where is Jap?"

Pavel clenched his teeth.

The sound of the chopper drew his attention and he watched the old army aircraft he had bought land in the middle of the pad, well away from the flaming remains of the terminal. Fofa and two other men carrying machine guns jumped out and ran to Pavel, the down draft from the four rotor blades rippling fabric jackets against their backs.

Fofa's eyes rolled in his head as he took in the devastation from up close. "Where is Jap?"

"How the fuck do I know?" Pavel waved his arms at the fountain of flame gushing from the top of the elevator shaft now exposed in the terminal's rubble.

"What do we do?"

"We fucking go nowhere without Jap!"

Other members of the crew surrounding Pavel voiced dissatisfaction with the decision.

"Are you mad?"

"Have you seen the furnace below?"

"So fucking what?" Pavel challenged. "We do not leave him here."

This time Fofa waved his hand. "And if he's dead?"

"We wait another ten minutes!" Pavel announced.

"The whole mountain is shaking," one six cried.

"It's full of fire," another voiced.

"I do not give a fuck! We wait! Tell the pilots to shut down the engine and stop wasting fuel."

As Fofa ran back to the chopper, the shudders from below and foreboding booming sounds continued. The mountain was trembling like a volcano about to erupt. The thought of the hundreds of rockets stored below numbed Pavel's thoughts but he forced himself to think only of Jap. If Plotnikov was still with Jap they would find a way out.

The helicopter rotors continued to spin lazily, ready to start turning full speed and lift off. Angrily Pavel sprinted to the aircraft.

Fofa was confronting two other thugs near the open door.

"We don't care!" Pavel heard. "He is dead or not dead. But we leave now or we are all dead!" Fofa's face distorted into a maddened animal mask.

He seized one of the gunmen by the hair on his head and smashed it against the hull of the chopper. The other one raised his machine gun and caught Fofa with the barrel across the face sending him tumbling down, blood gushing from his nose and split lips. Pavel instantly drew his gun and shot the man through the head at close quarters, blood splashing onto the chopper's door. Pavel turned his pistol and fired two slugs into another dissident six and then snatched the machine gun from the ground and emptied a volley through the open sliding doors. Men threw themselves on the floor as Pavel leapt inside, swinging his weapons.

"Out! Everybody fucking out! Pilots too. Cut the engine!" He let go a vicious kick into the cockpit door jamming it open. Men jumped from the helicopter as the engines died away. Pavel jumped out after them and helped Fofa to his feet.

"Bloody bitches!" hissed Fofa and shot another volley above their heads.

"Face down! On the ground! Face down!" Pavel bellowed fiercely.

"What are we gonna do, boss?" one six cried plaintively.

"Face down! Fuck you all! We go out with Jap or we all fucking die here! Face down, I said!"

The men had no choice but to obey. They sprawled on the concrete beside the two dead bodies. From the tunnel at the base of the Dome a wall of smoke arose, flames licking through it each time the mountain trembled from another explosion. The elevator pit behind them spit up another fountain of flame.

Pavel touched his face and saw the blood and black soot on his palm. He had lost track of time.

"What are we going to do, boss?" a voice came from the ground.

At Pavel's side Fofa was standing, cursing mightily, spitting bloody saliva. He pointed his barrel at the men lying around him.

"Wait. We're gonna fucking wait. For Jap."

Another explosion rumbled up from somewhere deep under them.

Climbing the first two hundred rungs was easy but in a few minutes Jap realized that he had only progressed a fraction of the way to the surface at the top of the Dome. The small bright hole beckoning from above seemed no closer, as unreachable as a star. His arms, wrists and ankles started to go numb.

He and Plotnikov had both torn away the shirts they had wound around their heads the better to breathe in more oxygen to feed the blood cells in aching muscles. Jap stopped for a moment feeling the cold fresh air streaming down from above. The fire consuming the core of the Dome created a powerful vacuum sucking in air violently through all ventilation ducts and tunnels to the outside. The wind was spreading fire in huge flame clouds of thousands of degrees throughout the enormous doomed nuclear storage and manufacturing facility.

It seemed to Jap he had been climbing for a century. Plotnikov was grunting somewhere beneath him. He forgot about the bright friendly spot of daylight far above, the numbness in his arms and legs. His entire life now was a simple movement, one-two, one-two, and his powerful survival instinct told him loud and clear that his life ends when the movement upward ceases.

Then something changed. The airflow in the shaft reversed itself. He felt as though claws were slashing his throat, his stomach twisted. Black smoke was rising now from below. Mad yells came from Plotnikov as the engineer's head pushed against Jap's feet. After all this, would the smoke kill them?

Plotnikov was in a far worse condition. Jap's body blocked much of the fresh air from the surface. He felt the fingers of the desperate man below him grasp at his trouser legs. Jap kicked down with each heave upward but his kicks lacked power, he needed all his strength to force his way toward the top. The Dome's engineer, on the contrary, placed his bid for life on an attempt to climb past and over Jap and in a shocking move he plunged his teeth into Jap's shin bone. The sharp pain whipped Jap's life force into a final proxysm of resolve and strength. He yelled and viciously kicked backward feeling his heel batter the forehead below. A second backward kick met only air. Plotnikov was gone. Jap did not bother to listen for the thud of a fallen body far below.

He was climbing again. The smoke became less dense for some reason but Jap was on the verge of unconsciousness. He fought the dreams running through his mind. Old round-shouldered Jackel with a golden sparkle in the corner of his wide open mouth was circling around him like a bird of prey. Then he vividly saw the courtroom in Moscow and the prosecutor in black uniform announcing,

"You are sentenced to fifteen years of climbing up and down."

Something hit him on the head. He opened his eyes. He was in a steel cube with long ventilating slits in the four walls. He could see snow-covered bolders outside. His numb hand reached for the AK-47. In a moment he inserted the barrel under the lock that held the cover on the roof of the shaft's cupola and tore it away. Another moment—and he was crawling on elbows and knees in the cool white snow, sparkling and crispy. Raising his head he saw the helicoter pad and after a few minutes of rest he pulled himself semi-erect and started to shamble toward the helicopter he recognized as one of the two purchased for his backup force in this operation.

None of the sixes, not even Pavel, recognized the man who appeared at the edge of the helipad, struggling towards them. He was naked to the waist, some rags hanging from his neck, torso red in the frost, face black with soot, disheveled black hair. His right arm was dragging a machine gun by the belt.

The sixes on the ground turned their heads at the apparition. Fofa was the first to react. He stripped the fur coat from one of the dead, rebellious gunmen, rushed to the man approaching them, and threw it over his back. Pavel was still gaping at him silently as the sixes started whispering, "Jap, it's Jap," to each other.

Jap took in the scene, a surprised look on his face. The mountain shuddered, the elevator pit erupted a geyser of fire and grinding tremors emitted from deep inside the Dome below them.

Jap smiled broadly and waved at the sprawled gunmen. "What brings you all here?" he asked.

"A training exercise," Pavel found his voice.

"Training for what?" Jap cast a glance at two corpses and Fofa's smashed face.

"Patience training," Fofa replied. "Some of the guys were a bit impatient, forcing certain events."

Jap was about to reply but the surface of the Dome where the terminal was burned out opened up, the asphalt cover blew into the air, and a long black crack zigzagged across the pad. Several sixes screamed as a fire ball rose out of the rent in the top of the Dome.

"Okay boys," Jap called out. "It's sort of getting hot here. Time to split. Now, in orderly fashion, one after another, we proceed to the helicopter. Pavel checks the tickets."

In three minutes the chopper was taking off, gaining height for some time, then it sped east and south. They were about ten minutes in flight when a flash behind blinded them. They all pressed their faces to the windows in the side of the machine.

A huge column of black clouds obscured the Dome. Pavel turned to the boss, his face gray. "It blew up Jap. The whole fucking scheme. Fuck!"

"Hiroshima," Jap replied indifferently. "After all, no witnesses. Every conterfeit dollar destroyed, including the ones the *ments* captured and gave to the American to use."

He started rubbing his shin.

"You've got a wound there . . .?

"Fucking Plotnikov. But I guess he saved me."

"Volkov?" Pavel asked.

"I think we lost a daring companion. But never mind, we'll find another greedy pig. They're all over the secret cities, the factories, the storage areas, the silos. In a few weeks we'll be back in business."

"Jap," Pavel said seriously. "Misha and Pop are dead. The American and Oksana got away."

Jap shrugged. "Well, I guess we still have some unfinished business before we start filling orders for our customers. I'm sure they'll be patient while we establish new sources of supply."

Jap leaned back on the canvas seat and put the flask of cognac Pavel had handed him to his lips, listening to the rotors of the chopper gyrating rhythmically above them.

CHAPTER FIFTY-THREE

eter murmured a prayer of thanksgiving as he gazed down at the Dome. Whatever the cause of the fiery eruption, and Peter smiled grimly as he thought of his chronolog, at that terrible moment he and Oxsana had faced almost certain death, the holocaust below had somehow discouraged the helicopter's final assault on them. He and Oksana stared incredulously as the airborne shooters turned away and unaccountably settled into the midst of the fire and smoke enveloping the crest of the Dome.

Now they were skimming over the rough terrain putting as much distance as quickly as possible between themselves and the pyrotechnics surrounding the Dome at Krasnov 86.

"I think we're going to make it, Oksana, all the way to New York," Peter called into her ear above the roar of the turbo engine and rotor blades.

"I was expecting to be with my mother," Oksana cried back.

"We have many years ahead of us together first." Then their lips came together and the rushing of air through the bullet holes in the helicopter, the beating of the rotor blades and the whine of the turbo engine were for some moments lost in oblivion.

Half an hour later they were nearing Irkutsk, an exhausted, emotionally drained Oksana, sinking into Peter's embrace. Their conflicts ceased to exist. The important thing was they had escaped Jap's aerial goon squad and the perils of the flaming maelstrom. Oksana now realized her anger at Peter had been petty. He really had saved her life.

As the helicopter settled in and landed, Peter helped Oksana out of the machine onto the ground. The calm and quiet of the landing zone deeply contrasted with what they had just been through. Peter went back into the helicopter to assist the wounded pilot out of his seat and onto the grassy landing field. The chief mechanic of the Irkutsk helicopter terminal came up to the chopper. His jaw dropped at the sight of the bullet-punctured fuselage, shattered windshield, and bloodsoaked interior.

"What the hell hit you? Where is Basil?"

"We need a doctor waiting at the hospital," Peter shot back in Russian.

Nickolai Martinov rushed up to the seriously damaged helicopter and threw his arms around his daughter. "What has happened since I left you this morning? You both look awful!"

Peter winked at him and said in Russian, "Long story, Comrade Deputy. I am sure you will not see your nice friends again until you all meet in the next world."

Martinov gaped at him. "What the fuck! I mean . . . I'm sorry, Oksana. He speaks Russian?"

Oksana smiled happily, wriggled out of her father's embrace and put an arm around Peter's shoulder. "As they say in America he's a fast study."

They heard what sounded like distant thunder and a white flash of lightning appeared in the darkening late afternoon sky. But a thunderstorm was hardly possible. It was late fall.

Peter turned back to the helicopter and reaching inside pulled his briefcase out from under the co-pilot's seat thinking, "What a nice souvenir this will be for the gang at Petrovka 38."

"Come, the car is waiting," Martinov urged. "I think you two need a good drink, some supper, and a long rest."

"What about our pilot?" Peter asked.

"Father," Oksana cried, "we can't just leave him here. There's room in the car to take him to the hospital."

Martinov stared at the miserable looking young man leaning against the fuselage of the helicopter for support, the belt still fastened around his thigh above the blood stained pants. He pointed at the pilot and two of his men went over and helped the boy off the field and into the front seat of the luxury sedan.

A gathering throng of people at the Irkutsk helicopter landing zone seeking news of what had happened out at the secret city of Krasnov 86 pulled at Peter and Oksana, asking questions and pointing at the rising black column of smoke to the northwest. As they made their way to the car, Peter clutching his briefcase in one hand and helping Oksana with the other, they could only repeat to the anxious inquiries of family members of the "screw-winged angels" that they were in the air, on the way back to Irkutsk when the explosion occurred. They didn't know what had caused it or how extensive the destruction was.

After leaving the wounded co-pilot off at the hospital Peter and Oksana bathed and changed clothes at Nickolai's apartment. They told him all they could about the explosions, as yet unexplained. Peter neglected to mention his chronolog which had initiated the destruction. It was clear to Nickolai that Jap and Pavel had ordered the deaths of Peter and Oksana. Much as he wanted his daughter to stay with him, Oksana's father urgently encouraged them to follow Peter's instinct to get away from Irkutsk and then Russia. Jap's men were everywhere, shadowing Volkov's family and two of them had been at the Irkutsk helicopter terminal when Peter and Oksana landed. Others were waiting further orders.

Nickolai drove Peter and Oksana out to the airport from his

apartment in time to catch the night flight to Moscow. "Take good care of my daughter," he said to Peter as the spacious car neared their destination. "I will miss her when she is living in America but she won't be safe in Moscow. Even if Jap is dead his *organizat- siya* is legion."

"Please call Colonel Nechiaev at Petrovka 38," Peter requested. "Ask him to have a police escort meet us. We will go directly to the American Embassy and pick up Oksana's visa, and then take the next plane out to the West."

"And I have to pack my clothes at the apartment," Oksana added.

Peter and Nickolai simultaneously shook their heads. "We can buy everything you will need in New York," Peter said.

"If any of Jap's people are looking for you, the apartment will be the first place they visit," Nickolai agreed.

"How could Slava have escaped?" she asked.

"It doesn't matter," her father replied. "One call from Pavel or another underboss to Moscow could set Jap's gangsters on you," he warned.

The airport at Irkutsk was an unprecedented scene of chaos. Besides the usual pandemoniun occasioned by too few seats for passengers unwilling to hazard the five day train trip to Moscow. As a matter of routine the flights were oversold and rumors of a nuclear accident were causing hundreds of people to leave the area. The airliners were on the verge of being taken over by mobs of unaccomodated passengers.

Nickolai Martinov, his driver, and the two guards who always drove behind his car stormed into the Aeroflot Booking Office, took its director by the lapels and dragged him from behind his desk onto his feet. In five minutes they intimidated him into issu- ing two first class tickets to Peter and Oksana. Although the air- port director protested that the tickets were no good and all seats had been sold for several days, Oksana and Peter prepared to board the airliner.

Escorted by Martinov's men through the milling crowd out to the airplane, Peter and Oksana joined the boarding party which seemed like more of an assault on an enemy fortress than passengers joining their flight. The numbers forcing their way aboard appeared to wildly exceed the load the Aeroflot airliner had the capacity to lift off the ground.

Peter's hands were occupied with clutching a suitcase and his attaché case as he made his way up the stairs, Oksana following close behind him. People around them were laden down with personal baggage and food of all sorts. A woman carrying a casserole with its cover tightly bound to it, tried to get around them but he and Oksana pushed upward.

In the passengers' fabric carrying bags, the outlines of liquor bottles were clearly visible. Customs and controllers virtually did not exist and check-in gates had been smashed. Departure times and flight numbers indicated on the tickets mattered nothing to anyone. Only when the vessel was full "up to the lid" and it was impossible for another soul to cram into the fuselage would the remaining passengers be cut off to wait for another plane.

To Peter the airport anarchy made matters easier. His plutonium sample was resting securely in his briefcase and in the melee there was no chance of the usual official inspection taking place. The next day he would deliver incontrovertable proof to Petrovka 38 and the highest levels of the new Russian government that Soviet nuclear material was now being acquired by organized crime and would be on the market for outlaw states to acquire and add to their terrorist arsenals.

Distracted by these thoughts, Peter absently pushed away a prune-faced old hag with a decaying shopping sack who was trying to force her way in front of Oksana. The wrinkled witch emitted a flood of obscenities and reached into her sack. Peter, concerned with the baggage in his hands, was unprepared when the *babushka* fell upon him screaming, a hammer in her hand. He barely snapped his head out of the way when she caught him with a blow on the left clavicle. The sudden sharp pain wrenched a cry out of him and Oksana shoved the crone away preventing a second hammer attack.

Enraged, the travellers on the stairs shouted at her and a huge man dropped his suitcase and smacked the old scold a powerful shot in the face sending her reeling into the crowd behind her. The granny lost her weapon and caught several sharp kicks to her bottom as she tumbled to the asphalt runway. It took her some moments to get to her feet and start a new ascent to the doorway into the airliner.

"How are you, friend?" the man inquired aimiably. "Pity I did not kill that ancient shit."

"Some passengers you've got," Peter muttered clutching his clavicle which pained him fiercely. It suddenly struck Peter that if Jap's thugs were out here they could easily dispose of him and Oksana. An old hag with a hammer in a shopping sack? Incredable.

Oksana helped Peter up the stairs, taking the suitcase from his helpless left arm. They worked their way into the plane already full, and struggled through the passengers and luggage to their first class seats which were already occupied by a family of five. Peter was close to fainting, perspiration running down his chalky face. Seeing the suffering written on Peter's visage the head of the family, a stocky wide Siberian gave up his seat to him. Oksana thanked him profusely.

"No trouble," he replied cheerfully. "It's a six hour flight. I used to stand longer in food lines."

A boy of about five was placed in the luggage rack above their heads and Oksana was seated as well, a three-year-old girl in her lap. And still the people kept crowding aboard. The steward at the plane's entrance was collecting double fare in cash for every missing ticket.

Peter leaned back in his seat staring up at a pack of cockroaches on the rack foraging impatiently for food. The plane had obviously not been cleaned for a month. With baggage jamming every passageway, movement down the aisles was a nearly unsurpassable obstacle course. Stewardesses were not taken aboard; it would have been impossible for them to perform their duties.

Peter turned to Oksana. "I guess, sweetheart, the next time we get into the restroom will be in Moscow."

She nodded. "How's your shoulder?"

"Fine," he said and then winced, his face twisting. "Oh God!"

The large man who had given Peter his seat nodded in understanding, reached into the bag at his feet, and produced a bottle of vodka. He uncorked it, his wife handed him a glass which he filled and passed to Peter. "Drink. It will help."

"Thank you. I would like to pay you."

"Come on, my friend. Were you not born in Russia? You do not pay. Drink! It is good."

It turned out to be the harshest moonshine Peter had ever tasted. He felt fire running through his veins but the pain retreated.

Throughout the plane, passengers were sipping at bottles and from glasses as food was taken from baskets and bags. An army of cockroaches swarmed toward their next meal. With the loading door finally jammed shut against the crowd inside and outside the airliner, the steward was counting and arranging a heap of battered banknotes with open pleasure.

Two burly bullies standing among the luggage at the rear of the first class section were loudly explaining to all within earshot that they were "brave falcons of Zirinovsky," that power in the state had been siezed by Jewish fascists headed by Yeltsin and they were going to Moscow and chop them all to pieces. Someone advised the loud-mouthed peasants to learn how to wipe their asses properly in the first place. The fight was prevented only by inability to reach an opponent.

The sound of the plane's four engines, one by one coughing and turning over, was greeted with shouts of appreciation. No one fastened seatbelts, there were few available in any case. Then as the plane suddenly lurched toward the runway the standing passengers spilled backwards into the luggage and the airliner taxied to its takeoff point. A rumor spread that out of three restrooms only one was functioning and none had doors. This news was ameliorated by the pilot's announcement from the flight deck that those who ran out of vodka could easily purchase bottles from the steward by passing the money to him along the aisle.

The engines roared at full pitch against the locked brakes, mustering all the take off power at the airliner's command.

Peter reached out for Oksana's hand with his good arm. "I love you, Oksana. If we do get airborne, and we do get home, I will never let you go again."

"And I love you, Peter," she said around the bobbing head of the child in her lap. "If we get through the rest of this day and night of our apocalypse I promise I'll never be parted from you." Between the child and Peter's painfully throbbing broken collarbone they couldn't kiss.

With the sudden release of the brakes, the plane sprang forward as half of those standing toppled over on each other cursing, turning over glasses, bottles and food spreads. Children fell shrieking out of the luggage racks onto those seated below. Somehow the airline with a capacity of one hundred and twenty-six people yet loaded with way over three hundred clamoring passengers wavered airborne as it came to the end of the runway and limped into the air. Slowly it gained altitude as the four engines delivering screaming maximum performance long after they should have been cut back to normal power settings. Peter and Oksana tightly clasped hands, expecting the overloaded plane to drop from the sky at any moment.

It took half an hour to restore some semblance of order but finally Peter's benefactor was able to pour another drink into a glass and hand it to him. Gratefully he downed it and once again the pain in his broken collarbone receeded.

When, after an hour of desperate climbing, the airliner reached its cruising altitude and the vastly overcrowded plane had leveled off Oksana and Peter finally breathed sighs of relief and tried to relax.

"What time is it in Moscow right now?" she asked.

Peter shrugged. "Well let me see Moscow is what, four or is it five hours behind Irkutsk?"

"Where's your chronolog? You promised to tell me its secret."

Peter shrugged. "I guess I lost it in the helicopter."

"No you didn't," she laughed. "You owe me an explanation."

"Okay. I left it back at the secret city."

"On purpose?"

He nodded.

"Why? It meant so much to you."

"How do you think that holocaust started?"

Oksana nodded wisely. "I suspected it didn't happen all by itself."

Peter shook his head solemnly. "No, of course it didn't."

"You did it?" she gasped. "How?"

"My chronolog was actually a miniature shaped charge."

"What's that?"

"The most powerful explosive material we have developed short of a nuclear device is packed in a concave configuration into a half-inch thick disk, like an outsized pocket watch."

Oksana cupped her hand. "Like this?"

"Exactly. When detonated the penetration power of the shaped blast from this relatively tiny bomb is about equal to an antitank gun rocket. Detonate it on the outer shell of an ICBM and it will ignite the unstable fuel inside. You saw what happened at the Dome."

"You did that?"

"If Hamster hadn't called the SS-25 Sickle missile back into the

Dome it would only have blown up Jap's aircraft and with my evidence the government of Russia, such as it is, would have had to prevent any further sale of missiles and nukes to terror states like Iraq."

"I wonder how many people died?" Oksana mused.

"I wonder how many people all over the free world would have been nuked by terrorists if the first missile or kilo of plutonium had been delivered to some mad Muslim dictator with more such weapons on their way?"

Oksana shuddered. "I can't even think through such concepts."

"We've had the most stressful day of our lives," Peter said. "Shall we try to get some sleep?"

"I just wish that right now we had a little more privacy together," Oksana grinned and pouted.

CHAPTER FIFTY-FOUR

E ight hours after leaving Irkutsk Peter and Oksana straggled into the domestic terminal of Moscow's Sheremetivo Airport. Peter clutched the attaché case containing the deadly nuclear sample in his right hand, Oksana carrying their suitcase.

Suddenly Nechiaev and Boris Berunchuk appeared on either side of them. Boris took the suitcase and Nechiaev reached for the attaché case.

"Careful!" Peter's voice was sharp. "The plutonium 239 sample is in there, one hundred grams! Enough to poison the whole city of Moscow."

"Okay, okay," Sly Fox replied taking the case.

"Where are we going?" Peter asked.

"Oh God! The ladies room," Oksana wailed dropping the suitcase and heading for the relief station.

"We're getting you two out of this country," Nechiaev said. "After a lot of talk General Bodaev got Oksana's visa from the American embassy. I have it with me."

"I've got a broken collarbone and I also need a restroom," Peter groaned. Briefly he explained the melee they had encountered boarding in Irkutsk.

While Boris waited for Oksana with the luggage, holding tightly to the case containing the plutonium sample, Nechiaev escorted Peter to a private Militsia office in the terminal. By the time he had finished using the toilet, a police first aid specialist had arrived and gently feeling the collarbone pronounced it broken.

"Can we strap it up long enough for him to get on the next plane to Frankfurt?" Rushail asked.

"I'd like to take him to the hospital and do it right," the medical specialist replied.

"He and the girl are getting out the soonest way possible," Nechiaev replied. Then to Peter he said, "The Ministry of Interior is trying to make the incident in Siberia nonexistent. But when we present your evidence of the sale of nuclear material you will be held for an indefinite length of time—if we can find you. So what do you want to do? I suggest you suffer a few more hours and check into a Frankfurt hospital."

"Exactly what I had intended," Peter replied. "We've also probably got Jap's people after us."

Sly Fox handed an open bottle of vodka to Peter who swallowed deeply and then nodded at the first aid man who began strapping his shoulders back.

Outside the terminal Oksana and Peter were bundled into the Militsia Mercedes. "We're going to the international terminal. Now tell me, what the hell happened out there?" Nechiaev demanded.

Peter tapped the attaché case Boris had taken charge of. "Here is incontrovertible proof that plutonium, rockets, and nuclear warheads were for sale by a ring made up of Dome factory director Volkov and Jap."

Peter refrained from implicating his future father-in-law. "You don't have to worry about Krasnov 86, but use the plutonium sample to force your government to stop the directors of other secret cities from making fortunes with the *organizatsiya* at the expense of the world."

"Does that mean that Jap is dead?" Nechiaev asked hopefully.

"Oksana and I are not betting our lives on it, but from what I saw I wouldn't count on seeing Yakovlev again in this world."

"He does have a powerful network of sub-bosses," Nechiaev commented. "What about Volkov?"

"He was only interested in the hundred dollar bills I gave him from the Militsia stash."

"Don't even whisper about it," Nechiaev barked. "What else happened?"

"He offered me missiles, warheads and plutonium 239 extracted from old warheads."

Peter patted the briefcase on Nechiaev's lap. "Oksana and I came as close to death as we ever will to get you this evidence."

"We'll keep it safe and use it well." After a pause Nechiaev gave Oksana a long look. "Do you think your father might have information that could help us understand what caused this cataclysm in his region?"

Oksana shrugged. "You can call him."

"He was never in the Dome the day it blew up," Peter said.

"Yes, yes, I understand. The State will go crazy as reports of the catastrophe come in and they have to cover it up. Fortunately you will not be around to be questioned about this accident." He gave Peter an owlish look. "If it was purely an accident."

"Come to New York someday and visit us," Peter replied. "Maybe I will be able to tell you what really happened."

With Nechiaev and Boris escorting them, Peter and Oksana passed quickly through customs. It was at the immigration counter that the sudden rustle in the air, followed by a sharp thud, startled them. A steel arrow had been fired at them, and was stuck in the barrier. Nechiaev whirled around and drew the gun from his shoulder holster, pushing his way through startled passengers as he pursued a man darting out of the terminal.

Peter turned to stare at the wooden stand behind which the immigration official had ducked his head. The thin steel rod with three tin fins at the end of it was sticking out of the front of the immigration stand. A strip of paper was taped around what he recognized as a crossbow bolt, a special kind of deadly arrow fired from a high-tech crossbow. He pulled the paper off the arrow and shoved it into his pocket while his eyes searched the area for an assailant.

Boris jumped to their side and shielding Oksana with his body, he took her elbow and hurried her away from the immigration station and behind the wall separating the boarding area from the terminal. Peter followed, still carefully watching.

"Thank you, Boris," Peter breathed. "And good luck in the coming Mafia wars. When this Dome thing blows over Oksana and I will be back to help. But next time I gotta make some money." Then to a pale-faced Oksana, "Come, Sweetheart, we're out of here."

Nechiaev returned to Peter and Oksana. "Whoever shot that arrow got away in the crowd. What do you make of it, Peter?"

Peter reached into Peter's pocket and pulled out the strip of paper that had been wrapped around the bolt. Nechiaev read the proffered message and shook his head. *"Glyady voba,* Peter."

"Both eyes open," Peter agreed solemnly.

Now, with Oksana at Peter's side sipping champagne as the Pan American flight winged its way from Moscow toward Frankfurt, she looked over his shoulder reading the note for the tenth time.

AND THEN THEY LIVED HAPPILY EVER AFTER? DON'T BELIEVE IN FAIRY TALES.

Oksana squeezed Peter's arm. "I am a big girl now and I can handle a gun. Remember?"

"Yeah. You got two notches already."

"What kind of a notch do I get for getting you?"

"That one will come from Tiffany's."